REVERIE OF WRATH

VOLUME 2

By Justin Ferrante

Table of Contents

Part 5: Arena Conquest

Despite the fact that it was a year later, not much had changed. It was now the beginning of April, and the old house was still there, with the same people still in it. In fact, Jareus was wondering whether or not he should get a new TV. He had worked a few one-gig jobs and saved up a bit of cash. After the Redaro incident, Adrenaline Corp. reported to the government that the whole gang had "helped" to get rid of the problem. As a result, the government turned a blind eye to them taking legal ownership of the abandoned house.

"What's this?" Jareus asked himself, watching TV while he was eating cereal. Jareus was eighteen now, therefore counting as a legal adult, although that didn't really change much in his life. He pointed at a commercial on TV advertising some sort of sporting competition, hosted by Adrenaline Corporation. They were accepting applications for the competition.

"Adrenaline Corp? We should join," Zach suddenly interjected, coming from the other room.

"Oh hey, Zach! How'd ya sleep?" Jareus asked. Zach yawned and stretched out his arms. It was still early in the morning.

"Fine, and also, we should get a new TV," Zach suggested. The TV they had kept going to static every now and then, and was a 4:3 aspect ratio.

"I was just thinking that!" Jareus exclaimed.

"But other than that, we should join that sporting competition. Looks like the top places in the tournament get jobs at Adrenaline Corporation, plus first place gets some cash," Zach explained.

"Yeah, I saw the commercial. I mean, I don't see why not," Jareus shrugged.

"Yo, Danny, what do you think of joining a sporting tournament?" Zach shouted to Danny, who was upstairs and still barely conscious.

"Hmmm-na erm... wha? Sports? I don't do sports..." Danny mumbled.

"WHAT?!" Zach shouted upstairs. Danny mumbled something again. Zach gave up on trying to hear Danny. "He said yes."

"His thoughts on joining a sporting tournament are: yes?" Jareus asked sarcastically.

"He's half asleep!" Zach told Jareus, winking. Yep, this is how they ended up joining a sporting tournament. They sent in their applications and the date for it was set: April 14th, 2014. It was there before they could even properly train for it.

"How did this even happen?" Cole asked as the whole crew drove out to the new Adrenaline Corp. Stadium on April 14th. In the end, Jareus, Cole, Danny, Zach, and Alex had entered the competition—they were the ones most pumped about it. Or, in athletically-challenged Danny's case, subjected to the dangers of his friends' hive mentality.

"That's a good question. And just making sure, you wanted to be dropped off in downtown Los Angeles so you could get some food before going in, right?" Jill asked. She was dropping them off, since she had the day off.

They had kept consistent friendships with Saskia, Jill, and Allison. Danny had gone to visit Lexus a few times as well.

"Yep, I know a really good place down here. It's got freakin' good Mexican food," Jareus bragged.

"I don't even like Mexican food," Danny grunted.

"Whaaaaaat? How could you not like Mexican food? It's delicious!" Jareus persuaded Danny.

"Delicious to you! Your opinion isn't fact!" Danny snickered, pretending to be serious.

"Heeeeey!" Jareus gibed.

"But why are you guys doing this? How did this happen again?" Jill asked again while driving.

"Well, Jareus and I noticed that we needed a new TV, and the way we were making money wasn't cutting it for what we had to keep up with. We saw the Adrenaline Corp. advertisement, and decided that if we can show off our skills in this tournament, we could probably get jobs. Also, if we win, we get a bunch of cash!" Zach explained excitedly. They were all ready and hyped to do something new for the time being.

"But who's going to win?" Jill asked with a smirk.

"I think I will…" Jareus was saying.

"ME!" Zach exclaimed. They looked at each other.

"Guys, guys… we all know I can probably beat you," Danny commented, not out of a desire to compete, but of a desire to instigate the others. His wish was granted—his comment only resulted in an argument, in which both Alex and Cole didn't want to get involved.

Eventually, Jill dropped them off at the Mexican food place and wished them luck. After a quick lunch, everyone headed toward the arena, which happened to be only a few blocks away.

"Alright, sign here and here. We're going to collect a small fee of thirty-five dollars per participant. This could be an all-day competition, depending on prizes and when events take place," The guy at a sign-in desk told the group.

"Thirty-five per person?" Jareus asked, concerned, seeing as they had five people there.

"That's a tiny fee!" The guy said, with a mutual sigh from the whole group. They decided to cough up the cash, knowing that if they won they'd get some more. Some Adrenaline Corp. personnel gave them a quick physical, just to make sure they were in good shape for the competition. After that, they walked into the whole stadium. The sun shone down, but it wasn't too hot. Only a few clouds were in the sky. The stadium was huge, with many rows for seats and some booths as well. The floor of the stadium was absolutely full of people—everybody that was competing was in the center of the arena. There were young adults of all different ages and backgrounds.

"Wow… I guess we aren't the only ones who want that money," Cole commented as they all walked further into the stadium.

"Well, no duh," Jareus started, "I bet everyone here is gunning for top position. Which will only be one of us."

"I'm sorry, Jareus, but I'm going to be on top this time," Zach told Jareus somewhat coldly. This was very out of character for Zach, and quite a bold statement.

"Oh, and what makes you so sure?" Danny asked, inadvertently making the situation even more intense.

"You all were the ones who got to Redaro, the way I see it… it's my time now," Zach told Danny, pointing at him.

4

"Well, that means I could win. Doesn't it?" Cole asked, grinning.

"I'm sorry, Cole, but I'm going to put up the best fight I can. If you beat me, honestly and fairly, then I'll accept you winning," Zach told Cole.

"Am I even old enough for this?" Alex asked out of nowhere, seemingly uninterested in the argument at hand. He was looking around, mostly seeing the older ages of people around him. As a sixteen-year-old minor, he wasn't even sure if he qualified.

"Alex, don't worry about it. I'm sure as of now they'll put us on teams or something, and you can be on our side," Danny told Alex.

"But if it comes down to it, I'll have to be the one on top," Zach muttered under his breath.

"WHAT'S YOUR DEAL?" Jareus asked Zach loudly.

"WHAT?!" Zach sneered back.

"What's with you and wanting to win so badly?" Jareus asked, more genuinely this time.

"Dude, I told you, I've been waiting for a chance like this for a long time," Zach told Jareus, a tad more calmed down.

"CONTESTANTS! We're going to need you to get into four corners! If you have been signed in, and completed the physical test… PLEASE choose one of the four squares in the corners!" The speakers suddenly blasted.

"We're gonna choose the same one, right?" Cole asked Zach, also darting his eyes over to Alex.

"Yeah…" Zach scowled. They all ran over to the green square—they had a good feeling that they would win there.

"Everyone grab the gloves laid out on the table! These gloves will act as disqualification indicators to whoever is out! Also, put on the strap harnesses. They have blue spots on them that everyone will try to hit with the gloves. If any of the blue spots on the harness get hit from the gloves, you're out! They're located on your front shoulders, sides, and elbows," The announcer explained over the speakers.

"Alright, you guys ready to kick some ass?!" Jareus asked. His team all posed, ready and behind him.

"Hell yeah!" They shouted in unison.

"Also, the way this game works is that you cannot get your own team out. But we can only choose four people from each team to advance!" The announcer explained through the speakers.

"HUH?!" Jareus exclaimed. The people in the seats above gasped along with the competitors there. Zach smirked—the stakes were high now.

"THREE... TWO... ONE... GO!" The announcer shouted. Zach ran off in his own direction, and so did Cole.

"GUYS LET'S TRY AND STAY—oh, whatever. THE REST OF YOU! Let's all stay in this one area, got it? If we group up, we might be the ones to move on to the next round from our team," Danny plotted out for everyone.

"I like that idea," Jareus approved.

"Me too..." Alex mumbled.

"You're FIRST!" Zach shouted as he slid under one guy, hitting his side spot right after. All the spots shone the color of the team each person was on. When Zach hit it, the lights all went out.

"Ah, what?! You're kidding me!" The guy yelled. Zach kept running behind him to stay on the move.

"When you get out, please return to the waiting area on the side of the Adrenaline Corp. banner!" The announcer's voice boomed through the speakers. He walked to the waiting area, but very begrudgingly.

"HEY!" A woman yelled as Cole did a jump over her, but hit her shoulder spot and tagged her out. *Tch, Zach's already ahead of everyone*, Cole thought.

"Okay, you got that! Ah—WAIT! Okay, I got this! I did it!" Jareus was wobbling around as he was getting people out. He, Danny, and Alex had made a sort of triangle. This would keep them from getting out, as they had their backs covered and they could see clearly in front of them.

"How's it goin'?" Zach boasted, waving to Cole as they ran by each other. Zach was smirking, but Cole wore quite the serious expression. He wasn't messing around. Yet somehow, Zach was still in the lead. What was it that drove Zach this way?

"GOT YOU!" A man went up and tried to get Zach out, but his scream was a bit too early. Zach had already slightly moved and his chop landed on Zach's bicep instead.

"Sure about that?" Zach scoffed and punched back, but the man was able to dodge. So Zach kept punching at the man. "You can't dodge forever!"

"Neither can you!" yelled another guy from the same team, going for one of Zach's upper body spots. But there was one little mistake they made, though.

"NOW WE HAVE YOU!" shouted the first guy, but Zach jumped and used his shoulder to pull himself over the guy, and when on the other side, he had the opportunity to swing around and get the two out at the same time.

7

"Jeez... they need to chill," Zach muttered as he ran away from the scene of the two dudes yelling at each other.

Meanwhile, Cole was having a struggle with some woman. She was quite persistent in trying to get him out, but Cole was trying not to go hard on her.

"WHY ARE YOU HOLDING YOURSELF BACK?!" She yelled at Cole. Cole remained silent, and when she finally tripped up, he went to take her out quickly. But before he could do so, she grabbed his arm.

"You fell for it," she sneered. Out of Cole's assumption that she was just some damsel in distress, he found himself in this situation!

"Wha?!" Cole was caught off guard as he watched her arm move toward him, about to be taken out.

"ALEX!" Danny yelled. Alex had broken from the triangle. Out of nowhere, Alex slid in toward the woman by Cole, and in his slide was able to tap one of her spots before she could get Cole out.

"Wha?!" She exclaimed, trying to tap Cole's spots, thinking that they just weren't working. After a few moments, she finally noticed that she was out. "HOW DID THAT EVEN HAPPEN!" She started to throw a fit at the electronics on her, shouting about how they were busted, as Cole and Alex just slowly backed away.

"Thank you Alex, I would have gotten out if it weren't for you," Cole told Alex genuinely, and gave him a thumbs up amidst the chaos.

"I saw you and Zach out there, and I couldn't help but think... that I also... want to win!" Alex cheered and gave Cole a thumbs up back, with a big glowing smile on his face. Cole smiled back.

"It's just you and me now, but that's okay, isn't it?" Danny asked Jareus, as they were back-to-back.

"Yeah, we got this. These first few rounds are when you have to rely on people," Jareus responded in a cool and serious manner, also getting in a defensive stance.

"First few rounds? I don't think you'll ever be able to get anywhere alone," Danny commented.

"I guess we'll see, especially with Zach being separated from us, won't we?" Jareus smirked.

"We will," Danny affirmed, blocking a jab from an incoming enemy team member. Together, they could outwit anyone. Taking care of people was easy for them, as long as there weren't too many.

"And you're also out!" Zach boasted, jumping by somebody and tapping their spot as he flew by.

"Aw, come on!" the girl yelled. Zach continued his winning streak, and most of the people were already out at this point. Cole and Alex were also helping out each other.

"Yah!" Alex yelled, trying to get somebody else out. He had almost gotten his spot, but he didn't manage to do so. They were swinging back and forth at each other, almost hitting each other. Every jab was a micrometer closer.

"I'll help you, Alex!" Cole yelled and went in to charge the guy, but it was too late.

"Wha?" Alex was dumbfounded. The guy had successfully hit the spot closest to his right shoulder.

"Sorry," He whispered sarcastically, and tried to then go after Cole next.

"TIME!" The announcer shouted. They stopped in their tracks, as the wiring with the spots around them made it hard for them to move. But it was clear who was in and who was out. "Everybody can exit to the sides, we need time to count up and rewatch the footage. Who was in and who was out determines nothing about who's moving on. It *does* have a say in whether or not you are, but it isn't the determining factor. So while you're all waiting, go have a drink! We've got refreshments!"

"I should have stayed put," Alex muttered, sipping the drink he'd just gotten.

"Hey, that doesn't mean you're out for good!" Jareus tried to cheer him up. He didn't seem to be feeling it. Jareus tried to go to drink his water from a plastic cup to alleviate the awkward situation, but it turned out he was trying to drink from an empty cup.

"Hey, you saved me. Without you, I would have been out," Cole told him, while Jareus snuck out to go get water.

"Thank you, but in the end, out of all five of us, I was the only one to actually get out. You all have a much better chance of moving on, anyways," Alex stated plainly, seeming down.

"Alex, you had resolve in your eyes. Don't give up just yet," Danny told him. Alex turned to look at him and smiled a bit. When Alex looked back to Cole, Danny smiled as well. *Well, at least I'll be in the next round. I do feel kinda bad, but I don't know what to say*, Zach thought. Cole told Alex he was going to get a drink and to sit tight, and he walked off.

"Hey, is this the—" Cole asked, opening the door to a small room.

"AGH! Why are you in here?" The announcer guy asked.

"I'm Cole Cidka, one of the contestants. And no, I'm not here to ask if I made it. I just wanted to say if on the off chance that I did make it and contestant Alex Kipper did not, I want you to give my spot to him. He saved me and deserves it more than I do," Cole told the announcer.

"Well, I don't know anything yet… There are judges reviewing the footage, and I don't even know if I'm allowed to influence the decisions. But I'll see what I can do. Unfortunately, I can't have you talking to them, as it would be against the papers you signed earlier." The announcer told him. Cole walked back outside, and then actually got water.

"GUYS! Look who I met in the line for water!" Jareus exclaimed to Alex, Danny, and Zach, sitting at a table and waiting. They all looked up at him.

"Sup!" Cole popped up from behind Jareus, and they both started laughing together. But only those two were laughing.

"Ha, ha, ha. Very funny." Zach groaned.

"Don't be such a party pooper!" Jareus told him, laughing.

"WE HAVE THE PEOPLE MOVING ON!" The announcer boomed through the speakers. This got everybody's attention, and everyone turned around to see them read off the names. He started, "From the red team, we have Harmony Hill, Carson Large, Adam Steel, and Seth Roadagen. From the yellow team we have Derrian Kendri, Miki Nikatala, Odessa Owens, and Archie Bomics. From the green team, we have Zach Artien, Jareus Dehayven, Danny Kipper and Alex Kipper. From the blue team, we have Thea Isia, Imani Gorgi, Anastasia Bruno, and Eva Wallay. Congratulations to all those moving on,"

"I knew it," Zach smirked, as Cole also smiled. He had accepted his fate, knowing that what he said may have affected the competition. The crowd was all riled up, many people were upset. Many people were walking out, and the people tuning in over television were on the edge of their seats, awaiting the next best thing.

"Cole…" Jareus slowly said. He went over and put his hand on Cole's shoulder, "You did your best. You're always still gonna be with us, so just wait! We'll kick butt in the competition for you!" Jareus cheered. Cole smiled.

"Thanks, guys. I know why I'm out, though, this kid Alex outperformed me! He saved my butt, and for that, he's going to the next round!" Cole convicted. He pointed to Alex and Alex was almost embarrassed. Alex was 16 around this time, so he was as old as Jareus and the gang when they fought Redaro, but he didn't think he'd get this much praise, being two years younger.

"Uh… ah! Thank you! I tried really hard, trust me. Growing up in a world where Redaro's king is no easy task," Alex thanked Cole.

"ALL THE CONTESTANTS THAT MADE IT, PLEASE COME OVER TO HALL F7 FOR NEXT ROUND PREP," The announcer boomed through the loudspeaker.

"I'll be watching you guys!" Cole smiled.

"You did great, Cole! So did you, Alex, but you still have to come with us. If Jareus can't, I'll kick butt for you!" Danny yelled to Cole, walking away. Zach, who seemed stone-cold, still smiled and gave Cole a thumbs up. They walked off, and Cole went to the stands. In Hall F7, they were seated in chairs, and people came around giving them water and toweling off their sweat, like this was a boxing match or something. There was also a table of fruits in the corner, but people were mainly focused on a little screen in the front with a video playing.

"Hello there! If you're hearing this, you've made it to the second round! Congrats! Anyways… in this match, all of you are going to be getting a sort of… Adrenaline Corp. bodysuit. It's pretty nice, and will increase your aerodynamics, because this next round is a race! But it's not just any race—in this race, you'll get exoskeleton legs. These legs will allow you to go much faster than regular human speeds, and if used correctly, will make your stamina last much longer. It will also allow for much more creative ways of winning the race.

"Now, this isn't just a regular race, but one with obstacles! Also, if you go outside the boundaries, the exosuit legs will stick to the powerful magnets lining the outside. This means your suit will stick you to the magnet, and you're out of bounds. Hindering others is allowed, too, just nothing too severe. Just simply complete in the three laps first, using any methods besides going outside of the boundaries, and you'll win. Good luck!" the woman on the screen monologued.

"Bodysuits?" Zach asked. A man walked onstage as he asked this aloud.

"Yes! These bodysuits! You can go pick them up at this table to the right of you over here!" A guy on stage wearing an orange-and-gray patterned, spandex-looking bodysuit told them all. It had a very computer-chiplike pattern, along with the Adrenaline Corp. logo in the front.

"This feels weird, but I guess I'm okay with it," Zach said about the suit. The group was all in line to get the exosuit legs.

"Yeah, it works. I thought it was just a whole suit, but bodysuit isn't the best term for it. It's two pieces, the pants are actually a little baggy, and the belt is quite large," Jareus pondered.

"Yeah, I'm guessing that this big gray belt is actually a secondary power supply for the exolegs," Danny explained. The rest of the gang agreed. After that, they got fitted for their exoskeleton legs, and were already at the track, standing around.

"Well, now what?" Alex asked aloud.

"Well, we have to wait for everyone to be done. They're still fitting some people," Danny told Alex.

"These things are weird..." Zach complained, looking at the leg parts. They consisted of a bunch of silver rods and what looked like a pneumatic system of parts. They had enough thrust for double jumping, where the user would jump once and the thrust mid-jump would give them a second jump. It was wired up to the belts, as guessed. They were also given gloves that had a button for the double jump function.

"These are a bit tight, but I remember how these work... kinda," Jareus thought aloud, stretching out on the ground.

"You REMEMBER how these work?" Danny questioned Jareus, who gave him a cold look.

"Yeah, I told you I stole one of these once. That was a long time ago. I don't steal anymore, of course!" Jareus said with nervous conviction.

"ALRIGHT! Hello viewers! These folks are about to take part in the second part of the Adrenaline Corp. Sports Tournament! This competition consists of a race, and that's it! Free-for-all, with exoskeleton leg attachments that allow a double jump! The only rule is that they can't go out of bounds! We'll get back to them right after this commercial break!" An announcer was explaining on the television. There were TVs around the arena, so they were able to see the broadcast.

14

"HAH! Look at those suits. Kinda happy I don't have to wear that," Cole spoke to himself, leaning over the safety rail by the stands. He was looking over, watching the tournament. There were many people around there, but there was only one person who was leaning on the safety rail with Cole. He was a tad older than Cole was.

"Hey, is that Danny Kipper over there?" The man asked aloud. Cole took a second to realize that this question was directed at him.

"Oh… yeah it is! He's over there with Jareus, Zach, and Alex," Cole told the man. Suddenly, he wondered, *How would he know Danny?* So he asked, "Did you hear about the Rownert incident?"

"The Rownert incident?" The man asked Cole.

"Oh, well, basically I thought you would know them because they helped contain the bomb threat of Rownert, or whatever the public news said about the situation," Cole told the man. *I don't know if I can tell random people about the Purged Souls,* he thought to himself.

"Ah, yes. I see," The man responded. He started walking toward where all the food stands were. *Wait, how did he know Danny then?* Cole thought to himself.

"I know about the Rownert incident!" another male voice sounded behind Cole. Cole was already apprehensive, and this voice caused him to jump. It came from a man he hadn't seen before. He had darker tan skin, a big smile, a completely white and short sleeve shirt, dark blue ripped jeans, a hoodie tied around his waist, and a sort of messy man bun.

"You know about the Rownert incident?" Cole asked. This guy looked about the same age as most of the gang.

"News gets around to people like me. I heard about the Purged Souls. I know you were there, Cole Cidka," the guy told Cole.

"What, how'd you know my name?!" Cole asked, shouting. The guy chuckled.

"Well, my name is Harlow Henry, if that explains it all to you," Harlow told Cole, closing his eyes and smirking.

"Actually, that doesn't explain much to me. Nothing, really. I'm bad with names, have we met before? I'm awfully sorry if we have," Cole apologized to Harlow. Harlow seemed very surprised. It was as if he had never met anybody that didn't recognize him before.

"Actually... we haven't met. Let me introduce myself properly. Hello! My name is Harlow Henry! I'm here watching the contestants of the tournament. You?" Harlow re-introduced himself. Cole was taken aback by this, Harlow already got so close.

"Uhh... I'm Cole, as you said. I was just watching my friends," Cole told Harlow.

"Yes, I've been keeping track of this tournament. Speaking of your friends, Zach has been quite cocky. But somehow it's deserved, he's in first place as it is!" Harlow exclaimed to Cole.

"I saw that he had the most points, but we'll see what happens when it comes to round two," Cole smirked.

"Ooo! Here it comes, actually! Let's watch!" Harlow spoke giddily. He wasn't wrong, they were all lined up to go. Everyone was in their Adrenaline Corp. suits, with the exoskeleton legs ready to go.

"Round two is about to begin, everyone! Our contestants are ready, are you?!" The announcer exclaimed. The audience was counting down with the

16

clock. 10… 9… Jareus, Zach and the gang were already readying themselves to blast right off.

"THREE! TWO! AND…" Harlow was yelling along with the countdown.

"ONE!" The announcer boomed. Everyone instantly launched off with their exoskeleton legs, boosting them into a running motion. Instantly, you could see that Danny and Zach were a little ahead of everyone else.

"I see you!" Zach yelled to Danny, who smirked. Zach tried to shoot the pressure of the exosuit legs off to the side, to throw off Danny's jump. Danny ducked, and it sent Zach a little off course to the side, bumping into some girl.

"Watch it!" She yelled, and shoved him. But he used her jump as a boost, by grabbing onto her leg and flinging himself forward. Jareus was using a technique where he tried to stay up in the air, but it seemed like just running fast was the way to go. The first obstacle was coming up, the pile of hay. Pretty easy, right?

"I'll just jump over it!" One of the other competitors shouted. He boosted ahead of everyone, and while jumping over it, the force of the boost was enough to make the hay lose shape, and it became a distraction for everyone.

"Gah! It's in my eyes!" Alex shouted, as he was closer to the back. Everyone was basically having the same problem, besides Jareus.

"Gahaha! That's where my experience shines!" Jareus taunted. HE boosted backwards into the dust cloud of straw, getting the back of his shirt covered in hay. However, his vision remained clear. Now he was ahead.

"Damn him and his experience, it got in my ear!" Zach yelled. Meanwhile, Alex was a little behind. He may have had hay in his eyes, but he pushed through it. Albeit, he was a little slower than the others. He wasn't in *last* place, though.

"Jeez…" Danny complained to himself. The first lap was nearly over for everyone at that point, with some people lagging behind, and Jareus still in first and only getting further ahead. But he wasn't ready for what was about to come next.

"LOOK AT THAT! This time, there are tiles that move on the floor! When landing, people are going to need to be careful of where they step!" The announcer shouted. The floor opened up to reveal the uneven tile mess.

"You're kidding me. Of course this has to be where I end up losing my advantage…" Jareus complained to himself.

"Hmph, I guess so," Zach smiled. Zach boosted right next to Jareus, he was able to catch up after seeing clearly.

"ZACH BOOSTS RIGHT NEXT TO JAREUS! THEY'RE NECK AND NECK! Danny Kipper is not close behind! Wait, what's this?!" The announcer shouted over the loudspeaker.

"Ya-hooo!" A woman's voice shouted. Danny shot his gaze right behind him, to see the same woman's shoes as she had already begun a flip over Danny.

"ODESSA OWENS TAKES THIRD PLACE! WHAT AN AMAZING FLIPPING TECHNIQUE! And I mean actual flipping, rather than using 'flipping' as emphasis!" The announcer commented on his own commentary.

"*Tch*—how'd you do that?!" Danny grunted as he was carefully boosting to tiles that were on the same level

18

as his feet. Each tile was slowly moving up and down, independent of the other tiles.

"Can't I also do that?" a guy further back asked himself. He jumped up and tried to do the same flip that boosted Odessa forward, but the incorrect angle he launched off at just made him fly just upward.

"IMANI GORGI MESSES UP THE SPIN!" The announcer boomed the second he flew up. This let Alex get ahead of him, but Alex seemed too focused on what he was doing with his feet.

"Ahh!" Alex almost fell off one of the tiles. *Jeez, I really have to make sure that I don't misplace my footing, it'd guarantee my loss,* he thought to himself.

"Can't go ballistic now, can you, Zach?" Jareus taunted Zach from behind him. Zach heard his taunts but tried to stay focused.

"But neither can anybody else, can they?" A voice sounded from behind Jareus. He was shocked by this and slipped.

"ODESSA PASSES JAREUS!" The announcer shouted as the crowd went wild. Odessa Owens, highly trained in gymnastics, knew how to boost well to complement her body's movements. She had a little bit of knowledge of aerodynamics as well. Zach, however, was still in front of her.

"I still have to get in front of these five!" Alex groaned under his breath. In front of him, even to get to where Danny was, he had Derrian Kendri, Adam Steel, Harmony Hill, Archie Bomics, Eva Wallay, Anastasia Bruno, and Seth Roadagen to get past.

"AND IT'S ABOUT TO BE THE FINAL LAP, AND THIS TIME THERE ARE MAGNETIC TRAPS TO PUSH THE RUNNER TO THE SIDE OF THE ARENA! IF THEY STEP ON OR FLY TOO

19

CLOSE TO ONE OF THE BLUE-TINTED TILES, IT MIGHT AS WELL BE OVER!" The announcer boomed. The tiles were now still, but some of them were slightly different colored, and had the ability to put you behind everybody else.

"This is where I can get ahead!" Alex yelled. Alex started to boost as fast as he could, and even past the magnet traps.

"Well said!" Danny grinned to himself, hearing Alex's cheer. Danny boosted up and stayed in the air, and waited for Jareus to do the same. While Danny was falling, he was able to do another boost under Jareus, hitting the ground and jumping off of it. He was able to do another boost, and just barely scraped by Odessa. He was now behind Zach, who was carefully dodging the magnet traps.

"DANNY'S TECHNIQUE PUSHES HIM TO SECOND PLACE! ALEX IS NOW IN FIFTH!" The announcer's voice filled the stadium.

"What the nut? Do you also have experience?" Jareus questioned aloud. Zach even heard this.

"Did you just say 'what the nut?'" Zach asked, yelling from ahead of them. Danny was unphased.

"Well, it's a public thing, man. Keeping it PG!" Jareus yelled to Zach, while jumping toward the right edge. He was so close to falling out, but boosted on specifically his right leg and kicked forward with it at the same time. This made him do a super fast boost, diagonally across the track to the left side. This got him in first place, and he successfully avoided the magnet trap in front of him.

"JAREUS JUMPS INTO FIRST PLACE! This makes Zach in second, and Danny in third!" The announcer updated.

"I'm coming too!" Alex yelled, as two contestants hit a magnet trap. They hit the ground and stayed trapped there.

"IMANI GORGI AND MIKI NIKATALA ARE HELD TO THE GROUND! ARE THEY OUT? WE'LL HAVE TO SEE WHO ELSE GETS STUCK!" The announcer chimed in. Adam Steel, who was behind them, was able to get over them and ahead of them. Going back to the front, Jareus was still in front, and just barely dodged another trap while maintaining speed. *I have to find a way to get in front…* Zach thought to himself. Zach boosted downwards, and hit Jareus's foot out of the air, causing him to spin.

"HEY! WHA—" Jareus started to yell, but he flipped around and accidentally hit Zach while one of his exosuit legs got trapped to the magnet. This caused Zach to also fly into one of the traps, and one of his exosuit legs went to collide with the magnet. But in the last second, Jareus was able to break the latch on it with his hand, before hitting the magnet and flew forward. He flew forward and hit Zach enough so he got hit off the magnet, and one of his exosuit legs also came off. They only had one exosuit leg each, but they were still in the competition!

"What the hell?" Zach asked aloud.

"WE HAVE NO TIME! I got us out of that situation, but we're going to need to work together if we even wanna stay in this race! Quickly switch sides with me!" Jareus told Zach. Zach was confused, but he went along with it.

"Do we have to do this?" Zach asked as he put his arm around Jareus, so together they made two exosuit legs.

21

"Try and boost with one leg, you'll probably break your other without the support. Together, however, we can make a pair of legs!" Jareus yelled at him.

"ALRIGHT! Whatever, let's go! I'm beating you in the next round, though!" Zach retorted. They counted down and boosted after every three. In the time they spent talking, Danny and Odessa had passed.

"Hey! You're a little too close for comfort!" Alex yelled behind him at Adam Steel.

"Am I now?" Adam yelled with a smirk. He boosted forward and grabbed Alex's leg, and threw him back at Derrian Kendri. They both got stuck to a magnet. He laughed, "Now just to get to the front!"

Suddenly, he was stuck to the ground as well. He had lost his footing and fell on a magnet.

"ALEX, DERRIAN, AND ADAM ARE OUT FOR THE TIME BEING! THEY WILL ALL BE RELEASED AT THE END OF THIS ROUND!" The announcer clarified for everyone stuck to the ground.

"You've gotta be kidding me," Alex complained to himself. Back at the front, Odessa was neck-and-neck with Danny, and Jareus and Zach were tied for third.

"JAREUS AND ZACH BARELY MANAGED TO ESCAPE DOOM! WILL THEY STAY NEAR THE FRONT? WHO WILL WIN?" The announcer was hyping up the audience. Then, Seth Roadagen and Anastasia Bruno crashed into each other while trying to beat each other, and flew into one of the magnets. The announcer was on top of that one with, "AND THERE GO SETH AND ANASTASIA AS WELL!"

"Hey, look out," A voice sounded. Danny was distracted for a second, and Odessa took the initiative and jumped ahead.

"What?!" Danny shouted in disbelief.

22

"I'm taking first place, I have to!" Odessa cheered. The finish line wasn't far ahead. The people stuck to the ground already were desperately trying to free themselves, but it wasn't working.

"Oh no you aren't!" Danny taunted back. He launched himself forward and hurt his leg, but he lept at just the right moment. While she was just regularly trying to get over the finish line, Danny dove and his arms crossed first.

"DANNY DID IT! DANNY WINS ROUND TWO! ODESSA OWENS IS IN SECOND, JAREUS AND ZACH TIED IN THIRD! The others to pass the finish line in order are: Harmony Hill, Archie Bomics, and Eva Wallay!" The speakers boomed with the announcer's voice, who sounded like he was going to break his voice shouting.

"What does that mean for us?" Derrian complained, still stuck to the ground. They were trying to get attention while still stuck to the ground.

"Hmmm... it looks like there's one more spot. OKAY! Everyone moves on... and ONE more person. HERE IS THE DEATHMATCH! Ready? First one to the finish line wins, no rules. Releasing in five... four... three... two... ONE!" The announcer said as the crowd was going absolutely nuts.

"GAH!" Alex reflexed as the magnetism stopped. *This is my one chance, I can't waste it!* He thought to himself.

"Now I'll get my chance!" Adam Steel yelled. But Alex couldn't let him take that chance.

"BWAH!" Alex's mouth made that noise as he instantly tried to spam the boost forward. Everybody was running for it at first, but Alex couldn't spam like he thought he could because of the delay in between boosts. *What the heck can I do?!* Alex's brain raced.

"Don't think you can just win without a fight!" Derrian yelled from behind Alex. Alex decided to bet it all on whether or not he could do the flip. He boosted up to Adam Steel, who was about to win.

"Watch out, Steel!" Alex yelled. He jumped, and almost as if it were in slow motion, Adam's face turned to terror as he saw Alex about to do the perfect rotation to boost himself forward. But fast thinking was on Adam's side. He almost instinctively boosted toward Alex halfway through his boost, and Alex's legs kicked him forward into the finish line, seconds before he got there himself.

"AND WE HAVE A WINNER! ADAM STEEL IS MOVING ON TO THE NEXT PART OF THE COMPETITION!" The announcer's voice filled the stadium as the crowd went berserk, and the other contestants who didn't make it were all angry and groaning.

"Wha…" Alex murmured to himself. *How? I had the perfect opportunity… and this guy just came in and ruined it…* he thought. Alex was kind of angry.

"Well… looks like he's out," Danny commented while watching it. Everyone from the race was still all tuckered out. Jareus and Zach were exhausted and gasping for air.

"Hey Alex, I'm really sorry about that! Don't sweat it though, you did the best you could!" Jareus yelled to Alex.

"Hey! What are you doing, being nicer to my grandson than me!" Danny exclaimed at Jareus. Jareus turned toward him and made a face sticking his tongue out. Danny sighed, "I'll go talk to him."

"Sorry about that," Alex told Danny as the contestants Derrian, Imani, Seth, Anastasia, and Miki exited the arena.

"Sorry about what? You did the best you could," Danny told Alex as he helped Alex get off the ground.

"Sorry for stealing Cole's spot and then wasting it," Alex admitted to Danny.

"No no no, you didn't waste anything. Okay? You helped Cole, and then just unfortunately ended up meeting a guy who'll do cheap tricks to win…" Danny started to trail off.

"Yee-haw! Yaw-hoo! Yippee!" Adam Steel was yelling to himself and jumping up and down.

…

"Well, what are you going to do now Alex? Stay with me?" Cole asked, as Harlow was still standing right beside him.

"Yeah, I guess I will. Who's this guy?" Alex asked Cole, coming back from returning the bodysuit and the exosuit parts.

"My name's Harlow! Harlow Henry! It's very nice to meet you! It was awesome watching you!" Harlow started spitting a bunch of greetings while smiling and shaking Alex's hand rapidly.

"THIS LAST ROUNDS WILL CONSIST OF ONE-ON-ONE FIGHTS UNTIL ONE CONTESTANT PUSHES THE OTHER CONTESTANT OUT OF THE RING! STAY TUNED!" The announcer's voice boomed.

"Aaaahhhow!" Cole complained. They were right next to the speakers, so the announcement hurt their ears.

"Let's move away from the speakers, it's for the best," Harlow told them both.

"THE FIRST MATCH WILL BE ARCHIE BOMICS VERSUS ODESSA OWENS! A FULL ADRENALINE CORPORATION BODY ARMOR AND EXOSUIT FOR EACH CONTESTANT! LET'S SEE WHO WILL PREVAIL!" The announcer cut in again.

"Hear that, Zach?" Jareus taunted him as they were putting on the armor in the lockers in the breakroom.

"We'll have to see who goes against one another," Zach sneered back at Jareus, pulling on his headpiece.

"There are eight of us left total, and there are about to be seven. If we all make it past this round into the prefinals, we're going to go against each other," Danny informed the other two while watching outside. The three were in the locker room, which had a hallway that led to the outside arena field. Zach had just put on all his gear, and Danny was watching the fight between Archie and Odessa. But Danny wasn't the only one watching their fight.

"You seeing this?" A voice asked the other on top of the arena, "Jareus and Danny moving on?"

"Yeah, it's annoying. I can't believe it," The other voice told the first voice, looking into the arena from the top.

"So what do you want to do about it, Jack?" The first voice asked again.

"I'm going to stop them from getting first place, Mark," Jack told Mark standing on top of the arena. Jareus and Danny were aware Jack was alive again, as Zach had told them how Mark had temporarily stolen the Wish Orb at one point. They had followed Jareus to the tournament.

"*THAT* is your master plan? Why did you want to come here anyways, Jack? You wanted to go to that Rownert place too, but never did! We could just like… forget about them. We could just live life without thinking about them!" Mark complained to Jack.

"They beat me up! I was supposed to be the prodigy, dude! I have this weird… almost innate sense that I have to get back at them! Or distract them… or something," Jack tried to explain to Mark, eyeing the recently-stolen Wish Orb in his pocket.

"Yeah, yeah. Alright, I get it, your pride was hurt or whatever. How do we get down from here?" Mark asked.

"We got up using the stairs, right? We'll go back down when we need to," Jack told Mark.

"You were so adamant about getting up here, dude. We had to sneak past guards and workers, just to view? We could have just snuck into the stands! Or even buy tickets! They're only like ten bucks, and taking money isn't *THAT* hard," Mark argued.

"What if they ask for my last name?" Jack asked dramatically.

"Dude, make one up. You can't be 'just Jack' forever. I'm Mark Taffe, last names can literally be anything. You can act offended if you get questioned about the legitimacy of it," Mark explained to Jack.

"I want to revel in the loss of people I don't like. I will be Jack Revel then!" Jack laughed wickedly.

"Uh… they usually aren't words. They're usually kinda like… weird vowels and…" Mark said.

"IT WORKS, OKAY!? If somebody asks, I'm Jack Revel! It's good enough, if Taffe is one as well," Jack commented.

"HEY! Okay, whatever, let's just go down there. The wind is bad up here and I really don't feel like falling that far today," Mark suggested.

"Okay, whatever," Jack affirmed. They started their descent. But back on the field, Odessa Owens had just won her battle with Archie, and Danny was going against Eva Wallay.

"GAH!" Eva dodged Danny, who nearly flew off the stage trying to push her off. They were both decked out in the exosuits, and had a bit of padding in their armor. The point of these rounds was not to beat up the other person, but simply get them out of the ring.

"ARCHIE BOMICS! Don't leave! There's prize money at the end for everyone that has made it this far!" The announcer shouted into the stadium. Archie was just trying to go home, but seemed happy anyways when he was told he was getting money.

"I've got you this time!" Danny yelled, bouncing back from the edge of the stage and launching himself again. It had already been awhile, since she was very good at dodging. Even so, she wasn't good at offense. Danny, however, knew how far to go when it came to offense.

"AH!" She sounded as Danny was able to push her up. She tried to use the boost to jump back into the arena, but as Danny almost fell out he used her to push himself back in the ring, and her out.

"DANNY KIPPER WINS THE SECOND ROUND! That was a long one, full of dodging and counterattacks!" The announcer boomed. Eva was already taking off the exosuit on the sidelines, and stormed into the lockers.

"Nice, dude," Jareus told Danny as he walked back to the room, with the crowd cheering behind him.

"Eva? Where are you going? You have to stay behind for your cash prize!" The announcer said. Eva was storming out of the place, she had already changed.

"MAIL IT TO ME!" She yelled, threw her bodysuit on the floor, and marched out. Jareus and Zach both reacted with a sigh. Danny felt almost embarrassed.

"Well... anyways... NEXT UP IS JAREUS DEHAYVEN VERSUS ADAM STEEL! Both contestants... come to the ring in the center of the field!" The announcer continued. Adam Steel was already at the side of the arena, with his taller composure, darker skin, longer hair, and orange eyes.

"Good luck, Jareus, hope I get to fight you soon," Zach told Jareus. Jareus looked back and gave him a smile and a thumbs up. Zach gave him a slight smile. Adam Steel got up on top of the stone ring without a word, and Jareus followed by a boost, jumping up there. It was a good six feet off the ground. They stared each other down as the audience seemed to get tense, watching them just look at each other.

"I know they're waiting for my countdown, but whoever moves first here will decide when the match begins! Go ahead whenever!" The announcer stated. But the staredown continued. Jareus was trying to think of a way he could beat Adam Steel while saving stamina for the next match, while Steel was already making plans of attacking before Jareus did.

"Watch," Adam Steel taunted. He jumped forward, and instantly hit Jareus in the side region, despite Jareus trying to dodge to the side. Jareus was extremely surprised. He followed up with, "I could tell you were deep in thought, and used that opportunity!" Jareus boosted backwards to try and survey the situation, but

Adam kept boosting toward him, so Jareus boosted upward.

"You don't give me too much choice, do you, Adam Steel?" Jareus grinned. Steel got right below him, just as Jareus thought he would. Jareus did a flip in the air, and boosted down right at Steel.

"A DIRECT HIT!" The announcer yelled. The crowd went crazy, as Adam Steel was already slightly damaged.

"That was good, Jareus was it?" Adam Steel asked, backing up. Jareus just smiled at him.

"Yeah, it was, Adam Steel. I've been watching and can tell you're pretty good yourself," Jareus responded with a confident smile, posed to defend himself.

"Really? Wow. I must say I'm impressed you watched that closely. I just wanted to come here and earn money for my family, but I think I ran into someone I actually respect," Adam told Jareus.

"You too. The uh… respect part! I guess I'm here because of…" Jareus trailed off. *Wasn't I here because we wanted to get a new TV? NO! That's lame, don't say that!* Jareus thought to himself. He continued, "I'm here because of a rivalry."

"Ah, I see," Steel said while boosting forward, "I hope that you two will settle that outside the arena." He went for a direct stomach shot, but Jareus dodged. Jareus looked up to try and hit Adam, but a glaring light from a reflection in the distance caught his eye.

"YES!" Jack cheered with his mirror.

"Was that really it? Was that what you wanted to do?" Mark asked Jack.

"NO! Don't be such a downer!" Jack yelled at Mark.

"AH!" Jareus yelled, almost falling over, but not before Steel kicked him and sent him flying to the edge of the arena. He was about to fall on the ground, but boosted up.

"Big mistake!" Steel shouted and charged at him in the corner of the arena, grabbing his foot in midair. Jareus had made sure his shoes were prone to flying off, however, so Steel grabbed just his shoe! The difference in the weight he'd expected when calculating the jump gave him too much force going forward, so Steel fell off the stage.

"STEEL IS OUT OF THE RING!" The announcer cheered, and the audience went wild. Jareus jumped down to him.

"Hey, you were pretty good! Let's talk after this whole sports tournament is over," Jareus told Adam Steel. He got up, brushed the dirt off, and saw Jareus's extended hand. He looked him in the eye, smiled, and shook his hand.

"I'm glad I got to meet you," Adam Steel told Jareus.

"The feeling is mutual," he told Steel.

"NEXT UP IS ZACH ARTIEN VERSUS HARMONY HILL! THIS WILL BE THE FINAL MATCH OF THE FIRST BRACKET!" The announcer called. Adam Steel started walking away.

"Oh, and by the way Jareus," Adam started. Jareus turned back to look at him. "Defeat your inner demons first, your rival second." Jareus thought about this for a second, and then nodded as Adam Steel went to the stands. He went back to where Danny was.

"Nice, dude," Danny told Jareus, and gave him a high five. It took Jareus a second to realize what had just happened.

"Wait, are you mocking me?!" Jareus questioned Danny, sounding peeved while Danny looked away from him.

"Nooooo, of course not," Danny said, grinning and looking right back at him.

"Oh. Okay," Jareus concluded as he looked out at the match. Danny smacked his palm against his face. Out in the ring, Harmony was doing leg stretches, and Zach was doing arm stretches.

"I hear you're a hotshot! I want to test that," Harmony testified almost triumphantly, annoying Zach and pointing right at him.

"You'll be testing nothing," Zach said, being edgy.

"FIVE... FOUR... THREE... TWO..." the announcer was counting down, as both Zach and Harmony got ready to battle. He finished, "ONE!"

"YAH!" Harmony exclaimed as she instantly boosted forward, going into a kick in midair. Zach wasn't even moving.

"Nice try," Zach muttered under his breath. Zach caught her kick with his hand and boost-jumped up, yanking Harmony with him. This made her lose her balance completely. He let go halfway into the jump, and she fell to the ground. She used her arms so she didn't crash into the floor head-first. Zach landed on the other side of the ring.

"HEY! You really could'a hurt someone! But not too bad... even if that's not going to dictate this fight," Harmony remarked. She got up and was ready again. She boosted forward, anticipated Zach's incoming punch, and dodged under it. She got a firm hit on him, and it pushed him back to the side of the ring. She taunted, "That all ya got?"

"Hah. Sure," He smirked, wiping blood from his mouth. Zach boosted forward and right before he was blocked, dodged under to the side, and hit her directly in the side. She used her arms to cover herself as Zach jumped up and tried to boost directly down on her. She barely managed to roll and dodge, but Zach saw right through this. Zach boosted toward her and kicked her rolling body right off of the ring.

"UNBELIEVABLE! Zach is the fastest winner, and stays at first place!" The announcer again screamed through the microphone.

"What?! What was that?" Harmony remarked, all roughed-up and dusty.

"We're going to have a break now, folks! Get ready for the next matchups!" The announcer informed the crowd as they had just ended their cheering.

...

"So who's still here?" Jareus asked Zach as he was finishing up drinking a water bottle. Danny had left for the bathroom.

"Uhh… well, technically everyone, minus that one Eva girl who did the real-life equivalent of a rage quit. The losers of the matches are still waiting around for their rewards at the end, around the edges of the arena," Zach informed Jareus.

"So you, Danny, Odessa, and I are the ones left in the one-on-one matches? I don't know about that Odessa girl. First she was really good in the racing round, and now she's gone into the semifinals of this," Jareus commented. Jareus and Zach looked on the field where Odessa was doing stretches.

"She is quite good. I wonder what her reason for coming here is..." Zach responded.

"What if she ends up beating us?" Jareus rhetorically asked.

"I'M winning, you can be beaten if you want, it'd just mean my guaranteed victory. Now can we focus on the tournament?" Zach sneered. Jareus was very confused by Zach's snideness.

"Hey, Zach, what's with the attitude?" Jareus asked, a little concerned.

"It's nothing, Jareus. I'm just going to be the one to beat you, that's all. Now stop—" Zach started.

"That isn't it," Jareus cut off Zach.

"Wha—what?" Zach sounded genuinely confused.

"You didn't act like this until this tournament. Yeah, there have been some times where you weren't feeling it, but you've been Hellbent on winning," Jareus explained to Zach.

"I know, I know, okay. You get to win everything, though, being in Rownert and getting recognition. I mean, why do you even want to win this?" Zach actually asked Jareus. He seemed a little more genuine now.

"When I heard about this sports tournament, yeah, I did think maybe we could enter because we needed money for a new television. But we both know neither of us are really here because of that. I've had multiple encounters with Adrenaline Corp. now. I want to get on the inside. I want to win this tournament, and prove that I can be one of the best with them! I want to get into the company and help coordinate protection plans, so more events like the Purged Souls taking over Rownert don't happen again," Jareus explained seriously to Zach. "So does that make sense? I just don't want things like that to happen again. I remember saying that I was ready for 'a new adventure,' before it all went down. I can't believe I didn't take it seriously. After what happened, I want to grow and make sure that it doesn't just become a game again." Jareus slowed down and realized how much he had been wanting to say that. It almost made him feel better saying it aloud.

"Well, that's good for you," Zach started, his voice quivering angrily. "I saw nothing but you getting awards, Jareus. For how you've been leading us, or whatever. I've always been left behind! Living off the streets, even. I refuse to let that happen anymore. This sports tournament... it isn't for the audience," Zach paused, "This tournament is for me, to prove to you... that I'm just as good."

"THE NEXT ROUND IS GOING TO BE ZACH ARTIEN VS ODESSA OWENS! EVERYBODY GET READY!" They could hear the muffled announcer in the locker room. Zach angrily walked out of the room, hiding what may have been tears from Jareus. Jareus was about to go after him, but then just sat down.

"Hey, what's been happening? I also got water, which may have taken longer than I expected," Danny asked.

"I think I made a mistake," Jareus told Danny quietly.

"A mistake? You seem to be doing good overall. Like, you did beat Adam Steel in that match pretty well," Danny commented.

"No... I mean like... a mistake in my judgment. A mistake in the way I carry myself, and treat people," Jareus admitted.

"THIS IS THE FIRST MATCH OF THE SEMIFINALS! GET READY FOR SOMETHING TRULY SPECIAL, FOLKS!" The announcer was hyping up the audience again. Zach was ready in one corner, looking at Odessa, who also remained silent.

"You ready for this, buddy?" Odessa smiled, taunting. She knew Zach was also the last one to fight, ending it pretty quickly. But she had gotten to see Zach do it, and now knew how he operated. Zach didn't say anything.

"THREE, TWO, ONE, GO!" The announcer started them off. They both charged toward each other, and their fists both hit each other. Their contact caused a bunch of sparks to go everywhere, as they had the exosuits on—which also meant their punches were equally as powerful.

"You're pretty good! Probably better than me, but I'm determined!" Odessa smirked, after she was pushed back by the force of the punch. Zach gritted his teeth. She jumped up and boosted in for the kick. Zach went to grab her leg, but she had already seen this done. It was a fakeout, and she kicked with her other leg. This sent Zach across the ring.

"No way! She just put the hurt on Zach!" Danny exclaimed from the sidelines.

"I don't know if he's emotionally stable. It might cause flaws in his judgment. But, I believe he deserves to win. So let's hope he can," Jareus told Danny.

"You... are also pretty good," Zach commented, getting up. He wiped the blood from his lip, and smirked. He went in for a punch and she blocked. He flipped to the right, and went in for another. This time, Odessa caught his hand and flipped him to the other side. She went in for the punch, but Zach caught her arm with his two hands, lifted her up by her arm, and was going to slam her on the ground. But halfway through the flip, Odessa boosted downwards, causing her fist to crash into him. They both fell over on the ground.

"Ahhh… jeez," Zach panted, more exhausted than before. He got his arms up, and slowly pushed himself up. Odessa got up as well. Zach commented, "Odessa, I understand. You're determined to show your use, aren't you?" An almost shocked expression appeared on her face.

"How would you know?" She spat as she got back in a defensive position. Zach chuckled.

"It takes someone like that to know one. I mean, you got those tired eyes, ya know?" Zach told her, smiling through his watering eyes. His face was all roughed up as well.

"From crying? Yeah, righ—" She was about to finish, yelling.

"You can't hide that. Eventually sooner or later, somebody's going to notice. Don't let your dreams pass by. Use that power of always wanting to be something better," Zach told Odessa. She was holding back her emotions, but somehow, she knew he was right.

"I… I know," she stammered, "I'll use this… fire within me," She got in a stance, even more powerful and determined than before.

"I like to see that! Because now that I see I'm not alone," Zach shouted, "I'm getting all fired up!" He stomped into his stance. She did too.

"IT SEEMS LIKE OUR CONTESTANTS ARE MORE READY THAN EVER!" The announcer shouted.

"LET'S GO!" Odessa shouted. She boosted forward, and Zach blocked her hit. She kept hitting, but Zach dodged and blocked the attacks, and then he jumped up high. She followed, and hit straight up. He knew this was coming, so he flipped and boosted right down at her. They crashed into the floor again, but this time both of them were on their feet, still sliding backwards.

"You know, Odessa..." Zach continued, "I think you've really taught me what it means to be determined." He smirked, and she smiled. They went back at it, crazy punches flying everywhere. Some hits landed, some did not. They boost-jumped all around the arena, clashing.

"WHAT A SPECTACLE! THIS FIGHT IS INSANE!" The announcer screamed. Zach then boosted into Odessa, pushing her to the edge. He jumped up into the air.

"Gah..." Odessa gasped for air. Zach jumped to the other side of the ring. He smirked and they both went right for each other again. But right before their fists clashed again, Zach boosted straight down and kicked Odessa into the air. She flipped around as Zach had expected her to.

"Okay! Come get me!" Zach yelled as she boosted down. But this time, he boosted right back up at her, taking the hit head-on. This she didn't expect, and it knocked her right out of the ring.

"ZACH WINS!" The announcer shouted, sounding almost muffled in the back of Zach's perspective. He smiled, jumped over, and helped Odessa up.

"You okay?" Zach asked her. She was not too badly hurt, so she sat up and smiled. She nodded, and he helped her up. He then told her, "You were the real winner there. I would have been done for, if I hadn't seen your resolve. It helped me remember my own."

"Really? I just… I don't know. I never wanted to be the BEST, I guess, but I know exactly what you meant. I just wanted to prove myself to my family," Odessa told Zach.

"I'm trying to prove myself to those fools over there, Jareus and Danny. So I get where you're coming from," Zach told Odessa as he walked her over to the sidelines.

"Those two? But you guys seem like really good friends," Odessa said tiredly.

"Yeah… I mean… we live together. It's just… the Rownert incident that they got all that credit for," Zach explained.

"Rownert incident?" Odessa questioned him. Zach was shocked.

"You don't know?" Zach asked.

"No!" She laughed, "And I'm pretty caught up on current events, so I'm 100% sure that it isn't as much credit as you think."

"NEXT UP IS JAREUS DEHAYVEN VERSUS DANNY KIPPER!" The announcer's voice came through the speakers. Jack and Mark had been watching this whole time.

"So when are you going to use *that* thing?" Mark asked. Jack looked at him, confused for a second, but then he remembered what he was talking about.

"Ah yes! Well… actually I want to see who wins in the Jareus versus Danny fight. But, I'll use it to mess up whoever wins," Jack smirked. He took the Wish Orb out of his pocket.

"That was one Hell of a task for me to steal it without anybody noticing. I mean, they also hadn't really used it in a year or so. There was dust on it. But I just think they're trying to protect it. Whatever you wish for, make sure the exchange works out," Mark went on.

"I know, I know!" Jack grunted. Unbeknownst to them, an unknown person behind them had taken note of the artifact they had in their possession, and ran off before being seen.

"ARE YOU READY?! THIS IS ONE HEATED MATCH BETWEEN TWO FRIENDS!" The announcer continued to hype the audience.

"More like housemates," Danny commented. He and Jareus chuckled a little, even while facing off against each other in the arena.

"You know, I've always wanted to see who'd win in a fight. I just never had a reason to start one until now!" Jareus smirked.

"Me too," Danny agreed. They were in a standoff.

"THREE, TWO, ONE, GO!" The announcer was almost cut off by Danny and Jareus rushing each other. They instantly hit both fists against each other, causing sparks. Danny threw Jareus to one side after gripping his arms, and Jareus jumped straight up, boosting in with a punch. It hit Danny to the side of the ring. Jareus ran low to the ground and tried to trip him, but Danny jumped to the other corner. Danny gripped a fist and boosted right to Jareus. The hit was received, but Jareus had to stand his ground. The hit impacted him, and he had to take all of the force, otherwise his body would have flown backwards. Jareus got low and kicked Danny's legs out from under him. Then he shoved his body to the other side of the ring, panting.

"Who would… have thought… we'd be even…" Jareus panted. Danny got up, breathing heavily as well.

"Yeah… I thought you would have fallen out already…" Danny commented exhaustedly. They ran toward each other again, and this time, they both went to knee each other and hit each other's shins.

"OW OW OW!" They both yelled simultaneously while jumping around on one leg. They both got serious again, and Jareus jumped as he heard Danny boosting, but he had no idea that Danny had boosted up as well. They both punched at each other and fought each other as they fell toward the ground. At that point, they both fell over, because their shins hurt a lot and the impact of the ground didn't help the pain whatsoever. Then Jareus had a weird idea as they both stood up again.

"This is getting quite tiring…" Danny panted, "But now when I…" He was cut off as Jareus threw his exosuit arm at Danny—he'd taken it off him. It hit Danny in the face.

"OW OW WHAT?!" Danny exclaimed. He couldn't see and ended up tripping on the edge of the arena.

"AND… Jareus wins?" The announcer half-shouted with a very questionable audience applause afterwards.

"Dude!" Danny yelled at Jareus as he peeked his head over the arena, almost laughing.

"Sorry man, you gotta do what you gotta do," Jareus told him and chuckled.

"Alright, whatever. I'm fine with you going up against Zach, but this didn't answer my question," Danny complained.

"What? Question?" Jareus asked.

"Yeah, who would win in a *fair* fight between us?" Danny teased him.

"Okay, well, the one thing you can find out by what happened is I'm willing to fight dirtier than you," Jareus told him.

"Fair enough," Danny told him as he started to walk back over to the sidelines.

"So, you guys wanna watch from the sidelines for this last matchup? Cuz I do!" Harlow Henry asked Alex and Cole.

"Really? We can do that?" Alex asked him.

"Dude, I own the place, let's go!" Harlow told him.

"Like, you own the building...?" Alex continued to question. Harlow sighed, and figured there was no use in hiding it anymore.

"I own Adrenaline Corp. Well... I kind-of own it. I'll tell you more later, let's go!" He grinned, and started walking.

The others snapped out of their shock and quickly went to the front lines, where the other fighting matchup contestants had been.

"EVERYBODY GET READY FOR THE FINAL ROUND, COMING IN JUST A MINUTE!" The announcer boomed as loud music played in the background.

"So... you know what to do, right?" The shadowy figure from earlier told another person.

"I know exactly what to do. We're gonna wait for their first move, though," He told the figure.

"THEY'RE JUST ABOUT READY! Waiting on confirmation... ZACH AND JAREUS ARE READY!" The announcer yelled and everybody cheered. Jareus entered, having refreshed himself, and Zach had as well. Zach entered from the opposite side of the arena, and they both slowly walked to the ring.

"THIS IS IT, FOLKS! THE WINNER OF THE ADRENALINE SPORTS TOURNAMENT ALL RESTS ON THIS!" The announcer told the audience, even though it was kind of implied.

"Jareus, when I beat you, I'm going to say that I told you so," Zach pointed at Jareus. Their suits shined, as they had been fed, rehydrated, patched up, and their suits all readied up again.

"Look, Zach, I don't know what to say to you... I know what you're feel—" Jareus was cut off.

"No, you don't," Zach scoffed, lowering his arm.

"Zach..." Jareus continued.

"Are you ready, Jack?! You should go now!" Mark shouted at him as he was getting out of his seat.

"I get it, I'm going!" Jack yelled back as people were starting to seem concerned. Even security saw him hop the wall into the arena, but they weren't fast enough.

"Zach, I... I've always valued you... I've even thought you were better than me..." Jareus spat out. Zach seemed almost shocked by this, and had to think for a second. But something stole his attention before he even had time to fully take that in.

"IS THAT JACK?!" Zach yelled suddenly, pointing and catching Jareus's attention, too. They all turned to him, as did everyone else on the field. Cole and Alex looked up, being on the actual field, while Harlow watched from right behind the first bench.

"I finally got to you guys!" Jack yelled, smirking. But before he could do anything else, another man appeared. He came out of a door that went right into the field and grabbed Jack's arm that was holding the Wish Orb. He looked older, with a bit of scruff on his face. He wore a necklace, a camo shirt, cargo pants, gray torn shoes, and two massive metal gloves that were different shades of dark green. Jareus and Zach could also see a shadowy figure in the doorway.

"I WISH FOR EVERYONE WITHIN THE FIELD OF THIS ARENA TO BE TRANSPORTED TO PLANET EQUINOX!" The man with the gloves yelled, extremely loudly. The shadowy figure stepped into the field as he was saying that, but they couldn't quite make out who it was in time. Suddenly, everyone on the field saw what looked like streams of light, galaxies of stars, and planets surrounding them, before the sensation wore off and they felt grounded again.

"Where... did they all go?" The announcer asked, gazing upon an empty field.

...

"Ughhh... where... am I?" Jareus asked. He looked around. He appeared to be on a beach of some sort, but the sky was a purple hue, and he could clearly see the galaxies beyond wherever he was. Somehow, he could breathe fine. Jareus panicked, "Hello?!"

"Wha... where are we?" Zach asked, getting up from the sand. He saw the same thing Jareus did.

"You think I know? Well, there's this beach... and it looks like there are some caves over there," Jareus described the place.

"Where's everyone else? I know he wished all of us here," Zach asked, looking around for any other signs of life.

"Well... it seems as if we were slightly further apart than at the tournament, so maybe it spaced all of us out a little more. That should mean everyone is that way!"

44

Jareus pointed inland, which was beyond a cliff that loomed over them.

"What are we supposed to do? Who was that? And... Why did *Jack* have the Wish Orb?" Zach panicked aloud.

"I don't know, but he's gonna get a proper beating for causing this. Freakin' JACK of all things! I knew he came back to life like two years ago, but I didn't expect him now, of all times!" Jareus complained.

"But it wasn't even him! I don't know what Jack was going to do, but it looked like that guy grabbed Jack forcefully against his will. I'm guessing that he wasn't affiliated with him, especially because Jack looked terrified," Zach snickered a little.

"Let's just go inland, get that orb back, and get home," Jareus commanded, and the two started walking.

"I... hope we have a good fight when we get home," Zach told Jareus. Jareus turned around and put his hand on Zach's shoulder.

"I'm sorry the police forced you out of Rownert, okay? I guess I was trying to play hero, and that was childish of me," Jareus admitted.

"Yeah... but apparently people don't even know about Rownert! I legit thought they did. But nah, not even Odessa did. I gotta thank her when we find her. So... apology accepted," Zach told Jareus, smirking.

"Is that all? Wow, okay. Let's go," Jareus stated. They kept walking. The only way up was through a cave.

"Are you sure this cave even goes up?" Zach asked Jareus, placing his feet carefully on the uneven ground below him.

"No, I don't! But it's our best bet," Jareus told him. They kept walking through the cave, and even heard some noises.

"Did you hear that? Sounded almost like a monster or something outside of here," Zach commented.

"Let's… speed up. Who knows what's happening outside of this cave?" Jareus questioned rhetorically. They started running, and they saw the other side of the cave. Jareus shouted, "THERE IT IS!" They exited the cave, and saw Alex.

"Alex! There you are!" Zach shouted.

"ZACH, JAREUS, HELP ME OUT HERE!" Alex shouted. Suddenly, a monster made out of bones with pieces of hanging flesh jumped out of a tree with a sword.

"What the heck is that?" Jareus yelled, actually terrified.

"Ah, so there *are* more. Welcome to Amar's arena, I have been ordered to try and eliminate anybody that comes around here by Amar," The bone monster spoke, pulling a sword of bone out of his chest.

"Eliminate?! Amar?!" Zach questioned aloud.

"No elaboration will be needed!" The bone monster shouted as he charged toward Jareus and Zach. Jareus and Zach boosted away, as they both still had the Adrenaline Corp. exosuits on. Alex didn't, though, so he was just running. The bone monster turned around and started going after Alex again.

"We gotta protect Alex!" Jareus yelled at Zach, but Zach was already on it. He boosted forward and kicked the bone monster's arm clean off.

"What do you think *that's* going to do?" The bone monster taunted as he started running for his arm, past Zach. But Jareus was in his way, so he yelled, "DIE!"

46

"AH!" Jareus yelled in response, and he ducked right below the monster's sword. The bone monster turned around, and almost stabbed him with it again, so Jareus jumped backwards. But Jareus hit a tree, and fell down off of a small cliff.

"JAREUS! ESCAPE AND FIND THE OTHERS! I GOT THIS!" Jareus could hear Zach yell as he continued to take on the bone monster. Jareus realized he was on a different part of the beach.

"OKAY, ZACH!" Jareus yelled, but now he didn't hear anything. They'd already sounded far away, but now they'd their battle elsewhere. Jareus just wondered what to do. This time, the beach connected to a big open plains area with bushes in the background, so he decided to walk toward it. *Amar must be the one with those giant green gloves*, he thought. As he kept walking, he realized the bushes formed a wall hedge of some sort, and saw an opening within it. It didn't look like there was anywhere else he could go, so he decided to go further into the bushes. The second he got inside, he realized exactly what it was.

"This is just like the labyrinth of leaves that's in Rownert! But it isn't underground... no. This is just a maze!" Jareus exclaimed to himself. He decided to go left first, and saw more options as he went on through the maze. Suddenly, as Jareus was going through, he felt something poke his back, something spine-like.

"What the..." Jareus turned around to see a cactus, "HECK!" He yelled and backed off. It was a slow-moving, living cactus creature. He was able to walk away easily, but thought, *this planet Equinox seems familiar... but it's really freaking weird*. He continued his journey through the maze, and found a more open area, and wondered what was there. He came to the conclusion that it had to be a dead end, at that moment, a small tornado formed in the area.

"AHH!" He screamed, and ran away from the plains. The tornado didn't move, and didn't even tear up any of the bushes. *That was weird*, he thought to himself, so he kept moving.

After jogging a bit further, he found an area that looked like a sacrificial altar of some sort, an area with stones, inscriptions, and a pit where they may have lit a fire. This terrified Jareus, and he wished he'd never seen that. But he had to continue through it, as that was the maze's exit.

"Ah... finally. Here's the exit!" Jareus cheered, seeing a big empty plain with some cliffs, grass, and mostly dirt. Suddenly, he heard growling behind him. This scared the heck out of him, and he turned around to see some sort of ice monster.

"AHHH!" He screamed again, and boost-jumped up to avoid it tackling him. It looked like a mixture between a gorilla and what most people would believe a yeti would look like. He yelled to himself, "WHY IS THERE A YETI?!"

The ice creature froze the land below it as it ran. Jareus landed on top of a small hill, and it turned around to try and tackle him again. But this time he ran forward, jumped off of its head, and boosted forward. Infuriated, the creature tried to rush after him, but it crashed into a bush. Jareus used this time to boost himself as he ran, and hid behind a rock. It turned and looked around, but it didn't even seem to have a nose, so it couldn't smell him. It went into the leaf maze, continuing to search for him. Jareus wiped the sweat off his forehead and continued down a dirt path he found.

"Wha—" Jareus started, tripping. He caught his balance, but heard the ice creature roar in the background, so he jumped down a small overhang and saw a small hut.

"Amar? Is that you? I thought you said you would leave me alone!" A humanoid creature exclaimed, taking out what looked like a gun.

"Hold it! Wait! I'm not Amar! My name is Jareus Dehayven!" Jareus yelled at him. He put the gun down and walked over.

"Hmm… it seems that you aren't. Forgive my eyesight, I cannot see well," He told Jareus. He looked like an older man, but his skin was a pale orange, not like human skin. His pupils were white, the rest of his eyes were black, and he was wearing rags.

"What is this place?" Jareus asked.

"You don't know? How did you get here?" The old man asked Jareus.

"I was on Earth, and I think this Amar guy wished us here. He's a bit older, right? It seems he wants us 'eliminated.'" Jareus responded.

"Ah, so you do not know what this place is?" The old man asked Jareus.

"Well, I know we're on planet Equinox," Jareus told him.

"DON'T use that cursed name! It was once known as Qiantam, and in my heart, that never changed," The old man told Jareus.

"Oh… what's the story behind that? I knew a man named Equinox once. My friend Danny and I had no choice but to kill him," Jareus told the old man.

"You were the killer of Equinox?! Here, come inside my house. I was formerly known as the 'Qiantam Elder,' but now I'm known only by my first name, Starayzo," Starayzo told Jareus, letting him into the small wooden hut.

"So you speak English?" Jareus asked him.

"Yes… well I learned. I was part of a research facility on the human world a long time ago. I'll tell you in just a second the entire story up to Amar, but shall I pour you a cup of Purflephic? It's similar to what you humans call 'tea' on Earth," Starayzo told Jareus.

"Uhh… sure," Jareus answered. He poured the liquid into a small wooden cup.

"Where was I? Oh yes… this is a long story, so prepare yourself for it," Starayzo started to explain, "Back a long time ago, while I was working at the human research facility, we decided that we would take two humans to conduct studies on. Small humans from what you call, 'orphanage homes.' After we successfully took them, we named them 'Equinox,' and 'Xenova.' They grew up as brothers, and we tried to integrate them into our society, since the Qiantam race and the human race were so similar. They had a couple of health scares, but generally they were okay."

"Mmhmm…" Jareus followed.

"As they got older," Starayzo continued, "they quarreled more often. Xenova would go on to become a 'wizard.' The wizards of this world were basically the police of yours, and yes, they could use what you could call 'magic.' But all magic works on the basic law of equivalency—I was once a wizard myself. At this point in time, we tried to take a third human, but he was said to have disappeared in an accident, so the human research facility and program was discontinued."

"Testing on people sounds messed up," Jareus commented.

"It was. I was against it, but..." He digressed, "Later, Equinox became jealous of Xenova's wizard power, and tried to become stronger on his own. To do this, he went into a restricted library and found a way to contact a dark power. The dark power first cursed him with strength and a different mind, and then tried to take over his body on its own. Xenova was somehow able to seal the dark power away, coming in at the last second to save his brother. Nobody knows where this dark power went, but it did not possess Equinox."

"Are you sure? That guy seemed demonic to me," Jareus laughed. He was met with a sad look from Starayzo. He sighed, "Joking."

"Even so, Equinox changed..." He ignored Jareus, "but of his own accord. He became obsessed with the very power that had attempted to take over his mind, and gained his own political platform and party. With that, he overran the world, causing a civil war that would eventually leave half of the planet annihilated. He killed almost everyone that didn't agree with him. Xenova fled to Earth after making an orb that could revive the friends he'd lost, although at a cost, and Equinox and his army chased him. That's all we know. The planet has been rural and basically empty for a long time since then. He did, indeed, rename the planet after himself... but I, along with most others left, do not respect that name," Starayzo finished.

"Wow... what happened is... I don't know about Xenova, but I found Equinox looking for the Wish Orb with my friend, Danny. But it seemed as if Equinox had become frail, he yelled about how weak he had gotten thanks to Xenova," Jareus butted in for a second.

"That means… Xenova might still be alive… but I doubt he remembers who he is." Starayzo commented. *Forgetfulness is a nasty thing. Even Cole doesn't remember who he is, and that's caused him all kinds of problems,* Jareus thought.

"Anyways, a person named Amar suddenly showed up on this planet and started making these… arenas. He told us that as long as we didn't interfere, we wouldn't be killed. Everything he did seemed almost robotic, and he demanded a way to get to the planet Earth at one point. After threatening me with his giant gloves, I gave up an escape pod I had from the civil war and he used it to go to Earth. Amar's nothing but bad news," Starayzo finished up.

"Then I have to stop Amar! First Jack, Minister Destructo, Redaro, and now Amar have all contested us, trying to protect the Wish Orb. We've had to get rid of them one way or another," Jareus spoke loudly.

"I knew Minster Destructo… he used to be a good guy, generally, until he met Equinox," Starayzo told Jareus.

"I know, he was the worst! When I get home, I'm throwing that stupid boot he's trapped in into space!" Jareus told Starayzo.

"A boot…? Well, it would be what he deserves. Also, I think I saw one of your friends pass by here earlier. He went toward the forest, but I sensed something bad about him. It may just be me fortune-telling like a crazy old wizard, but it seems as if he'll lose someone important to him. At this rate, you must defeat Amar, Jareus. It doesn't matter what you have to do, we here on Qiantam are on our last limb of life. Do whatever you have to," Starayzo told Jareus. Jareus got up and opened the door.

"I'll do everything I can, Starayzo!" Jareus yelled. He was already off, going to find Amar. Starayzo could finally rest peacefully. *He must have been talking about Danny, losing someone? Let's make it so he won't! When I get to the forest, fate's gonna eat my butt!* Jareus thought. He jumped right into the forest and heard something.

"No! I do not think that there's water here!" Cole was yelling at someone.

"We might as well try it if we're really stuck here! I mean, what else are we going to do? Just lay down and die?" Odessa's voice responded.

"Cole, Odessa!" Jareus yelled as he crashed into the dirt, coming from above through some trees.

"Jareus, what are you doing? Where are we? I have a weird sense of déjà vu," Cole explained. Jareus got up off of the dirt.

"Cole, I promise I'll explain to you later. As of right now, I have no clue what Amar's motives are, but Amar is the guy who teleported us here. He's the guy with the green gauntlet gloves, and wants us dead! I don't want to kill Amar, but to get home and set the Qiantam free… we might have to," Jareus explained to them.

"Wha—what the hell? Why am I here? How did he teleport us?" Odessa asked.

"I think you were consequently teleported. I'm pretty sure he's after us, and it has something to do with the Wish Orb!" Jareus continued to explain.

"But I have nothing to do with that!" A different voice shouted.

"I know you don't, Odessa!" Jareus yelled back, looking around for possible ways to go.

"Jareus… that wasn't me…" Odessa told Jareus. Jareus panicked for a second, and he turned around. His eyes widened when he saw who had talked to him.

"That was me, Jareus. I've been waiting to fight you again! Unfortunately, I don't have the Wish Orb, I think it was teleported elsewhere," Jack yelled. Jareus's face got serious.

"Jareus," Jack sneered as he stood there.

"Jack!" Jareus scoffed, walking forward.

"Oh ho! So you're gonna come right to me? After all this time, I don't even have to convince you?" Jack taunted Jareus.

"I can't beat some sense into you without being direct," Jareus growled at Jack, as Odessa and Cole watched awkwardly. They clashed, their two fists hit each other, and the sparks sent Jack flying backwards. Jareus still had the exosuit.

"That isn't all I got!" Jack smirked.

I never thought it was, Jareus thought to himself. Jack ran up to him and slid, but Jareus kicked him, and he flew against a tree.

"STOP FOOLING AROUND! Amar, the guy who used you earlier, could still have the Wish Orb!" Jareus yelled at Jack.

"WHAT DO YOU SUGGEST I DO, HELP FIND IT?!" Jack yelled back at Jareus. Jareus smacked his face with his palm.

"Jack… you literally *earned* what happened to you already. Think about what you tried to do. Just come help us, and maybe we can just get over what's already happened," Jareus told Jack. Jack gritted his teeth.

"FINE!" Jack yelled in his dirtied white clothing. He started walking toward them and pointed forward.

"Hmph… that was a lot easier than I thought. Let's get going," Jareus said aloud.

"Did… I just hallucinate?" Cole asked aloud, following Jareus and Jack.

"Nope, I saw it too. I don't know what's going on, but that was *Hella* weird," Odessa commented. She and Cole started snickering.

"We should split up to try and find the Wish Orb, if you want to, Cole… and… whatever your name is," Jack told everybody.

"It's Odessa, and sure. I guess I can go with Cole, so Jareus can keep a watch of you," Odessa said, smirking.

"Ugh, whatever, sure," Jack scoffed. Cole and Odessa went down a different way through the forest, while Jack and Jareus continued down the same path.

"I never thought I'd be in this situation. We—meaning you and I, meaning I'm with JACK right now, of all people—are working together on a different planet, trying to find the Wish Orb. How is this even possible?" Jareus thought aloud.

"Hey! Look, it could be worse. You could be with Redaro or whatever his name was. Or killed by him, or something," Jack retorted. They continued to look around, walking through the forest.

"What's this?" Jareus asked. There was a wall of trees with a small path through them, and it went down in elevation by about ten feet.

"There's only one way to find out!" Jack gloated, walking in gleefully. Jareus followed, and their eyes widened in shock when they saw what lay before them.

Below them was some sort of an arena. It looked like a giant bowl-shaped area of just dirt and walls of trees, and three entrances were in the walls. Within the arena, Harmony Hill was on the ground, and Archie Bomics was fighting someone with Adam Steel. The person they were fighting looked like someone in their early twenties with very pale skin, a gray fedora with a blue stripe, a plaid red and black button up with a gray shirt under it, and brown-ish cargo shorts with a sash.

"Oi mate! This ain't funny anymore!" Archie told this man, who happened to be wielding a pole-like weapon. He whacked Archie right down.

"ARCHIE!" Adam yelled, and he charged the man with the pole. He successfully blocked the pole with the exosuit he luckily still had on.

"STEEL! I'm here to help!" Jareus yelled and jumped in without hesitation. As soon as Jack realized what Jareus had done, he followed him.

"You really think you can enter the arena of Scar without permission? I'll beat you senseless," The man, who Jareus guessed was named Scar, yelled. Scar jumped forward and hit Jareus with the pole dead in the center of his face.

"GAH!" Jareus let out a sound as he was pushed into the ground.

"You know? Amar told me to kill someone with your exact description. In the past, I wouldn't murder. But after this place became rural and it wasn't relevant anymore, people thought I died or something. I became an assassin. I'll do whatever I need to do to survive, and Amar's made it easy for me, so I'm going to do what he wants. Do you know what he wants to be done to you, Jareus?" Scar monologued.

Is he the third human they tried to get from the Quintam program? His pupils are normal! Jareus thought.

Scar attempted to stab the pole right through Jareus, but Jareus boosted up, dodging it.

"Why does Amar want me dead?!" Jareus yelled, dodging upward and finding his footing.

"Beats me, but I heard something about Redaro!" Scar yelled back at Jareus. Jareus was shocked for a second, wondering how exactly Redaro was connected to this.

"I don't know how Redaro is related to this issue… but Amar and you, Scar, just suddenly jumped into this whole equation! Which means I'm going to have to get rid of you to proceed!" Jareus yelled back at Scar. Jack was about to jump on Scar, but Scar hit him in the face and he hit the ground. Scar turned his attention back to Jareus.

"You're gonna get rid of me? Huh, a funny story. I've heard it all before, but once an assassin knows his target, they're already dead," Scar spoke loudly as he jabbed upward at Jareus, who was dodging his pole. Jareus jumped up and over Scar.

"It seems you've already tried to get rid of Adam Steel, but he still looks fine. Guess your target switched!" Jareus taunted. Scar grunted and jumped forward to try and surprise-attack Jareus.

"YAH!" Alex yelled, jumping out of the trees. He hit Scar in the head with a single exosuit arm, knocking him out cold. When Scar fell over, they could see a bunch of scars on his back.

"Alex! Where did you come from?! Where's Zach?!" Jareus had already started firing questions at Alex. Alex was panting.

"Zach and Danny… are fighting…" Alex was still catching his breath, so he couldn't make full sentences.

"They're fighting... each other?" Jareus seemed confused.

"They're fighting *Diadem*," Alex told Jareus. Jareus's mind flew back to Rownert... *did they ever find Diadem's dead body?* He thought. He remembered the Adrenaline Corp. personnel looking for Diadem and noting his disappearance. *No,* he continued, *we just assumed he died...*

"I'm coming with you, so show me the way..." Jareus told Alex, almost stumbling as he approached him. He hadn't even realized how tired he was. Jareus continued, "I'm guessing Diadem just never really died back in Rownert, and now Amar's recruited his help."

"They do seem to be working together, but we haven't yet seen Amar again. He seems to be MIA. But we're already caught up with Diadem so it's nice to only have to deal with one... also, why is Jack here?" Alex asked.

"I was brought back, obviously. I just got teleported here like the rest of you guys, so I'm helping Jareus look for the Wish Orb. We were fighting this Scar guy," Jack explained.

"Oh, okay. Well, let's get over to Diadem... Zach's gonna need this exosuit arm back," Alex said.

"Thank you for helping with Scar! We'll meet you over there, we're just going to make sure everybody's recovered!" Harmony yelled from the other side of Scar's arena.

"Really, Jareus, thank you for looking out for us," Adam Steel smiled and gave him a thumbs up.

"I'm done playing hero, guys! It was all of us!" Jareus told them as they left.

"That's good, mate, that's good," Archie said, stumbling out of the arena. Scar was out cold, but he wasn't dead. Jack, Jareus, and Alex started running back to where Diadem was. *Diadem was that shadowy figure, I'm guessing… What does Amar have to do with any of this?* Jareus thought to himself.

"Ohhh, maybe I can use this sword to fight with Diadem!" Alex smirked and pointed to a dagger he'd found lodged in the floor. Jareus slowed down. He had a bad feeling about that dagger. Alex picked it up, but suddenly he started spazzing out. His whole body jittered and he fell to the ground.

"ALEX!" Jareus yelled and went over to help Alex off the ground.

"I…! I'm okay!" Alex exclaimed. The sword he picked up had fallen, and it was so fragile it had become dust.

"That… seemed like a trap. Bad idea to pick up anything random. When we get there, I'll give Zach an exosuit arm. You'll need at least one to protect yourself with," Jareus told Alex. They crossed paths with Cole and Odessa, who started running with them.

"How are you guys doing? Any luck in finding the Wish Orb?" Odessa asked as she and Cole joined the group running through the forest.

"Nope, but Zach and Danny are going to need all of our help. They're fighting a being we know as Diadem," Alex told everybody. They kept running, but when they rushed into an opening, Danny and Zach ran into them.

"Wha—what are you guys doing?" Zach asked as Jareus took off one exosuit arm and threw it to him.

"We were coming to help you! Where'd Diadem go?" Jareus asked Danny and Zach. The group stopped—they'd suddenly felt a stone-cold presence.

"Well, if it isn't everybody all huddled together?" Diadem's voice sounded. He and Amar descended, floating above all of them. Amar held the Wish Orb.

"Now, we can finish Redaro's plan, Trevor Amiraga," Amar told Diadem. Everybody watched the two of them.

"Go ahead with what should be done, Amar," Diadem, who Amar called Trevor, said. Amar held out the Wish Orb.

"I WISH TO RETAIN MY YOUTH!" Amar shouted. Suddenly, his body's age started to regress rapidly, and he stopped at what looked to be around the age of eighteen—they could tell because he looked like the spitting image of Jareus.

"What the?!" Jareus yelled.

"Huh?!" Everyone else exclaimed. Diadem pointed at Jareus.

"You are Amar, Jareus! The Redaro of the future hypnotized him quite well! The same Redaro that Alex ran from, the same timeline where you all died and Alex escaped to the past. Jareus, you never died in that timeline. According to what I've heard, you were quite damn persistent!" Diadem exclaimed. He shook his head. "But here you are, a slave, after trying to attack Redaro. I'm here to keep the spell on him! Nobody's getting older because I am the equivalent exchange of the wish! The debt of age was paid by me, but I cannot die naturally! I knew your father quite well, Jareus, we were good friends. But what your father *didn't* know when we messed around with a ouija board many years ago was that we were going to become the Purged Souls! So controlling you will be easy."

"Are you saying I'm *him*?! Because… err… I'm having these weird… flashbacks…" Amar started to hold his head tightly.

"Now, now… hold on—" Diadem started to tell him.

"DIADEM!" Amar randomly shouted. Diadem tried to take the Wish Orb, and did so successfully at first. But he only held it for a few seconds before Amar socked him hard in the face, sending him flying. The Wish Orb was released from his grasp and went flying in a completely different way. Amar jumped out of his float to the ground and ran toward Diadem.

"Now is our chance! Get the Wish Orb!" Alex shouted. Everybody started running in different directions. Jareus was still shocked about the information revealed to him, but tried to table his processing for later, running to try and find the Wish Orb. Jareus continued to look through the rubble, still not spotting it. Everyone was almost scattered now, and they could hear Amar fighting Diadem in the background. Jareus saw Odessa and started looking with her.

"What's become of me?" Jareus asked aloud.

"What? What do you mean?" Odessa asked.

"I'm no leader. I'm a slave. And looking at this future me, I'm a monster," Jareus stuttered.

"Woah, wait! *You* are not a monster! I don't know what the HELL is going on, but I know that Amar isn't *you*," Odessa talked some sense into Jareus.

"I'm destined to be a monster, and a slave to one too…" Jareus started chanting as if in a trance, not hearing anything.

"SNAP OUT OF IT!" Odessa slapped Jareus. Jareus finally began to listen to her. "Forget this destiny crap! What you do now is all up to you! Obviously that you is *not* this you, and we are going to find the Wish Orb!" Odessa shouted at Jareus.

"Okay… okay…" Jareus said, almost panting.

"You good?" Odessa asked.

"Yeah… good enough," Jareus told her. They continued to look around, and they heard the other people in the distance yelling as well. Out of nowhere, Diadem came out from behind a tree. He'd used the shadow limbs in order to climb around the trees.

"It took some work. I had to *DRILL* his purpose back into his thick skull… but Amar and I are on good terms again. With the power you gained, Jareus, I will eliminate you and your friends! This is bigger than you, so getting you out of our way will finally end things," Diadem spoke down to Jareus and Odessa.

"WHERE'S AMAR? WHAT'S HE DOING?!" Jareus shouted right back up at Diadem.

"Your friends have to deal with him now. And seeing the ability he has from Redaro, they won't be beating him," Diadem scorned.

"Uh… Odessa! We're going to go right through this guy! You hear me?!" Jareus shouted. She was almost stunned. Jareus boosted forward, and Diadem made his shadow limb into a giant knife. Jareus's exosuit arm clashed with the knife. Jareus boosted upward, and then down, sending Diadem crashing into the ground. Diadem went for Odessa, but Odessa grabbed his arm and threw him successfully.

"Looks like that Adrenaline Corp. sports tournament paid off!" Odessa smirked. Jareus then went in and punched Diadem in the gut.

"How dare you!" Diadem remarked, shooting his knife upward. It slightly cut Jareus's shoulder on his unprotected arm.

"GAH!" Jareus shouted, grunting in pain. He kicked up and snapped off Diadem's shadow limb, leaving him writhing in agony. Jareus took his other arm and slammed Diadem's head into the ground. Diadem cut Jareus's foot with his regenerating shadow limb, which caused Jareus to jump back.

"How could you do this to me... and so quickly... Jareus..." Diadem asked while his shadow limb transformed and hoisted him up into a tree.

"You're messing with fire! You should have been dead a long time ago!" Jareus shouted back at him.

"Gotcha!" Odessa shouted, kicking him out of the tree. Diadem fell into the dirt, right below Jareus, bleeding and angry.

"Jareus... you'll never be free from being a monster," Diadem coughed up.

"A monster to you, maybe," Jareus spat.

"No, no, wait! Hey, don't—!" Diadem shouted as Jareus jumped up and boosted down right on his spine. Diadem's eyes closed, and he laid on the ground.

"Is... he dead?" Odessa went over to where Jareus was.

"He's passed out from the pain, that wouldn't kill him. But if we leave this place, it'd be funny to think about him being stranded here," Jareus declared, walking in the other direction.

"Where are you going?" Odessa asked him.

"We're going to go save everyone from Amar, so follow me only if you're determined to do that," Jareus told her, still walking the other way. Of course, she ended up following him. They ended up boosting toward where the noise was. But the second they got over the hill, it wasn't a pretty sight. They saw Jack, Cole, and Alex on the floor. Jareus ran over to them.

"You guys okay?! I didn't see what happened... I'm guessing it was Amar," he said.

"Those fists pack a punch... but we're not dead. Alex is helping Jack right now... Amar didn't treat him nicely. Alex also is feeling a little sick, and after trying to fight, he threw up a little. I just straight up ran out of energy," Cole told them, his voice sounding dry.

"We're going to go help Danny and Zach, then. Only come back in the fight if you really feel well enough!" Jareus told everyone, while moving closer to the sound. Odessa followed him.

"YOUR FISTS CAN'T BE THAT TOUGH!" Danny yelled. He boosted right to Amar's face and tried to kick off one of the metal gloves, but the metal stopped his kick. Amar yelled, punching Danny off of him, and Danny landed on the ground. Zach was still looking for the Wish Orb. Danny yelled to him, "Have you not found it yet?!"

"STILL LOOKING!" Zach yelled back. Amar charged toward Danny, but he dodged to the side.

"You gotta remember me. Jareus would. You haven't said anything since you charged us all again. Why were you fighting Diadem? Aren't you tired of being used?" Danny taunted Amar. Amar yelled again and punched at Danny, but Danny boosted backwards. The metal fist crashed into the ground, kicking some rubble up.

"This is something I must do…" Amar muttered.

"What was that? Couldn't hear you," Danny scoffed.

"I DON'T HAVE A CHOICE!" Amar shouted, hitting Danny's leg out of the air as he tried to dodge, "I HAVE TO DO THIS!" Danny crashed into a tree.

"I shouldn't have provoked a puppet," Danny groaned. Amar started to run toward the tree, and Danny's expression turned to terror.

"YAH!" Jareus yelled, kicking Amar to the side. Jareus ran to Danny, got him out of the tree, and asked, "You alright?"

"Hah, I've been better. Whatever Redaro did to you in that future, it really screwed you up. He even heals fast," Danny panted.

"He what?!" Jareus exclaims.

"I'll take him, Jareus. It looks like you have a fight to get to," Odessa commented. Amar, who had crashed into another tree, was steaming with anger.

"Where's Zach?" Jareus asked.

"Looking for the orb, he'll come in if he needs to," Danny told Jareus as Odessa took Danny to go rest. Jareus readied for battle.

"So you're me, huh? I don't remember… in fact, I don't *ever* remember being that weak," Amar scoffed, "You're you. I became a new man." He jumped forward and Jareus blocked the hit, but it smashed a part of the electronics in the exosuit. They punched right into each other. Jareus jumped up to dodge, and Amar launched himself off the ground, kicking Jareus after gaining height. Jareus fell backward, but flipped back up. Amar charged toward him, but Jareus grabbed onto Amar's head and threw him into the ground, using him as a stepping stone to boost over.

"Looks like I don't even know my own fighting tactics," Jareus commented. Suddenly, Amar jumped out of the smoke and went to hit Jareus. Jareus dodged and punched right through a chunk of Amar's actual arm, making a side of it come straight off with the force of the exosuit.

"AHHH... AH..." Amar was panting and shouting. It looked like a bunch of steam was leaking from the wound. The muscle almost even appeared to bubble and boil as suddenly, the tendons restrung themselves and the skin grew back.

"What the hell? So *that's* what Redaro can do for you? No matter... I don't know how many people he intends on sending to this timeline, but the tech we've made without him here surpasses what he can do!" Jareus gloated.

"Is that so?" Amar whispered. He looked right up with his red eyes. That was their only glaring difference in physique. Amar's pupils were tinted bright red, while Jareus's own were a soft brown.

Amar charged Jareus faster than before, and drove the metal fist into where the cut on his shoulder was. Amar attacked with the arm that was still healing, but it was still powerful enough to take Jareus's unprotected arm right off, letting some of his fast-healing blood seep into Jareus's fresh wound.

"That's what Redaro can do. But now... it seems I've shared blood with you... It doesn't matter, you'll be dead before you can realize any power!" Amar punched Jareus in the face with his big metal glove, and Jareus, in shock, fell to the dirt. As his vision began to fade, Jareus saw a figure. It was Zach, arriving on the scene as Jareus lost the fight.

"Zach… please do your best…" Jareus gasped. Zach had seen the fight go down as he approached.

"AMAR! You'd go so far as to kill a past version of yourself?! All this for what, Redaro and his conquest? Or does it seem like it's yours? Was your whole idea to take everyone from the sporting tournament, and to destroy them in your little arena conquest?!" Zach shouted, teary-eyed. If only he'd made up with Jareus earlier.

"It isn't that simple, Zach! While I needed those involved with the Wish Orb, the others in the tournament were just bystanders that happened to be there! Pity for them!" Amar yelled.

Wait, he knows my name! Zach thought. *If I can get through to him while fighting him… and preventing him from being a threat to anybody else… we might be able to wish ourselves back and get Jareus to an ambulance on time…*

"Well, it sure seems like it!" Zach yelled, holding back his tears. *But Jareus couldn't even get through to basically himself… but he didn't seem to be using emotional responses, rather basic memories. And over time, maybe it wears off and Diadem would have to do something about it again? We'll give it a shot, all or nothing!* Zach decided.

"ERRRR…. YAAAHH!' Amar ran forward and slugged his metal fist forward. Zach dodged and punched Amar in the face, sending him back a bit. They collided with their fists. The two went crazy, punching and dodging and blocking. Zach boosted back, already a little battle-damaged. Amar's little cuts were healing themselves. Zach jumped up into a tree, seemingly up to something. Amar didn't like whatever Zach was up to, so he started throwing stones at him, but Zach dodged to the next tree every time one would come his way. Amar started to chase Zach through the forest, as he hopped from tree to tree. Zach jumped out of the way after priming all of the trees to fall over on eachother.

"I made all of the trees unstable, so they should be..." Zach was cut off by the domino effect in practicality. By landing on the rather skinny trees, he had shifted them to lean to the side, all in a row. Eventually they all started falling down in a path which headed right to Amar. His eyes widened and he started to run from them, but then he turned around. Amar braced himself for impact, and caught the tree.

I WAS NOT EXPECTING THAT! Zach's brain shouted in his mind. Amar got angry, picked up a tree, and threw it toward the tree that Zach was on. Zach flipped out and jumped off the tree into an open area zone.

"GET BACK HERE!" Amar yelled. Zach saw a giant mountain-like area in the plains he was in, and if he lured Amar up there, everyone else would be clear from him. Zach started to boost-jump up the rockier area, and Amar grabbed onto the rocks, gaining on Zach quickly through sheer determination. Once Zach reached a flatter area on the mountain, he stopped and turned around. Amar jumped up, shouting, "I'm going to be Redaro's hero!"

"I thought you were done playing hero... Jareus. I thought you had *finally* just wanted to be real and transparent! Did you *EVER* get to do that?!" Zach shouted at Amar as he was about to charge once more.

Amar stopped for a second, but shook his head and kept charging. Zach caught Amar's fist. *Damn, I think I had him... but only for a second*, Zach thought. Zach jumped up, and let Amar fly to the other side with the amount of force he was exerting. Amar swung around and hit Zach. Zach slid under Amar, jumped up, and hit him with a nice uppercut. Amar put out his hands and hoisted himself onto a rock. He jumped off, swinging his fist forward, and Zach went to block his attack. It was a fakeout—Amar stuck out his leg and kicked Zach in the face. Zach fell over.

"How'd you like that?" Amar scoffed. Zach was coughing out blood, so he decided it was best to dodge, and boost jumped into a tree.

"What are you trying to prove?!" Zach yelled back at Amar. Amar stopped and thought about it for a second. Zach took that pause to boost off the branch and directly into Amar's chest, sending him flying back into the dirt.

"I'm going to be a savior!" Amar yelled. He got back up and went to charge Zach again, but Zach ducked and sent both of the exosuit arms into his rib cage. Amar held his chest and backed up a bit. Zach, with a stern look and blood dripping down his face, stood there.

"You aren't going to be a savior," Zach told Amar coldly, "Do you even know why you're fighting me?"

"I'LL KILL YOU ALL!" Amar shouted. He grabbed his own head, as if there were great pain occuring there.

"WHY WOULD YOU WANT TO KILL THOSE THAT YOU'VE ALWAYS VALUED?!" Zach yelled at Amar, struggling to disassociate him with Jareus. Amar charged forward, seemingly weaker and more regretful than before. He tried to kick Zach in the chest, but Zach caught his leg and flipped him onto the ground. His attacks were not as tough as they seemed to be. Zach looked at Amar dead in the eyes.

"You know why you're fighting me?" Zach asked. "You've always been afraid… that maybe I was better than you… and you never had any time to test anything—"

"Until now…" Amar spat out instinctively. He looked surprised that he'd even said that.

"We can stop this…" Zach started.

"AMAR! KILL ZACH AS SOON AS YOU CAN!" Diadem cut him off, crawling up the mountain and barely clinging on to life.

"GAHHHH! AHHHH!" Amar shouted as if the pain in his head had returned. He held his head down, and then flipped it back up like a madman. Amar turned around and set his sight on Diadem. Zach was pretty beat up, and he didn't know if he could take any more hits from Amar.

Amar screamed at Diadem, "SHUT THE HELL UP! NO MORE TELLING ME WHAT TO DO!" He was out of control—whether he was being manipulated or not, Amar was crazy.

"What?!" Diadem shouted, almost squeaking. Amar jumped up and stomped on Diadem's hand, crushing multiple bones. Diadem, infuriated, wrapped his shadow limb around Amar's leg. But Amar saw this, picked up Diadem, and threw him on the ground. Diadem tried to stop Amar from punching him, but it was too late. Amar started to beat Diadem senselessly, crushing his jawbone and ruining his teeth.

"THIS IS WHAT YOU GET FOR PRETENDING TO BE REDARO!" Amar yelled in his craze.

"That… isn't what I was waiting for…" Diadem croaked through what was almost his last breath. Diadem pulled himself close to Amar with his shadow limb, but Amar caught his fist. In that moment, the world suddenly seemed to blur, and once-stagnant forms had lost their definite shape. The colors inverted, and it was as if you could see multiple frames of reality at once. After a second, reality returned to normal, but it distracted Amar and Zach for a second.

Diadem smiled. "*That was.*"

"ZACH! I FOUND IT!" A voice yelled in the distance. It was Adam Steel, on the same mountain.

"NO YOU DON'T!" Amar shouted, dropping Diadem and starting to run toward Steel, as Zach did the same.

"Finish the job..." Diadem spoke with a condescendingly dry voice. Amar couldn't stand the feeling of being controlled anymore, so he turned around and grabbed Diadem by the neck. At this point, Zach had arrived.

"Thank you *so* much, Adam Steel!" Zach yelled, grabbing the orb. At this point, Amar had thrown Diadem, but was still looking in his direction.

This is my shot, let's do this right! Zach's thoughts raced. Zach held up the Wish Orb and yelled, "I WISH THAT THIS PLANET AND ITS NATURAL INHABITANTS WERE TELEPORTED FAR AWAY IN THE GALAXY, AND THAT ALL HUMANS WERE SENT BACK TO THE SPORTS TOURNAMENT BESIDES DIADEM AND AMAR! KEEP THOSE TWO RIGHT IN THIS VERY POSITION AS OUTER SPACE ENVELOPES THEM!"

Amar turned around and sprinted at Zach until... Suddenly, he wasn't. The planet wasn't there anymore.

"GAHHH... AHHH! THIS IS ALL YOUR FAULT, DIADEEEMMMMM!' Amar shouted as he and Diadem succumbed to the vacuum of space, meeting their demise.

Meanwhile, the arena competitors had woken up on the floor, in the exact same positions they had been before they were spirited away. They were all back at the Adrenaline Corp. Stadium on Earth.

"THIS JUST IN: THE CONTESTANTS HAVE REAPPEARED!" The announcer yelled in shock. Harmony, Archie, and others were on the floor.

"MEDIC! MEDIC! WE NEED A MEDIC!" Zach shouted, while Jareus was down and unconscious beside him.

"It looks like... JAREUS IS UNCONSCIOUS! THIS MAKES ZACH ARTIEN THE WINNER OF THE ADRENALINE CORP. SPORTS TOURNAMENT!" The announcer boomed, but there wasn't much applause. Most people had gone home, and the audience there were a little more concerned about the actual people who'd just randomly reappeared.

"WE NEED A—wait. What the heck?" Zach was yelling, until he looked down at Jareus. His arm was fine—it was back. Zach put two and two together in his mind... It was because Amar's fast-healing blood had been in Jareus's system. It wasn't long until they had a bunch of people back on the field, and those who were better changed back into their regular clothes. Harlow, who hadn't been teleported, even stopped by to congratulate everybody. They all got each others' contacts as well.

"WHAT HAPPENED TO ALL OF YOU? WHERE DID YOU GO?" A news reporter yelled, genuinely curious. The contestants were confused... they didn't know what to say.

"There were these two terrorists, they were experimenting with teleportation tech, and they tried to kill us! That kid that ran onto the field earlier was trying to save us from them! But we got them instead, and we were sent back here," Odessa stepped forward and told the news reporter. Everybody else just nodded in agreement. In not long, they were interviewing Jack.

"So Jack… Revel, is it? What was happening on your end during the terrorist attacks?" The news reporter asked Jack for the camera.

"Well… I knew these guys, and I didn't want them to be victims of the terrorists I thought I'd seen in the hall earlier. So I jumped down there to try and stop them," Jack told the camera. He heard Mark in the stands of the arena.

"Well, thank you, Jack, that was interesting…" The reporter continued. But Jack went back to Mark, and started to explain the actual story.

…

"So you're better now?" Zach asked Jareus out on the street, while the five of them who'd gone to Los Angeles were awaiting Jill's pickup.

"Yeah, that was… one trippy day. Oh yeah, Cole!" Jareus exclaimed aloud, looking at Cole.

"Yeah, what?" Cole asked.

"Do you know the name 'Xenova?'" Jareus asked him. He instantly seemed to zone out. Jareus made sure he was okay, grabbing his shoulder. "Cole?"

"You know… I have been having these weird flashes of memories. I think I know what you're talking about. I think I know Xenova somehow," Cole said.

"You *what*?!" Alex exclaimed.

"I'll tell you guys tomorrow, I'm freakin' tired," Jareus told everyone. Alex was shivering a little.

"I can't believe it's almost midnight… We got up so early today… and I thought I was going to die. When I heard Redaro mentioned again, I almost had a heart attack. I didn't know that me going back in time like that would link our two timelines, either. I had no idea you were alive all that time, Jareus," Alex explained.

"What about you, Jareus? I know Zach just asked, but we basically just had to fight you... in a way," Danny chimed in.

"Yeah... that was weird. He somehow even gave me his power of fast healing. But I guess there was one main difference between the two of us..." Jareus thought aloud.

"What would that be?" Zach asked.

"Amar, unfortunately, was a slave to fate. He tried so hard to beat Redaro, I bet. But fate played against him. While I... don't play by the rules of fate. I was fated to not tell you my feelings regarding the whole situation. I was fated to take credit for things that were the work of my team... but not anymore..." Jareus told them as he looked into the sky, "I value you all, and I already think you're better than me." Danny was about to say something, but Jill had just pulled up.

"Get in, you've got some explaining to do!" Jill yelled at them.

"Jilllll, you ruined a moment," Alex told her.

"I'm tired as heck, okay? Just get in so we can go home," Jill told them. They all started laughing amongst themselves as they got into the car. On the way home, they told Jill the whole story. The sports tournament, the one-on-one matches, the friends they made on the way, Amar and Diadem, and the cash prizes at the end.

"I agree with you, Jill... it's weird how all of that can happen so fast," Alex commented.

"Zach, I think we made bank. We got the best prizes!" Jareus told Zach. They started laughing together as they pulled up back to their house.

"I'm going right to sleep dude, probably for fourteen hours," Danny yawned and went right inside. Alex followed him.

"Me too, today's been quite a day. I'm gonna need to process this well so I can remember it well!" Cole quipped as he walked inside.

"Yeah, yeah. I'm tired, let's go," Jill complained.

"WAIT!" Zach exclaimed as Jareus was about to enter the house.

"SHHHH! Dude, it's late! What is it?" Jareus asked Zach as Jill went inside after locking the car.

"We have enough money to buy the best brand-new TV now!" Zach told Jareus. They laughed hysterically as they walked into the house. —*END OF ARENA CONQUEST*

Fun Fact: Amar and Jareus were originally supposed to share a body and swap between personalities. What a headache that would have been.

Part 6: Paradox Glitch

So what's this story all about, anyways?

This is just about all my mistakes, right? Jareus thought, looking down at his neighbor's house from a wall in his backyard. They were partying it up. He lived vicariously through their celebration—Jareus had been rather bored since the whole sports festival. He didn't feel like he could ever be enough. But that's exactly what this story is all about. It's about trial and error, and not just taking what life gives you. Most importantly, it's about never giving up, despite impossible odds.

"Yep, I give up!" Jareus grinned, shouting as he jumped off of the wall to join their party. He was only wearing pajamas, as it was late. It was now November of 2015—a long time had gone by, and Jareus thought that maybe he was now finally living what people considered to be a "normal" life... although, maybe not. Truly, there was no such thing as normal and he didn't even know it.

"Hey, you! I know you! Decided to join the party, Jareus?" His neighbor asked as Jareus stumbled into his backyard. There were a bunch of college kids all around the yard, with cheap beer everywhere.

"I gave in. I'm really stressed... I have to give a speech tomorrow. I might be needed as a director for a whole company... at only nineteen years old." Jareus told his neighbor. His neighbor offered him a can, which he initially turned down. Eventually, the college kids had their way with him, and chanted him on while he drank.

"Hello?" Danny rang the doorbell. Most of the others had moved out of the group house, but Jareus remained living there. There was occasionally another when Saskia needed a place to crash. Jareus had finally bought the property with some help from Harlow Henry, the owner of Adrenaline Corporation. Jareus got out of bed, slightly hung over, and looked at the clock. It was nearly 7:30.

"HOLY CRAP!" He yelled, terrified of the numbers on the alarm clock, and jumped out of bed. Danny heard all the ruckus from Jareus's front porch, and wondered what was going on.

"Jareus, if you aren't ready, then just open up!" Danny yelled through the front door and jiggled the door handle. Seeing that it was locked, he knocked again. "OI! JAREUS!"

"I'M COMING!" Jareus yelled right before he opened the door, with the same pajamas from the night before still on. There were some stains on his shirt, and he had bags under his eyes. Danny stared at him as he walked out onto the porch that cloudy morning.

"You gotta be kidding me. We gotta go by eight, dude… I don't know what you're going to do to clean this up," Danny scolded.

"Yeah, yeah, I know, I know. Look, give me, like, five minutes… WAIT! The speech…" Jareus was about to run inside.

"Recite some of it to me, now!" Danny grinned.

"Bahhh! I can't do that! Uhhh… In today's world we need the… authority? To be able…" Jareus tried.

"THAT SOUNDED LIKE A QUESTION!" Danny shouted.

"WELL, I GOTTA CLEAN UP!" Jareus yelled, dashing into the house and avoiding any further comments about the speech. Danny could hear him frantically getting ready upstairs.

"You know, Jareus, it's been awhile since we've gotten everybody together. This is going to be the first time in months and you're *this* ill-prepared? No wonder Cole left," Danny sighed.

"Cole saw oppwitunity iwn anowther awea!" Jareus tried to talk while brushing his teeth.

"Yeah, I guess Regiment Legion sounds kinda cool. I don't blame him either, since Adrenaline Corp. didn't hire him on the spot like the rest of us. Had he given us time, I'm sure we could have gotten him a job there. But I'm sure he's doing well in Regiment Legion," Danny just kinda spoke to himself. Jareus spat out his toothpaste.

"Enough about that! I'm so nervous because Harlow wants to let me take 'control' of the company... he's done it for a while now! We've been working every day to create this new prototype perfectly, and *now* he puts the pressure on me by telling me I have to give a speech to get investors on board and introduce our creation?! I've never had to give a real speech in my life! What the hell does he think I'm gonna do, be amazing on the first try?!" Jareus ranted.

"Dunno. It's up to you now," Danny seemed uninterested in his rant, and dragged him out of the house as soon as he was ready. Danny had agreed to drive him the other day since Jareus's car was in the shop. They drove directly there, running short on time. So

Jareus, all tidied up now, ran up the steps of the Adrenaline Corp. building in downtown Sacramento.

"Jareus! There you are! The man himself has arrived! You're totally ready for today, right?" Harlow Henry, one of Jareus's now close friends and work partner, asked him.

"Yeah… We'll call it that," Jareus seemed kinda nervous.

"Great! I'll be watching!" Harlow cheered on. *Jeez, he's always so positive. I don't know if I've seen him nervous. How come I, the nervous one, have to give this speech?* Jareus thought to himself. Harlow interrupted his silence, "Good luck, too!"

"Guess I just gotta suck it up and do it," Jareus commented to himself. He walked up the steps and listened into the meeting room in front of him. He heard some voices that were familiar, and some that weren't. He straightened his fake tuxedo suit and walked right in. People went silent as they saw Jareus walk in. Investors were there, many higher-ups were there, and Zach, Danny, Alex, and Harlow were there as well. He adjusted the bowtie on the suit, stood in front of the table, and took a deep breath.

"In today's world, we need somebody to truly take authority over the situations that aren't controllable by the public military's standards," Jareus started. "What could I possibly mean by that? Well, let's take a look at two separate situations this company has been involved in. The Rownert Incident of 2013 and the sports tournament in 2014 are two prime examples of situations that required intervention beyond regular governmental protocol. This presentation will enable you to learn how to prevent future incidents such as those, and how I can lead you all in doing so."

Jareus went on to discuss more effective business models on production, how Adrenaline Corp. could keep ties with the government for most of their funding, and their role as a private military corporation. He'd captured the audience's attention so far, and he tried his best to maintain it.

"Just because I'd be the leader in this situation does not stop me from being in the fight. I don't plan to stop—I'd still be part of our dispatch squad, and Harlow and I have actually been working on something for just that. For the past six months, the two of us have been perfecting what we call the Untethered Non-Periodical Exoskeleton Suit, or the U.N.E. Suit." Jareus finally stopped as Harlow got up from his seat and wheeled the thing in. It was a full-body exoskeleton suit, displayed in an upright, standing position. The only lack of coverage it provided was that of the head. The suit was very slim, and wouldn't get in the way as much as the previous models had.

"Woah!" Everyone was surprised by Jareus and Harlow's new suit design.

"What do you mean by non-periodical?" One of the investors asked.

"It's viable for many long term missions. Due to its ability to use solar power and its powerful charging capacity, there would be little to no charging breaks. I can demonstrate it," Jareus told them. He undid a hidden knot on his fake tux and it fell, revealing his red t-shirt and blue cargo shorts underneath. He pressed a button on the suit and backed up into it, letting it close in all around him. Soon, he was wearing the exoskeleton arms with shoulder guards, brown military gloves, and the suit which reached past his ankles. It went a tad under his shoes as well, for jumping capabilities. Everyone was awed at the sight of the new suit model in use, but Danny spotted something out of the corner of his eye.

"As you can see, we have a solid state battery on the back here, making for easier—" Harlow was showing everyone the features of Jareus's suit at the same time.

"Guys… you might want to see this," Danny stated as he looked through the window, sounding very concerned.

"WHAT THE HELL?!" Alex shouted as he laid eyes on what Danny was seeing. Everybody crowded around the window to see what was going on down below—they were a few stories above the ground.

"Let me see!" Jareus made them move, still wearing the exosuit. Down on the grass and approaching the building, there was a figure. It was entirely white, apart from its black hands that transitioned into gray on the wrists, and the black reaper-like hood covering its face.

"That… that thing looks slightly different, but… it's pretty similar to how Redaro looked when he first came to my world! Redaro had more eyes, though, rather than none…" Alex started to go on. Suddenly, two cyan-blue eyes lit up from its blank hooded face.

"Do you think it's another demon?" Danny asked in a panic.

"Another demon like Redaro?! I don't… well… I guess it could be," Alex muttered. He was scared, and it was showing. The investors and people inside the room were all panicking, with the few of those oblivious to the existence of demons still in denial.

"Guess we're going to have to do an early test run," Jareus grunted. *This is the only way I'm going to be able to show off leadership skills now, but can I really go up against that?! Especially since this suit has had like one field test so far...* Jareus thought.

"You're going to *what?!*" Alex questioned in horror.

"We'd better get going, then!" Danny quipped. In no time at all, Danny and Jareus were running down the stairs, Danny struggling to catch up, thanks to Jareus's improved speed from the suit.

"Shouldn't we stay here, where it's safe?!" Zach yelled.

"HEY, WAIT UP!" Harlow yelled, following them. Alex felt guilty at the thought of staying on the sidelines, so he reluctantly followed them as well. Jareus was ahead of the rest, and beat them to the floor with no problem. He walked out of the building just for the demon-figure to confront him right outside.

"Identify yourself!" Jareus shouted, and the thing stopped walking. Despite having cover from the paper-white hood, its cyan eyes were able to be seen even from afar. They were bright, almost like headlights.

"It seems I've finally found you, and in the right time as well," The being's voice was distortedly glitch-like and femininely high-pitched. Its body structure also resembled a female human adult.

"I told you to identify yourself! What do you mean by *'in'* the right time?!" Jareus readied himself, just in case.

"Jareus, you forgot the radiative pistol!" Danny yelled just as he exited the building with Harlow. Something unexpected happened at that moment. The creature started to move unexpectedly fast, appearing to glitch through the battlefield. Jareus was only able to turn around in time to see the thing slash right through Danny's side, causing him to bleed through his shirt. Without a second thought, Jareus boost-jumped toward his opponent. He kicked the head of the entity that had just attacked Danny, and the being flew backwards several feet, but caught itself midair and planted its feet on the ground.

"DANNY! ARE YOU OKAY?!" Jareus yelled, planting himself in front of Danny and Harlow. Harlow was already looking at Danny's wound.

"Yeah… yeah, I think I'm okay. It's just a deep cut," Danny admitted.

"That seems about right. You'll definitely need stitches though," Harlow agreed. The creature went in for a second attack, targeting Danny again. But this time, Jareus stopped it, actually managing to kick it in the hip, giving it a small scratch. Some of its blood flew out, hitting Danny's side.

"AHH!!! THAT STINGS!" Danny yelled in pain as the entity's blood fused with his own. Jareus was infuriated that it kept trying to go for his less-protected friends.

"Get him inside, Harlow! And YOU! You're fighting me!" Jareus yelled, remembering that he had an authoritative reputation that he now had to live up to. Harlow did as he was told.

"I was getting to you, Jareus," The creature affirmed.

"Then what should I call you, creature?" Jareus quipped back.

"Creature?! You've seen Redaro, have you not? I'm no creature. I'm the demon Escarere," Escarere announced. *So she is a demon!* Jareus internally freaked out.

"Redaro? How do *you* know about Redaro?" Jareus questioned the new demon.

"I don't have to answer any of your questions, Jareus. All I know is that your friend here must be put to an end—you've been a disruption to Redaro's plan for the timeline. But clearly not enough of a disruption to stop me, you see?" Escarere taunted.

"You leave me no choice! This is a prototype and it hasn't seen combat yet, but with this suit, I'll have to take you down!" Jareus cheered himself on through his fear.

"Oh? Is that so?" Escarere clearly enjoyed acting as an instigator.

"YOU BET!" Jareus yelled, boosting himself forward. Escarere grabbed him mid-kick and threw his body to the ground. He jumped up from the ground and instantly rebounded into a punch. Suddenly, Escarere's body seemed to glitch around him and dodge the punch. Jareus caught himself before he hit the ground and turned around to stop one of Escarere's punches.

"Not bad, messy boy," Escarere commended as she kicked Jareus to the side. Jareus, panting, still got up. *Crap, what am I going to do against a* demon*? Is she just toying with me? There's so much I want to know and so little I'm figuring out!* Jareus's mind was racing, frustrated.

"You okay, Danny?" Harlow asked as he bandaged Danny's side. They had also become good friends after the sporting tournament, perhaps because of their relation through Adrenaline Corporation.

"Yeah, I'm fine now. I just wonder if Jareus is still fighting that being or whatever," Danny told Harlow.

"He really is fighting a demon," Alex, wide eyed and terrified, told them as he walked back from watching.

"Are you sure?" Harlow asked Alex.

"She introduced herself as Escarere, and she somehow knows about Redaro!" Alex nervously informed.

"We have to at least stand by and make sure Jareus is alright, if he's really fighting a demon," Danny commented.

"You really don't have much of a chance, Jareus. I'm sure you could just come with me if you really didn't want to die. We could figure something out between just the two of us," Escarere taunted as she dodged more of Jareus's attacks.

"You're a *fool* if you think I'll leave my friends behind!" Jareus shouted back at her, actually landing a hit on her arm. She reeled back from the blow, but then grinned. This time, Danny saw something odd. Suddenly, the world around them warped in slow motion, and everything appeared to be blueshifting. This was accompanied by an odd sound that could only be described as a wine glass violently shattering, as if to smash the time barrier. Jareus, even with the suit on, wasn't moving fast at all, but Escarere moved at a normal pace behind Jareus and hit his back. Just as she made contact, Jareus was flung forward, but he didn't lose balance. *Did... I really just see that?* Danny questioned in his head. But he witnessed his vision stop blueshifting and return to normal as Jareus and Escarere's battle continued. *It's... not her moving fast... It's gotta be...*

"How much longer do you think you can survive if you don't come with me?" Escarere sounded almost giddy. She threw a punch, which Jareus dodged by boosting straight up into the air. But this maneuver damaged one of the exosuit legs, and it started letting off smoke. *Crap,* Jareus thought, *I knew it needed more field tests before combat!*

"JAREUS! SHE ISN'T GAINING A TEMPORARY SPEED BOOST! IT'S TIME! SHE'S MANIPULATING TIME ITSELF SOMEHOW!" Danny yelled as loud as he needed to so Jareus could hear him. *Time? Is this demon really slowing down time for herself?* Jareus thought nervously.

"Well, we've certainly got a keen eye over there," Escarere commented as Jareus tried to boost down on her. She dodged, then started again, "I'm no Time Demon, but my power does help me outspeed my opponents."

"For some reason... that gate over there leading into our parking lot, it seems to be emitting... energy, it looks like? Magenta energy?" Danny stated. The other two looked at him as if he was crazy. Danny followed up, "No, seriously! I think having close contact with that demon must have done something, because I can see when she slows down time! So maybe I can see other time-related things as well," Danny tried to explain. He still received plenty of weird looks.

"That's *it*, Escarere! I want you out of here!" Jareus yelled as he boosted straight into her, faster than she could use her time powers.

"Jareus, try throwing her into that gate! The magenta one!" Danny shouted, pointing at the gate he was referring to. He was still the only one able to see the gate's aura.

"Uh... okay?! It's... actually gray..." Jareus was confused, but boosted up nonetheless. *What could they be talking about? Why a gate?* Escarere thought. Jareus boosted down, but Escarere dodged. This time, however, Jareus anticipated it and grabbed onto her arm. Jareus flung around and tossed Escarere toward the gate. While midair, Escarere saw the magenta energy that Danny had. *Shit,* she thought, *how did he know about that?!*

"Could you see that too, Danny?! Answer me!" Escarere yelled, infuriated. At that point, it was too late—she was about to hit the gate, but her body seemed to mysteriously disappear just before she made contact with it. Jareus, confused, was panting with his hands on his knees.

"Good thing that was there... Now I need to... Fix this thing," Jareus told himself as he fell over to lay on the ground.

"There really *was* something there!" Alex exclaimed.

"Told you," Danny said. The three ran outside to where Jareus was.

"Could you have beat that demon, had it come down to it?" Harlow asked as Jareus coughed.

"As I currently am... no. And can you unhook this one part here? If I leave the leg like this, it's kind of a fire hazard..." Jareus asked Harlow.

"Oh, sure thing," Harlow got right on it.

"Jareus... could you see when Escarere was able to bend time? Or the magenta energy? I had a gut feeling that the energy around the object meant that it was also a time-gate of sorts..." Danny asked.

"No, but I *do* think you're right about her having time powers," Jareus said, climbing out of the exosuit. There was dirt all over him.

"There was never a demon like this in my timeline... I never saw anything like that," Alex was still frantic.

"Let's regroup inside. I'm sure after handling that as well as you did, you'll get to lead Adrenaline Corporation, Jareus. We'll have to make immediate plans on what to do if Escarere comes back, and get our best research team on this case right away," Harlow commanded.

"Yeah... we definitely should," Danny commented as they went back inside, Harlow helping Jareus walk for a second.

"The pain went away. I healed quickly, I guess... you don't need to help," Jareus told Harlow.

"Don't you remember? We think you got that ability from Amar somehow," Harlow told Jareus.

"Yeah, yeah, I remember. But I don't want to rely on that," Jareus rolled his eyes. The three walked back in to receive their much deserved gratitude.

ALTERNIS - 11 NOVEMBER 2015, 8:36 PM

"Are you new around here?" A bartender asked the only guy in his bar. The bartender didn't recognize him, and yet usually he recognized the people that walked in.

"Not exactly. But this is the first time you would have seen me," The man told the bartender. This was confusing, but the bartender didn't pay it any mind. He had come in and ordered wine, which most men his age wouldn't do. Another person walked in.

"Ah, if it isn't Bobonson! How do you do?" The bartender asked as Bobonson, wearing a backwards net hat and blue flannel, came in. The new man's eyes darted toward Bobonson, and Bobonson froze when he saw the man, but continued slowly.

"I'm... good! But, eh, who's this here?" Bobonson asked nervously. He seemed as if he recognized him.

"Why don't you ask him?" The bartender told Bobonson, sliding him a Chicago Martini, Bobonson's favorite drink. Bobonson caught the glass, sitting next to the man.

"Are you… Ja—" Bobonson was asking.

"No," The man told him, cutting him off.

"Oh, well, you certainly look like… never mind," Bobonson sighed, sipping his drink. There was a bit of awkward silence.

"I'm gonna need your help, Bobonson," The man said suddenly. This man had a hood over his face, so it wasn't easy to see him. He had a black zip-up jacket, with the sleeves tinged only slightly more gray, and a black bandana tied around his neck. A backpack was slung over his shoulders. One thing was clear to Bobonson, though—his eyes were red.

"How did you know my name?" Bobonson asked. Another awkward silence for a second.

"The bartender said it," The man said obviously.

"Then how do you know you're going to need my help?" Bobonson pestered. The man grinned.

"Alright, I need someone who can help me fix a mistake I made. Just one thing, though, I need you to prove to me you can do that. Duel me, prove yourself. No rules, besides no killing your opponent. Oh, and bartender, don't call the cops. Sound like a deal to everyone?" The man suddenly put forth. Bobonson just nodded and got up. The bartender looked like he was in shock, but then calmed himself.

"I expect a GENEROUS tip!" He yelled as he closed the front door. The man grinned and got up.

"On the count of three, then. One…" the man started, with Bobonson holding something on his waist, "…two… three!" Bobonson instantly shot at the man, who dodged the bullet. Bobonson had carried a pistol with him this entire time, right on his belt. The man was somehow already at Bobonson's side, and he kicked him into the bar. Bobonson did a handstand on the barstools for a second just to see the man suddenly draw a knife. Bobonson pushed up with his hands and let them fall into the man. He attempted to shoot again while in freefall, but missed. Bobonson's bullet grazed his shoulder and he fell on top of the dude.

"Stop, stop! This is making too much ruckus! Don't you see that Bobonson can help you? Now let me open these doors!" The bartender scolded them. The man's hood fell off.

"Yes…" the man was somewhat dizzy from being clobbered by Bobonson's body.

"Hey, wait! You look just like that guy I met at the park!" Bobonson remarked. Memories came flooding back—Bobonson accidentally shooting with that old antique gun, meeting Jareus and company, and Jill using him to figure out what was going on.

"About that… I'm who you're talking about, but also not who you're talking about. I'd say his name, but I'm not that man any longer. You can call me Amar," Amar told Bobonson.

"You sure you aren't Jareus? Wait! Didn't you go missing during the sports tournament? Yeah! Adrenaline Corp. had to shut down the whole thing after the contestants went missing and never came back!" Bobonson told Amar. They both got up and sat back on the seats of the bar. Bobonson listened closely as Amar filled him in.

"Well… it's a weird story. You see… I come from a different timeline than this one. A demon named Redaro took over in that timeline. I have reason to believe that there may be another demon again, but we'll get back to that.

"I was the old dude on TV that teleported everybody away. Redaro sent me back to get rid of the threats to him, and he thought it'd be poetic if I were my own undoing. I can't really remember that much... sometimes it comes back to me. But what I *can* remember is that there was this weird flash of light on the other planet. There was a guy named Diadem who was pissing me off, and partially controlling me. But after that flash of light I threw Diadem, knocking... I think Zach... out of the sky. It's still kinda blurry, but the Wish Orb was whacked out of anybody's reach."

"Zach... he was friends with those guys..." Bobonson made the connection.

"Yeah. Diadem had me kill every person on that planet like some sort of damn mutt... but after I had seen what I had done... I couldn't help it!" Amar started to speak louder, tearing up, "I smashed Diadem's face in, and wished myself back to this planet, and I wished for that orb to stay trapped in space..." Amar wiped his face. Bobonson was in shock.

"That's horrible! Oh my... jeez! But uh... where do I come into this? How did you know me?" Bobonson asked, his shaggy hair poking out from under his hat.

"Oh, right. Well, in my timeline I got to meet you, but then that Redaro guy split us all up at one point. I was that timeline's version of Jareus. And you come into this because... I need help. Just like I said originally. I'm responsible for killing those guys, they were our best shot at fighting any demons, and now there might be a new one so..." Amar got out of his seat and bowed to Bobonson, "I beg of you!"

"Woah woah woah, no need to be so formal! I guess I told you about this bar, but you never got to see me become a mercenary in your timeline then?" Bobonson gloated. *I do remember the text about a great bar when I'm of age... but I'm not of age... this is a fake ID!* Amar thought, snickering. He remembered what Bobonson just said.

"Eh...? Mercenary...?" Amar questioned.

"Yep! Usually, I'd make you pay me big time... but since Jareus is gone and there's a demon... I'll help you. But where's the demon?" Bobonson asked. Amar grinned.

"Thank you, Bobonson. As for the demon, I was being pursued for a long time. I don't know how exactly it knew me... or why it was after me... but it reminded me too much of Redaro. I had a close encounter, and it looked like a female demon to me, to be honest! But... it just said that something was wrong and left. It seemed to be able to periodically speed up too, so if we're going to find this thing and figure out what's going on, we'll need a bit of a group!" Amar explained.

"Oh, well then, I think I've got the next best guy!" Bobonson smiled. Amar grinned back at him, and in no time at all the two had headed to a junkyard, but not before Bobonson paid for any little damages caused in the scuffle—plus extra—to the bartender.

"Uhhh... are you SURE you have the next best guy?!" Amar was not too sure of Bobonson's decision anymore.

"I'm sure of it! I got word of this guy being great in hand-to-hand fights as a mercenary!" Bobonson assured Amar.

"WHO'S IT WHAT?!" They suddenly heard. Bobonson turned to face the source of the sound.

"There he is!" Bobonson pointed out. Amar looked over and saw a younger tan man wearing a gray hoodie with stains all over it, and white basketball shorts. His hair was smooth, but very short. He was sitting on top of a bunch of trash, holding a small stick of beige bamboo.

"Who's that?" Amar snarkily asked.

"WHO DA HELL YOU TALKIN' TO?! I'LL FIGHT YOU!" The dude seemed to have just woken up, although he clearly had a lot of energy.

"Please don't fight us," Amar sighed.

"My apologies! I've heard a lot about you, Hosea! We just wanted to talk to you," Bobonson was much more polite.

"You're on my territory!" Hosea yelled back at them.

"LOOK! We're just here to—" Amar was slightly annoyed.

"Have some fun?" Hosea suddenly smiled, holding up the bamboo stick.

"Yes—wait no, I don't... think? ANYWAYS! We're gathering people to do a hero's work!" Amar triumphed.

"That sounds stupid," Hosea lost all his hype and sat back down.

"OI! I'm still making the offer!" Amar yelled at Hosea.

"Go home," Hosea told off Amar.

"Look, Hosea. Amar here is trying to gather a few people to be able to take on a demon that he spotted, and we think that your fighting ability might be able to—" Bobonson started.

"WE GONNA KILL THINGS?! I'M IN!" Hosea suddenly jumped back up.

"Oh, so *now* you're in," Amar sulked.

94

"Let us introduce ourselves first!" Bobonson intervened. The three talked for a bit and decided that starting the next morning, they'd be off on a journey. But first they'd sleep, and Hosea provided them with the absolute best the junkyard could offer. While Amar was fine with it, having been mainly living out of his backpack, Bobonson could hardly sleep. Amar had started his journey to his own redemption.

PRIMARIUM - 14 NOVEMBER 2015, 10:03 AM

"So Jareus, it's been a long while since we got that new TV. You think you could beat me in a fight now?" Zach asked as he was putting together a model home in the Adrenaline Corp. building's conference room.

"What are we talking? Like a street fight? Do I get to use the U.N.E.?" Jareus didn't even question it.

"If you fix it, hypothetically," Zach jeered back at him. He just stood there for a second.

"Well… it *is* gonna need to be fixed if Escarere comes back anytime soon… and we'll need more! You wanna help?" Jareus asked.

"You're lucky that you even *got* a smooth transition into leadership after pulling that stunt! You're lucky that Harlow is doing all of the actual CEO work as well. You're like one of those Spartan leader-heroes or whatever—a figurehead. But you're gonna need my help, so I'm going to offer it to you," Zach said. Jareus gave a nervous smile at Zach's snippy offer, and he scratched the back of his head.

"Alright, but when we fix up those suits, let's field test them instead of fighting right off the bat. We'll make

Danny and Alex come out with us as well," Jareus proposed.

"Sounds fine with me," Zach agreed.

In little to no time at all, they were on top of a building in San Francisco, jumping around like maniacs.

"YOU LIKE THE NEW SUITS?!" Jareus yelled to Danny and Zach midair as they all aimed toward an open street.

"WHAT?!" Danny tried to respond. Zach just gave up on conversing. The exo absorbed all of the ground impact, and three landed safely.

"WOOHOO! That's some field testing!" Jareus smiled. Danny was basically shivering. That had been terrifying—and exhilarating, too.

"Don't make me do that again anytime soon," Alex told Jareus, walking over to where they landed. He'd been around just in case something had gone wrong, so he'd be able to call backup if needed.

"Maybe I will," Danny grinned evilly.

"Don't you love me, Grandpa? Do you hate me or somethin'?" Alex expressed.

"Oh c'mon Alex, it's not half bad!" Zach smiled, cheerier now. Alex shook his head and held his stomach.

"Jeez, Alex… are you so afraid, you feel like gonna throw up at just the thought of it? Wanna go back and get some antacids or something?" Jareus offered.

"No… it's not that…" Alex had one hand on his mouth and one on his stomach, seeming like he was in pain.

"Hey… Alex… are you alright, bud?" Danny voiced his concern. Alex shifted both of his hands to grab his head now. As his head whipped up, a dark energy started to surround his head and his hands, which then

96

manifested into a physical form. Alex suddenly morphed a head that resembled Escarere's without the eyes, and demon-like claws.

"THE HELL? ALEX?!" Jareus was now very concerned. Alex looked up at them and seemed ready to attack.

"Ready yourselves!" Zach shouted as Alex jumped forward, trying to claw the three. They all boosted out of the way in opposite directions.

"What's going on, Alex?!" Danny demanded while in midair. Alex was making growling noises like a demon.

"Is this some sort of attack by Escarere?! Is he being taken over by a demon?" Zach added.

"Alex is being… taken over by a demon?" Jareus repeated. Alex lunged out at Jareus, but Jareus boosted upward. Somehow, Alex followed, jumping just as high. Jareus air-dodged quickly, flying down the street. Some people started screaming when they saw what was going on. Danny was running down the street, trying his best to keep up with the fight.

"Everybody stay calm! We'll handle this!" Danny shouted. Jareus landed on the ground and was about to block, since Alex was so close behind him, but Zach hit Alex out of nowhere.

"Thanks for the help," Jareus smiled.

"It wasn't for you, get better at blocking," Zach murmured.

"Eh?!" Jareus exclaimed in confusion before Alex stood up again, after he had been bashed into the floor. He roared like a demon.

"How exactly did this happen?!" Danny asked, catching up with the two.

"WE DON'T KNOW!" Jareus shouted back at him, turning around to see Alex still rampaging toward them.

"LOOK OUT!" Danny jumped and shoved Jareus out of the way. Alex seemed like a bloodthirsty animal to people running down the streets of San Francisco. They could even see a trolley from where they were.

"Hey, do you guys need help?" They heard a call from a distance, but nobody could see where it had come from.

"SIR! WHEREVER YOU ARE, STAY BACK! THIS IS A BIT OF A SITUATION!" Danny shouted.

"Why should I?" The stranger revealed himself, walking around the corner. He had piercing yellow eyes and hazel colored hair that exploded in all directions, wearing a combination of an orange and gray jumpsuit with large shoulder pads. It had parts of an exoskeleton implemented into them and a clear visor. His gloves and boots looked ready for combat as well. He smiled and continued, "I'm not an amateur!"

"Who-who-who are you?!" Jareus sputtered out fearfully, while dodging an attack from Alex.

"Harlow has really sheltered you, hasn't he? The name's Toshi. Toshi Enoch," Toshi smiled while pulling out some rope from behind him.

"Making more friends, are we Toshi?" A woman came from behind him. Her eyes were a light blue, and she had the same jumpsuit pants, but had a cyan tank top on instead. Her hair was very light pink.

"I'm just doing my job, Kami!" He smiled as he shouted.

"Wait... you're both from..." Zach started as the three looked at their costumes. They had the Adrenaline Corp. logo on their pants.

"ADRENALINE CORP!" Jareus and Danny jinxed each other right after Zach had finished speaking. Alex crashed into Danny, sending him flying into a nearby building.

"Let's fix this up!" Toshi yelled as Jareus tried to advance to where Alex was. Toshi sprinted forward and beat Jareus to the punch, knocking the wind out of Alex. Next, Kami came right as Toshi threw up the rope, and instantly went to work tying Alex up. Alex realized what was happening and started to struggle.

"I wonder… What happened to him? I've never seen anything like that," Kami commented as they saw Alex struggling on the ground. Jareus, Zach, and Danny were in total shock. *How did he move faster with inferior equipment?* Jareus wondered.

"Hey! HEY! What…? What am I…?" Alex started to regain consciousness, but remained in the demon form. He looked down at his own arms and saw the demon appendages.

"He's coming back!" Danny shouted, running forward, but Kami held out her arm, keeping Danny from getting closer.

"Let me… LET ME OUT!" The demonic side of Alex started getting stronger again. Eventually, however, he tired himself out, and the demon parts retracted to let Alex breathe on his own.

"He seems to have calmed down… now. What the heck happened to him?" Toshi asked, turning to Jareus, Zach, and Danny.

"You think we know?" Zach rolled his eyes.

"Hmm…" Toshi thought and looked up at Jareus, "…oh. And you're our new Greek hero-leader aren't you?" Toshi pointed at Jareus.

"Greek hero-leader? I... guess? You're also from Adrenaline Corp. right?" Jareus seemed confused, recalling how Zach had said something similar to him earlier.

"It seems Harlow has kept you in the dark. You've been in the economic and support sectors of Adrenaline Corporation, but there are actually three sectors in total. He appointed you the leader of all three without ever really showing you around the third sector? Well, it's the military branch, and I don't know how they feel about Harlow putting some new guy in charge," Kami suddenly cut in, explaining. Jareus had already been thinking that Harlow was hiding something, but knowing this didn't make him feel any better.

"I ran into the military branch a couple of years ago," Jareus told them. "He hasn't shown me much, but at least I've encountered them." Kami nodded, looking a little bit relieved.

"I think we can untie him now," Toshi pointed to Alex. Alex was tuckered out, panting.

"Are you okay Alex?" Danny asked, concerned.

"I... I couldn't control it... until the end there..." Alex was still panting.

"What?! You could control it?!" Zach shouted, asking.

"Yeah... just a little. Yet... I don't know how it happened..." Alex was exhausted.

"We should get back," Toshi suggested. Kami nodded and Toshi said, "Try and prove yourself. Okay, rookie?" Jareus nodded his head uncertainly as Toshi and Kami walked away.

"So Jareus... I guess you're gonna need to talk to Harlow before we can have any kind of match. I knew about them, but I guess we didn't really meet everyone yet," Zach told him. Jareus knew this, but he had no idea what to do about it now.

"Yeah… just let me think. Also… help Alex up," Jareus told them demandingly.

ALTERNIS - 14 NOVEMBER 2015, 2:12 PM

"So Amar, who're you taking us to? And why does this house look abandoned?" Bobonson asked as he, Amar, and Hosea all approached what would have been Jareus's house in that timeline.

"I knew this would be here. It used to be my house in my timeline," Amar smirked. They jumped into the backyard.

"Are we gonna break in?" Hosea asked, holding up his bamboo stick. Although they called it a stick, it was more of a segment of a branch, since it was rather thick. It was hollow on the inside.

"Hosea, we're…! Wait, yeah. Actually, we're breaking in," Amar realized halfway through the sentence.

"What? What?!" Bobonson was concerned.

"YUS!" Hosea triumphed.

"Why would we break into a random house?" Bobonson questioned.

"It's abandoned now, but it used to be mine! Now shut up, you're gonna scare the neighbors if there are any," Amar shushed them. They hopped over the fence as discreetly as they could do so in plain daylight.

"Well… why are we breaking in?" Bobonson questioned right as they were approaching the side.

"Well… there's someone trapped inside a boot here. I think we should be able to convince him to—" Amar was saying.

"Oi. Did you just say that somebody was in a boot?" Hosea was bewildered.

"Oh… yeah. You guys probably don't know about stuff like this, but we're gonna have to fight a demon. So maybe you should get used to weird stuff," Amar told the two.

"Wait… so you're serious? All that timeline stuff and Redaro and all that?" Bobonson questioned.

"Yeah. I was!" Amar was a little ticked off that they weren't taking him seriously.

"How is he inside the boot? Nobody can fit inside a boot," Hosea proclaimed as if he had just cracked a theory wide open.

"Can you just shut it and see what I mean?" Amar rolled his eyes. The two begrudgingly followed Amar into the house as he opened one of the windows, so they could sneak in through the side.

"Okay, so where are we gonna find your boot?!" Hosea yelled once they got in.

"Calm down Hosea, the booze is in the other room," Amar pointed, just trying to appease. Hosea smiled and skipped like a happy little boy into the kitchen.

"But where's the boot?" Bobonson genuinely wondered.

"I can go get it. I'm sure it's in the other room," Amar told Bobonson as he walked off into the laundry room. Bobonson just stood patiently, staying in the first room they'd started in.

"AUGH! WHAT? WHERE?" Bobonson heard from the other room, followed by what sounded like a smack on the head. In the kitchen Hosea was happily pouring rum into his hollow bamboo stick. The top of it was removable.

"Yo. Destructo," Amar greeted him after whacking him on the head in the laundry room. He had thrown the boot against a wall, and out came Minister Destructo.

"JAREUS! YOU WILL RUE THE DAY YOU EVER—" Minister Destructo started to yell just as Amar whacked him on the head again.

"Nope. I don't go by Jareus. Call me Amar. I've been through quite a bit," Amar commanded him.

"Wha—what's going on?!" Minister Destructo questioned. Amar grabbed the Morph Stone Destructo had and broke it.

"It's been a few years. Cole trapped you inside a magical boot, but I let you free because I think I have a use for you," Amar told Minister Destructo.

"You think my loyalty to Equinox would be—?!" He started as Amar hit him on the head again.

"Equinox has been dead for, like, ever, now! Also, the Qiantam that are left are living peacefully on Qiantam. I refuse to call it planet Equinox. So quit complaining and listen to me," Amar talked down to Minister Destructo.

"Why would I listen to you?!" Minister Destructo asked. Amar and Destructo went back and forth with this banter for a while, with Bobonson listening to Amar hitting him on the head every now and then.

"So it's settled. You'll be coming with us. Also I'm just gonna call you Destructo," Amar triumphed after a while.

"You don't have to, my real name is…" Destructo was saying. But he suddenly realized that he didn't remember.

"Hm? What is it?" Amar asked genuinely.

"Never mind! Call me what you want. I'll come with you if you just let me live. What did you say about a demon?" Destructo asked just as he finally got up off the floor.

"Ah, yes! I have friends in the other room with me that are going to help us take on a demon, so this will be your chance to redeem yourself for trying to claim Earth," Amar smirked. He opened the door out into the main room, where Bobonson was playing cards with Hosea.

"Oh. Hosea, look who's finally back," Bobonson pointed, without looking up from his cards.

"There 'dey are. Don't matter right now," Hosea scoffed, looking at his cards.

"What are you...?" Amar asked. Then the two showed their hands.

"HAH! THREE OF THE SAME CARD!" Hosea shouted. They were playing five-card poker.

"It's three of a kind. And damn, I thought my two pairs would win," Bobonson complained.

"YOU GUYS! LISTEN! THIS IS—" Amar started to yell. Bobonson finally looked over.

"IT'S MINISTER DESTRUCTO!" Bobonson got out his gun and pointed it.

"WOAH WOAH WOAH! CALM DOWN! I forgot that you were already acquainted with our friend Destructo here..." Amar waved his hand to signal not to shoot.

"Who?" Hosea was just confused. Amar had to calm Bobonson down and find an understanding between them all.

"NOW THAT WE ALL ARE IN AGREEMENT... I think we have to discuss the threat here," Amar finally said.

"So I just have to burn the boot and get rid of Bobonson? That'll be easy..." A voice echoed from the other room.

"WHO WAS THAT?!" Hosea suddenly burst out.

"I just needed information," The voice echoed again. The four of them ran into the other room.

"You're too late to burn any boot!" Amar scoffed. Nobody was there. The four stood by the couch and near the glass door going to the backyard, but suddenly, a hand waved from behind the curtains covering the glass doors.

"Huh?" Destructo questioned, but the hand just waved again, like it was a prank or something.

"You think this is funny?" Bobonson complained irritably.

"I DO!" Suddenly, a paper-white demon burst out, trying to grab Bobonson's gun. They were caught off guard by her cyan eyes.

"YOU!" Amar shouted, kicking Escarere right as she managed to get the gun free. This made Escarere drop the gun, and it slid over to Destructo.

"WE KILL 'EM?" Hosea asked.

"YES!" Amar yelled, jumping and going after Escarere again, but Escarere escaped right over the couch and into the kitchen. Destructo picked up the gun and looked at it for a second. He suddenly pointed it at Bobonson.

"WHA?!" Bobonson was flabbergasted.

"Oooh, do we have a traitor?" Escarere provoked. Destructo grinned, and fired the gun as he turned. The bullet hit Escarere right in the shoulder and sent her flying into the kitchen counter.

"I don't know this demon's name, but that's the one!" Amar shouted. They all charged toward her. Bobonson sighed, thinking he was gonna be caught in the crossfire. Escarere got up, angered by the commotion.

"What business do you have with me, slave Jareus?!" Escarere questioned. Amar froze for a second, and Escarere launched herself off of the counter in the back of the kitchen.

"Wha—" Amar had no clue how the demon knew who he really was. Escarere then crashed right into Amar and right into the ground. Destructo shot at Escarere again, but she dodged and got right up. Hosea swung with his bamboo stick, but Escarere grabbed his arm.

"NAH!" Hosea yelled, punching her with his other fist. Escarere didn't even flinch, and hit Hosea back right in the gut. Hosea flew into a chair. Bobonson went up for the neck punch, but Escarere blocked and kicked Bobonson into the window which, thankfully, didn't break.

"Damn…" Escarere sighed. Amar got up again and shoved Escarere into the other room through the other kitchen door. Destructo went through the first kitchen door and shot at Escarere a few more times.

"How do you know me, demon?!" Amar shouted his question as he ran forward and punched Escarere.

"It's Escarere, remember me?" Escarere hissed. Amar froze again for a second, as Escarere kicked up and hit Amar. Escarere instantly phased through the air and flew upstairs at an insane speed. *I remember that name… but I can't remember the memory! It's blocked… like a lot of my memories of the other timeline…* Amar thought.

"Amar! What was that?!" Destructo yelled at Amar.

"I froze up, let's still push forward," Amar got up. They charged up the stairs, only to see that Escarere wasn't there. Suddenly, she broke through the double doors that used to go to Jareus's bedroom. Destructo immediately shot again at Escarere, who seemed to actually take a bit of damage again.

"Escarere, just what are you trying to accomplish?" Destructo questioned as Amar went in for a punch.

"I just needed info. I can't ignore the insatiable hunger that drives me, but you might help me as well," Escarere's voice was hard on the ears. She punched Amar in the gut and knocked him down the stairs.

"What info?!" Bobonson shouted from downstairs.

"Predicting the next move of someone else! I also just need to buy more time!" Escarere shouted back. Destructo suddenly came in with a barrage of gunshots, knocking Escarere over. Destructo went to Amar, and Amar grabbed his hand. He pulled Amar to his feet. Escarere's eyes widened, and she looked at a nearby wall. She threw herself at the wall and suddenly disappeared right through it, as if it hadn't been there.

"What the hell?" Amar questioned, getting up after he'd been knocked onto the stairs. He turned to Destructo to talk to him. "Thanks. At first I was a little scared, but I think we can count on you."

"WHERE IS THE BASTARD?!" Hosea ran up the stairs in anger. He looked right at the wall where she was.

"That was the demon. Her name was Escarere, and it seems she doesn't want to mess with us anymore, but maybe she's now after someone else..." Amar said, also trying to put his hand through the wall. It didn't work for him, though.

"I'm sure to kill her next time..." Hosea complained, opening his bamboo stick and taking a drink.

"Hosea?! What the heck?! You DRINK from the bamboo stick?!" Bobonson questioned aloud as he walked up the stairs.

"It's handy," Hosea commented.

"Where do you think Escarere went?" Destructo asked Amar seriously.

"Well… if you're really still in it to help us… we'll all have to figure that out," Amar smiled. Destructo nodded, ensuring that he would help.

"We're gonna save whoever Escarere's going after then?" Bobonson asked.

"That's the plan for now," Amar ensured.

PRIMARIUM - 15 NOVEMBER 2015, 1:14 PM

"Who still lives back there, anyways? Just you, Jareus?" Zach asked. Zach and Jareus were on their way to Jareus's old house.

"It was basically just me, with Saskia sometimes crashing in that other room by the window in the front. She doesn't do much now," Jareus told Zach as he was driving.

"Why'd ya take me along, anyways? Wouldn't it be better if I was back with the others, just in case Alex turned back into that demon thing?" Zach asked.

"I don't think he will again anytime soon. Plus, Danny and Toshi are there, just in case. After that whole incident, the rest of the day kinda went on, and I saw the military branch of Adrenaline Corp. They pretty much just ignored me… so I've got aways to go. Basically, I wanted your help," Jareus told Zach.

"We do have a long way to go, and what help?" Zach asked again.

"I'm gonna put the Wish Orb somewhere safe in Adrenaline Corp. Also, I might talk to Jill for a while. She's going to be coming, so if I'm taking forever, you can just take the orb back for me," Jareus told Zach. They drove the rest of the way to the house, but just as they were pulling up the hill, Saskia ran out of the house.

"JAREUSSSS!" She shouted prolongedly.

"What, something wrong? You're lucky I let you move back in…" Jareus sneered, looking out the window he just rolled down.

"It's the demon!" Saskia shouted. Zach and Jareus's eyes immediately widened and Zach jumped out of the car.

"Take this, I'll be there in a sec!" Jareus shouted as he threw Zach a gun and drove up into the driveway. This was no ordinary gun—it was a laser handgun. Harlow and Jareus had spent a month perfecting the design so it wouldn't combust from overheating. Zach ran into the house toward the source of the noise, just to see something terrifying. Escarere was dragging Jareus's oven out of the house, into the backyard. From the back porch, she chucked it into the wilderness, and it exploded. Horrifyingly enough, Zach swore he'd heard something that sounded like a screech.

"Oh Hello, you! I've gotten rid of your potential ally by destroying that boot with an oven, and I've already taken care of that Bobonson guy, in *this* timeline…" Escarere smirked evilly. Zach shot toward her with the lightspeed lasers, so when Escarere tried to dodge by slowing down time, it still wasn't enough and it hit her directly on the shoulder.

"I don't know why you thought killing our old enemy, Minister Destructo, would be of any help to you.

109

And why Bobonson? You sure are sadistic," Zach spoke down to Escarere. She was furious, and Zach fired more. She raged through the damage inflicted on her and continued to jump forward. This was just like her movements in the other timeline—this was her experiment.

"WHAT happened?!" Jareus yelled as he burst through the front door, having just put on the exosuit arms.

"Escarere just killed Minister Destructo by burning his boot!" Zach yelled back.

"Why...?" Jareus looked in confused disgust at Escarere. Escarere was also rather confused, as she had been thinking that they would have tried to recruit Destructo, like Amar had. Zach and Jareus were thrown for a loop by this new demon's random actions. She had the entirety of Adrenaline Corp. on red alert.

"Don't pretend he wasn't a potential ally!" Escarere shouted back. Zach and Jareus looked at each other.

"If he was a potential ally, why did we seal him inside a boot?" Zach asked rhetorically. Escarere, perhaps realizing that maybe Destructo *wasn't* their ally and the two timelines may have been massively different, was now thinking of a way she could attack one opponent without the other interfering, now that they were in a triangle.

"Anything else, Zach?" Jareus asked.

"Escarere also mentioned something about 'taking care of' Bobonson," Zach mentioned to Jareus.

"Taking care of Bobonson? Killing him? I haven't talked to Bobonson in, like, a year! Escarere, why are you going after people just *loosely* associated with us?" Jareus asked, legitimately curious. But he knew the second that he moved, there would be an opening for Escarere, so he stayed put.

"I just thought maybe they'd help you. I can't have anybody protecting my targets—they'll be hard enough to kill on their own. If you two are so heroic, why not offer yourselves up so I can go home and get rid of this unquenchable thirst for blood?" Escarere asked with a demonic and sinister undertone. *What the hell is that supposed to mean?* Jareus was shocked by the very idea of offering himself up.

"As if we would, demon!" Zach shouted, shooting multiple shots at Escarere and causing her to dash for the front door, where Jareus was. Jareus immediately responded by jumping up and using the strength of the exosuit arms at point blank, punching Escarere to the ground. But at that moment, Escarere used her time-bending ability to make Jareus's next attack almost freeze in the air, while she escaped through the front door and through the outlet to the mountains. She had a new plan.

"What just happened?" Jareus asked, stopping himself from hitting the floor. Zach noticed that the door was a left slightly ajar, and the two ran outside. Panting, they realized it was a little too late to do much.

"What the hell was THAT?!" Saskia yelled, a little crazed. Zach and Jareus had a lot of explaining to do. A few days before Jareus had suddenly jumped into the next-door neighbor's house to join their party, Saskia decided to crash at the place during that time.

"…So that's what's been happening since we met Escarere for the first time, and now she showed up at our house," Zach finally finished explaining. Saskia still seemed a little confused.

"Uh, Saskia, actually... if you want to get back into a job... we could always use more mechanics at Adrenaline Corp. ya know? People are usually more interested in the soldier side of things, since we essentially have 'super' soldiers. But if you wanna help us create some support items, that'd be sweet," Jareus added, since she wanted to regain her financial freedom.

"Really?! Sure! I'd love to help, I'm bored as heck at the house. Also, how's Alex?" Saskia was delighted, but still had a question.

"Alex is alright, but under watch. He was overcome by a supernatural ability that somehow manifested after our encounter with Escarere. Danny still hasn't figured it out, but he was somehow able to use the same type of time-bending ability that Escarere has," Jareus explained.

"Is that so?" Jill suddenly asked, pulling up in a cop car.

"Jill! It's been a while!" Saskia immediately greeted, with Zach and Jareus smiling at her arrival as well. They went inside, and all chatted while Jareus also cleaned up the debris from the missing oven.

"Yeah... I had gotten a lot of news from Adrenaline Corp. I'm friends with a few of the people there, so I know your general situation. But the demon appeared for the second time just now? Damn... I wish I could have gotten to see it," Jill explained.

"Nah, it wasn't fun to see," Saskia immediately shot down her interest.

"As a cop, I think it would be interesting at the very least," Jill tried again.

"Interestingly *terrifying* at least," Saskia squinted.

"That's about all the scraps left over. I can't believe Escarere threw an oven," Jareus sighed.

"Good thing you finished that up, because tonight is when we start the military training program," Zach mentioned.

"Oh! Good thing you reminded me, I almost forgot," Jareus replied as he came over and sat down with the other three.

"How've you been, Jareus?" Jill asked.

"Stressed with all that's going on, but I think I've finally accepted that I'm just never gonna live a 'normal' life. You think I'd be most stressed about Escarere, but actually I think it's more about proving I'm worthy of my spot in Adrenaline Corporation," Jareus told Jill.

"I'm mostly stressed about Escarere…" Zach muttered.

"What do you mean by proving worthy of your spot?" Jill asked.

"Well… basically what's happened is Harlow Henry, the CEO of Adrenaline Corp., appointed me as the new leader. For some reason he saw something in me, I guess. I'm not entirely sure what he was thinking. There are many more capable soldiers in Adrenaline Corporation—we just happened to build the new model of the exoskeleton suit together. I talked to him about it earlier today. I was the CEO, but I was asking him why I wasn't doing the work, and he was still largely in charge of it as a company. It's because his idea is that he was going to make me… like a symbol or figurehead of some sort. I still don't entirely know what he means, but when he starts on this stuff you really can't stop him," Jareus explained.

"A symbol?! That's crazy!" Saskia told him.

"You've certainly got a lot to live up to," Jill commented. Zach just gave a little bit of a shocked look.

Harlow must have some reason. What is it with Jareus and stealing the spotlight? I can't help but feel for those high ranking soldiers in Adrenaline Corp... Zach thought. The four chatted for a while. Jareus and Jill seemed to be hitting it off a lot better than they had used to. Zach and Saskia were kinda forced to talk to each other because of this, but they did get closer as a result. Later on, Zach showed Jareus what time it was, and basically dragged him back to the car so they could go back to the Adrenaline Corp. building at about 4 PM. Half an hour later, they were there.

"I'll make sure to contact Saskia for you, Jareus. So... is that all that happened with Escarere?" Harlow asked as he took Zach and Jareus through the Adrenaline Corp. building.

"Yup. It's weird what Escarere's doing. It seems her plans are very scattered," Zach mentioned.

"That is rather weird, I'll make sure to talk about it. You two should go to the cafeteria, though. It's where everyone is going to get ready for the military training program. Danny's already there," Harlow told the two. They continued their walk down the long hallway, and Harlow wished them luck as they entered the cafeteria.

"Look who's here!" One of the men in the cafeteria shouted as the two entered. All the eyes in the cafeteria went to Jareus and Zach. This particular man seemed to be in Danny's face.

"Look, it's our wanna-be-leader!"

"Harlow's little love child!"

"It's the brat that thinks he can tell us what to do!"

All these people were yelling, making snarky remarks. Jareus knew it was bad, but who knew this'd be the case. Zach couldn't say anything, because as much as the vocal ones were bullies, he understood how they felt.

"I think Jareus is a fine fit for the spot he's in," Someone spoke up finally. Everybody was turning their heads to the back of the crowd. Jareus's eyes widened. His defender was a face from the past they hadn't been sure they'd ever see again—Odessa Owens.

"If it isn't Odessa!" Zach shouted, waving. She waved back, smiling. This silenced the whole room and the rest of the crowd seemed to back off from talking. As Zach and Jareus walked over to her, they all went back to talking to each other. Danny caught up with Jareus and Zach as well.

"That guy earlier was being a complete meathead. He was like 'you have no right to just come in and tell us what to do!' I was just relaying Harlow's message to be done with dinner by 5:15," Danny complained.

"Well… it seems like people are against us because of him," Zach pointed to Jareus. Jareus was now extremely nervous, unsure if he could live up to this.

"Hey! Don't do that! Jareus is probably… already nervous enough," Odessa observed.

"Thanks, Odessa," Jareus spoke softly. Although he was trying to hide it, he really was freaking out a bit. They got reacquainted, but were interrupted soon after by another.

"I'm sure it must be hard, having to live up to that," Another voice spoke. It was Adam Steel.

"Adam Steel?! You were also hired?! That's awesome!" Jareus exclaimed, going over to greet his old rival.

115

"It has been a while," Adam was almost embarrassed to be seen around Jareus, and as they caught up, another man came up and questioned him.

"Does that mean you aren't gonna be on our team?" The man asked Adam.

"Sorry, Jareus, I already have my team chosen," Adam Steel told Jareus. The other guys around Adam seemed to claim him as theirs.

"We're doing teams?" Danny suddenly asked. Jareus and Zach were taken aback by this as well.

"Oh, sorry, I forgot to tell you! I came over in case you guys needed another team member!" Odessa mentioned.

"What number of people can be in a—" Jareus was about to ask, but he was cut off by Zach.

"SORRY GUYS! It looks like those two need a third!" Zach suddenly announced, going over to a group of two girls.

"Groups of three," Odessa told Danny and Jareus, as they watched Zach walk away.

"What the heck was that?!" Danny was baffled by what Zach just pulled.

"I get it, he doesn't wanna be lumped in with me," Jareus was moping.

"Don't be so sad, Jareus! You got me! Plus... I was originally coming over because I thought you would need two groups, considering Cole and Alex. Where are they?" Odessa asked.

"Cole... isn't working with Adrenaline Corp. Something weird happened with Alex, so he's staying back. They have him in a medical ward right now," Danny explained.

"Well, it's good you two got me!" Odessa cheered while grabbing the both of them. They all ate after that, readying themselves for that night. Jareus really felt bad about Zach joining another group. Zach was a social butterfly and Jareus knew that, but also he partially knew that he had a giant metaphorical red target on his head to most of the people there.

According to Odessa, Harlow had said that they would be in teams of three inside of a giant artificial indoor jungle. Here, they would fight a simulated terrorist group. Any groups tagged by the terrorists would become accomplices, and would help the terrorists throughout the match. The exercise was meant for teamwork, but also a test of trustworthiness and character—any team could be working for the terrorists.

"Ehem," Harlow cleared his throat as he got on a stage in front of the entire cafeteria. Jareus was feeling uneasy as everybody looked the way of the stage.

"He's right on time," Zach commented.

"Hello, all Adrenaline Corporation soldiers! I'm sure you all know why we're gathered here. Recently, we've encountered something we did not think would be a problem we'd be facing right now. Yes, crime rates have gone up significantly, but that actually isn't the point I'm making. Not too long ago, Adrenaline Corp. HQ was attacked by what we think is a terrorist posing as a demon. We've seen what seems almost like supernatural capabilities as early as the Sporting Tournament, but this attacker is something else," Harlow started to announce to everyone.

A terrorist posing as a demon? Is this just a cover up for what's going on here... Jareus thought. Harlow continued, "Of course, we're going to take our best

117

measures against whoever this is. She calls herself...
Es-scare-ray," Harlow finished, clearly reading the
demon's name off of a cue card. He pointed to a screen
that slid down behind him, revealing a photo they got of
Escarere with the caption, 'ESCARERE - EXTREME DANGER
LEVEL.' *This could cause a bit of danger, not telling people
about her abilities with time...* Danny thought.

"We gonna go and teach this chick a lesson?!"
Some barbaric guy rose up and shouted.

"We will have to take care of the situation
somehow, yes. That's what this military training program
is about. You should all come out as better soldiers than
when you went in. It's an area of ten square miles that is
mostly wilderness. I told some before, but the teams will
go in 'uninfected' by the terrorists, and try to find good
areas for themselves. Then, I'll send in a group of
terrorists, and the first group they find will automatically
become part of the terrorist side.

"Sheesh," Danny sighed.

"The only way to stop all the terrorists is to
handcuff them all, with a bag of handcuffs given to each
person," Harlow continued, "But if the terrorists use their
tagging guns, your exosuit will temporarily disable for a
few seconds and you will then be counted as part of the
terrorist team. The exercise continues until either one of
the teams wins, or the time limit of fifty hours is reached.
You will all be given a lite variation of the new U.N.E.
exosuit, which I'd like Jareus Dehayven, your new leader,
to share a few words about it,"

All eyes turned to Jareus as he froze. He saw
Harlow motioning to him, so he stood up and walked to
the stage as all the eyes around him silently judged him.

As he walked by Harlow, Harlow whispered, "Show 'em that you're here!" Jareus stood awkwardly on the stage.

"The… lite… variant of the U.N.E. exosuit… features a much lighter build that can sustain itself for about 71 hours on a full charge. This is achieved due to its much lower power consumption, since it isn't really meant for heavy combat. It's meant mainly for supplemental stamina, a feature of the main suit. Running shouldn't tire you. Occasional boosts are also doable, but they can't be chained in succession…" Jareus was so nervous that he just started rambling about the suit. Harlow put his palm to his face.

"Did you ramble your way to the top?!" An annoyed soldier from the back suddenly interrupted. Jareus kinda just froze.

"Hey! That was uncalled for!" Odessa shouted. Danny got up and agreed with Odessa. Zach didn't really wanna get involved. But basically, the entire crowd erupted in arguments and shouting. *C'mon Jareus. Do something…* Harlow thought.

"Enough," Jareus finally spoke prominently into the microphone, much louder than before, "I'll just have to show you. I'll see you in the training program," He bowed, and walked off the stage as people stopped talking and sat down in silence.

"Thank you for that, Jareus. Are you all ready for this?" Harlow took center stage again, just to get great applause, unlike the man before him. In no time at all, they all funneled outside to where they had tents set up. This was to provide everyone with a lite exosuit. From there, they had a car for each team of people that were ready.

"That was a good recovery," Danny affirmed Jareus as they and Odessa got in the car.

"Thanks, but I doubt it was enough. I now have to live up to what I said..." Jareus was nervous about that part.

"We'll have to show them all!" Odessa cheered. She was more ready than both of them to make that a reality, "Zach helped me out a lot back at the sporting tournament. Unfortunately, we'll have to see if we can trust his team if we cross paths."

"Our best strategy would be to get a good home base and defend from there. Since I practically have a target on my head, they're all going to be going after me. We could survive the fifty hours or just cuff anybody that tries to come at us," Jareus strategized. The other two decided that they'd go with that plan as they approached the training grounds. The teams all gathered in the center, where the drivers of the car all dropped them off, each with a bag of handcuffs.

"Alright all! Look at the few screens in the center, and that will count you off. Go find a good spot to hide, and good luck to all 20 teams!" Harlow's voice came on over a loudspeaker. It seemed they were in the middle of what looked like a big forest. They were on a circle of concrete and a pillar with screens on each side. It was counting down from thirty. All of the soldiers from Adrenaline Corp. were ready to make a dash for it. Zach, partnered with two new people, thought, *I wonder if Jareus is really going to prove himself?* Meanwhile, Jareus wondered, *How the Hell am I gonna prove myself?*

"You two ready?" Odessa looked at Danny and Jareus as they observed the three primary groups around them, full of entirely diverse subgroups.

120

"As much as I can be…" Jareus commented. They watched as the screen's timer counted down to one.

"Three… two… one," Danny mouthed with the timer. At 10 PM, it started. A large rumbling noise occurred as everyone tried to run. Suddenly, the cement circle started to retract and it revealed a ravine with water circling it at the bottom.

"It wouldn't be a good hiding spot if you were all out in the open like this, would it?" Harlow's voice taunted. Some people just started to jump across, with two falling into the pit.

"USE THE SMALL BOOST!" Jareus shouted, suddenly running ahead of Danny and Odessa. He jumped and boosted midair to make it across. When people saw him do that, he became an example. Right after him, Danny and Odessa followed by boosting over. The rest of the people started to immediately do the same, and scattered in all different directions. Danny and Odessa caught up with Jareus.

"Any idea where you're going?!" Danny shouted while running beside him.

"Not a clue yet. We'll probably want to hide around the outskirts. That's where it's hardest to get to!" Jareus shouted back at him.

"Getting far away is our objective for now!" Odessa shouted at both of them as they continued running. Usually, they'd expect to get tired, but with the help of the suit, it seemed as though they could run endlessly. The layer of trees started to become thickly packed, though, so they had to get through the many bushes and layers of forest. The ground wasn't flat either—they had to change course due to sudden cliffs. With the lite exo, they couldn't boost over cliffs, but only downward or to the side.

"Hold on!" Danny suddenly told the other two to stop.

"What's up?" Odessa asked. Danny had noticed they were in an area with little slope to the ground and relatively short trees around—especially two that were low-hanging, whose trunks snaked to the side.

"We're going to make our base here," Danny suddenly demanded. The other two were shocked.

"I thought we were gonna go to the sides of the area?" Jareus asked, trying to exercise his leadership.

"No, I see how we can actually use this area right here for an advantage. They said nothing against building, so we can build a little fort. Our defense will be much better than the others," Danny explained.

"That's not a bad idea," Odessa put her index finger to her mouth, thinking.

He isn't wrong... I guess we should just go with it, Jareus thought.

"Alright, let's get to work. Maybe we can actually sleep in it, too. I'd rather not sleep in the trees, which I'm pretty sure was everyone else's plan," Jareus admitted.

"Leave it to me," Danny smirked.

"When did you learn so much about building?" Jareus teased, smiling.

"The internet is an amazing tool," Danny proclaimed. *THE INTERNET?* Jareus thought, now wondering if this was a good idea at all.

"How can I help?" Odessa asked. The three quickly got to work, ripping small wooden chunks off of the nearby trees to make bootleg wooden planks. They piled them all up next to the two trees with sideways trunks.

122

The next step was to prop up the two trees with wooden planks planted in the ground. Then they lined the two trees' upper side with planks all across it—and finally, with planks around the rest of it and a small hole acting as the door, it made for a little space that they could fit inside.

"Who knew that'd work out so smoothly?" Danny rhetorically questioned as Jareus returned from the wild.

"I got the carpeting!" Jareus exclaimed, throwing a bunch of decent-looking leaves onto the ground.

"Nice going, we'll be high-class living out here," Odessa stated, laughing. The three went inside and shared a few stories. Danny talked about the time he'd spent in the economics department of Adrenaline Corp. before all of this. Jareus discussed how much he'd learned while helping design and build the U.N.E. exosuit. Odessa told them how Adrenaline Corp. had scouted her after the sporting tournament. Harlow Henry talked to Jareus and Danny personally, but as for Odessa, she had been taken in with Adam Steel by a regular recruiter. After a while, they all dozed off, tired from all the work they'd done that day. However, even in their rest they couldn't find much peace.

"OI! Is that a hut?! What the hell?! Who thought of that?! No, seriously… it's a hut," A voice from outside commented in awe. Odessa was stirred by this commotion, but Danny and Jareus remained asleep. She went right away to shake them awake. But just as the two got up, their hut was trespassed upon.

"Gotcha! Look at these fools," A girl with purple hair and a black bodysuit tore down the door, "Oh my. Two guys and a *girl*? You three weren't doing anything weird in there… were you?" She teased.

"AS IF!" Jareus shouted. He was definitely awake now.

"Who are you?!" Danny asked immediately. It was still dark out, but the sun was going to rise soon.

"Oh… I'm Tanya. Horse-face over here is named Devon," Tanya chuckled as she introduced her partner.

"Tanya… What do 'ya want? Where's your third person, anyways?" Odessa was over it already.

"There's no third person. We're the original terrorists, and now you're teaming up with us!" She said as sweetly as possible.

"WHAAAAT?!" Odessa was really riled up now.

"Yeah, this fort thing, it TOTALLY gave you guys away! And OI! I do not have a HORSE FACE!" Devon shouted at Tanya as she continued to laugh about it.

"Anyways, you guys don't need the handcuffs anymore. Take these instead. You'll need to use them at practically point blank range for them to work, though," Tanya threw three guns, one for each of them. Jareus's gun hit him in the head.

"OW! Uh… thanks," Jareus didn't know what to think of it.

"No problem, leeeader!" Tanya seemed like she was teasing him again.

"Yeah! The leader man! We got the leader man!" Devon suddenly cheered, just as the sun started to come up.

"My plan ended up not being so good… I guess…" Danny was looking at the ground, feeling bad.

"It's fine. Now if those two will stop making fun of me, I'll lead them by crushing them all!" Jareus was grinning evilly. Odessa was a little scared of this side of Jareus.

124

"THAT'S THE SPIRIT!" Tanya evilly grinned with Jareus. They all went outside, and sat on the roof of the hut, figuring out what to do. The two of them also brought snacks, so everyone had their fill.

"We can keep this as a home base actually, this still works out. It's a lot easier for us to tag them than it is for them to tag us. If Tanya and Devon start by trying to tag other people rather than staying with us, we can trick people into thinking that we're a group running from them," Danny started muttering.

"You're absolutely right! Absolutely right you are!" Devon cheered Danny on.

"Sounds like a plan! I love sneaking up on people, don't you?!" Tanya was clearly obsessed with the idea of being a spy. So after a bit of time, they split up again. The three acted like they were trying to avoid contact, but were secretly listening in hard for any kind of sound. Jareus knew exactly what the suits sounded like as well.

"Pretty sure I just heard someone boost to our left," Jareus alerted the rest of his group.

"How many did you hear?" Danny asked as the three changed direction as to where they'd heard running.

"I heard one, but who knows how many are there?" Jareus questioned as they headed over, but as they quietly approached the area, they realized it was someone taking a leak in the wilderness.

"That's Adam Steel!" Danny whisper-shouted as the three hid.

"My idea is that I run from you two while you're making loud noises, and tell him that the terrorists are behind me. Adam will come to help, but then I'll deactivate his suit, and I'll leave him to betray his teammates," Odessa suddenly brainstormed. Danny and Jareus were immediately on board with the idea.

"Jeez... I'm starving..." Adam Steel complained as he zipped up his pants. He turned his head to the sound of multiple exosuit boosts. *I've gotta go tell the others!* He thought. He turned, but then heard a very familiar voice.

"Adam!" Odessa shouted, running on the ground.

"Odessa! What are you doing?! Where's your team?!" Adam shouted at her.

"They got them! They're coming this way!" Odessa yelled, and just as she thought, he let her catch up with him. They started running at the same pace.

"We gotta get back to my group fast then... they—" Adam was cut off by Odessa pressing the gun against his side and firing. It did nothing but freeze his suit. "You... were with them?!" Adam didn't know what to say.

"Yeah, and now you'll help us out by bringing the rest of your team to our side. It's also best to travel as a group, so others won't be suspecting. The suit will let you move again in a few seconds. Good luck and sorry again," Odessa explained, boosting off toward where Jareus and Danny were again. They started to run the other way, not wasting any time.

"That worked like a charm!" Danny exclaimed, smiling as they ran through the forest once more.

"Yeah, and now they'll also go bring other people on our side as well!" Jareus cheered.

"Aw, stop with the compliments, you two! I'm just getting started!" Odessa grinned. But Jareus suddenly stopped as they were running, with Danny and Odessa quickly following suit.

"Huh?! What's up?" Danny questioned.

"We aren't here alone. I could have sworn I heard a boost sound from right by here," Jareus was suddenly on the alert, looking in every nearby direction that he could.

"In that you'd be right, Jareus!" A familiar male voice sounded from nearby. The three of them looked for where the voice was coming from, but couldn't find anything until someone stepped out from behind a tree on top of a small hill near them, saying, "You still did want to find out who'd win a fight now? Right?" It was Zach.

"Zach! What the heck? Where are your other teammates?! Don't tell me you're on the terrorist side!" Danny pretended to accuse him.

"I'm not an idiot. You forgot to carry around a bag to even look like you still had handcuffs. You can't even play the part of 'innocent.'" Zach pointed out. *Crap! He's right! Why didn't we think of that!* Jareus's brain panicked.

"Alright Zach, you really wanna fight so badly that you'd abandon your other teammates?" Jareus asked him.

"Of course I wanna, we got robbed of it in the sports tournament. But don't get me wrong, my teammates are here. They'll be ready for a surprise at any time," Zach talked down to Jareus, Danny, and Odessa, who all had their backs to each other.

"You think you can take him?" Odessa asked.

"I could have in the sporting tournament, of course I can," Jareus whispered back. Odessa didn't look certain about his statement.

"How about we back you up, and also ready for an outside attack?" Danny suggested.

"Sounds good to me," Jareus grins, "Alright Zach! We'll have a fair fight!" Jareus readied himself.

"I knew you'd say that," Zach smirked. Danny and Odessa split up as Zach jumped off of the hill and boosted right toward Jareus, who blocked his kick by putting his arms in an X formation on his chest. Jareus's feet dragged backwards in the dirt, then broke Zach's attack while going in for a punch of his own. He hit Zach dead on, causing him to retreat a bit. Suddenly, another person with a hood on boosted in from behind a tree to try and kick Jareus, but he ducked.

"They're here!" Jareus yelled.

"We know!" Danny yelled back, as they were also ambushed by another hooded person. *Who are these people?* Jareus thought to himself. He felt like he recognized the person who had just come in. Suddenly, they both retreated into the shadows behind the trees.

"Do you recognize those two?!" Jareus asked Danny. Danny suddenly realized what Jareus was talking about—he remembered their faces.

"You caught on so early?" Zach smirked, charging in for an attack. He kicked Jareus down.

"*Augh*, so we do know these people?" Jareus let out as he hit the ground. Zach backed off.

"Alright, I've let it slip, you can reveal yourselves," Zach shouted toward the shadows. The two boosted out, taking off their hoods. It was Allison and Lexus.

"Lexus?!" Danny shouted in surprise.

"Allison?!" Jareus also shouted, equally as surprised. The two girls both took advantage of their shock and opened up the handcuffs. *Crap! She's gonna cuff me this fast?!* Jareus panicked. He was able to boost out of the way, albeit barely, while Lexus cuffed Danny.

"You gotta be kidding me!" Danny shouted as his hands were clasped together.

"We're not gonna let you win!" Zach boasted.

"Allison, why are you against us?!" Jareus shouted.

"Why haven't you been updating us? Lexus and I had to practically *beg* to get into Adrenaline Corp. in order to get here!" Allison questioned Jareus.

"Jareus, we've gotta retreat," Odessa demanded.

Shoot, I forgot to text Allison! Jareus thought.

"Who even *is* she?!" Allison questioned. Jareus said nothing in response, and boosted backwards. He grabbed Odessa's hand and ran out of there with her.

"Sorry!" Jareus yelled as they retreated. Allison was a little peeved that Jareus still hadn't explained anything, but Jareus really hadn't known what to say. He had meant to keep up with her, but he'd ended up just saying the bare minimum to her because of how busy he was.

"Danny... what's happened since we last saw you...?" Lexus meekly asked. Zach sighed.

"Don't go easy on him, he deserves to explain everything to you," Zach smirked as they all approached Danny.

"I swear, I was trying to stay in touch, but I didn't know what I could or couldn't tell you! I didn't know what was supposed to be top secret!" Danny tried to explain.

"We literally basically became friends with Odessa on live TV, you at least ought to explain what happened between the sports tournament and now to them. They've come all this way!" Zach taunted Danny.

"Right now? We're in the middle of an exercise..." Danny complained.

"Danny, we worked this hard to get in here! We just wanted to know what was going on with you guys!" Allison scolded him.

"Fine, fine... Well after the sports tournament, Harlow introduced himself to all of us and he recruited some of us for a job. I guess Odessa and Adam Steel also were approached. Cole had already been scouted by a different regiment, so he was moving away regardless. Jareus and Harlow instantly hit it off and became good friends, since Jareus expressed his interest in making an exosuit. They spent a while on that while Alex, Zach, and I did a bunch of the company's busywork. We've been getting decent pay and things have been normal-ish, but now things are getting out of hand. Happy?" Danny explained. They sat there absorbing the info for a second.

"We'll talk about this more later. But for now, we're going to try and find more allies," Allison accepted begrudgingly.

ALTERNIS - 16 NOVEMBER 2015, 8:23 AM

"I can't believe that we still have to find a new place to sleep every night. Can't we just find one good place?" Amar complained as their group of four left a motel. They always had enough money to just barely scrape by.

"We could stay at the junkyard!" Hosea charmed in. It seemed Hosea missed his little group of homeless friends.

"I don't know if I'd really want to sleep with scrap metal..." Destructo scratched his head.

"Why didn't we just sleep at your old place, Amar?" Bobonson asked.

"I don't deserve to be back there..." Amar mumbled.

"Look at mister emo boy over here! Is that really all?!" Destructo prodded Amar.

"Okay, not really. We also needed to go somewhere where we could make some cash in order to keep this thing going. This motel is just the halfway point, and we don't have a car. Bobonson would be the only likely one out of us that'd actually have a car... but..." Amar explained.

"Oi! I usually have one, but being a mercenary requires that I often switch cars..." Bobonson justified.

"So no junkyard...?" Hosea seemed disappointed.

"No," The other three said in unison. And with that, they were off to the destination Amar had in mind, bantering all the way there.

"...As I was saying, that's probably the easiest way to bake without an oven," Bobonson concluded as they were close to the destination.

"I didn't have the same cooking tools as you do... but just from context I can tell using a 'microwave' for everything doesn't sound like a great idea..." Destructo voiced his concern.

"It isn't! At least use a freaking toaster or something!" Amar convicted Bobonson.

"I like using fire," Hosea smiled.

"You say that now, Amar, but you'd be the kinda person to throw waffles in the microwave because you don't wanna wait for them to toast," Bobonson chuckled.

"WHAT ARE YOU SAYIN'?!" Amar rebutted.

"Amar, are we here?" Destructo interrupted. He pointed up to a sign—they were at a harbor on a small river connecting to the ocean.

"Ah yes, this is where I was planning on going," Amar boasted.

"Are we going on a boat?" Hosea seemed confused.

"Nope, but we're going fishing," Amar announced. Everybody looked at him funny, their expressions reading something along the lines of: *Has he lost his mind?*

"Why are we going fishing?" Hosea questioned.

"If we catch some decent-sized fish, we could actually make a profit by selling them. With the four of us, we could probably get some decent cash if we have some good luck and a lot of skill," Amar explained.

"Oh, that's why we're here," Destructo understood.

"Well… what about gear? Where are we gonna fish?" Bobonson asked.

"We'll go rent the gear and make the money back easily. We'll fish in many spots, but let's start across that bridge by the ocean," Amar pointed. They proceeded to go get their gear, and went fishing for the day.

PRIMARIUM - 16 NOVEMBER 2015, 12:34 AM

"Odessa…? Is that you?" A familiar voice asked.

"Tanya? What's up?" Odessa asked. She and Jareus were in a small cave, discussing what they should do next now that Zach's crew knew about them and Danny was out for the match.

"We've got quite the amount of people. I'd say there's an epidemic of terrorism out there, so go lead your people, dummy," Tanya shouted. It hit Jareus like a truck. *I have to prove I can lead, so if we even have like a good half of the people out there, then it may be enough to win!*

"You're exactly right, Tanya! Is there a group of people out there?!" Jareus suddenly felt the urge to act.

"The terrorists are working together to make a bigger group. You should join 'em," Tanya suggested to Jareus. Jareus started to break out into a sprint without a second thought.

"WAIT UP!" Odessa shouted at him as she started after him. The two of them ran. *I need to do this! I have to be the leader that Harlow Henry saw inside of me!* Jareus thought as he sprinted. He ran to the edge of a hill, and looking over the hill, he could see a group of people all frantically running around with the exo-disabling guns. *They're incredibly disorganized... if they could just figure out how to attack as a group,* Jareus thought. He remembered Harlow showing him multiple battle simulations and what the leader would do in them. They'd taken battle tactics into consideration when designing the abilities of the U.N.E. exoskeleton suit.

"Are you all on the terrorist side?!" Jareus shouted to the group. The non-terrorists suddenly saw him alone, and changed direction. Two guys came in to try and cuff Jareus, but he boosted to the side and kicked one down as Odessa caught up and crashed into the other one, shooting him at point blank.

"Look! It's mister privileged!" The other soldiers made fun of Jareus. But as that was said, another group of non-terrorists came in and started to arrest a few of the group.

"Your movements are too sporadic and contradictory to each other! Nobody's planning what they're doing!" Jareus brought the heat with his criticism—this made some people realize that he was right.

"Then allow me," Aaron Johnson walked out of the crowd, "continue the attack on them!"

"Aaron?! Do you not remember me?!" Jareus spat out the second he saw Aaron.

"Eh? You're that Jareus guy, the one Harlow likes," Aaron stated simply.

"Do you *not* remember Rownert!?" Jareus was a little peeved. It hit Aaron all at once.

"Oh yeah! You were also that crazy guy!" Aaron had a laugh, but stopped as he realized that the crazy guy from 3 years ago now had a higher rank than him. "Wait, that's you?! Figures..."

"Yeah, Aaron! Why else did you think I knew your name?!" Jareus shouted back. As the other soldiers were doing as Aaron said, another man came in, and instantly handcuffed a few of them. He went back, to back, to back—moving faster than the rest. It was Toshi.

"Nice to stop you here, terrorist scum!" Toshi smiled, giving a thumbs up. Jareus and Aaron were flabbergasted.

"They've sent out their strongest soldier already, attack that one, everybody!" Aaron shouted.

"That won't work on me, Aaron!" Toshi smiled like a true hero, and continued to dodge multiple attacks.

"Aaron, if you're gonna beat somebody like Toshi, you're gonna need a better strategy!" Jareus shouted. As Jareus called out, Odessa suddenly blocked another oncoming attack.

"Who's this?!" Odessa grunted as she blocked a kick. It was Kami—she backed up and got into a fighting position.

"She fought alongside Toshi when we first met him, so don't underestimate her!" Jareus shouted, also getting ready. She, without hesitation, jumped right into action and consistently boosted in for attacks, jumping forward and then backwards. Odessa and Jareus had to put up their best defense.

"No kidding! But you gotta do something about that clown, they're dying over there!" Odessa shouted to Jareus. *You're completely right…* Jareus thought, seeing the chaos that was unfolding.

"HEY! Get in a circle, all of you!" Jareus suddenly shouted, boosting toward the plethora of people on the same team as him. People ignored him at first. *What the hell is he thinking?* Aaron thought, but after further assessing the situation, he saw exactly what Jareus was planning. An all-out defense circle would be fully advantageous, because the suits couldn't jump vertically. The exo-disabling guns would work a lot better than the handcuffs in that situation.

"Well, what are you all doing?! Do as he says!" Aaron shouted. People started to notice after Aaron shouted it, finally thinking that maybe they should. Suddenly, they all retreated in a back-to-back formation, making a circle. Odessa even joined the circle, smiling at Jareus as he dodged another one of Kami's attacks.

"I see… a defensive circle. That's not bad," Kami stated to herself. Toshi jumped in right next to her.

"But with all three of us, it's not going to be enough," Toshi gave another smile, while pointing with his thumb behind him. With that, another person burst through the trees. Landing next to Toshi was none other than Martin.

"I see who you've decided to side with!" Aaron smirked.

"Long time no see, Aaron," Martin also smirked. Martin and Aaron instantly went to battle, originally going in for a punch each, but they both switched to a block on each other.

"The rest of you, stay in formation! Together, we can take down Toshi! Even if he's the best," Jareus shouted, trying to prove himself.

"Why are we listening to that guy…" One of the guys in the circle complained.

"Probably because it's the best course of action…" Odessa grunted, a little frustrated with some of the soldiers being numbskulls. As she said that, Jareus and Toshi both boosted around the circle while the other members of the circle reached out. They tried to get close enough for the disabling guns to work, but they were always just out of reach.

"We can't just circle around here forever, Jareus," Toshi taunted as they both bolted around, changing directions occasionally as if to play cat and mouse. Toshi would have been just about to catch Jareus if it hadn't been for Odessa suddenly breaking the circle and kicking him out of the way. But he didn't stop smiling as Martin and Aaron were still dueling in the background. Kami came in and tried to grab Jareus as he boosted, but crashed into the ground.

"I can't do this without all of you! Circle around them now!" Jareus shouted, with the side of his face now bleeding. The people finally started to see that he really meant business.

"Aye aye," One of the girls affirmed as the rest nodded and charged forward, suddenly trapping Toshi in the circle. They tried to trap Kami as well, but she boosted out of the way at the last moment. Jareus jumped after her, and by diving right under where she was, he was able to get close enough to disable her exo, bringing her to the terrorist side.

"Kami!" Toshi yelled. He was done messing around. He grabbed two guys after him, smacked them into each other, jumped out of the way, and boosted out of the circle while sliding under someone else that tried to boost into him. Jareus was about to disable Toshi's exo as well, but he knocked the gun out of his hand. Jareus and Toshi dodged around each other, boosting over and around each other every second they got the chance. As Jareus tried to get back to the gun, he blocked the way every time.

"Take this one!" Odessa yelled, throwing him one of the guns. But Jareus couldn't catch it, as Toshi smacked it out of the air. Jareus tried to dodge, but Toshi boosted in the same direction, knocking Jareus onto the ground.

"He's down!" Aaron yelled.

"What?!" Martin turned for a second, giving Aaron the opportunity to boost up and disable Martin's exosuit. Then, as the dust cleared, it could be seen that Jareus had been cuffed by Toshi, but just barely.

"Sorry, Jareus," Toshi whispered in his ear. Jareus felt bad, but then remembered something. Toshi must have had tunnel vision to be that focused.

"What are you waiting for? Let's go!" Odessa took over, and the rest of the mob there charged Toshi at first. He could dodge well, but it was only a matter of time.

"I'll get you!" Aaron distracted Toshi, coming from the opposite way where he originally was going to escape to. Toshi was able to pull off an impressive last-second side boost, but Odessa had figured he was going to do that, and told a few people to go around that way.

"Here I am!" Odessa yelled, distracting Toshi for just a second as a group of three came in from behind him, finally bringing him down.

"Fine, fine... you got me!" Toshi laughed, getting off of the ground. He looked over to Jareus, who looked incredibly defeated. He sat on the ground in his chains. Toshi yelled over to him, "Oi, Jareus. You got me, okay? Look. The people you rallied together took me down." Jareus looked up, and his expression changed from frustration to a slight happiness.

"Good job, taking down our best," Jareus smiled at the other soldiers. They started to see a little of what Harlow saw in him.

"Now since that's all over, you think we ought to go get Zach, Allison, and Lexus?" Odessa asked the other soldiers. It took a while, since they were hiding, but the rest of the Adrenaline Corp. soldiers found their group and ambushed them. Since it had spread that much, it was inevitable that the terrorist side would win. Jareus got his first taste of leading, and on the way out, he personally thanked Tanya.

ALTERNIS - 16 NOVEMBER 2015, 6:17 PM

"I can't believe we got a white seabass! Who would have thought?!" Amar boasted, laughing to himself as he and the crew returned their fishing equipment, smelling like the fish they'd caught.

"I honestly didn't think that we would make any money, but here we are..." Destructo was incredibly surprised. They'd claimed quite a large sum of money after turning everything in, including their catches.

138

"Excuse me… what do you call yourself, sir…" A voice suddenly said behind Amar.

"Oh, I'm Amar, and these are…" Amar started, but he stopped as soon as he realized the person behind them was definitely not friendly. Whoever it was suddenly drew a dagger, and Amar instantly reacted, shoving the others out of the way.

"What the hell? Who are you!" Hosea was instantly pissed off. The man was in a dark green trench coat with the hood over his face.

"You're the one from the Adrenaline Corp. sports tournament, aren't you? I was wondering why you looked just like that one contestant…" The man with the dagger said.

"Yeah… I am, but first let me ask… who are you?" Amar questioned while everybody else was staying back.

"MY NAME IS HARLOW HENRY!" The man shouted, seemingly filled with rage, "AND I NEED TO KNOW WHAT HAPPENED THAT DAY!" He approached quickly with the dagger, but Amar instantly pulled a sword out of his backpack.

"You see this?" Amar asked, blocking Harlow's sword, "This is the first thing I stole when I came back to Earth, after being under a demon's control. I stole it to kill myself, you see. But I thought, since the participants of the tournament were killed by my possessed hands… The least I could do is try to protect the same world they were trying to protect," Harlow's expression fell into despair.

"So… they *are* dead. Adrenaline Corp. practically fell apart and went bankrupt after that. You took all those lives, and you can find it in your sanity to blame it on that?!" Harlow angrily tried to slash again, but Amar blocked.

139

"What would he have to gain from lying?!" Bobonson questioned, pointing his gun at Harlow just in case.

"Something to help his conscience, I guess. I've been looking for the man that teleported them all away for some time now, and I get reports of a Jareus lookalike, and they *just* happen to be the same person? Why do you look exactly the same?!" Harlow was confused.

"I'm from a timeline where we lose to the demon Redaro, and I was under control, I swear. I still feel guilty about everything I've done, Harlow! But my decisions were never a factor in this matter," Amar was nearly losing it.

"Then you ought to be ready to give your life for the ones you took!" Harlow shouted through tears. He had nowhere to go anymore. The company in this timeline was gone, along with all of Harlow's dreams. As Harlow went for Amar's neck, Bobonson instinctively shot at Harlow's left leg, causing him to fall to the ground and scream.

"What'd you do that for?! He could have ducked!" Destructo yelled at Bobonson.

"I'm not taking chances, and we can patch this guy up," Bobonson told Destructo, taking out some medical supplies from Amar's backpack. He had a first-aid kit in his bag ever since the incident with Escarere. They patched him up as quickly as they could, but swiftly had to be on their way out before the police got there.

"I'm sorry... let me make up for my own past," Amar whispered to Harlow right before the rest of the gang took off.

"Today's the day where we're throwing a little celebration for the inventors of Adrenaline Corporation. We're calling it the 'Invention Convention.' Cute little name, I know. But Jareus, I'd like you and Danny to come with me during that time. It's something that should definitely remain private," Harlow Henry of the Primarium Timeline told Jareus and Danny. Jareus seemed gloomy for some reason.

"I don't know if he'll try and keep anything private again…Allison chewed him out a little after the military training program, and she wants to talk to him again later," Danny commented.

"I see… Then Jareus, you can spend the time with Allison if need be. I don't want to rob you of your other personal relationships. Danny and I will check it out and tell you afterwards," Harlow offered.

"Thank you, I guess I'll take you up on that offer. I feel so bad for leaving her in the dark," Jareus admitted.

"I got to talk to Lexus earlier as well, but she seemed a little more chill about it," Danny mentioned.

"Well, she didn't seem the type to want to get involved in the first place!" Jareus pointed out. They both stopped talking for a second, realizing that he was right.

"Well, let's walk down to the first floor and see what people are doing for the invention convention, at least. I'm sure seeing the cool tech they have on display will take your mind off of other stress for now," Harlow offered, trying to put on a smile to calm the other two.

"Let's do it," Jareus agreed, and with that the three went downstairs to check out what was going on. It was like an adult version of a school science fair. There was one station downstairs where a person was demonstrating how strong the suction on a sticky grenade was, by shooting it onto slippery and wet surfaces. He further tested out the amount of force it could withstand by sticking it to a fan and turning the fan on full power. There was also a girl with the laser handgun that Harlow and Jareus had designed, and she was showcasing the accuracy of it by shooting tiny targets straight-on, whereas standard bullets would usually suffer from a little bit of air resistance and drift. A third exhibit they walked by had a man with the U.N.E. exoskeleton arms on, lifting objects of different weights that went all the way up to a three-row minivan. The last was one Jareus was particularly interested in, since Saskia was there as well.

"Hey Saskia! What's been going on over here?" Danny asked as the three guys stopped at where Saskia was stationed with another girl.

"Oh hey! I got on this project at the last moment, so I couldn't really help all that much besides setting up this area," Saskia told them. It was a rather large area that was the length of a bowling alley, with a fake tree at the end.

"So I'm guessing this is the grapple hook I've been hearing so much about," Harlow boasted, showing off his prior knowledge.

"Grapple hook?!" Jareus questioned excitedly.

"Yep, and it works with your exo, Mr. Dehayven and Mr. Henry!" Saskia nodded.

"Here! Why don't you all try it?" The other girl asked. As she turned to them, Jareus recognized her as Tanya from the earlier competition. The three of them looked at each other with smiles.

"Grapple now!" Saskia shouted, as Harlow was the first one to try on the suit with the new attachment. He had just boosted upward and pointed his arm at the place on the tree he wanted to grapple to. There was also a rather large part that had to go on top of the shoulder—in Harlow's case, the left shoulder. He was left-handed. This part acted as a shock absorber, counteracting the force of the grapple hook and keeping it completely inside the suit, as to avoid breaking any arms.

"Woah!" Harlow exclaimed as the grapple pulled him toward the tree. The grapple diverted the force to the torso section of the grapple suit, avoiding any limbs from being pulled on unequally, which again prevented the grapple force from breaking any limbs. As Harlow hung onto the tree, he yelled, "This rocks! You all gotta try this!" Danny and Jareus tried it out, both having similar experiences.

"We gotta get this on our exosuits as soon as we can!" Jareus told Saskia, laughing from his enjoyment of the grapple hook. He swung from the tree like a spider. After they had all tested it out and had some fun along the way, it was time for Danny and Harlow to split ways with Jareus.

"Allison wants to meet me in the break room…" Jareus told the other two while looking at his phone.

"Then Danny and I have got some special testing to do. We'll tell you the results afterwards," Harlow told Jareus.

"But what is it?" Jareus asked.

"It's a surprise," Harlow responded.

"It… it is?" Danny questioned nervously.

"Well, whatever it is, you two better tell me about it after, I really gotta sprint… she's expecting me so… I'll see you two after!" Jareus loudly explained as his slow pace away turned into a full jog.

"So… er… Harlow. What's this surprise?" Danny asked after a few seconds of silence. Harlow turned to him.

"As much as I made it out to be a fun surprise, it's actually quite serious. I think I found out how Escarere escaped the first time, thanks to one of our better experimental scientists here. I think you met him earlier—his name is Devon," Harlow told Danny seriously.

"He's a scientist here? Does this involve my ability to see in slowed down time?" Danny questioned Harlow.

"Yes, we found the object that Escarere escaped through. You said you could see it glow like, ehhh… a pinkish color, right? The point is that it suddenly emits a strong radiation every now and then, and we can't seem to find a reason for it. But it seems to be the area rather than the object itself," Harlow explained to Danny.

"It's a magenta color. So you're saying that Escarere escaped through a portal?" Danny asked.

"Well, we also get unique radio signals near the area, which don't appear around us other than when it's emitting the radiation. For that we have to believe that it's…" Harlow was saying.

"An entirely separate world…" Danny finished.

Meanwhile, Jareus had just arrived to talk with Allison in the break room.

"Hey, sorry I was a minute or two late… I was talking to Danny and Harlow about the invention convention going on right now," Jareus apologized as he entered the break room.

"It's… fine. Just seat yourself, dummy. I'm gonna demand a lot of answers," Allison sighed. Jareus gulped and took a seat.

"So…" He tried to break the awkwardness, but just made it worse.

"So? Why haven't you been telling me about this corporation stuff? You just said that you were 'doing fine' and 'just working a lot.'" Allison questioned Jareus.

"That isn't false, I was working a lot. But it was mainly because of how busy I was…" Jareus started, but Allison cut him off.

"Busy isn't a great excuse, Jareus. I was wondering what was up!" She scolded him.

"…and because I still feel terrible about putting you in danger all those times," Jareus finished his sentence.

They sat there for a second. Jareus hadn't seen her in a long time, so he just stayed in silence, looking at Allison. She wore a dark red short sleeve shirt with high-waisted gray jeans, and her blonde hair was as long as it always had been.

It was a moment of clarity in the mind of Allison.

"You weren't the one putting me in danger, Jareus…" Allison started, putting her index finger up before Jareus could retort, "It started with me putting *you* in danger, ever since our times in the gang. Now you're going out and living this grandiose life. You told me you just wanted to live a normal life, but your actions have contradicted that. I don't want you to apologize for giving up living a 'normal life.' I just don't want you to push me out of your life out of worry!" Allison expressed, a little bit worked up.

145

"Allison… it's dangerous doing this now. Didn't you hear about the threat that Harlow talked about?" Jareus asked her.

"Yeah, and I can handle myself. Everyone here is in equal danger, besides you! You keep throwing yourself on the front line, and if anything, it's me that's worrying more about your safety. The fact that you didn't tell me anything didn't make my worrying go away, it just made me even more anxious, knowing that you were up to something. I mean, knowing you, there's always something you're up to," Allison explained to him.

He didn't even know she'd cared about him this much. He always saw her as someone he'd needed to protect, but seeing it from her point of view made him think twice.

"I'm… sorry… but NOT for that thing you told me not to apologize for! I'm sorry for just not telling you the full truth, and not being transparent. I shouldn't have… underestimated you," Jareus told her, feeling his guilt permeate his entire being.

"Jareus… it's okay. Let's just… work together instead of trying to work for one another, okay?" Allison proposed. He nodded his head confidently. Once she was satisfied with his answer, she also demanded, "Now you gotta tell me all the details! Tell me what's been going on up to now."

Allison and Jareus started to get into a long conversation. Jareus's heartstrings suddenly felt pulled in two directions. He was left asking himself if he still liked Allison, or whether or not he had moved on to Jill.

Meanwhile, Harlow and Danny were setting up a machine for Danny to try and contact the other timeline through the magenta energy of the time-gates.

146

"Is the thing up to speed?" Danny asked about the machine he was right next to. He and Harlow were in one of the back rooms of the Adrenaline Corp. Headquarters.

"Yeah, you should be able to just walk into that wall, as long as you can figure out how to use the same time power that Escarere had. I tried, but I can't go through," Harlow assured Danny. Danny had a little machine on his neck that would theoretically be able to amplify the amount of energy that his time power gave off. It'd help Danny's body get accumulated to using his newfound ability, as well as make it easier for him to travel to the other timeline.

"What'll be on the other side you think? A magenta world?" Danny asked, smiling as he faced the wall. Harlow chuckled.

"I'm not sure. For now, just try and gather information on the other timeline when you get over there. You'll be able to talk to me through the machine you have on. If need be, I have a lever right here that should be able to bring you back to here," Harlow continued assuring Danny.

"Alright… here I go, then. Let's make sure I don't forget this just in case…" Danny said as he picked up a laser handgun. If there were people hostile to him in the other timeline, he would need to take them down.

"Also, if you can, try and find the origin of the split. If my theory is right, the timelines should be the same up until a certain point. Alex told me this when I was talking to him the other day… so I don't even know if I can call it a theory. You know what I mean," Harlow told Danny.

"Wait… what if it's that timeline that Alex said is all screwed up? Like a future where Redaro won?" Danny asked Harlow, now quite worried.

"If it is, I'll pull you out of there as soon as possible," Harlow reassured Danny. He nodded and tried to walk into the wall, smacking his head on the concrete.

"Ow, what the heck?" Danny questioned.

"Uh... just... try a little harder I guess," Harlow shrugged, making a fake smile as Danny looked at him, wondering what happened. After a few tries, it actually did work, and Danny's vision turned completely white for a few seconds, before fading away to a familiar surrounding.

ALTERNIS - 17 NOVEMBER 2015, 11:56 AM

"So? What do you see?" Harlow asked through the speaker of the machine that Danny had on.

"Well... it's a closet," Danny told him.

"What?" Harlow was confused.

"Yeah, hold on," Danny told him, walking out of the closet. He seemed to be in a dressing room area of some store. He informed Harlow of his surroundings.

"Well, can you figure out where exactly you are?" Harlow asked. Danny walked out of the store and realized that it was a clothing store nearby the neighborhood where Jareus lived.

"Yeah, actually, I think I could get a ride to Jareus's house from here. I'm sure that'd be interesting. Plus, this world's versions of us could inform me of something," Danny told Harlow through the microphone.

"Wait, wouldn't that cause a paradox or something?" Harlow asked.

"No way of telling, and besides... if these *are* two different timelines, then they shouldn't be the exact same people as we are. Also, there are people walking around on the street—so I can confirm that no demon has destroyed all life here," Danny informed Harlow. He walked to the bus stop across the street from the store.

"You heard of a portal, Hosea?" Amar asked. They had come back to Jareus's old house, in search of somewhere to hide out. They were all laying around on the couch.

"Yeah, I got a call from a buddy who lives around this ranch, right? It's called Orange Grove Ranch, and they do weddings there sometimes," Hosea responded.

"That's the most competent sentence I've heard from you," Destructo poked fun, laughing.

"HEY! YOU WANNA GO, PUNK?!" Hosea held up his bamboo stick. Destructo had access to a small shotgun, though. He'd gotten it from Bobonson.

"You two, stop messing around for now," Bobonson intervened.

"Yeah, what about this portal?" Amar asked. Hosea sat back down, and tried to calm himself.

"Yeah this little pond thingy turned pink. They say that er… rabbits just fall into it and don't come back. They tried rocks, I guess, too," Hosea explained.

"You're really competent when you want to be," Destructo instigated.

"OI!" Amar and Bobonson both yelled at Destructo.

"Sorry… sorry…" He apologized.

"Anyways… What do you want us to do about it, Hosea?" Bobonson asked.

"We ought to go to it! Is-scary guy might be behind it!" Hosea shouted.

"You mean *Escarere*? Well… you could be right. Why don't you three go check it out? I'll go get food or something, I'm tired," Amar proposed.

"Why do *you* get to stay back? I could be tired too, you know. Or I could betray them!" Destructo threatened.

"Well, are you tired?" Amar asked.

"No..." Destructo admitted.

"Well, I don't see you betraying us. You have no reason to, as it is. You should go," Amar shooed them.

"Alright, alright, why don't we go, guys?" Bobonson asked. They all eventually agreed, and the three of them were out of there. Amar planned to chill for a bit before going out to get some food.

Meanwhile, Danny was headed to their very location.

"Alright, I just got off the bus. I'm glad I'm alone—Jareus would have hated to use public transportation. I don't know why he still hates it. Maybe he doesn't like the germs or something," Danny told Harlow through the microphone as he walked up the hill to Jareus's house.

"Guess I should go do something, now?" Amar asked himself. He got up off of the couch and started to go down the driveway, but freaked out when he saw someone he recognized walking up the driveway. *I see... Danny...* Amar's head was pulsing. They both stopped and stared at each other. *But... I killed Danny... I still have the painful memory of doing it personally...* Amar was freaking out.

Is... that Amar?! His eyes... they're red. He couldn't possibly be alive... but this is another timeline... Danny's mind was racing as well. They remained staring at each other, motionless.

"You there!" Danny shouted, pulling out his gun and aiming it at Amar, "Does the name Jareus sound familiar to you?"

150

"I… definitely know him," Amar backed up.

"Then let me ask you this… is your name Amar?" Danny asked.

"Busted," He shrugged, smiling nervously. Danny shot a warning shot, and Amar freaked out. "Wait wait wait, I can explain!"

"Then do so!" Danny yelled.

"Wait! What am *I* supposed to explain?! I *killed* you, how are you alive?!" Amar asked.

"You killed me?!" Danny shouted.

"Your name is Danny, right?" Amar asked.

"Yeah. Are you planning to kill me again?!" Danny shouted back, pointing his gun right at Amar.

"No! I can't believe that you're alive. I regret everything about what happened!" Amar shouted back to Danny.

"What?!" Danny questioned.

In no time, they were sitting on the couch while Amar explained everything to Danny, and Danny explained everything to Amar.

"I can't believe that flash of light that Diadem was waiting for was a timeline split. Escarere's probably been here ever since… speaking of other timelines… you literally just got here from a different timeline? And Harlow's with you there?!" Amar asked. Danny pointed to the back of his neck as the speaker activated again.

"Yep!" Harlow's voice spoke.

"Oh. Well, I think maybe I should go investigate with the others about that portal," Amar said.

"Yeah, I have a few people already there. You can come back if you want, Danny," Harlow stated.

"YOU have people there?" Danny asked.

"It's acting the same on this side. It seems to be a portal, I should tell them that," Harlow said.

"Well, I'll go tell Bobonson and the others as well. It's a shame that Escarere already killed them in your world," Amar said to Danny.

"Yeah... we just need to focus on figuring out Escarere, and if we have to... killing her as well," Danny affirmed. Amar understood.

"Are ya ready for me to pull you back?" Harlow asked.

"Yep! And Amar..." Danny started, "I'm sorry that you had to see those memories of what you were forced to do. Try not to feel too guilty over it," Danny smiled as he was warped back into the other timeline.

"Yeah! With our combined knowledge, we can take down Escarere!" Amar cheered. Danny disappeared as he said that. Amar sighed and headed over to the others.

"Can I jump in?" Hosea was bantering with the other two. They had been standing around the pool of water for a while now. It wasn't too far from where Adrenaline Corp. Headquarters was in the Primarium timeline. They were in a grove of trees, but there was beige concrete surrounding the pink-tinged pond.

"Sure, you can jump in!" Destructo was ready to shove him in.

"Let's... not try that out right now," Bobonson sighed.

"Hey guys! That really *is* a portal!" Amar yelled, running over. "I was going to buy groceries when I ran into Danny Kipper, of all people. I *did* kill this timeline's one... but that portal leads to a different timeline where, as unfortunate for me as it is, I died and the others lived. Danny just went back, using some sort of machine."

"Woah woah woah, what?" Bobonson was confused by the information overload. Amar briefly explained to them about what just happened to him.

"So that's where that bastard Escarere escaped to…" Destructo muttered to himself, but Amar heard.

"Escarere should actually be in this timeline right now. But… we also don't know for sure. She has more freedom to move in-between the timelines than any of us," Amar expressed.

"Prove it! Take this, and take pictures!" Hosea yelled at Amar, giving Amar his beat up flip phone.

"Uhh… alright?" Amar questioned while taking the phone.

PRIMARIUM - 17 NOVEMBER 2015, 2:38 PM

"It's in an orange grove ranch, right?" Alex asked Zach.

"It better be, because we're already there!" Zach snarkily replied to Alex. Those were the two people that Harlow had sent to go investigate rumors of a "portal" in a park. They walked around the area, seeing a plethora of orange trees and different paths. There was a ditch where there had used to be a stream, which had snaked around the whole place. A small hedge maze adorned the place too, accompanied by a few statues. There were many dirt paths with benches, and even a windmill.

Eventually, they arrived at what seemed like a big puddle, but the concrete around it was accompanied by a purple coloration. But just as Alex and Zach got to it, Amar had just jumped in from the other side. They witnessed him coming out upside-down, since he had jumped in feet first, not expecting gravity to change on him. They only

153

saw him for a split second as he suddenly fell head-first back into the portal.

"Was that Amar just now?!" Zach exclaimed, stepping back from the portal. Alex stepped forward.

"I think it was! His eyes..." Alex remembered the appearance of the guy's face, "...they were red!"

"Alex... I didn't think we'd encounter any threats. I didn't bring anything. If Escarere intends to use this timeline's population against us, and Amar is one of those people... I think as we are now, we'd be crushed by him. If I had an exosuit, it'd be a different story. Maybe we should run," Zach backed up as he nervously explained to Alex.

"There's no need..." Alex mumbled, "I don't want to jeopardize the lives of other civilians. I saw what happens if these evils go unchecked!" He shouted, bringing back that darkness from before.

"Alex... do you think you could control it?" Zach asked him.

"I... I don't think I can at first... but me going ravenous on him shouldn't be a problem," Alex was instigated from a memory of the past, taking what some would call unnecessary measures.

"What if he doesn't come back? Don't act too rash!" Zach yelled at Alex, but it was too late. The demon claws and head had come back to envelop Alex's body, just as Amar jumped through the portal to land the right way.

"You two! I thought you two were dead as well..." Amar stated, not thinking, then seeing what was in front of him.

"So he *did* want us dead... get him, Alex!" Zach shouted. Alex, in his demonic form, screeched and charged forward.

"What the hell?! Are you helping Escarere?!" Amar shouted, dodging out of the way. *Helping Escarere? Why would Amar ask whether or not WE were helping Escarere? Sure... Alex looks a little like a demon in that form... but by attacking him if he were on Escarere's side... that'd be hurting Escarere, wouldn't it? Unless...* Zach's mind raced.

"AAAARRRHHH!' Alex's demon form raged. He wasn't controlling it. He swiped at Amar, but Amar was fast as well. *Shoot... I could just retreat and get back to the portal... but he's blocking my way! Why is he attacking me?* Amar thought, but then realized what this timeline's version of him had likely done to terrorize them. They were attacking because they were still expecting him to be hostile. Alex raged on, clawing at Amar, but Amar turned his back and tried to dodge by jumping onto a tree. Alex clawed the tree and it fell over, with Amar jumping off as it hit the ground.

"Guess I don't have a choice!" Amar yelled, grabbing his sword. As Alex sent his strongest punch toward Amar, he blocked it with his sword. He was just barely able to hold Alex back. But Zach noticed that Amar didn't seem like the same person as before he had fought him. Amar managed to shove Alex off of him and swung his sword a few times, only for Alex to dodge and then parry his attacks. Alex, screaming with every move, punched Amar directly in the gut, sending him crashing into a tree.

"Zach, can you hear me?" Harlow's voice came from Zach's phone. He had just picked it up, and Harlow continued, "Amar might be at the portal over there, but don't freak out. He was under a spell of sorts during the sports tournament. He's also fighting Escarere!" Zach didn't know what to say at first, assessing the situation.

"Yeah... about that..." Zach nervously started. Meanwhile, Amar just dodged out of the way while Alex clawed right through another tree, making it fall over.

"You're Alex, right?! I thought you'd be fighting against Escarere!" Amar shouted. Alex stopped for a second, but it didn't take him long to get back to clawing whatever was in front of him. He was incredibly fast as well, making him highly dangerous. Amar could barely handle him on his own. Amar took another hit, sending him into the ditch where the creek had used to be. Amar crashed and rolled into the leaves, "Ow ow ow..." Amar mumbled to himself as he got up. Just as he resumed his fighting position, Alex came charging right in, slashing at his arm and wounding him. Steam began to pour from the bloody wounds. *I forgot that this happened now...* Amar vaguely remembered his ability to heal quickly due to Redaro's bloody experiments on him. Still, most of those memories were foggy. Alex was coming in to slash him again, but Zach suddenly came in and kicked him to the side. *The hell? I thought they were together...* Amar was confused.

"Sorry for immediately assuming you wanted our heads—I heard where you were from. But this kid can't really control this power... so if you wanna talk, let's calm him down first," Zach told him.

"I don't think a regular kick will put him down for long," Amar told Zach.

"Look, I don't have any bullshit superpowers or any overpowered technology right now. I have to be strategic, so you'll be doing the majority of the 'calming down.'" Zach motioned air quotes on the last part there.

156

"So you're giving me all the work?" Amar questioned, giving him a scowl. But there wasn't much time for banter.

"Now's your chance!" Zach yelled at him, running out of the way. Amar clashed with Alex once more, and Alex grabbed onto Amar's sword. Amar, using most of his strength, was able to raise the sword up, cutting through the demon claws. Alex backed up a bit. While he was distracted, Amar kicked, sending Alex back for a second. But he recovered quickly, and went back for him again.

"Alex, your grandpa Danny wouldn't want you doing that!" Zach shouted. Alex actually stopped, letting Amar back up a little more. *Hey, that's actually working...* Amar thought.

"Alex, we're all fighting Escarere together, right? We don't want any more demons taking over, right? I've been hurt by Redaro too," Amar reasoned with Alex. Alex finally started to breathe a little harder.

"I'm... sorry..." Alex was able to get out. He was still panting pretty hard. The demon form distorted his voice.

"Alex, can you control it? It's not going away this time!" Zach exclaimed.

"Yeah... I finally have control over myself. It's exhausting, though. I want to try and maintain this form, so I can use it later," Alex was able to spit out as he looked down at his demon claws.

"Oh, that's too bad. It was fun watching you do my work for me..." A chilling voice taunted from behind the three. They all froze as Alex slowly turned around. Escarere kicked him, sending him crashing into the dirt.

"SHE'S HERE!" Zach yelled. Amar drew his sword. *What is it with her, and why does she seem so familiar?!* Amar thought.

"With Alex's demon form, maybe we could take her on together!" Amar shouted.

"Did you not see what I just did to him? You must be blind..." Escarere taunted Amar.

"Why are you after us?! How do you know Redaro?!" Zach started to shout questions at her.

"Why am I obligated to answer that?" Escarere spat. Alex got back up and rushed toward her.

"I WON'T LET YOU KILL THEM!" Alex shouted. Amar saw this as the perfect opportunity to come in and help. He slashed low at Escarere's legs as Alex prepared to claw at her at full force. There was only one problem—the sword stopped entirely when it hit Escarere's ankle, and Escarere caught Alex's punch.

"You think you two are good enough? Even with that third teammate of yours, it's no use... and I'm really starting to get hungry..." Escarere told them. *Hungry?! Is she gonna eat us?!* Zach thought.

"We're booking it!" Amar yelled, grabbing Alex's arm to turn him the other way. They both ran, and Zach followed. At that moment, Escarere slowed down time to catch up with them, tripping Alex. When time resumed, they were all running up a hill, with Alex about to fall back toward Escarere. Amar turned around and grabbed Alex's hand before he could fall, hoisting him to the top of the hill. They continued to sprint as Escarere became annoyed. Using her time powers to catch up with them once again, she put herself in front of them, but they split up, running left and right around her.

"Where are we running?!" Zach shouted to Amar.

"As I see it, you guys have a much bigger chance of finding the way to beat her in this timeline with an entire military corporation behind you! I'll find a way of distracting Escarere in my timeline!" Amar shouted. Zach and Alex were aware of what that meant—they were approaching the portal.

"Then leave it to me!" Alex yelled. Turning around, he realized that Escarere took longer to use the time power again. He boasted, "So slowing down the flow of time really does use up your stamina, doesn't it?!" Escarere didn't respond, instead going in for an attack. But Alex ducked, and shoved Escarere right to Amar. Amar grabbed her, and the two fell right into the other timeline.

ALTERNIS - 17 NOVEMBER 2015, 3:17 PM

"He is coming back... right?" Bobonson wondered. The group had been sitting there for a while.

"I swear if he lost my phone... he will die!" Hosea was complaining to himself as he played with ants in the dirt. Out of nowhere, Amar came flying through the portal, with Escarere there as well.

"WHAT THE HELL! AMAR?!" Destructo questioned. Escarere instantly sent him flying into a tree again.

"Don't let her go back!" Amar yelped, taking damage from his spine smashing against the hard wood of the tree.

"What are we supposed to do?!" Bobonson yelled, taking out his gun and shooting Escarere multiple times. She took a bit of whiplash from it, but it was nothing that could pierce her skin. Destructo took out the shotgun, but

159

even as Escarere got close to him, all he could do was push her back with the gun's shot string.

"You know... I'm not feeling as hungry anymore. Except for you, the one with big talk..." Escarere pointed at Amar, "But if you get out of here now, maybe I could satisfy myself with the deaths of one of the others for now."

"I'm not going to let you do that!" Amar yelled, getting off of the tree and drawing his sword.

"You think you're hot stuff... don't you?" Escarere's chilling voice traveled to the others' ears.

"YAH!" Hosea smacked Escarere with his bamboo stick. But she took no damage and simply kicked him down.

"Why are you doing this?!" Amar asked, as if he was yelling for help. This got Escarere to stop. She suddenly trembled, looking too frightened to hurt Amar.

"I guess I can just wait it out, then. See you," Escarere taunted, dashing backwards and disappearing into the shadows of the trees.

"Wait... what?!" Hosea appeared to be infuriated. "What the hell?! Does she think she can just run from us?!"

"She just intends to use a different way of getting back to the other world. I don't see why she's so intent on killing, though," Destructo commented.

"What's she even got against us?" Bobonson wondered.

"There's certainly that to worry about. We were trying to make up for the lack of a group, right Amar? People who protected other people? Aren't we just protecting ourselves?" Destructo asked.

"Well... right now, I guess we've got to protect ourselves, along with the people in the other world.

Escarere wants us dead for some reason, I don't know what her plan is for that exactly… but we have to at least neutralize the immediate threat to us," Amar told the other members of his team.

"We just have to protect each other. Is that not what this is for?" Bobonson smiled.

"But… isn't Escarere just after me? I feel like I'm putting the rest of you in danger just by association. Maybe I should just go on my own," Amar spoke honestly.

"No, you shouldn't," Bobonson said. Hosea and Destructo didn't seem to react.

"Wha—why?" Amar asked.

"Well… being a mercenary is cool and all… but it makes life seem kinda… pointless? After having the thrill of one job over and over again, it just got kinda boring, and money became meaningless. This… this feels like it has meaning to it," Bobonson admitted. Amar had never thought of it that way, and he saw Bobonson in a new light.

"Yeah… er… well, I guess if I were let out and left alone, I wouldn't exactly have any direction in the world either. I think you even said something like that. So… I guess you were a little bit correct," Destructo begrudgingly admitted. After a few more moments of silence, Hosea finally spoke.

"I guess it's a little more fun than the junkyard," Hosea shrugged. They all gasped.

"Who would have thought you'd get anything nice from Hosea?" Bobonson taunted, leaning on Hosea's shoulder.

"OI!" Hosea shouted.

"Yeah, I thought that we were forcing you to be with us and you only wanted to go back to the junkyard?" Destructo smirked, leaning on his other shoulder.

"OIIII!" Hosea yelled again, going into a rant against the two. Amar couldn't help himself from bursting out into laughter. It was a feeling of bliss he didn't know he'd ever feel again. But mainly, he felt cared about. It was a refreshing sentiment. *Thank you, guys...* He thought to himself.

PRIMARIUM - 20 NOVEMBER 2015, 7:24 PM

"So... what's up? There seems to be something going on with you..." Jill seemed concerned. She and Jareus were in an office together.

"It's nothing. I've just been thinking about what it means to have to lead all these people..." Jareus told her. He was pensively staring out the window at the rain. It had been raining for a bit, and there had just been a bit of awkward silence between the two. Jareus rolled a pen around with his index finger.

"You must be feeling the pressure, then," Jill told Jareus as he continued to stare out the window. He flinched as she came and put her arm around him. The two had been seeing each other in a kind of romantic context, but neither of them had officially confirmed anything. Even though—or even because—she was older than him, Jareus felt that she could understand him more than anyone else he knew. They'd both felt the pressure of being in charge, and they'd both had to kill against their wishes. Jareus had finally forgiven her for what happened when they'd first met, and they had been generally okay at working toward a mutual romance until recently. Jareus

162

tried to push the thoughts of Allison out of his head, but it wasn't working.

"Ye-yeah…" Jareus stumbled over his own words, "I think I ought to close up the place for today, Harlow already went home. I think it's just Danny and Alex left in the lobby now…"

"I guess you're right. Are you sure you're feeling alright?" Jill asked as Jareus got up and started to walk toward the door. He froze.

"I don't really know. I'm going to try my best though, okay? This is something I really have to think about by myself…" Jareus told her as he left to walk out of the building. She felt like she should do something, but couldn't really put her finger on what.

"So? We're still having fun with the grapple hook here! Why do we have to go?" Alex asked Jareus after he told him and Danny to go home.

"Well… I guess you can have the key, Danny. But I have a work-in-progress project in the back there… so try not to crash into it," Jareus gave them the key and headed out.

"WOOO!" Alex shouted, grappling across the room. The two were just having fun.

"Alright, let me do it again. I've had enough of just watching," Danny grinned, and Alex handed over the grapple hook suit. Danny flew across the room as Alex watched him with interest—it was like seeing Danny become a kid again.

"Who would have thought I'd get to see my own grandpa like this? He doesn't even feel like a grandfather as he is right now," Alex was talking to himself as he noticed the project in the back of the room that Jareus had been talking about. "What exactly is this that Jareus is working on?" He wondered

"Hey, Alex! He said not to touch that!" Danny yelled, grappling close to Alex and landing.

"Really, he told us not to crash INTO it. Not 'don't touch it.'" Alex was being a smart-alec. He took off the cover to reveal a silver android with a bunch of different shades of dark gray, and what seemed to be a fake beanie and goggles to go with the look. The android's face bore a resemblance to Jareus's.

"WHAT the heck?" Danny questioned as the two backed up, "Is this some sort of robot?" It had the Adrenaline Corp. logo on its chest as well, a new one that Harlow revealed recently. The logo was an upside-down "A" with "wings" on the top right and left.

"Let's see what happens if we turn it on..." Alex said to himself as he looked at the computer next to the robot, which had a bunch of wires plugged into it. He looked at the name files on the computer and said, "He's called the Adrenaline Droid. Apparently he should be able to function?"

"Alex, we really shouldn't turn it on... but I do want to see what it can do," Danny said mischievously. Of course, they turned it on.

"The Adrenaline Droid, now running at about 7% power, nice to meet you," The droid said in a robotic voice. It did a little wave motion.

"That's cool, so it responds to voice? Adrenaline Droid, go make me some coffee," Danny tried it out.

"My purpose is not for beverages, rather for combat. I can understand attack and defense terms," Adrenaline Droid told them.

"Alright, what are your commands, then?" Alex asked, ecstatic. Suddenly, the robot stopped speaking for a moment and froze.

"Incomplete," it stated after a few seconds.

"What?" Danny reacted.

"Incomplete. Parts incomplete. Search for completion commencing," Adrenaline Droid spoke, suddenly running toward the exit.

"This is why he didn't want us messing with it…" Danny muttered to himself, using the grapple hook to get in front of the robot and pushing it back. "The parts are in here!"

"Part search unsuccessful in the vicinity. Must continue looking," Adrenaline Droid claimed. *Jareus must have not finished the parts yet, and now this robot is going to go on some rampage looking for parts that don't exist,* Danny thought.

"Power down!" Alex shouted, trying to grab the robot. The Adrenaline Droid shook him off, sending him flying into the wall.

"Power down will commence after parts are found. Currently in emergency mode," The droid said. *Emergency mode? Maybe they intended for it to maintain power during battle, even if it was damaged or its parts were missing…* Danny concluded in his head.

"It's stronger than it looks…" Alex spat out. The impact from his crash had made a dent in the wall. Danny stood firmly as the droid tried to dodge past him and run to the exit, but Danny pulled it and threw it to the ground. It instantly recovered and tried to continue forward. The basement they were in was filled with pillars, though—pillars that could be used to one's advantage.

165

Danny grappled toward one of these pillars, kicking the droid down once more and killing its momentum.

"You're coming with me!" Danny yelled as he started to drag the droid backwards. Its legs retracted too fast for his hands to continue holding them, and the droid tried to make a break for it again. This time, Alex jumped out from behind a pillar, activating his demon powers.

"YOU WON'T BE GOING ANYWHERE!" Alex roared.

"Don't you think that's a little excessive?!" Danny shouted at Alex. The Adrenaline Droid went to try and shove Alex out of the way, but Alex grabbed both of his hands, pushing back. The two of them were at a stalemate.

"I CAN CONTROL IT NOW!" Alex's voice yelled distortedly. Danny backed off, a little afraid now. The Adrenaline Droid didn't even seem to falter as it continued to push back, its emergency mode compelling it with urgency. Eventually, it got the best of Alex, tripping him up. It continued to run toward the exit, without seeing that Danny had already hid behind one of the pillars near the front.

"Nice try," Danny spat as he grappled toward the Adrenaline Droid, trying to pin him down as he landed. The Adrenaline Droid kicked up, sending Danny flying, but giving Alex the perfect opportunity. Alex grabbed at its legs, dragging it back about thirty feet before it kicked hard enough to get free. But Danny was back up again, and hooked the grapple hook to the robot, pulling it back toward him. It was still slowly pulling out the hook's wirelength, getting further toward the door.

"I'll help!" Alex's distorted voice came in, and using his demon powers, he grabbed the chain and started pulling as if it were tug-of-war. It still was able to persist for a bit, but suddenly, the robot's body went limp and they flung his body toward them.

'AH!" Danny shouted as the both of them ducked. The Adrenaline Droid flew slightly over the two, and fell on the ground. Its battery had run out. The two were standing there, panting. The demon form receded off of Alex.

"Jeez… I… can't believe… it was that strong…" Alex barely got out.

"Yeah… let's put it back and get out of here," Danny said, and they got right to it. However, it wasn't enough to cover up their tracks.

"Are you for real? Why did you turn it on?" Jareus was up and at it, scolding them early the next morning.

"Look, we didn't know you meant DON'T turn it on…" Alex tried to explain himself, but it wasn't working.

"That *is* what I meant, but I'll let you two off easy for today. It *did* prove that we have something good for the battlefield, as well as proving the usefulness of the grapple hook. And while that was not exactly an experiment I was planning on doing, it did prove that your power—while still unexplainable—can be helpful," Jareus told the two. "Now for today, Harlow's taking us to do some team-building activities with the military branch. They're all great soldiers on their own, but we're pretty much the only ones with defined teams. Although, Toshi may still have one as well."

"Our team? What's our team?" Alex asked.

"Ya know! Like… us three, Zach, Allison, and Lexus as well. But Lexus is most likely going to transfer to the support branch. There, I will have her, Saskia, and Tanya all work on a way to attach the grapple hook—that we proved useful—to a new version of the U.N.E. exosuit.

Now let's get going, we don't want to leave Harlow waiting," Jareus explained.

ALTERNIS - 21 NOVEMBER 2015, 11:44 AM

"Are we just going to wait around, then? We've basically fished out the ocean. We need to do something else," Bobonson suggested.

"We can live in the wilderness!" Amar suggested.

"No," Hosea and Destructo jinxed each other.

"Then there are plenty of other jobs to do!" Amar told everyone as they suddenly heard a knock at the door. They weren't expecting any visitors, but they went to the door anyway. Amar opened it and greeted, "How can I help you?"

"Are you the one that Harlow ran into?" The man at the door asked. He had giant eyebags, and was wearing nearly all black.

"Eh... the guy at the harbor...?" Amar couldn't really remember. Suddenly, the other guy—out of pure anger—punched Amar dead in the stomach. Amar suddenly shouted out in pain. "WHAT WAS THAT FOR?!"

"YOU'RE THE ONE THAT MADE THEM DISAPPEAR, AREN'T YOU?!" The man shouted, taking out a knife and trying to stab Amar. Amar jumped to the side and grabbed his arm, forcing him to stay still. Amar looked down, shadows covering his face.

"Yeah... it's my fault. He probably told you what I look like, didn't he? Well... I'm here to tell you the story, then," Amar sneered.

"I HAD A CHANCE! A CHANCE TO TURN MY LIFE AROUND! I DON'T EVEN CARE IF I WAS NEVER HIRED, YOU TOOK THAT AWAY FROM—" He started yelling.

168

"I get it. Okay? I never wanted this either. Just let me tell you the story, okay?" Amar asked him seriously, removing the knife from his hands.

"What…?" He started. Amar took the man over to the couch, while the other three in Amar's team watched from the kitchen.

"I owe this to you, and I know how you feel… It all started without a trace of memory, and teleportation to another planet. But I'll tell you what I can recall. It all started with a flash of light, one that seemed unexplainable at the time… but it was something that defined my fate…"

In Alternis, during the fight on planet Equinox: Everything was the same up until the flash of light.

"That… isn't what I was waiting for…" Diadem croaked. But the flash of light he WAS waiting for then occurred. After the flash slowly dispersed, Amar and Zach were distracted for a second. "That *was*," Diadem finished his thought, smiling. The flash of light was *what he'd been waiting for*. Diadem must have known a much bigger part of Redaro's plans than Amar had.

"ZACH! I FOUND IT!" A voice yelled in the distance. It was Adam Steel, on the same mountain.

"NO YOU DON'T!" Amar shouted, dropping Diadem and starting to run toward Steel, while Zach was doing the same. This was where everything blurred. Amar beat Zach to Adam Steel and snapped Adam's neck. Amar obtained the Wish Orb and killed Zach soon after. All of those that got in his way died, no matter what they tried. It was only after the massacre that IT happened…

"Wonderful job, Amar! This is amazing, exactly what you were created for—if only you'd listen to me

more. Redaro's three-step plan is now one step in!"
Diadem gloated. But Amar didn't like that one bit, and
killed him too. Only then did Amar feel completely in
control of his actions, since Diadem had been controlling
him. He'd seen everything that had happened, and broke.
He then went back to Earth, to buy a sword and originally
end his own life. But... something else happened instead.

"You... couldn't do anything? You tried?" The man
asked Amar. Amar shook his head. The man put his hands
to his face, "Ever since then, I was going to try and get
some revenge too... on you. But now that I know what's
happened... I can't do anything."

"I'm sorry... I wanted to do something so badly..."
Amar was just as frustrated. The two sat in silence.

"No, I'm sorry! I shouldn't have pent up all that
rage. But... after seeing all those people disappear... I
couldn't do nothing. Harlow and I became friends
afterwards, both looking for a new purpose or to-do list.
This is just what ended up happening," He told Amar, and
started to head out.

"Wait, what was your name?" Amar asked.

"Derrian. Derrian Kendri," He told them, leaving
them behind.

"I'm sorry... Derrian," Amar really wanted to
express his sincerity to him, but he was gone.

PRIMARIUM - 21 NOVEMBER 2015, 1:13 PM

"JAREUS! Bring some people over to the side!"
Harlow yelled. Jareus had actually just been making
friends with people in the military branch, and Harlow
was sort of interrupting this. Jareus walked over, pouting.

"Ya know, they were finally treating me with some respect!" Jareus started to shout.

"I did say to bring SOME people over as well, didn't I?" Harlow seemed to have more important things in mind.

"Fine, fine, but what's so important? I *do* have to be the leader you cracked me up to be, ya know," Jareus quipped back at Harlow as he started to walk back.

"Well… there's an actual robbery going on, and I thought us taking care of it would make for good press coverage," Harlow stated nonchalantly.

"Actual robbery? What's the situation?" Jareus was finally interested in what Harlow had to say.

"Go get some people and get out there! They were discovered by the police, and they were inside with civilians! We can't let people die if we could have done something about it," Harlow explained to Jareus, but he had already started running back.

"Danny! Toshi! Can you two come with me really quickly?" Jareus asked, waving from a distance.

"Hm? What's up?" Toshi asked, Danny also looking out at Jareus. Toshi had his signature getup on, while Danny wore cargo shorts with an orange hoodie.

"There's… a robbery we're gonna take care of," Jareus told the two.

"Robbery?!" Danny questioned. His inquiry was never replied to—in no time at all, Jareus had rushed the two out on Adrenaline Corp. private transport. Not public transport, of course, since Jareus hated the very idea of that. They pulled up to the scene to see the police surrounding the building, and checked in with the police closest to the action.

"Adrenaline Corp? Yeah, sure. Since you're here, we *do* need some way to take the robbers out of the situation without shooting. That would be our last resort. He's been in there since he tried to escape the first time. He saw cop cars and holed himself up in there," The cop gave the three the briefing.

"As part of the Adrenaline Corporation, we soldiers gotta deal with this kinda thing too! It isn't always a demon-level threat, but this is still serious!" Toshi flashed his signature grin.

"Your smile is too much, Toshi! We have to focus on removing the robber from the situation," Jareus pointed out as Toshi's smile gleamed like a hero's.

"We should use the grapple hook," Danny suggested.

"Yeah! Like you did last time!" Jareus was still a little peeved about the robot incident.

"Look, it *did* prove that he can use the grapple hook well, didn't it, Jareus?" Toshi asked.

"You're too easy on him, but yes," Jareus admitted, squinting at Toshi.

"So maybe give Danny a chance to explain his plan," Toshi told Jareus. *He's being all nice now... How come he didn't want to hear my plans out back then?* Jareus thought.

"Alright, Danny. You've got the spotlight," Jareus pointed to Danny. But just as he was about to start explaining, they heard police commotion. When they looked over, they saw that the police were approaching a robber that had been shot down. *Did they have to shoot him?* Jareus thought.

"Don't worry about him—we may have shot him, but it shouldn't be lethal," A girl started to say to the police officers. She was a little on the shorter side, and she wore blue jeans and a black shirt that had a butterfly design on the front. She had black hair in a ponytail, and her skin was somewhat tan. Another man with her had a fedora and glasses on. The most mysterious part of their features especially caught Jareus's attention—they had their own versions of an exosuit equipped.

"DID THEY JUST BEAT US TO IT?!" Jareus questioned aloud.

"Calm down, Jareus! The people are safe now!" Toshi tried to quiet him down.

"Amber here took care of him. It's just a tranquilizer dart," The man beside her told the police.

"And who gave you two the right to get involved?" The chief of these police asked the two.

"We're from Regiment Legion," The lady held out an official ID card, but Jareus didn't even notice what they were saying.

"You need to chill, dude! It doesn't matter that we came all this way! Those people are safe!" Toshi yelled, trying to pull Jareus from breaking their cover. Danny was helping him as well, but Jareus broke out of their grasp.

"YOU TWO MUST SERIOUSLY UNDERESTIMATE ADRENALINE CORPORATION! YOU DO KNOW THAT WE WERE HERE FIRST, RIGHT?!" Jareus came out, scolding.

"Oh…! I'm sorry, it's just that we decided to take immediate action. I didn't mean anything by it, economy-dog," The lady told him. Jareus was fuming.

"Wait… is that you? Jareus?" The man with the darker skin beside the lady asked.

"I AM NOT AN—wait. You know me?" Jareus went from shouting to genuinely asking. The man beside the lady took off his glasses and black fedora to reveal himself.

"COLE?!" Danny shouted from the back of the whole situation.

"Long time no see!" Cole Cidka himself boasted, wearing white cargo shorts and a blue short sleeved shirt with a surfboard design. He was also boasting an exosuit of his own, but it had a lot more wires and tubes connecting the parts, as well as a bigger battery pack in the back without a big chest piece.

"I... I didn't think it'd be you... Cole. And who is she?" Jareus greeted in disbelief.

"This is Amber Ranatrix, the leader of Regiment Legion. She's appointed me as second-in-command, since I've shown myself to be useful," Cole chuckled.

"You three were also assigned to this job? Even though you're a private military? What are you doing in public affairs?" Amber immediately questioned Jareus.

"Nice to meet you too," Jareus nervously stated. They got the whole situation figured out after that. Jareus explained that in spite of being a private company, the government paid them to serve on both the state and federal level. Cole wondered who Toshi was as well, so Danny introduced the two while Amber was still chewing out Jareus. Toshi was his usual self, putting on a big smile and acting like some kind of hero. Cole seemed to be his usual self as well.

"You know, Cole. It's a good thing I ran into you two today," Jareus told Cole, turning to him.

"Hm, why is that?" Cole asked.

"If you and Amber will come with me for just a second, I can explain," Jareus told him. The two Regiment Legion soldiers looked at each other and nodded.

"You think he's telling them about the Escarere situation?" Toshi questioned aloud.

"Yeah, just in case they don't know," Danny was sure. They watched as Jareus began to tell them what had been going on.

"…and we're going to launch an attack on that demon, Escarere. If you can, we'd really appreciate your help," Jareus finished explaining to the two. He was genuinely asking for aid, without doing so in some petty way.

"An attack? That could be dangerous without a defense plan…" Cole commented on Jareus's explanation.

"Actually, we absolutely can't help you if it's relatively soon," Amber put her foot down. Both of them looked at her, almost as if they were told they'd been denied a dream job.

"What?! Why not?" Jareus questioned, seemingly begging now.

"Regiment Legion is going to be involved in getting supplies for a Naval Base's training exercise. This means we'll be helping out as well—I don't know if I can condone a risky plan like that… either," Amber told the two firmly.

"I'd only need Cole! If he were by my side helping, I'm sure that we could come out victorious!" Jareus was starting to sound like a narrator. Cole nodded vigorously, giving Jareus a thumbs up.

"Are you sure it isn't *just* because you two just want to hang out?" Amber pointed out. Both of them gave a look that captured the very essence of the word *busted*.

"I promise you! We *do* need more soldiers!" Jareus tried to sound confident again, but it came out as nervous.

"As long as it's just Cole, and just that day as well," Amber finally gave in. The two jumped for joy together as Amber sighed.

"Are you guys all done?" Danny asked. He and Toshi were bored in the background, and interaction between them had been getting a little awkward.

"Yeah, I'll be joining you on the Escarere attack mission!" Cole cheered. The two almost looked confused.

"Escarere… attack… mission?" Toshi questioned slowly.

"What attack mission, Jareus?" Danny sounded like an angry mother who had found her child doing something naughty.

"Hold it, hold it! I didn't come up with it!" Jareus sighed, "Well, since the cat's out of the bag… I might as well tell you what Harlow's come up with. I don't know if I agree with it 100%… but it's most likely gonna happen." All of them sat in to listen as Jareus told them of what was to come soon. That was all the action for that day, though. The way Jareus described it was pretty mundane—the rough idea of the plan was to attack Escarere first, and throw a bunch of attackers at once to overwhelm the opponent.

ALTERNIS - 24 NOVEMBER 2015, 7:22 PM

"Five hundred dollars says that Hosea can beat every single one of you fighters!" Amar yelled, entirely drunk.

"Are you sure he can beat even me? You must be insane to put down that much money!" One of the fighters yelled back.

176

"CHILL OUT, AMAR!" Bobonson grabbed Amar, pulling him back from the other guys.

"Let him go, it's entertaining," Destructo commented. The four of them were in a fighting club in the suburbs of Northern California—a low-key place, and hardly legal. Moments earlier, Hosea had hopped in the ring out of a pure adrenaline rush. The other fighter didn't object, and the two battled until Hosea was the victor. He drank out of his bamboo stick, which he made the waitress fill with more booze.

"YEAH! TAKE ME ALL ON! I TAKE YOU ALL DOWN!" Hosea was on a rampage, still standing in the ring.

"He's an entirely different person with a little bit of alcohol in his system. It's like day and night," Destructo laughed. Amar finally got away from Bobonson, putting his five hundred dollars in the betting pot.

"Alright, well, I'm betting against him!" A random girl in the bar yelled. A bunch of people started to bet against Hosea, seeking to make an easy profit, since there were three more fighters left.

"I wouldn't do that! Hosea is great!" Amar shouted at all the people running to bet against Hosea.

"Amar isn't the same when he's like that, either," Bobonson sighed, giving up on controlling the situation.

"HOSEA… What's your last name? HOSEA ESPOSITO VERSUS BOBBY BROWN!" A man beside the ring yelled.

"Really? Your last name is…" Hosea's opponent was asking.

"Maybe you didn't think it 'cuz my first name but actually, I'm Italian." Hosea spat out, his words barely sounding like English.

"START!" Other men started to chant. Just like that, it became a horror fest for most people watching. Hosea didn't look like it, but he was a VERY strong man. After knocking the first guy's teeth out, Hosea continued to beat down his opponents. Every other person besides Destructo, Amar, and Bobonson were all cheering and hoping for anybody besides Hosea. Nobody could retract their money, but they got to watch it go as Hosea punched his final opponent's lights out.

"YEAHHHHH! HOSEAAA!" Amar shouted.

"HOSEA ACTUALLY JUST DID THAT! WHAT!" Bobonson shouted. Destructo just nodded, having known what was going to happen the entire time.

"YEAAAAHHHHHH!!!!!" Hosea shouted at the top of his lungs. The entire crowd lost it, and Amar took the pot of money, spitting in everyone else's faces. They all shouted back at him, but technically, he'd won all that money fair and square.

"Thanks for the good times, chiefs!" Amar shouted as Bobonson dragged them all outside of the club.

"I did it! I DIIIIID IT!" Hosea shouted, a little bloody and bruised, but victorious.

"I can't believe you two…" Destructo said, smirking. They were all celebrating as Bobonson noticed a shady man walking toward them.

"You guys, stand back," Bobonson warned, pulling out a gun to the man. He started to wave his hands rapidly.

"Woah woah woah, you guys—I'm not here to threaten you!" The guy stated in the shadows. The four of them, although a "little" drunk, were still cautious.

"Okay, who are you then?" Destructo asked. He came forward, and Amar might have been the only one that understood the situation immediately.

"I think I need your help," Jareus told them. He held out his hand. It was weird—for Amar, it was like looking into a mirror. Amar shook Jareus's hand. It was uncanny.

"We do!" Alex shouted suddenly from behind Jareus.

"Wah! Who's that?!" Bobonson asked.

"I'll explain it all. That's Alex, by the way," Jareus told them. They all gathered round, and Jareus talked about his plan. He told them all of the plan to attack Escarere all at once.

"You need us from *this* timeline? We can leave?" Boboonson asked.

"The Bobonson and Destructo of our timeline are dead. Escarere already killed them. We need as many strong soldiers as we can get," Jareus told them all.

"Should we go with him?" Bobonson asked Amar. Amar was still pensive. Hosea was wondering about all this as well.

"If it's to kill Escarere... then yes. I guess we will have to go with you. But I can't say I've had the best experience in your timeline," Amar admitted begrudgingly.

"I can't blame you for that one," Alex shrugged nervously. He was the one that had originally fought Amar. That wasn't a good intro to another world.

"It's getting late, so meet us at the portal tomorrow. How does two in the afternoon sound?" Jareus suggested. They all agreed on that, and thus the time was set for the convergence of the timelines.

"I'm going to go with Danny to the portal later, Jill," Jareus told her. They were hanging out in his office, and it was raining outside of the Adrenaline Corp. building.

"Don't you think this plan is a little reckless? What if you get hurt?" Jill asked Jareus.

"Harlow and I have discussed this. I won't be in the first wave since Escarere seems to be targeting people like Danny and I. But we're doing this now, because recently Harlow and I were wondering why Escarere wasn't attacking right away. We figured at first that maybe she got lost, but after recounting the events, there's no way that that's possible—especially for such a long period of time. If anything, we've got accounts of her struggling to use her time powers, and she might be training them to perfection. We need to throw everything we have at her next time, or we may not be able to win against an entirely time-stopping demon," Jareus explained to Jill. They sat in a weird silence for a moment.

"Alright. I got it. But you could easily put the police in this situation! I'd even go myself!" Jill offered.

"They are. They'll be called in while the battle is going on. We still don't know where Escarere is right now, so we're just going to tell all the police chiefs in the area to be fully ready to go at a moment's notice," Jareus told Jill. She was at a loss for words. Suddenly, she walked over to Jareus and hugged him.

"Thank you for understanding. I really just wanted to make sure I was there so you all were safe," Jil told him. Jareus froze. He wasn't sure that he felt comfortable in the slightest. Jill noticed his unrest, pulled away, and asked, "Is something wrong?"

"Don't get me wrong Jill, I do care about you. But…
I feel like I don't want to get you mixed up in my
confusing minefield of feelings. Especially not right now,"
Jareus told her sternly, looking her in the eyes with a
serious expression.

"Bu… but why are you feeling that? Are you
worried? Everyone you know will be fine! There's no
reason to get yourself hung up over that," Jill suddenly
protested as she thought of something from the past, "Is
it him? From when we first met? Do you… hate me?"

"No. Jill, I don't hate you. I told you already, I
understand that you did that out of instinct and because
of what you had been told. But right now, everything is
here at once, and I can't really navigate my own mind at
the moment. I don't want to break under the pressure
and end up having you in the crossfire," Jareus told her.
He was not backing off. She stood back.

"Okay, I get it," She told him, almost tearfully.

"I have to go find Danny. We should probably get
going," Jareus said, getting out of his chair finally. He felt
how tense the situation was, and wanted to put an end to
it.

"Oh, okay," Jill said.

"Take care of yourself, I'm still counting on you to
be there during that battle. I'm sure things will go back to
normal after that," Jareus told her. She seemed to be less
upset, and nodded to him as he left. As Jareus was
walking down the stairs, he felt a little guilty.

*I shouldn't have put the blame entirely on this
situation… I mean, it was less hurtful to put it like that,* he
thought. *This situation* does *have my mind all over the
place. But mainly, I just don't feel the same way.
Especially after seeing Allison again, I can't make myself*

feel something that I don't. Maybe I shouldn't have said that last part... I don't want to give her false hope... Jareus thought. He walked down the stairs, over to the support rooms where Danny and Alex would be.

"...after that, Harlow instantly grabbed a mop, and started wiping the floor like, 'SORRY! THAT'S MY BAD!'" Odessa was talking to Alex and Danny. They were having a good laugh over whatever story she was telling.

"Oh, hey Jareus! Odessa was telling us about how Harlow, while usually very telling, gets embarrassed pretty easily," Danny saw Jareus, inviting him into the conversation.

"Yeah, he accidentally elbowed my drink and it fell on the floor, and he was quick to get a mop and clean it himself rather than leaving it to one of the cleaners. His face was bright red the whole time," Odessa laughed.

"That's something he didn't tell me about. But Danny and Alex, I need you two," Jareus seemed rather serious. The other three seemed to notice immediately that he wasn't in the laughing mood.

"Eh, and why not me?!" Odessa questioned. *Because I don't need more people knowing about the timeline situation until later,* Jareus thought.

"Well... you know we need as many people as we can here preparing for the plan of our attack, so I'm just taking these two," Jareus lied to Odessa.

"Speaking of that plan," Zach interrupted out of nowhere, coming in with a shirt that had horizontally striped fall colors and a mug, "I heard you've got one person in front as bait for Escarere."

"Zach! I didn't see you were around here!" Jareus started. *Crap, I can't bring Zach now that I just told*

Odessa no, he thought. "Yeah, but Danny, Alex, and I really have to go."

"Why can't it be me? I could easily be the bait to lure Escarere out," Zach asked.

"Don't worry about it, Zach! You're in the first wave of responders after that. Plus, I'm having a robot be the bait, so nobody will get hurt," Jareus nervously told Zach. *Wait, isn't he talking about the robot he said he couldn't repair?* Danny thought.

"We'll talk about it later, I can tell you're in a rush," Zach told Jareus, going the other way.

"Just don't worry about it, Zach!" Jareus yelled to him again.

"Hey, Zach, wait up!" Odessa yelled to him, following him. The time had come for Jareus, Danny, and Alex to head out. Jareus had brought an umbrella for the rain, since they knew they would have to be at the portal at two. Alex also thanked Jareus for talking to him seriously last night, since Jareus had brought only Alex along. They got to talk seriously one-on-one.

"So Alex, what did you want to tell me?" Jareus asked. They had started a conversation while they were walking to meet Amar.

"I still don't know why entirely… But I think I have a little bit of the reason for the demon form," Alex told Jareus.

"Hm? What is it?" Jareus asked him.

"You have to promise not to tell anybody," Alex told Jareus. Jareus nodded, agreeing to Alex's terms. He continued, "Well, you see, I might be partially demon myself. Danny from… that timeline… told me. Remember who Equinox cursed to have Jack? Yeah… she's my grandmother. Her child could still have been a partial

demon. Which if her blood counted as half... that would make me one eighth." His words were still on Jareus's mind. But on the way out, a man shouted at them.

"THERE YOU ARE!" He yelled. He had a gray fedora on, as well as a red and black plaid flannel with a white shirt underneath. He also had brown cargo pants on with a backpack on his back. There was something about a signature scar on his face that seemed recognizable.

"Yes? Here we are?" Danny questioned, looking weirdly out at the man. It took him a moment, but Jareus did recognize the man.

"SCAR?!" Jareus shouted. Danny and Alex instantly realized it as well—it was Scar from Amar's arena.

"Yeah, what about it?! I've been trying to find you guys forever now! I finally got some intel about the Jareus dude being some big higher-up at Adrenaline Corporation, so I came here because of that! Took me a damn while, too!" Scar started to yell at them, taking an axe out of his backpack.

"Zach *did* wish all humans back to Earth, didn't he..." Jareus muttered quietly.

"What? You mean Scar's human?!" Alex questioned.

"Yeah... an old man I met on that planet told me about how there were three humans brought there. One of them was Equinox and the other was Xenova. One had 'disappeared' in an 'accident,' but I doubt that's the case. Right, Scar?" Jareus asked.

"Oh *Hell* no! I made a living by fighting the strongest people they had and making myself the best! That's the only thing I could rely on, since a bunch of idiots stole me away. But that doesn't matter anymore! You trapped me here, where I almost starved because I had nothing, and now, I want payback. And mainly, I want a good fight. Being an assassin who kills in one shot is boring," Scar ravenously yelled, as if his hunger was for blood.

"So that's what this is about…" Danny commented.

"You two, hold him off real quick. I'm gonna try a new feature of the exosuit," Jareus told the two. They nodded. Alex immediately brought out his demon form.

"Woah! What in the Hell is that?! Looks strong to me!" Scar grinned, rushing forward with his axe. Alex jumped forward and clashed with Scar's axe, creating sparks. His demon hand was durable enough to withstand it.

"YOU WON'T BE GETTING THROUGH THIS EASILY!" Alex's distorted voice shouted. Scar's axe knocked him back, yet he kept attacking.

"Neither will you," Scar grinned as Alex jumped forward. He started to run forward as well, but he jumped up and bounced off of Alex. He did a flip and then landed on the ground, as Alex got a faceful of concrete. Scar immediately took a turn, and was running to the back of Alex's neck with his axe. Danny saw this and freaked out. There would be no way he could be there on time to stop it.

"ALEX!" He shouted. But everything around him started to slow down. His surroundings color shifted. It looked like he could easily make it to Scar on time. *Is this… the time power?!* Danny thought. He took no chances, running forward and punching Scar in the gut as time resumed its normal flow. Danny noted in his mind that stopping time felt similar to holding his breath, and was a little exhausting. Scar got knocked back to a wall, since Danny had technically hit him at an insane speed.

"What was that? You all a bunch of mutants now or somethin'?" Scar groaned, getting off of the wall.

"It's done!" Jareus yelled suddenly. The parts of the exosuit all came flying out, surrounding Jareus. They all stuck together at once as Jareus spread his arms apart. He then adjusted the pants of his suit a little, as it fit a little tight.

"That's a little fancy," Scar commented. Jareus held out his hand, and using the magnets on his suit, his gun came to him.

"Don't make me do this, Scar," Jareus threatened, holding his gun out. Scar laughed.

"Try me," Scar grinned, suddenly running toward Jareus. Jareus shot, but Scar could predict these things and had already ducked out of the way as Jareus fired. He ran forward with an evil grin, ducking and dodging until he was right in front of Jareus. Jareus started out blocking his axe with the exosuit arms, until he was able to hit Scar off of him. He boosted forward, going to kick Scar. But in this instance, Scar had jumped to the side. Alex had already been there, though, and he slashed at Scar. Scar somehow dodged at the last second.

"Hey! You guys aren't too bad!" Scar smiled. Jareus instantly tried to shoot again, but Scar wasn't phased, jumping up for his next attack. Jareus boosted up and kicked him. Scar couldn't react on time, and he actually took a bit of damage, hitting the ground. Alex almost slashed at him again, but Scar was quick on his feet. Danny attempted to use his time power on Scar again, but this time, he couldn't hold it the entire time. Scar realized that Danny was right behind him, turned around, and tried to chop him with the axe. Danny luckily ducked for this, and retreated right after as Scar went back to trading blows with Alex.

"Danny! Grab on!" Jareus shouted, grappling to the pillar and swinging around it in the air. There was no way Danny could make it to his outstretched hand on time, until he realized what Jareus was thinking. Danny used the time powers again to quickly get over to Jareus, and grabbed his hand. He resumed the flow of time as he grabbed Jareus's hand. Jareus pulled him off the ground and swung him directly into Scar, using the grapple line on his other arm. Scar was knocked backwards, hitting the concrete and bloodying his nose.

"Had enough?" Danny taunted as the two slowed down and jumped to the ground. Scar could barely stand.

"Maybe for today," He still grinned as they knocked him to a roadway. As a van came by, he grabbed onto the back of it, standing on the back bumper.

"HEY! WHAT!" Alex shouted, his demon form receding. Scar was making fun of them as he retreated. The rain started to clear up as well.

"We might as well take this opportunity to go, we need to be at Orange Grove Ranch in like ten minutes if we're gonna meet Amar at two," Jareus mentioned.

"TEN MINUTES?!" Danny questioned.

"Could you help us slow that down? I saw that you figured out how to use that time power of yours," Jareus smiled.

"I… I don't think it works like that," Danny told him honestly. Alex and Jareus had a good laugh at that reaction.

ALTERNIS - 25 NOVEMBER 2015, 2:05 PM

"Didn't they say they'd be here by now? Or am I crazy?" Destructo commented.

"No, you're not crazy. They said they'd be here five minutes ago," Bobonson affirmed his concerns. Just then, Jareus hopped through the portal.

"Woah!" He shouted, landing with his exosuit on.

"THE HECK IS THAT METAL ON YOU?!" Hosea immediately asked.

"Oh… this? It's an exosuit. You wanna try one when we get over to the other timeline?" Jareus asked, grinning.

"NO WAY MAN. It looks scary," Hosea commented. They all had a laugh about Hosea's reaction, except for Amar. He was sitting on the concrete, looking pensive.

"Alright, well, let's get going," Jareus concluded, pointing to the portal in Orange Grove Ranch.

PRIMARIUM - 25 NOVEMBER 2015, 2:35 PM

"We brought 'em here, Harlow!" Danny shouted as he and the rest of them entered the back of the Adrenaline Corp. building. The people from Alternis were looking at the building in disbelief, since it was a different building in the world where they were from.

"Woah! It's a mirror image!" Harlow pointed to Amar and then to Jareus. They both kinda nervously laughed at that. Neither of them knew exactly how to feel about it.

"WE GONNA KILL THAT DEMON, RIGHT?!" Hosea shouted his question.

"Yes, at least I hope," Harlow laughed. The four from Alternis went to follow Harlow while Jareus, Danny, and Alex went inside the other entrance.

"What do we do now? What's the plan?" Danny asked.

"We wait. We have to figure out exactly where Escarere is, so we're all going to sit back for now. When we figure that part out, we're going to call both the Regiment Legion and the police immediately. For now, we have to have everything ready to go. So let's get to work," Jareus told them. Danny sighed, but also smiled after knowing that they were good for now. Meanwhile, Harlow was showing the four where they were going to stay.

"These rooms are for you guys. You can stay here as long as you like, and there's a cafeteria downstairs I'll show you later," Harlow pointed.

"Seriously? You're just going to give all of this to us?" Destructo asked.

"Well, yeah. We need you guys to be ready the second we figure out where Escarere is. So feel free to do whatever until then," Harlow told them.

"I'm gonna watch that TV all night, Amar!" Hosea's eyes lit up.

"You better turn the volume down, then," Amar was already dreading it. Bobonson laughed at Amar's reaction, but Destructo entirely agreed. Amar and Destructo just wanted to sleep.

"We can also wash your clothes," Harlow told them. They all were satisfied with that, and given some Adrenaline Corp. jumpsuits in the meantime.

"Harlow… I just wanted to ask you one thing about the plan," Amar told Harlow right before he left, since they had just finished the tour basically.

"Hm, what is it?" He wondered.

"We four are going to be in the first wave, right?" Amar asked.

"Yeah…" Harlow responded.

"Get on with it Amar, tell him the idea already," Destructo commented.

"I WAS!' Amar shouted back at him. Turning back to Harlow, Amar continued, "Anyways, I say that the four of us be used as a back wall. We'll go around back, and make sure Escarere doesn't retreat, even if it is a low possibility." Amar and Harlow discussed this plan until they worked it out between them. They eventually agreed on what they were going to do.

"Are you all sure you don't need any of the exosuits?" Harlow asked.

"Save them for the close combat troops that can't fast-heal. Besides Hosea, he just doesn't like how they look," Amar told Harlow while Hosea nodded.

"Hey! I'll take one!" Destructo said.

"I'm a ranged fighter, so I think I'll be okay," Bobonson said.

"Okay then, I'll get one for Destructo if we have an extra, sound good?" Harlow asked. They all agreed on that, and the four of them, after going on that giant tour, were ready to settle in for the night. Hosea was fascinated by the TV for hours. Meanwhile, Jareus was locking the building for the night.

"Looks like we have everything in place," Danny commented as he waited for Jareus to finish up. Jareus put away his keys.

"Yep, even with the people from the other timeline. Looks like it's just something we have to do if we don't want an enemy we can't beat. If this turns out

190

badly… we might just be the first in her way, but the world might become like that in Alex's timeline if we don't do something now," Jareus said.

"You really are worried about that, aren't you?" Danny asked.

"Well, yeah. I also want to live up to expectations. Harlow told me that I'd be a good leader to give the people hope. If I want to do that, I can't let Escarere destroy us all," Jareus told Danny as they walked away from the building.

"I never thought you truly wanted 'just a normal life.' You used to go on and on about that," Danny mentioned.

"I really did think that was what I wanted, but then when things even got close to it, my actions seemed to always contradict what I said," Jareus admitted to Danny. "I felt like I was doing the right thing, though, so I had to question that. So I gave up on that. I decided that instead, I wanted to live up to what I should be,"

"But you can't always think about others, you should also live the way that you want to live," Danny told Jareus. They walked in silence for a bit.

"I'll try to do that, too," Jareus finally said.

PRIMARIUM - 29 NOVEMBER 2015, 10:42 AM

"There isn't a lot for anybody to do. Shouldn't we send out everyone to look for Escarere?" Allison asked Jareus.

"I don't want massive amounts of people out there. Something might alert her, and that's the last thing we want," Jareus told Allison. The two of them were in his office. She had gone up there to tell him that people were looking for things to do. Jareus wore a red short sleeve shirt that just said "Adrenaline Corporation" in white across the chest.

"Alright, then what should I do then, Mister Mess?" Allison started to joke around. Jareus smiled though, he hadn't heard that in a while.

"Who thought it would have been like this?" Jareus grinned.

"Been like what?" Allison wondered.

"I was always under your supervision. Now, it's like we've switched places. I came all the way to you before Rownert, and now you came all the way to me by joining Adrenaline Corp. It's like a mirror," Jareus told her.

"Well, you're right when you put it like that. But don't think this means you're ahead of me now! I was experienced before you, so I'm still the master," Allison proclaimed. Jareus laughed, but also felt guilty. He knew something that he thought nobody else knew.

"You're right, Allison. You have always been there around me, and for me. Even if I didn't really deserve it..." Jareus trailed off.

"Oh don't be silly, you deserved it! You came back for me at first, remember?" She asked, but when she turned to him he had his head on his desk, facing down. She walked over, wondering what was up. She heard quiet sniffling.

"I didn't really deserve any of this. I was just thrust into this position, expected to be a symbol," Jareus could barely spit out, lifting his head, "How the Hell could I be a symbol?! What does that even mean?!" Allison realized how frustrated Jareus must have been.

"Be quiet," Allison ordered him as tears flowed freely from his eyes, "You did everything you could. You're right in the fact that Harlow kinda thrust you into this situation. But you did what you could. Did you see yourself? You inspired people! You got people together, even taking down Toshi!" Allison told him with a smile.

"Yeah, but I'm no symbol if I can't even—" Jareus started.

"Shhhh," Allison shushed him, "Toshi came with you and Danny recently, didn't he? He respects you guys, and I'm sure Kami, Tanya, and all the other people from Adrenaline Corp. respect you too. You didn't do anything wrong," Allison ran her fingers through his hair.

"Isn't it my fault? Why does Escarere want us specifically? I don't want people to be in danger because of me…" Jareus mumbled.

"We're all by your side. We're going to fight with you," Allison affirmed. He felt it, but he was still determined to do one thing.

"Okay," Jareus finally gave up. He let Allison hug him, and he fell back into her. He let himself feel that, just this once.

"JAREUS!" Harlow shouted, running into the room. The two fell onto the ground.

"KNOCK NEXT TIME!" Jareus shouted at Harlow.

"IT'S ESCARERE!" Harlow showed him. It was a picture that had just been uploaded to their servers. She was by Lake Tahoe. Harlow continued, "Should I send the alert to everybody now?!"

"By Truckee, California, huh? We should. We might not get an opportunity like this," Jareus concluded. They went into preparation mode. Allison turned to walk away toward the stairs, and Jareus started to follow her.

"Jareus? Aren't you coming with me? The first wave is going to be deployed this way," Harlow asked Jareus.

"I gotta go set up that robot!" Jareus told Harlow. Harlow gave him the thumbs up as Jareus caught up with Allison.

"You've really got to go, don't you?" Allison asked him as the two of them reached the bottom of the flight of stairs. He had to go to the basement, but she was staying on the floor they were on.

"Yeah, but Allison! Thank you... really... I needed that," Jareus told her.

"No problem! You gotta get ready, Jareus!" She yelled back to him, running in the other direction. Jareus really didn't want her to.

"Allison, wait! I love...!" He started to shout, but Allison couldn't hear him. She had already joined the crowd of people ahead of them. Jareus was left standing there, reaching out. He thought that maybe he'd try later, and left to go set up the robot, like he had originally planned to do. He'd only hesitated to do so because he figured that the robot was irreparable to that degree.

"Alright, are we all ready to head out?!" Harlow asked as all the people finally gathered on trucks. All the trucks gave the signal to move, except for one.

"Danny, where's Jareus?" Zach asked. Danny shrugged, and didn't know. The truck driver told Harlow to go over to the truck.

"The only person we're missing is Jareus," Danny told him.

"What?! Where is he?! There's no way he's still in the building." But Allison, also in the truck, realized something.

"Harlow, can you check the security cameras from your phone?" Allison asked.

"Why now?!" Harlow didn't seem on board with the idea.

"Actually... She has a point. Check them, Harlow." Danny told him. He decided to do so, although he really didn't want to. But at close inspection, they saw Jareus going to the basement, ignoring the robot and putting on a full exosuit with two grapple hooks attached. He then ran out the front, and got in a car.

"Don't tell me..." Harlow started.

"Jareus made himself the bait... didn't he?" Zach asked.

"No... he wanted to prove himself that badly," Allison said out of instinct.

"What do you mean, he wanted to prove himself?! He better get back here right now!" Harlow yelled, dialing in Jareus's number on his phone. It went straight to voicemail.

"Ever since he was appointed leader by you, he felt he had something that he had to live up to... I think this is his way of confirming if he can," Allison told Harlow.

"This isn't what I wanted... I didn't want him to feel like he really even had to do much! We have to start the operation now. Tell all trucks to move out!" Harlow shouted.

...

"I see you've found me, but you're an idiot for coming alone," Escarere told Jareus with her back turned. The weather was cold, and the sky was covered in clouds. Despite the storm clouds ahead, Jareus continued forward.

"We have unfinished business. I'm only going to be here for a limited time, so I want answers in the meantime. If you answer them, I won't have to kill you," Jareus told her.

"You won't HAVE TO kill me either way. You aren't going to. Why should I answer your questions?" Escarere finally decided to turn around. But as she did, Jareus shot something right at her, which stuck her right in the leg. She didn't have time to react to it.

"Why are you doing this?" Jareus demanded.

"Okay, FIRST OFF, what the hell is that?!" Escarere questioned Jareus.

"I made a drug— it's kind of a gamble. I know that Danny said he couldn't use the time power well when exhausted," Jareus told her as she suddenly began panting.

"What a cheap tactic... but one I wasn't expecting, at that. But that won't be necessary for me to kill you," Escarere complained, taking out the drugged dart and crushing it.

"Back to my question, why? Why do you want to kill us? You talk about it like it's hunger, why is that?" Jareus asked, putting away the single-use dart gun and taking out the laser pistol.

"That's simply all it is. There are a few people I have to kill to satisfy this feeling. Do you know what it's like to starve, Jareus?" Escarere approached.

"I guess I don't. But I also don't understand why your hunger was specific to us," Jareus aimed right for Escarere's head.

"Let's just say I was MADE THIS WAY... Jareus. I don't have any choice in the matter, if I want any chance at living and not going entirely insane... I knew that I'd have to kill you next time I see you," Escarere's voice crackled.

"I'm sorry to disappoint you then," Jareus fired the gun, but Escarere ducked to the side. Escarere started sprinting toward Jareus as he boosted up. They fought on the borders of a small forest, next to a giant plain by the freeway. The scattered clouds in the sky blocked some of the sun's rays, making spotty patches of sunlight on the ground below.

"You're not disappointing anybody," Escarere grinned, her blue eyes showing again. She tried to wait below Jareus, with her claws ready to tear through him, but he used the grapple hook to fly over toward the trees. He bounced off of it and boosted straight down into Escarere, shoving her down a small hill, where she was on the verge of losing her balance. Jareus aimed the gun and shot a few times to ensure that she fell over. Boosting forward, Jareus shot his grapple toward the ground by Escarere. But she saw this coming, and she clawed at the hook while off of the ground, causing it to become undone. Jareus started to fall toward the ground, with Escarere preparing to kill him the second he hit the floor, but Jareus used the other grapple hook to cling to the ground a bit further away.

"Having two grapple hooks is pretty great, isn't it, Escarere?" Jareus gloated, "See, you aren't just fighting me, but the creation Harlow and I took months to make. That, along with some new tricks," Escarere rushed Jareus out of anger, and Jareus shot at her. She used her time powers to dodge to the left, but could only use it a little bit before stopping. She kept trying to go toward the plains area. *She's trying to take the fight away from the trees, since I have the inherent advantage there,* Jareus

197

thought. He boosted further toward the plains, and used the grapple hook to get further out as well. He then had Escarere in his line of sight with the trees behind her. This was the perfect line of attack to push her back into the forest area.

"I'M SO HUNGRY, JAREUS!" Escarere screamed. Her eyes lit up a darker blue, and a mouth started to rip through what looked like the solid surface that was her face.

"You're getting more desperate, aren't you?" Jareus beamed. She started to sprint even faster toward him, looking ravenous. Jareus shot his grapple toward the forest behind her so he could come in with a sweeping kick, but Escarere hopped up and cut the grapple line of his left hook while he was midair.

Shit, what can I do?! Jareus panicked as he tried to use the other grapple. Escarere was able to use a little bit of the time power, though, and slashed him right out of the air. Jareus crash landed on the ground, rolling in the dirt until he stopped himself. He boosted up slightly to get himself back on his feet. *Her time powers are starting to slowly come back, so I need to keep overwhelming her with attacks right now!* Jareus's mind raced.

"You're my prey," Escarere grinned. Her face was getting more and more gruesome. Jareus aimed down the pistol sight and started to fire as rapidly as he could. Escarere couldn't run forward due to all the knockback, in addition to the damage she'd obtained from the burn factor of the laser technology. Jareus boosted straight toward her, delivering a blow directly to her cheek by kicking her in the face.

"That had to sting," Jareus grinned, not letting up on the barrage of lasers as Escarere attempted to keep herself from falling in the dirt. Suddenly, she moved entirely too quickly to keep up with again. *I might have run out of the drug's effect time already. It would have worked longer on a human, but what was I expecting anyways...* Jareus thought. She went in for the slash, but Jareus blocked her with his exosuit. But at this point, she was so obsessed with killing him that she was strong enough to rip off a part of the exosuit arm.

"AH-HAH!" Escarere triumphed. Jareus boosted backwards—his suit was beeping, giving him a warning. But at this point, he had to ignore it.

"You didn't even cut me," Jareus spat. Escarere went forward for more attacks, but Jareus boosted upward, aiming down with his gun and taking a few shots. She was able to use her time power in order to get out of the way. Jareus used the other grapple to go toward the forest. Instead of being smart enough to retreat, Escarere followed instinctively.

The second the grapple activated, Jareus shouted in pain. It felt like the arm that had been broken out of the suit was being tugged out of its socket. He bore with the pain and made it to the trees, though. From there, he leapt downwards, kicking Escarere in the face. She fell backwards, but reversed the knockback by slowing down time to recover. She looked like she would destroy him at that point, even with the cuts all over her from the gunshots. Jareus had no choice but to grab her arms as she tried to slash at him. She still managed to cut through his skin, and he bled from his arms.

"Now I did," Escarere excitedly commented. He kicked up, sending her back for a second, and used the grapple up into another tree. She tried to claw at him, but now he was boosting from tree to tree, over to a small but rocky mountain in the plains. He had a final plan.

"You really can't keep up, can you?" Jaresu taunted, having the advantage in an area with trees. This just made Escarere use her powers to try and keep up with him. She barely could. He grabbed onto the mountain, checking to see if a boulder nearby him would budge. It did start to move.

"GET BACK HERE!" Escarere shouted, starting to scale up the mountain. Jareus jumped right off to the bottom again, making her turn around and rush right toward him. Out of nowhere, he threw his gun at her. She dodged, wondering why he would do something so stupid—that was his only ranged weapon.

He then used his grapple on the boulder, and instead of retracting himself to it, he yanked on the cord as hard as he could. As Escarere ran toward Jareus, she slowed down time after seeing what he was doing. She looked up, seeing that a boulder was slowly falling through the air. If she hadn't slowed down time, she would have been hit by it. Escarere stepped back in slowtime so the boulder wouldn't hit her. Escarere felt the cold metal of Jareus's gun on her back in slowed down time, and froze. Jareus had thought about trapping her through the distraction of the boulder, so he'd made a safety net with the magnetic gun handle. As Escarere let time flow normally again, the gun smacked into her back, sending both her and the gun flying right under the boulder. Jareus panted, bloody and exhausted. His stamina and gun were now broken.

"Prey, am I? I just smashed you with a boulder. I guess that's how a leader would do it..." Jareus slowly got out, breathing heavily. He looked into the sky, but the sun had not yet come out from behind the clouds.

"YES, YOU ARE." Escarere, who was all scratched up at this point, lifted the boulder. She threw it off herself and claimed, "You've been hitting me with the same force as a transport truck. Why would a boulder crush me?"

"Oh…" Jareus let out, bracing for impact as Escarere launched herself at him again, taking off a part of the exosuit's other arm attachment. Yet again, it beeped, and Jareus didn't know what to do anymore. He boosted up, thinking that he'd grapple toward the forest. Escarere grabbed the piece of the exo she had just torn off, saw how sharp the ends of it were, and lobbed it at him. She threw it so hard, it took off Jareus's left arm, and he lost balance and crashed into the ground.

"I'm sorry—this is what I was made for," Escarere told him, dragging his bloody body across the field. As he tried to move, she clawed at the back of his neck, and it caused the exo's muscle-predicting mechanics to stop entirely. It became too heavy for Jareus to move.

"Why are you being apologetic now…?" Jares groaned, barely able to talk.

"Bloodied. Battered. I remember something like that. Someone like you. Now… now I'm not hungry enough to kill you," Escarere admitted, throwing Jareus into a small divot in the mountain. As Jareus spat out blood, he still managed to shoot out his grapple hook right into Escarere, dragging her to him. He bit her hand, even with the blood seeping out of his mouth.

"I'll kill you even if I have to eat you. I caused all this by finding that stupid orb in the first place. I have to take responsibility…" Jareus coughed out.

"You will. I can't kill you, but a lack of food will," Escarere took the grapple hook out of her and threw it on the ground.

"You know… my friends are on the way… you're as good as dead," Jareus was able to chuckle barely.

"If that's so, then goodbye." Escarere kicked the rock in front of the divot, trapping a one-armed Jareus inside the small indent with no exit. She even felt a little guilty about it before she left him behind.

…

"Screw it, how long is it going to take to get there at this point?!" Amar shouted at the truck driver. He looked at the GPS.

"Going at this speed, about ten minutes," the driver told them.

"That's crucial at a time like this," Destructo commented.

"Yeah, you know what, let me drive," Amar shouted at him.

"I'm sorry, I can't sir, this is—" The driver stopped speaking after Amar took out his sword and Bobonson took out his gun. He yelped, "GO AHEAD!" Amar drove them off the road in a direct line.

"TRUCK 3! WHERE ARE YOU GOING?!" Amar heard Harlow's voice come in through the truck speaker.

"This is my gang, Harlow. As much as I'd love to obey traffic laws right now, that isn't my kinda thing when it comes to demon hunting," Amar told Harlow through the speaker.

"I'LL HAVE YOU KNOW—" Harlow started to shout. Amar stabbed the speaker with his sword, cutting Harlow off.

"That's property damage, you know," The truck driver told Amar.

"I'm sure saving some lives will be well worth the pay," Amar grunted. They continued forward, passing everybody, and Escarere saw the truck on the plains.

"WE'RE GONNA GET YOU, DEMON!" Hosea shouted as Amar drove the truck right to Escarere, pushing its fastest speed.

"GET READY TO JUMP!" Amar yelled at everyone, letting go of the wheel.

"WHAT?!" Bobonson shouted.

"I'M GONNA DIE!" The truck driver shouted. They all jumped out of the truck as it rolled over and exploded as it hit Escarere.

"It was a little greeting present I thought of," Amar shrugged as they got up off of the grassy ground. The truck driver just started running toward a gas station by the freeway.

"YOU'RE INSANE, AMAAR!" Bobonson shouted at him.

"I thought this was a good idea for once," Destructo smiled, taking out his shotgun. Escarere walked out of the fire, barely scratched.

"Well... maybe that was a necessary greeting present," Bobonson took aim with his rifle.

"DEMON KILLING TIME!" Hosea shouted. Escarere still approached, and they waited for her to get within range.

"Let's go for another big attack," Amar handed Hosea a grenade. He brought two of them, "Bobonson and Destructo, shoot the grenades when they get near Escarere. Try and go for a collateral if you can, I'm terrible at timing this kinda thing."

"Me too!" Hosea agreed. They counted down to Amar and Hosea throwing the grenades. Bobonson and Destructo both aimed and shot them midair. They didn't expect Escarere to go forward so fast, but Escarere didn't anticipate the blast being as powerful as it was. The force of the blast sent her flying forward to Amar's group, immediately putting them in a close-combat situation.

"HERE SHE IS!" Amar shouted.

"I GOTTA GET RANGE!" Bobonson yelled, running back while Amar slashed at her. She dodged his attacks as Hosea came in, smacking her with his bamboo stick. Somehow, the attack landed. Destructo fired his shotgun, and his close range to Escarere sent the densely-packed shot string flying into her. She fell backwards.

"It's so painful. It's *so* painful. It's so painful," Escarere started to mutter as she was on the ground.

"This'll be easy!" Hosea shouted. As he swung down, he noticed that he didn't hit. It took him a moment to notice that his hand was missing, but when he did so, his reaction was catastrophic. "AHHHH!!! WHAT THE HELL! WHAT THE HELL DID YOU DO TO ME, YOU BITCH?!" Hosea shouted.

"What'd ya call me?" Escarere asked calmly as she walked toward Hosea. Destructo went to shoot her once more, but without warning, she used her time power to teleport behind him. She stabbed right through his back, holding him up like a trophy as he bled out.

"DESTRUCTO!" Bobonson yelled. He shot at Escarere, but Escarere used Destructo as a shield, and then threw him down.

"Amar, Amar—I need you, Amar," Escarere seemed like she was in a trance as Amar stood speechless and terrified. He couldn't make himself move. His muscles were all on fire.

"YOU CAN'T DO THIS TO US!" Hosea shouted, trying to smash her head in with his left hand, which was wielding the bamboo stick this time. Escarere stabbed his back and kicked him, making him tumble down a hill.

"Amar, hold me," Escarere demanded, almost softly. She pushed herself onto him, grabbing onto him as they both fell to the ground together. Amar was in shock.

"AMAR?! AMAR, ARE YOU THERE?!" Bobonson yelled. Destructo had gone entirely quiet, and Hosea was bleeding out.

"I just wanted to be like this with you one last time, Amar. I'm so hungry, I have to kill you. But I feel so bad for doing that. What I felt killing that other timeline version of you hurt too much," Escarere started explaining, seemingly even weeping. Amar didn't know what to say, or what to do.

"What... am I to you?" Amar barely mustered out.

"You're my love," Escarere whispered. Suddenly, those words activated what Amar had been forgetting. He remembered exactly... who Escarere was.

TIMELINE OF REDARO'S VICTORY - MEMORY

"I have to at least try and do something, Daphne," Amar told his wife. They had just been "married," which had consisted of a makeshift celebration of just the two of them, as there had been no way to officiate a marriage after Redaro had taken over. Amar had found her in an abandoned farmhouse while he had been trying to find tools to defend himself. While his other friends had thought he'd died initially after Redaro had started his takeover, Jareus had actually survived and given up his old identity. He wandered the now-destroyed Earth, known to others as Amar. Only his wife knew of his original name. Amar was still in his original and older body as well.

"But why do you have to do anything, Amar?! We could just try and live our lives away from the demons," Daphne begged him.

"I can't go down without a fight, Daphne. Plus, with these gloves and this sword, I'm sure I could probably face Redaro. But for today, I'm just going to go out scavenging for food," Amar told Daphne.

"Dad, if you're just going out for food, can I come with you?" Amar's son, Sam, asked him.

"It's dangerous to go outside, honey, I don't think you should…" Daphne warned.

"He's going to need to be a man of his own at some point, so he ought to come with me!" Amar laughed. Daphne barely agreed to it, so they spent some time foraging. After a while, they were headed back with supplies from an abandoned warehouse when they heard a shriek.

"Sam, I want you to stay here, okay? No matter what you see, do NOT come out of hiding until I come get you, okay?" Amar asked of his son, who could only nod.

"AMAR! AMAR HELP! PLEASE!" Daphne cried as Redaro held her by the neck.

"Too late, Jareus," Redaro taunted as Amar's memory turned red, suddenly transitioning to another time. A month or so later, Amar had discovered where Redaro was. A hate within him, a vengeance within him compelled him to slaughter Redaro at all costs.

206

"I'll murder him... I'll murder him and every last thing he stands for..." Amar hungered for his death. He was right behind a few rocks, and Redaro was right in front of him. Amar jumped out, and had a clear line to slash Amar's neck. Redaro didn't even notice he was there, it was the perfect opportunity.

But something punched Amar, sending him crashing into the dirt. Amar looked up, and saw a demon like Redaro. This demon... was Escarere.

"Nice try, Jareus. But I needed a companion, specifically a female one. I wanted to see if special demons like me could procreate, honestly. Seems the answer is no, but at least your little Daphne has become a valuable slave to me," Redaro gloated.

"REDARO! I'LL SLIT YOUR THROAT WIDE OPEN! I'LL GOUGE OUT YOUR INSIDES!" Amar shouted as Escarere pinned him down.

"You wouldn't yell like that in front of Daphne, would you?" Now quiet down, I think I've figured out time travel... So we can chase that Alex kid..." Redaro complained.

"SHUT THE HELL UP, YOU DISGUSTING PIECE OF FILTH!" Amar still screamed, looking at Redaro as Escarere held him down.

"Fine, I'll make you my slave too, if you want that so badly. I'll have you go back in time to kill everybody I want dead. If you fail, I'm sure your wife here'll succeed, seeing as she's a demon like me now," Redaro gloated. Escarere covered Amar's mouth as he tried to scream, but Redaro had already started to put him to sleep. Redaro angrily spat, "I'll have you pledge your loyalty with the blood of your own son, Jareus."

Amar did as he said.

"I loved you…" Amar looked at Escarere with tears in his eyes. The clouds still covered the sun above them. Amar still had on the gloves he had made in that era of his life.

"Looks like our time is up," Escarere frowned. The rest of the trucks had just gotten there, and she went to stab through Amar. Amar pushed himself off of her and rolled down the hill.

"GOTCHA!" Bobonson sniped Escarere, and her limp body flew toward Destructo's corpse.

"That hurt a little," Escarere got up, picking up Destructo's shotgun and shooting at Bobonson. It wasn't enough for it to reach him, though. Bobonson ran toward the forest, and Amar had just made it far enough as they all realized what was happening.

"WAVE ONE! GO!" Harlow shouted. Odessa, Zach, Kami, Toshi, Danny, Cole, and Alex were all lined up with giant rocket launchers. They fired them all simultaneously.

"Supply chain, let's go! Quickly get these soldiers some guns! Laser rifles for the Wave One soldiers!" Tanya shouted at the support branch, who were acting as the suppliers in this situation. Escarere was damaged, but still walked out of the situation alive.

"FIRE!" Harlow shouted as they all shot at Escarere, hurting her, but she started to use her time powers to teleport around.

"I didn't think that'd be of help, but maybe it *did* do something," Devon shrugged.

"It better be doing something!" Adam Steel shouted from the line of guns. They saw Escarere disappear into the smoke.

"I thought this'd happen. Toshi, Kami, and Odessa—I need you three to boost around quickly and protect the back. Having Escarere take out a few of us and then retreat would be the worst possible outcome. We need an unbreakable wall back there, so Toshi, you'd better not disappoint!" Harlow ordered.

"Roger that!" The three of them rushed around the field. Harlow turned around to the rest of the soldiers.

"I need you all to create a ring around the area, no matter which way Escarere is coming, you need to inform other people of her location," Harlow ordered.

"YES SIR!" They all chanted in unison.

"The rest of the Wave One people, I need you on the field immediately," Harlow pointed to the remaining four.

"Have you seen Jareus anywhere?" Alex asked.

"I haven't, but that bastard better be alive, I'm using his stupid ring technique," Harlow commented. In no time, they were out on the battlefield.

"YOU'LL ALL SATISFY ME!" Escarere shouted in glee. Alex activated his demon form, Danny readied himself, and Cole and Zach stood back-to-back.

"NEVER!" Alex shouted. Zach and Cole were the first to fling themselves into action. They both boosted themselves forward, kicking each side of Esacrere.

"Not bad for the first time in a while," Zach grinned.

"That's for sure!" Cole agreed, running around the other side of Escarere. As she ran toward Zach, Zach boosted up as Cole smashed into her back. Zach then took advantage of this and boosted straight down onto Escarere. She got angry and threw them both out of the way.

"MY TURN!" Alex shouted. He grabbed Escarere's hands, and they pushed back and forth for a bit before Cole came back in, sliding under Escarere and dragging her. This gave Alex the opportunity to go haywire on her. She jumped out of the way and used her time powers to speed up and try to stab Alex. Alex's demon form wouldn't allow it, and he tried to hold her off until the time was right.

"NOW!" Danny yelled. Alex jumped out of the way as Danny activated his own time powers and boosted straight down onto Escarere. For a moment, Danny and Escarere were moving at the same speed in slowed-down time, but Danny outlasted her in his stamina to control time. As she relented, the slowtime was left under his control. Danny was able to land a pretty sizable hit, kicking Escarere toward the forest.

"POWER MOVE!" Toshi suddenly yelled, kicking Escarere in the gut from out of nowhere.

"WHY YOU...!" Escarere shouted back, trying to stab him as Alex grabbed her and they tumbled down the hill together. Escarere full-force punched Alex and he went flying away. As she got up, Escarere noticed two hooks in both of her sides.

"PULL!" Zach shouted. Cole and Zach tried to pull her apart by pulling on both sides with their grapple hooks. It didn't work, though, and Escarere pulled both grapple lines toward each other. Zach and Cole crashed into each other.

"I'LL FINISH THIS!" Danny shouted, jumping into action. He grappled onto Escarere and used the time power at the same time as her. He crashed into her, and they flew in normal time as the rest of the world slowed down. They crashed into the dirt at high speeds.

"If I had known… not one… but TWO of you would have gotten powers from my blood in the beginning… I would have waited until I perfected slowing down time, rather than attacking when I found you…" Escarere barely got out as she started to trade blows with Danny. She wasn't strong enough to break the exosuit anymore.

"Expect the unexpected," Danny glared at her, unleashing both of his grapple hooks at once. He flung Escarere up and then smacked her back into the ground, yelling, "WHAT DID YOU DO WITH JAREUS?!"

"Only the same thing that Redaro made me hunger to do to you too," Escarere was furious, breaking free from the grapple lines. She tore off one of her own fingers and threw it at Danny like a dart, and it stuck right inside his chest. Then she went to grab Danny's neck, holding him up for everybody to see.

"I HAVE TO DO THIS!" Escarere shouted. Her outburst even managed to make Amar turn around.

"What can we do?!" Adam Steel asked Harlow from the sidelines.

"YOU CAN'T FIRE ANYTHING, SHE'S GOT A HOSTAGE!" Harlow yelled at him. But Amar turned and saw this. This same figure, holding Danny up by the neck. The same way Redaro held up Daphne. His fighting instincts kicked in, and he sprinted toward them with every ounce of strength he had.

"AFTER THIS, I—" Escarere began. She suddenly couldn't speak, and let Danny go. Danny coughed, laying on the ground.

"I'm sorry, but it pains me too much to see you like this. Especially if you're going to repeat the process. I hope you go to heaven, Daphne," Amar was wide-eyed and furious. He had stuck his sword right into Escarere's neck. Everyone battling her had worn down her defenses enough, allowing Amar to take over. He shoved her on the ground, standing on top of her while still holding the sword. He took it out, and stabbed it in yet again.

"Amar... I think... I think you did it," Danny sighed. The sun finally shone down on them.

"YOU CAN NEVER BE TOO SURE!" Alex shouted, slicing into Escarere with his demon hands. But they cut her easily—she had no defense anymore.

"Calm down, Alex..." Danny panted out.

"Her first mistake was thinking that bringing back those memories would do her any good," Amar's eyes remained open wide. He was in an emotionless state of shock.

"Did they do it...?" Adam Steel asked from the sidelines.

"I... I think they did. MISSION COMPLETE!" Harlow shouted through a megaphone. Soldiers on the side were all celebrating as Harlow ran toward the center of the field.

"Amar...Destructo and Hosea are..." Bobonson looked down as he tried to bring himself to say it.

"All I have is blood on my hands. I know," Amar told Bobonson.

"That isn't your fault, Amar! Escarere just tore through us... unlike previous times, she was actually going straight for the kill this time!" Bobonson's voice wavered as he shouted at Amar.

"Danny? Are you okay?" Harlow asked Danny.

"Oddly… I feel fine," Danny told Harlow. Harlow looked down at Danny's wound, where Escarere implanted a finger, but it had completely vanished. "Maybe her attacks disappeared when she died."

"I guess that's possible. I'm not doubting anything anymore," Harlow commented.

"Guuuyyys! Guys! Guys, where is he?! Where did he go?! Wasn't he here before all of us? Where's Jareus?!" Allison started to shout at people in distress. She had been with the many soldiers during the time of the battle. Everybody went silent around her. Even Amar had memories of who she was. She continued, "Why won't any of you tell me?!"

"Allison. There's no easy way to say this…" Amar started. He didn't even finish his sentence. Allison already broke down, knowing exactly what he meant.

"We didn't find a body yet! That's harsh, Amar!" Bobonson scolded Amar.

"No… she deserves to know the truth…" Danny barely got out as well.

"Are they kidding me?! Are they KIDDING ME!" Zach shouted, kicking a rock, "I told him that I WOULD DO THAT! He lied to me, he lied to my FACE and told me a robot would be the one to face her." *And I knew the robot didn't work… but I had faith in him…* Danny thought to himself. He would take that to his grave.

"Jareus… is… gone?" Cole could barely grasp the reality of the situation. The glue that had brought them all together had vanished entirely.

213

PRIMARIUM - 1 DECEMBER 2015, 6:55 PM

Two days had passed since then. They had scavenged the entire field, but found no traces of a body—even so, Jareus was legally "dead." Barely anybody could really come to terms with what had just happened. Everybody found out about the news quickly. Adrenaline Corp. had a new symbol of hope, a symbol of what could be done and what to look up to. Escarere had killed the symbol aspect of it, for sure.

During the day that everybody took off, Harlow went to investigate the portals. It seemed the timelines' closeness had been caused by Escarere herself. After Escarere died, the main portal in Orange Grove Ranch had disappeared. The day they came back, they all held a funeral for Jareus. On that day, it snowed.

"I just don't know what to do now... I feel like it's all my fault," Harlow admitted to Danny after the funeral, when most people had gone home.

"Don't put yourself at fault. Jareus knew what he was doing, and went in over his head. I just wished he'd said something before going..." Danny said back to Harlow. The two exchanged a moment of silence.

"Nobody knows what to do anymore. This new and exciting symbol of hope for Adrenaline Corp. disappeared so quickly... Nobody has someone to look toward now. I can't even be that person. If I could do that myself, I would have a long time ago. All the exosuits are still from his mind. The logo even came from him," Harlow started to ramble on, destroyed by what had just occurred.

"I want to try and do it. Be a symbol, I mean. For Jareus. He'd like that of me, don't ya think?" Danny asked. Harlow was hesitant to answer at first.

214

"I guess he would want you to do that," Harlow finally answered.

"So what do you think?" Danny asked. Harlow thought about it for a moment.

"I guess you can do that," Harlow agreed. Danny smiled weakly. He and Harlow shook on it before Harlow had to leave. He decided to start Christmas Break early for Adrenaline Corp. after the first day of december. But as he was leaving, he saw Amar in the back, piquing his interest.

"You two deserved so much more," Amar was barely holding back tears. He and Bobonson were the only ones there.

"Hey… Amar. Are you good?" Harlow asked.

"NO, HARLOW. DOES IT LOOK LIKE I'M 'GOOD' TO YOU?!" Amar suddenly burst out.

"Amar… he didn't mean anything by it…" Bobonson whispered. Amar took deep breaths to calm down.

"I know, obviously none of us are good. But I just wanted to make sure you were somewhat holding up," Harlow told the two.

"Yeah, the only thing right now… is that for Jareus the 'symbol of hope…' he gets a whole funeral dedicated to him." Amar muttered, unable to hold back his strong feelings. "What do my boys get? What did Destructo and Hosea get? They got graves. That's it. No soldiers even came to pay respects to their fallen comrades. They're all assholes."

"Amar, they aren't assholes. They just didn't know any of the deceased… besides their legacy as the truck that went off course," Harlow told Amar.

"NOW LISTEN HERE, MR. HENRY. THESE TWO WERE LIKE FAMILY TO ME, AND YOU'RE GONNA TELL ME THAT PEOPLE *THINK* THEY DIED BECAUSE I WAS TRYING TO SAVE ANOTHER PERSON?! YOU DIPSHITS SHOULD HAVE FOLLOWED US!" Amar started to shout.

"AMAR! LANGUAGE! I'm terribly sorry for him… but it's really not kind of you to play down other deaths like that," Bobonson shouted at Amar and told Harlow.

"I'm really sorry, that isn't what I meant," Harlow told them.

"Well have fun with Adrenaline Corp. I'm gonna go find something to do with what's left of the life I have," Amar walked away in the snow. He took a piece of black cloth sewn together from Hosea's and Destructo's clothing. Using that, he made it a bandana around his neck as he walked away.

"I'm sorry, Harlow. Hopefully we'll see you when he's less angry," Bobonson told him.

"No it's alright. You two take care," Harlow waved goodbye. They were all gone. The Adrenaline Corp. building, while covered in snow, was empty… besides Danny.

"So now it's my turn…"
—*END OF PARADOX GLITCH*

216

Part 7: Conflicting Divide

It had only been a few months since the incident in which Jareus had been lost. Most situations had been sorting themselves out with the rest of the crew, but things were heating up between Adrenaline Corporation and Regiment Legion. The Regiment Legion had been growing in size, with Cole still working alongside Amber. They were another military corporation much like Adrenaline Corporation, but made specifically by and for use alongside the army. But Adrenaline Corp. had been working on something secret—an idea to make Adrenaline Corporation the most superior army was being put into action. Something in Danny's head had manifested.

Amar had to stay in this timeline. It had become stable again, and access to Alternis disappeared after the death of Escarere. Not even Danny could return there, even with his time powers. Amar had started to wear that bandana around his neck regularly, and he also still had his black zip-up jacket with gray sleeves.

He was heading back to his hideout, which was on a mountain outside the Adrenaline Corp. HQ. He wondered how far Regiment Legion HQ was from there, as it wasn't really common knowledge where it was. Amar jumped a fence as the moon dawned over the sky. It was dusk—dark blue light shone from above. Amar jumped up onto a large stone, stuck in the dirt and gravel below. From there he jumped on to a tree and stepped through the branches, just to get to a little slope on a big hill. He ran up the slope to a little cave. There was a torch inside. This is where he had been living—this was his hideout.

"Tomorrow is the day. The day of the conference. Something's up, and I can tell... I guess I'll see tomorrow," Amar whispered to himself. He retreated into his cave to stay the night. The moon rose as February 17th, 2016, ended.

Adrenaline Corporation 1: Manifestation

The next day began like any other, with everyone getting ready for the day. Danny, as the new CEO of Adrenaline Corporation, called a meeting. Zach got up just like any other day. He put on his shirt, pants, and shaved some beard hair off. Nobody had been quite the same since Jareus's unfortunate departure, but they were managing. Zach went to the meeting as scheduled. He went to the building right through the rotating doors, and saw a familiar face inside.

"Oh hey, Zach," Amar said. He was looking gloomy, as per usual.

"'Sup, Amar. Any luck fitting into this world?" Zach asked Amar in a more upbeat tone.

"Eh. Not really. I've been living in a cave," Amar told Zach. He had brightened up a little bit.

"What brings you around, then?" Zach asked Amar. More Adrenaline Corp. soldiers were coming in for the meeting.

"Danny invited me. I haven't exactly been nice, but I've decided that I'm not going to turn that down... now, c'mon. There are people going into the meeting," Amar explained to Zach. Zach nodded and they went with the rest of the people funneling into the next room. After showing ID for a bunch of people guarding every doorway, and Zach vouching for Amar, they had made it into the conference room. Aaron and Martin were there, along with a bunch of other higher-ups all sitting around a big table. Danny was sitting at the end of it, and Alex was already in there.

"Hey, guys! Come on, sit right down. We got two seats right at the end of the table," Alex told Amar and Zach. Everybody was sitting now, but Danny was turned away from the table, working on his laptop. When everyone was in, some guards came in and closed the doors. They pressed a button, and lights came on and blackout shaders went over the doors.

"Woah, what's going on?" Zach asked.

"Sorry to suddenly spring this on all of you, but the information I will talk about in this meeting is largely private. I invited you, Amar, to show you some trust. Perhaps you'll show me a little trust in return and join Adrenaline Corp?" Danny asked.

"I'll have to see. Where's Harlow, anyways?" Amar asked. He was still skeptical of the whole situation.

"He's been under the weather, and I can do most of what he was doing anyways. In fact, I'll be doing more. This is actually what we're here to discuss, since I'm actually going to be leading this company in a more-than-symbolic way. But quickly, since I'm going to see Cole shortly afterwards," Danny explained.

"Alright, then what do you plan on? Things haven't really been different around," Zach commented.

"Not that you've seen, Zach. But I've been working on a lot in the background. Martin and Aaron know a little bit," Danny eyed the two of them.

"What's that supposed to mean?" Amar asked those two.

"We've just been helping him set it up, and I think his newer ideas are going to be brilliant for the company's next steps," Aaron mentioned.

"You see," Danny started, "Adrenaline Corporation is a fine, strong military. But what happened when one decently-strong demon showed up? The whole thing was seemingly powerless against it. We had nothing set up for an enemy so powerful. We were just lucky that such an enemy had a personal vendetta against us, and didn't pop up somewhere else in the world. So that's why I'm announcing my plan for phase two of this great corporation, and it all starts with coverage.

"We need to be prepared, even if unlikely, for the possibility of an attack like that. Not only HERE do we need to be prepared, but in a few specific locations that could relay information about large areas back to us. This includes possibly working with Regiment Legion. Cole will be here soon for us to discuss that. Not only this, but I've also been working on brand-new weaponry that could help destroy any demon we come in contact with," Danny informed the group.

Zach started to clap.

"Very impressive, Danny. And here I got the feeling you were about to tell us bad news. What are we talking about? More Adrenaline Corp. buildings across the US? More laser pistols like the one Jareus used? If I recall the way those were made, they were legal," Zach complimented. Danny lost his smile after that last sentence.

"Well first, I'd like to tell you about our new spheres of influence. Yes, we're going to have more US buildings, but Harlow already planned for that. What I'm talking about are buildings in Europe and Canada. That will relay us most of the information from countries with less development. I'd like to make talks with China and Japan as well, but they seem less open to the idea. The weapons I've been making mostly include ranged ones. I see no reason to change the U.N.E. with the grapple attachment. Starting very soon we'll be producing parasite ammunition, incendiary ammunition, and poison—" Danny was explaining.

"Hold on, WHAT! I don't even know what parasite ammunition is, but I DO know that incendiary weapons are a war crime!" Zach slammed his hands on the table, cutting Danny off. Amar and Alex turned to him, almost shocked.

"Ahh… I knew something like this would happen. Look, I understand the laws. I get that they're trying to protect people from unnecessary pain in fights. But for the thick skin of something like a demon? We NEED this kind of weaponry! Normal bullets just don't cut it!" Danny shouted. Everyone else hesitantly relaxed their bodies.

"We were able to handle Escarere, though, and the likelihood of something like that happening again seems pretty low to me," Zach argued.

"That's what we said right after finishing off the Purged Souls! *'There won't be any more strong enemies like that.'* Time after time we're proven wrong. I just want to be ready for it this time, so we don't have people dying like Jareus again!" Danny shouted back.

Zach fell silent. He knew that doing this kind of thing was wrong, though. Danny's actions didn't seem to all line up.

"Although," Amar suddenly cut in, "We didn't *need* to have any incidents like that. Jareus isn't the only one who died, but I know his mistake. We both made the same mistake. Only my friends got caught in the fire instead of me, and they didn't deserve that. If anything, *I* deserved those deaths. I made the mistake. I'm sure Jareus knew that if he couldn't beat Escarere—"

"That's enough, Amar..." Danny cut him off, "Mistakes always have to be calculated for. You're right. Jareus didn't have to die, only if we'd had better weapons for him to defend himself with. Which we will, now!" Zach suddenly got up.

"Then, if you don't mind... I'm leaving," Zach announced, getting up from his chair suddenly.

"I *do* mind, Zach. This is confidential information," Danny glared at Zach. Zach made a break for it, kicking down the door and sprinting.

"AFTER HIM!" One of the guards shouted from outside the door. Both of them ran in the same direction as him.

"Ugh... well, that ruins that. You get where I'm going, right?" Danny asked the rest of the room.

"Yeah, but after seeing that I'm afraid to tell you that I'm going to wait it out to see if I want to join or not," Amar spat, putting his feet up on the table.

"Amar..." Danny angrily grunted.

"He'll join in time, but for now, get your feet off of the table," Alex scolded Amar. He opened one eye and shrugged, getting up.

"Now, if you'll excuse me..." Danny angrily said, standing up and walking down the same way Zach went.

Meanwhile, Zach was still running. *Where am I gonna go after I escape?!* Zach wondered. As the guards shot darts at him, Zach jumped over the railings and jumped down the stairs, ducking and side-stepping out of the way at any point possible. He looked out the window and figured out what he wanted to do. *I have to get out there!* He thought, grabbing the railing above him and smashing out the second floor window. He rolled, taking little damage. But the glass had still cut him up.

"Zach?! What's going on?!" Cole shouted. He and Amber had just arrived at the Adrenaline Corp. facility.

"Cole… let me join you… it's Danny…" Zach groaned out. Meanwhile, Danny was trudging down the stairs.

"Let me handle this, alone," Danny told the guards, stomping all the way down to the first floor doors. Danny flung open the doors, beholding the sight of Zach with Cole and Amber. "Leaving us already, Zach?" He questioned.

"Danny… I understand that you're trying to make up for losses. But, I can't agree with the fact that you're trying to make biological and incendiary weapons. I know 'parasite bullets' are slang for bullets that can target their host with specific diseases," Cole made public. Danny gritted his teeth, feeling alone in this situation.

"You too, Cole? I was just about to ask Regiment Legion for some help. What are you going to do if some demon shows up? What we did last time wasn't exactly the best situation. Even worse, what if a *few* show up?" Danny questioned Cole.

"I'll defend us!" Cole spat, holding up his fist and shoving Danny back, "I understand that you're hurt by the losses we suffered, but don't let them cloud your judgment!" Danny stood back, his chest tight. His friends had betrayed and abandoned him—it was like nobody understood what he was trying to prevent.

"Are you trying to fight?" Danny spat back, shoving Cole. Amber pulled Zach back.

"Cole, I think it's time we go!" Amber shouted for Cole. Cole looked back, but he couldn't just walk away.

"I will—as soon as I settle things here," Cole said, walking toward Danny. Both of their hearts were pounding. "I don't wanna have to be the one to come stop you when the government finds out about what you're doing, so knock it off!"

Danny snapped and punched Cole. Cole held his gut.

"Are you kidding me? You're going to *tattle* on me? What kind of bullshit is this? I'm the one who's trying to save BOTH OF US!" Danny was infuriated. Cole punched Danny back, right in the side.

"You're letting your anger cloud your judgment," Cole groaned.

"YOU'RE THE ONE WITH CLOUDED JUDGMENT!" Danny shouted back as a small brawl broke out. Danny slowed down time, and managed to get a hit in. Cole took the attack, and broke through the pain. He was bigger than Danny, though, so he still managed to make up for it in brute strength.

"What are you two? Kids?" Amar asked, suddenly breaking into the fight. They both stopped, panting, and looked at him, "If you two keep fighting, then *any* demon would get the best of both of you…" Amar walked up to Danny and flicked his forehead, "Even your overcautious cranium wouldn't survive." Danny punched Amar right in the side as he tried to walk away.

224

"WHY ARE YOU AGAINST ME?!" Danny shouted at Amar.

"Danny! Don't involve him!" Cole shouted, running to try and stop Danny.

"You're just not over what happened yet!" Amar shouted at Danny, going in to punch him back. But Danny slowed down time, stepped out of the way, and punched Amar directly in the cheek, knocking him to the ground.

"I JUST KNOW WHAT HAS TO BE DONE!" Danny shouted, going for another punch on Amar when Cole restrained him.

"Stop this!" Cole shouted, but Danny whipped his head back, crushing Cole's nose.

"What's going on here?" Alex came out of the main building and promptly freaked out at what he saw. Danny stepped back, moving over to Alex.

"Forget them, Alex. They're not going to help us," Danny whispered to him, sounding disappointed as he walked back into the building.

"Alex! You don't need to deal with that, you can come with us," Cole offered him, holding out his hand. Alex stared at it for a bit, and saw Amar coughing on the ground. He almost wanted to.

"I can't. I've seen what can happen to the future if you aren't cautious, Cole. Plus, I'm sure governments would understand when they know our use for the weapons," Alex smiled eerily, and walked back inside.

"Need a hand?" Cole offered out to Amar. Amar got up on his own, ignoring any help.

"I can't side with either of you yet. I'm sorry, Cole, but I still need to wait," Amar told Cole.

"That's fine, don't worry about that," Cole told Amar, although he still sounded disappointed.

"But if Danny does anything scandalous, you better tell us!" Zach shouted at Amar. Amar half-grinned.

"I'll try to," Amar waved as he walked back toward the mountains. Cole took a deep breath and turned to Zach and Amber.

"So what should we do now?" Amber asked.

"We have to tell everyone inside of Adrenaline Corp. what's happening. We'll also need to see what kind of weapons they're producing…" Zach said.

"Well, let's get a video ready to send to the employees then. I don't like the fact that Danny isn't telling them this," Cole agreed. While they were making plans and leaving the area… Danny was in the back, already holding one of the incendiary munitions. Alex watched as he put a test model in a case.

"Alex, what are you doing?" Danny asked as he observed Alex peeking around the corner.

"Uhhh… nothing. Nothing at all," Alex answered, turning around.

"Look, I know you think what I'm doing is bad, but they just need time. After I prove the effectiveness of the weapons, I'm sure they'll come back. They just don't understand yet," Danny told Alex genuinely. Alex shrugged and gave a little twitch. He walked away rather robotically. Danny wondered what was going on with him, but the business he had to take care of remained at the forefront of his mind.

"Breaking news! Two unidentified deaths are being blamed on Adrenaline Corporation! We'll gather more information here today with our guest, now ex-Adrenaline Corp. member, Zach Artien!" A newsman announced while sitting at a table, live on television. Zach came into the picture.

"About that sir, I'm pretty sure that the public opinion is that Adrenaline Corp. is at fault. While it isn't entirely true from what I know... I *do* know that they died during an Adrenaline Corp. mission," Zach admitted to the newsman.

"Were you there when these two were killed?! Is it part of the reason you quit?" The newsman questioned him.

"Although Adrenaline Corp. and I aren't on the best terms now... I'm going to have to say 'no comment.'" Zach told the newsman. Meanwhile, Danny was at Jareus's old house, watching this whole thing unfold.

"He's not exposing the truth. He's being vague enough to make it seem like it was my fault. That's dirty... throwing us under the bus like that. I'm sure we'll get nothing but negative coverage because of that," Danny commented. Zoey was sleeping right next to him on the couch he sat on. Danny got up, put on a coat, and was headed for Adrenaline Corp. HQ. Meanwhile, Zach had beaten him there.

"The next step is getting the model files for those illegal weapons," Zach muttered to himself. He was already at Adrenaline Corp. HQ, arriving there right after the TV interview had aired. Zach had a version of the Regiment Legion lightweight exosuit on. He boosted up and grabbed onto a wall. He used these suction-cup devices to climb his way to the roof. He found the roof entrance, and used a tool to blow the door handle right off, getting him access to the inside without making too much noise. He ran right down the hall, knowing where everything was since he had been there many times before. He headed straight for the computer room. But as he ran through another room as a shortcut, he encountered a familiar face.

"Uh…" Alex seemed confused. He had gotten there before Zach. He was just sitting in a conference room with the door wide open, eating a sandwich. Zach froze when he heard Alex. He turned and his eyes met Alex's.

"Hey Alex, are you here?" Danny's voice projected from downstairs. Danny had just arrived. Alex looked down, and thought for a second. He agreed with Danny's mentality, but didn't think he was entirely in the right. Alex just hoped that he'd get over this whole chemical weaponry thing. So Alex didn't say a word, and instead pointed Zach in the direction of the computer room. Zach's expression lit up, surprised. He gave Alex a thumbs up and was on his way.

"Yeah, I'm up here!" Alex shouted, getting up. Alex stood at the top of the stairway as Danny climbed the stairs. Alex stood suspiciously in the way of the hall toward the computer room as Danny walked up to him.

"Uh… what's going on?" Danny asked.

"Nothing, really," Alex avoided eye contact.

"Well… I need to get to that office so—" Danny started.

"No! There's a huge mess in there! Oh shoot did I say that? I wanted to clean it up before you saw," Alex made the best excuse he could think of.

"A mess... huh? I don't really care. Just go make my computer accessible for a minute. I'll be right in there," Danny mumbled, walking the other way to go hang up his jacket. Alex ran right into the room, slamming the door behind him.

"I don't know what you're doing, but make it quick!" Alex told Zach.

"I'm just getting the files for the chemical weapons. I'm just about done. Please cover for me like you did earlier!" Zach shouted as he grabbed a USB drive and opened up the window just to jump out.

"Why did I hear voices?" Danny asked, slowly creaking open the door. Alex sweat nervously as Danny gave him a certain look. Meanwhile, Zach had successfully copied the files and was running away outside, but a gate closed on him. Danny was out there in no time at all. He asked Zach, "Where do you think you're going?"

"You think you're going to stop me now?!" Zach shouted at Danny. Then Alex ran into the mix, getting in front of Zach.

"Listen... Danny...!" Alex started.

"Look Alex, this is something I have to do so..." Danny glared, "Don't interfere."

"If what you're doing is so 'right,' then why are you afraid if others have even a *look* at it?" Alex questioned Danny.

"It's something I made. It's a secret to me! Don't make me explain why I don't want those weapon files getting in the wrong hands," Danny scolded Alex.

"The wrong hands...?! Why you..." Zach didn't like what he was hearing.

"Just let him take it. If it's truly going to be for the greater good, they should just see that you're bending the rules a bit... but making it to the safest possible degree, right?" Alex questioned Danny.

"It's not for them to have, Alex! Are you an idiot?! He's going to use that just to get at us!" Danny shouted at Alex. But this was the last straw for Alex. Alex got his right arm ready and started to throw a punch at Danny. But Danny slowed down time, and dodged the attack. Danny grabbed his arm, and threw Alex out of the way as time resumed its normal flow.

"WHATEVER!" Alex shouted, running back into the HQ. Danny looked at Zach, and before Zach could boost out of the way, Danny grabbed the drive.

"This is mine," Danny spat at Zach, glaring. He walked back into Adrenaline Corp. HQ. Zach didn't want any stories of Regiment Legion attacking Danny, so he stayed his ground.

"Fine, keep your stupid renders," Zach pouted, but then smiled, "I have a copy, anyways." He grinned as he jumped away. Danny caught a glimpse of this, though.

"I should have known!" Danny angrily shouted. Danny ran after Zach as the sun started to set. But Zach was easily ahead of him because of his exosuit. But then...

"REGIMENT LEGION!" A voice shouted. A bamboo stick suddenly flung up, hitting Zach out of the air.

"What the hell...?" Danny asked himself. What he saw was beyond his understanding. He had seen this man die before.

"Regiment Legion keeps taking parts of my territory. And you're part of Adrenaline Corporation, aren't you? I'll keep you hostage for some money," The man grinned.

"Hosea... is that you?!" Zach questioned.

230

"How do you know my name…?" Hosea questioned. It was the Hosea from the original timeline. He had never met Amar, so he was still his old self. But he was strong, indeed.

"I used to know you," Zach smiled, getting off the ground.

"You know what, I don't care. If I take you two as hostages…" Hosea started, pulling out a gun, "Then maybe I'll get you Regiment Legion punks off of my territory with some cash as a bonus!"

"Move!" Danny shouted, punching Zach out of the way. Hosea shot but missed both of them, "Just for this once, I'll team up with you. I don't want to be taken hostage by this fool," Danny told Zach. But Danny wasn't really thinking about teaming up. He just didn't want Zach to suddenly leave him there.

"Well, that was a quick change," Zach commented, jumping forward and going head-to-head with Hosea. They exchanged blows, and started to fight. But Hosea was incredibly strong, even for someone who fought regularly.

"Who do you think you're taking hostage?!" Danny punched him in the mouth, slowed down time, and kicked him backwards. But Hosea still got back up.

"I don't think you two have what it takes!" Hosea tried to shoot again, but Danny slowed down time once more, and ran in to take the gun away from him.

"Are you still going to resist?!" Zach shouted. Hosea picked up the bamboo stick he'd thrown earlier.

"Because you're on my turf, then yeah!" Hosea shouted, going to hit Zach with it. Just then, it occurred to Danny that he could use this situation. Zach was fighting one of the people that he'd allegedly killed. Plus, now

Hosea was disarmed. If Regiment Legion wanted to play the media coverage game, then Danny had just found a way to play right back.

"Just give up already, Hosea!" Zach shouted, kicking Hosea. His wounds were beginning to bleed. But Danny stayed back and began to record the whole interaction. Hosea kept fighting Zach until he suddenly stopped and grabbed his side.

"My… what is this?!" Hosea shouted. He had lost enough blood for his consciousness to start fading.

"Hosea! Just give up!" Zach shouted. But Zach didn't realize that his vision was also fading. Hosea then fell on the ground after losing consciousness, and the concrete he'd fallen on gave him a major head injury.

"That's all I need…" Danny stopped recording.

"HOSEA?! WHAT HAPPENED?! DANNY, CALL AN AMBULANCE!" Zach shouted.

"You do it. I didn't continue beating up a helpless man," Danny shouted at Zach.

"He was a threat to both of us! I just didn't realize that he wasn't like the other one. Now if we can quickly…" Zach started to panic.

"YOU DO IT!" Danny shouted, walking off.

"What the hell, Danny…? Fine," Zach gritted his teeth, and hopped in the ambulance as they got to the scene. But Danny went inside, and Alex was sitting on one of the couches.

"You won't believe this, Alex! I've got video footage of Zach killing one of the guys who was originally believed to have been murdered by me!" Danny gloated, watching the video on his smartphone again.

"Who…?" Alex didn't want to talk. He didn't like what had happened earlier that day.

232

"The Hosea from our timeline wanted to hold us hostage. I guess Zach just went a little overboard on him," Danny showed Alex the video.

"But nowhere in the video does Hosea say anything about being the first to attack…" Alex commented.

"And that's exactly the way I wanted it," Danny grinned. Later that night, Hosea died in the hospital. The head injury he'd taken on had been too severe. Guilt permeated Zach's entire being when he was finally told the news in the hospital waiting room. He didn't even know that Danny had been the one who created the wound that ultimately killed Hosea. Danny's kick had ruptured some internal organs and caused a severe amount of internal bleeding.

Regiment Legion 2: Legionaries

Amar didn't even know that there had been a second chance for Hosea, but felt a weird sadness for some reason. He went to a bar alone that night, just thinking of when he had Destructo and Hosea by his side. He genuinely missed the two, and ended up getting a little more drunk than anticipated. The bartender even asked him about Bobonson. It was a melancholy night all around. He had a huge migraine when he woke up the next morning.

"Uhh… now what…" Amar questioned himself. He woke up in a little cave area. This is where he was living, away from everyone else. He told himself that he had to get stronger, so he spent the day doing push-ups, sit-ups, and even punching trees. The first time he punched a tree, even with his gloves on, it just hurt him. He spent all day working on it, and eventually could make a dent in the tree. He started to realize that the more focus that he put into his punch, the stronger it would become. It was like a source of energy that he could concentrate there. Later that night, Amar found that right over his mountain, there was an easy access way right into Adrenaline Corp. that Regiment Legion could use. He was always in for a little fun, so he went down to civilization and called up Cole. Cole told him that he'd have a few of his soldiers meet him the next morning at Amar's little cave hideout.

"Wake up, doofus," Bobonson smiled. Amar's eyes opened. He saw Zach and Bobonson standing on the rocks above him.

"Sup," Amar grinned as he was getting up to greet them.

"You're living in… a small cave?" Zach asked. Amar turned around to realize exactly what it was he was sleeping in.

"Well… it's a pretty crappy home. I think there's even like… a gopher's nest in there or something. But I have no problems with it currently. I've just been staying out of trouble up here," Amar admitted.

"Why don't you come with us to Regiment Legion? I'm sure we've got a better place to sleep there," Bobonson offered.

"You think you're going to drag me into this corporate crap that easily?" Amar questioned.

"It's not a request to join. You can just come with us to see the place," Zach informed Amar.

"You sure you want to trust me with that? I could be a traitor…" Amar joked around.

"I'm sure the last thing you want to do right now is join Adrenaline Corporation. Especially after that meeting," Bobonson pointed out.

"Fine, fine. I'll go with you two. I just want to see what the Regiment Legion HQ is like," Amar finally gave in. Bobonson and Zach grinned as the three of them took off in another direction, over the mountain and through the grass. They ran for a long time, until they got to an abandoned water tower where Bobonson and Zach stopped.

"This is our entrance," Zach grinned. Amar looked down, wondering what Zach meant. *This freakin' water tower?* Amar thought.

"Uhhh… you don't mean…" Amar pointed to the rusted water tower as Zach and Bobonson smiled at his bewilderment.

"Yup! This is where we enter when it's only a few of us at a time. Come with us," Bobonson went through a small opening in the water tower. Amar, while in shock, just decided to follow him. When they were inside, Amar noticed that the bottom of the tower was metal.

"And here we go!" Zach cheered, pressing a button. Suddenly, the floor started to move. It was like an elevator descending.

"What the…? How do you get large amounts of stuff in here at once if it's just this one lift?" Amar asked as they descended.

"There's another entrance that we barely use. It's for trucks and stuff. The 'empty' warehouse on the other side of this mountain is actually ours as well," Bobonson commented, just as they reached the bottom. It was a huge underground base. It had a giant room of computers, with hallways going either way to other places as well.

"This place is enormous! It's all underground?!" Amar exclaimed, looking at the vastness of the halls.

"Yup. How do you think we stay mostly hidden?" Zach asked, laughing. Amar walked forward, and looking all around, he saw a curtained area off to the right.

"What's over there?" Amar asked, pointing to the curtained area.

"Actually, bedrooms. We have a lot of people in training staying over there. We get a lot of people from the military as well, and since they were living at a military base beforehand, we need to give them a place to live. There's even a cafeteria and such here," Bobonson added.

"Is that back there?" Amar pointed backwards. Behind the elevator that they had just come down, there was mostly just a giant wall beside a closed door.

"Well… actually, no. That's a digging project we're doing. I'd tell you, but usually we'd have to ask Cole or Amber. They're not here right now. They're on military recruitment for the day," Zach explained.

"Oh come on, it couldn't hurt to show him. We've already shown him the base," Bobonson nudged Zach.

"Maybe if he were to join Regiment Legion…" Zach added.

"You know… I think Danny and Alex were out for the day as well," Amar commented, looking around. Zach and Bobonson looked at each other, knowing that this might be a chance for them.

"I *did* need to go back to try and get the source files for their weapons. You know, the other drive I had got destroyed in a…" Zach started to realize that Amar wouldn't be on their side if he mentioned Hosea, so he stopped himself from revealing his name, "…fight I was in."

"Are you saying we should go back?" Amar asked. Zach looked at him, grinning. Without hesitation, they began to run back to Adrenaline Corp. HQ. The other two followed Amar back to his original position at the beginning of the day, and the three of them ran through the wilderness to the back of the Adrenaline Corp. building.

"Aren't the cameras or sensors going to go off if we enter here?" Bobonson asked.

"This is a blind spot," Amar commented, jumping up and vaulting himself over the fence. Zach and Bobonson jumped over as well, following Amar. Just as they were about to reach the building, something unexpected happened.

"STOP RIGHT THERE!" A voice yelled. They looked up. There were two people that ran out from the HQ to defend it. The three from Regiment Legion were shocked by who it was.

"JACK AND MARK?!" Zach exclaimed. Jack was wearing an Adrenaline Corp. uniform, as well as Mark. Jack held a handgun while Mark held a shotgun. Zach and Bobonson both took out handguns as Amar stood behind the two of them.

"What are you two doing here?! Why join Adrenaline Corp. now?" Bobonson asked them.

"Why should I trust either of you? Danny seems like the most trustworthy guy at the moment," Jack put his opinion forward.

"What do you mean the MOST trustworthy?!" Zach sounded betrayed.

"If you *must* know, I was also curious about his plan regarding the weapons he's building. Mark just came with me," Jack retorted.

"I'd never betray you, Jack," Mark grinned, aiming his shotgun. The tension between the two groups was high.

"So what brings you here to the back entrance? Were you going to try and rob us?" Jack asked, smirking.

"*Tch.* It's of no use for us to be here right now," Bobonson spat. Amar walked forward.

"You *do* realize that Danny's most likely gone off of the deep end, right? He seems mentally unstable to me, despite his calm exterior," Amar declared.

"Are you in any position to shout? Mister unarmed and indecisive?" Mark taunted Amar. Amar gritted his teeth.

"All right, then. Then I'll tell you right now that I'm not on your side," Amar growled, turning back and walking back toward the fence.

"Amar? Where are you going?" Zach asked him.

"Let's go back to base. I'm sick of being unable to do anything," Amar said, hopping the fence. Jack lowered his gun, and Mark followed.

"Go ahead. If anything, it's bad publicity for you to be here anyways. You might as well leave now," Jack shooed them. Zach and Bobonson looked at each other, nodded, and then left with Amar. The three of them would soon return to Regiment Legion, after Amar had finally decided where to side himself.

Adrenaline Corporation 2: Call for a Deal

"Why do they continue to play this?" Danny snarled. He was watching the news intently from Adrenaline Corp. HQ. They continued to cover stories of Adrenaline Corporation. None of them were being cast in a good light. Suddenly, Danny felt weird.

Guilt? I don't feel guilt. Danny's brain decided. But a little voice in the back of his mind asked, *Do you ever?*

Danny didn't think twice about this second voice. *Not necessary,* he answered. *How unlike the old you,* the voice commented. Danny sighed, "I thought I had somebody send in the clip of Hosea dying? Oh well… I guess I'll have to do it myself."

"Are you talking to yourself?" Alex asked, walking into the room. It was sunny outside, and it had been a day since Amar and the others had tried to invade the place. Danny and Alex were simply looking at another building with real estate agents. They turned them down.

"It's a good way of forming your own thoughts, Alex," Danny told him, getting up, "Now if you heard what I said, let's get going."

"Sure," Alex responded. They got in the car and left. Danny was weirdly quiet the entire time. The second they got to the new station, Danny barged in, asking nobody for permission. Alex shouted to him, "Danny, wait up!"

"Why do you keep airing negative news about Adrenaline Corp?!" Danny shouted, walking into the studio with two guys sitting at computers.

"Wha-?! Sir who let you in?!" One of them asked.

"The CEO of Adrenaline Corporation let me in. In other words, I let myself in. So why do you keep badmouthing me?! I didn't kill two people. In fact, I had someone send you a video of the one who actually did kill someone," Danny scolded the two.

"Well... I guess we can see your video," The other answered as Alex caught up to Danny.

"Grandpa! What are you doing, barging in here like that?!" Alex seemed annoyed.

"He's your... grandson?" One of the newsmen asked.

"Pay him no attention. He gets delusional sometimes. Here... watch this video," Danny pulled out his phone, showing the two the video of Zach "killing" Hosea as Alex angrily looked off in the other direction.

"Sir, this video is way too dark to really tell what's going on..." One of the newsmen told Danny.

"WHAT?! But you can clearly see... THAT'S ZACH ARTIEN! That on the ground is HOSEA'S BLOOD!" Danny shouted.

"Sir, we're going to have to ask you to leave," A body guard entered the room. Danny put his phone back in his pocket.

"C'mon Alex. Let's get out of here," Danny walked out. Alex angrily followed, not saying a word. The drive back to Adrenaline Corp. was terribly awkward. The two walked back into HQ together.

"JACK AND MARK, COME WITH ME!" Alex shouted at the two of them, who were laughing together on a bench about something.

"It seems like Alex isn't happy," Martin commented, one of Adrenaline Corp's many soldiers. He stood next to Danny.

"Martin, make sure that Alex isn't making them do things unnecessarily out of anger," Danny commanded Martin.

"Y-yes sir!" Martin stuttered, walking outside to go watch Alex. Danny sighed and took out his phone. He had just gotten a text.

This is something you need to build, the voice told Danny. *Why?* Danny's mind asked the voice. *It's in my instinct,* the voice replied. *Instinct? What instinct?* Danny's mind asked. Suddenly, Danny appeared in a land full of rocks. It was a land that had just materialized in his mind. There was a pool of blood in front of him, and the sky was the same color. The pool of blood contained a body torn to shreds in it. *This is what happened when I last ignored those instincts,* the voice told him this as he woke back to his senses in the outside world.

"Okay," Danny simply said aloud, looking down at the text once more. It told him to meet another person outside. He somehow knew that this man would have the parts he needed to build this "thing" that the voice inside of his head told him to. It would protect them, he believed. So Danny went to the man, outside of the building.

"So, do you have enough for this? It wasn't very easy to get my hands on all these metals. What do you plan to do with them, anyways?" The dealer asked. He was a shady guy with a black baseball cap and a half-grown beard. He wore a black coat and owned a smart watch.

"In money, I can guarantee you 75 shares of Adrenaline Corp. stock. I haven't even gone public yet, but it's my plan. Would you want that to appreciate, or would you rather just take the money?" Danny asked the dealer.

"The Hell do you mean *stock*? I just wanted cash. Do you not have enough or something? If so… the deals done. It's going to be at least 75 grand for what you're ordering," The dealer told him.

"Exactly. I figured. I was thinking they'd go for 1000 dollars a share," Danny explained to the dealer.

"But you don't *know* that. I need some capital where I know I won't be scammed," The dealer made his demands.

"Understood. I don't have the cash at the moment, as taking that kind of money out of any bank would be rather suspicious. So give me a few days. In turn, you can have this," Danny told the man, holding up a key on a string.

"The Hell? You want to give me a key?" The dealer asked.

"It's the key to the Adrenaline Corp. basement. Worst comes to worst, you could probably find stuff worth a lot more than 75 grand down there," Danny grinned, putting the key in his hand.

"I'm going to see if this works," The dealer demanded, swiping the key and walking over to the basement door. To his surprise, it actually did unlock. He continued, "I get it. You really do need this, don't you? But why me? Why don't you ask the government?"

"They wouldn't like my ideas. But I know they're for the greater good," Danny told the dealer.

"Got it…" He was almost frightened by how determined Danny was. The dealer pressed a button on his phone as he walked off, which made a drone drop a suitcase. Danny opened the suitcase, and it contained exactly what he needed.

"Mr. Kipper, could you come here for a minute? Alex says that there's something you should see," Martin told Danny. Danny nodded and followed. It was an hour after the deal. They went upstairs to where Jack and Alex were on a computer.

"Danny, you should hear this. It's from when I came in contact with Amar the other day," Jack told Danny.

"What did he say?" Danny asked. Jack responded by turning on the audio clip he had prepared. It was Amar telling them that he had decided to join Regiment Legion.

"So this happened when we were gone," Alex told Danny after the clip finished playing.

"Damn, even Amar? How sad. Soon enough I'm sure even Allison is going to want to go," Danny commented.

"Is everyone coming back soon?" Jack asked.

"Yes. Right after I finish something," Danny said, leaving the room.

"Wait, no comment on Amar or anything?! Aren't you going to say SOMETHING?! We have to fight back and gain their trust, but honestly, it's hard for ME to even trust you!" Alex ran after Danny, shouting at him as Danny picked up the suitcase from earlier.

"Oh? Why is that?" Danny asked. He sounded like a robot.

"You're still keeping a lot from me! I can tell! What's this project you're even trying to complete anyways?!" Alex shouted at Danny.

"It's nothing you need to—" Danny started.

"SEE! You can't even tell me anything and we're FAMILY! I literally came back from a desolate future to SAVE YOUR ASS! You can't even... rely on me a little..." Alex troubled himself getting that all out.

"This is just for business..." Danny started.

"When are you going to stop lying to me? I need to be able to TRUST you! All the people here at Adrenaline Corp. need to be able to trust you! When Harlow gets back, who knows what will even happen?!" Alex continued to yell on the verge of tears.

"JUST GIVE ME TIME!" Danny shouted back at him, silencing the room, "Just give me time..." Alex ran away. Danny walked out the other way with the suitcase. Nothing had been resolved. When Alex ran outside, he saw a man—the man who had just done business with Danny.

"Hey, man. I just tried this key again. It must have been unlocked the first time, or you changed the lock or something. But basically, I just need money quickly. I don't care if it looks suspicious. I can cover it up. Even if we make it a robbery or something," The dealer told Alex.

"So you just made a deal with Mr. Kipper, didn't you?" Alex asked him. He nodded.

"Look man, just let me see the guy. I see that you work here, you just came out of there," The dealer told Alex. Alex let him inside.

"Just wait here for a second," Alex told him. He stayed there for a second while Alex left quickly, but then came back, "He isn't feeling well."

"LOOK MAN! I JUST SAW HIM EARLIER! GIVE ME THE MONEY OR I WILL CALL THE POLICE RIGHT—" The dealer shouted. But he was cut off by the suppressed sound of a bullet.

"How disgusting…" Alex commented. Alex shot him right in the head, and dragged his body off somewhere. He got rid of the security footage as well. For now, not a soul knew.

Adrenaline Corporation 3: Sided Against

"Is that Amar?" Danny asked himself. It was one day later, and he saw Amar up on the hill behind the Adrenaline Corp. HQ. Danny went outside, looking up at where Amar was in the wind. Amar didn't notice him, so Danny shouted, "AMAR! GET DOWN HERE!"

"WHAAAAT?" Amar shouted. He turned around. He could barely hear Danny through all of the wind.

"GET! DOWN!! HERE!!!" Danny shouted to him at the top of his lungs. Amar shrugged and hopped over the fence, running down to where Danny was, right outside the HQ.

"What is it?" Amar asked Danny.

"I heard that even after saying that you'd be independent from all this business, you joined Regiment Legion," Danny poked at Amar.

"What of it?" Amar asked, knowing that Jack would have probably told him about the encounter at that point.

"I'd appreciate it if you stayed away from Adrenaline Corp. property. I see you up in the hills all the time. Even just now," Danny seemed irritated.

"But that's just some little cave that happens to be by Adrenaline Corp! I was just sleeping there for a while!" Amar was a little angered at Danny's provocation.

"But you see, I've purchased the land surrounding the HQ as well, so we can not only expand but kick off people trying to spy—like yourself," Danny spat at Amar.

"Is that how it is? You're really just turning your back on old friends of yours?" Amar questioned angrily. Danny looked away. They both stopped at this tense moment. Danny looked back at Amar, and Amar expected him to be furious or disappointed. However, this was not the case. Amar only got a glimpse of his face before he turned back around. It looked like he was in… pain. Danny just walked back into the building.

"HEY! IS THAT ALL?!" Amar yelled at Danny. He didn't know what to feel besides frustrated—or even almost remorseful. Amar just ignored this, and looked for something at their base. He did feel angry, and wanted just to kick something over to make Danny come back. But instead… he found the Adrenaline Droid. Amar saw a button to turn it on, and did so without knowing the consequences. He left quickly after, and so did the droid, which wandered out into the world without supervision. Danny noticed that the droid was gone shortly after.

"ALEX! WHERE THE HELL DID THE ADRENALINE DROID GO?!" Danny shouted across a hall.

"HUH? Grandpa, I have no idea. Why would I be the first person you ask, anyways?" Alex snarkily responded.

"YOU'RE THE ONLY OTHER PERSON HERE!" Danny shouted at him. Alex was about to lose his cool.

"I heard you shouting at Amar earlier. You think he'd just go quietly?" Alex gritted his teeth. Danny looked confused for a second, and then exhaled.

"You're right. I'm sorry," Danny admitted.

"The last time that robot was on, it tried to escape, looking for parts that didn't exist yet to complete itself. Did you build them recently?" Alex also calmed down.

"No. Its solar recharge function will probably run out before anything else. It'll search endlessly until it stops working at this point," Danny explained.

"So what are we going to do about that?" Alex asked.

"Nothing. We don't need to do anything," Danny affirmed.

"What? Then why did you get so worked up about it? Why was it even out in the first place?" Alex got a little annoyed.

"I was studying it to make my own. Turns out I can't exactly understand how Harlow or Jareus—or whoever built it—made it work. It worked, but when I tried to do the same thing, it didn't work. So I was going to do something else, anyway," Danny explained.

"Speaking of, where is Harlow? Shouldn't he still be around? How come he hasn't been here?" Alex asked, suspicious of Danny.

"I don't really know myself. At first, Harlow told me that he was sick. But just a day or two ago, he told me that he wouldn't be back for a while. There was no explanation this time. Even when I texted him about it, he never responded," Danny told Alex.

"I see. So now what?" Alex asked.

"I was just about to test a prototype weapon outside. That's when I saw the robot missing. I'm just going to get back to that. Wanna come with?" Danny asked, putting on a backpack that was hanging on a peg on the wall.

"I guess I'm not doing anything else," Alex responded. The two continued outside, out to about ten meters away from the little cave Amar was staying in.

"Watch and learn, Alex. This is going to be a spectacle," Danny grinned, taking aim with a gun that looked rather like a grenade launcher, but without any grenades.

"What are you going to do? Shoot Amar's cave and leave dents in the walls?" Alex asked. Right after, Danny pulled the trigger. It had very little recoil, and a micro-sized bullet came out. But on impact, it made an explosion that shaved off some of the walls of rock and caused a fire in the small cave.

"That was a success," Danny grinned.

"WHAT THE HELL WAS THAT?!" Alex questioned Danny.

"It was explosive ammunition. We've made it nearly perfect," Danny grinned, getting the fire extinguisher out of his bag.

"How is that even humane?!" Alex shouted.

"It isn't," Danny started as he went over and started to put out the fires, "This kind of thing was outlawed in battle by the 1868 Saint Petersburg Declaration. But we'll be using it against demons, so it doesn't matter," Alex listened to Danny as he walked with him.

"You're walking a fine line between righteous and illegal," Alex commented.

"I'm fully aware," Danny responded.

A few hours earlier…

"DROP! ONE HUNDRED PUSH-UPS!" Amber shouted. Regiment Legion was doing training drills.

"Gah… uh… yes ma'am!" A soldier shouted as he followed along right next to Amar and Bobonson, who were also doing drills.

"Look alive, Steven. You're training with the big leagues right now," Cole looked down at them, standing next to Amber, "Right by you are Amar and Bobonson. These people participated in the battle against Escarere that only we, Adrenaline Corporation, and the United States Government know of."

"Oh… is that so…?" Steven gasped out as he was doing push-ups.

"Nice to meet ya!" Amar exhaled while also doing the exercises. Soon they would be done with that, and ready for what was to come next.

"Amar, I'm going to take Steven into the field for the first time. Can I trust you with guarding the base?" Cole asked Amar.

"Sure thing," Amar grinned at Cole. Cole gave him a thumbs up, and rushed Steven and Bobonson into the other room.

"Eh… What was that? Cole?" Bobonson questioned, confused.

"The three of us are actually going to do a raid on Adrenaline Corp's base. I just needed to keep it mostly a secret. The only people who know are the people who worked on it, us three, and Amber," Cole started to tell them, but his explanation was missing some vital bits of info.

"Sir... what is 'it?'" Steven asked.

"Oh! Right... Well we've been working on a secret tunnel to the basement of Adrenaline Corp. This'll get us right through. To be honest with you, I'm glad to say I think Danny's forgotten about the Wish Orb. But Jareus hid it somewhere in Adrenaline Corporation, and I can't rest knowing that it's there. We have to at least try and steal it back!" Cole started to explain.

"Oh! So you mean the tunnel is a secret!" Bobonson exclaimed.

"Why keep it a secret from our own men, sir?" Steven asked.

"Who knows if even them speaking amongst themselves will somehow get leaked through an audio file or something. This is our ace against them, we need to keep it secret," Cole grinned.

"Adrenaline Corp. is just down this tunnel? It looks like a mineshaft or something," Bobonson commented.

"No worries. It's structurally sound, so let's head over. Just before this another one of our soldiers told me that it's practically empty now," Cole explained.

"Let's go then!" Steven shouted. The three of them started to run down the tunnel. There was an odd feeling of moisture in the air, as it was a dirt tunnel with only wood flooring and support beams. There were lamps every so often that made the tunnel visible.

"You're *sure* this is safe?" Bobonson asked Cole again, just to reassure himself that the tunnel wouldn't collapse.

"Of course. We wouldn't rush to build a tunnel that'd just collapse. Plus, it has to meet California architectural standards due to earthquakes. So don't worry about it, we're almost there," Cole explained just as they were nearing the end of the tunnel. The Regiment Legion base was not that far from the Adrenaline Corp. base. They saw a steel door at the end of the tunnel.

"Is that… a door?" Steven asked as they ran toward it.

"Well, yeah. But behind that door is a wall. We're going to break through the wall and do whatever investigation we can manage. We'll try our hardest to find the Wish Orb," Cole proclaimed. The three of them reached the door. Cole took a key out of his pocket, and unlocked the door. They stepped through to where the dirt met the wall of the basement. There was a tool left there on the floor—a blowtorch.

"Are we going to use this to get through?" Bobonson asked, picking up the blowtorch.

"You bet. That isn't any regular blow torch. Its heat should be enough to cut through the wall and make a temporary entrance. Now the area we're entering is actually going to be a small hallway, meant for people repairing the air conditioning units. I'm just going to guess that even when we leave, nobody's going to look at that part of the wall," Cole explained.

"Then let's go. We don't have much time," Steven butted in. The other two nodded, and Bobonson got to work opening up a square in the wall with the blowtorch. It was as Cole said, when they pushed through to the other side, they saw a small metallic hall which led downstairs to a door that would enter the basement.

"Alright! It's time to split up and look for the Wish Orb! This will be our test to see if we can successfully go in and out of Adrenaline Corp. HQ without alerting anyone," Cole proclaimed, taking out a gun out of the tunnel they had just gone through. He threw one to

Bobonson and Steven as well, and the three of them split up, looking for the orb. Bobonson spent most of his time looking through the basement. Steven snuck around the first floor while Cole looked into the third floor. While up there, Cole went to the main computer, and found something he wasn't expecting. It looked like an android, but it didn't seem like the robot from earlier.

Cole's phone buzzed, and he looked at it. Bobonson had sent a message saying that he couldn't find anything. Cole, looking back at the screen, saw that the Wish Orb was in the blueprints for the robot without explanation. Suddenly, Cole looked out the window toward the outside of the building. Danny and Alex were on their way back. Cole started to erase the footage of their break-in, and when completed, started to run.

"SIR! I THINK THEY'RE COMING!" Steven shouted to Cole as Cole ran down the stairs.

"Could you find anything?" Cole questioned Steven.

"No... not even a clue," Steven answered.

"I have a weird feeling that it's either specifically hidden... or not even here," Cole told him as they ran back to the basement.

"THEY'RE COMING, BOBONSON!" Steven shouted as the two of them ran to Bobonson in the basement.

"Got it... what a backfire..." Bobonson muttered to himself as the three of them ran back.

"Well... there's some certainly interesting information I found out," Cole mentioned as he welded part of the wall back. The three of them escaped without much of a trace—at least not enough for Danny to notice. Cole saw something quite suspicious, and the test actually ended up proving that they were able to break into

Adrenaline Corp. HQ. But it was quite clear that chemical weaponry wasn't the only thing that Danny was working on. Later, when Amar heard news that Danny was working on something else suspicious, his doubts about whether this was the same Danny he had known only grew.

Adrenaline Corporation 4: Flow of Betrayal

Danny was sitting in his office. It had been a few days since the Regiment Legion break-in that he remained unaware of. There was something else more pressing on his mind. Recently, Adrenaline Corp. had been expanding outside of just the United States. Danny saw that political tension was getting high in the United States, and that the government wasn't always going to agree with his actions. So, he sought to spread Adrenaline Corp. out. There were now Canadian, Italian, Brazilian, Nordic, and Japanese Adrenaline Corp. regional bases. They were small compared to the main one, but they provided good means for shipping and a good backup plan in case they had to escape the United States. But recently, there had been reports of defecting soldiers at the Canadian base. Danny paced back and forth, waiting for the phone to ring. Eventually, he couldn't take the anxiety, so he dialed the number he was thinking of himself.

"Hello… Danny. I was just about to call you as you had asked," A familiar voice told him.

"Yeah… Jill. I was wondering about all these reports of defecting soldiers," Danny told Jill. Jill had quit her job as part of the police to join Adrenaline Corporation, and Danny had put her in charge of the Canadian base.

"We've heard, Danny…" Jill stated in an unempathetic tone, "…I don't know why you weren't the one to tell us… But I don't think I can agree with violating laws in order to increase security. Can't we do that with our regular weaponry?"

"Jill, I don't know if you understand… but the last time we tried to use regular weaponry on a demon, it did close to nothing. Maybe a nuke would work, but nobody wants to use a nuclear bomb on their own country," Danny responded.

"So it really *was* your decision…" Jill trailed off, clenching her teeth, "Look, Danny. I don't really know what to say, other than just telling you how it is up here. I learned from Cole what was happening down there. I was the one to read a text from him aloud, and the news spread like wildfire. I don't think anybody here agrees with what you're doing," Jill put it as it was, and Danny stood cold for a few seconds.

"I see. So you're all defecting," Danny commented. Jill started to respond, but Danny hung up before she could finish her sentence. Danny walked out of his office and said, "Aaron, cut off communication with the northern base. They're a bunch of damn traitors."

"Wha—sir—are you sure?!" Aaron was suddenly surprised. He was just standing guard, as per usual, while all the soldiers were at Adrenaline Corp. HQ. Danny nodded as he resumed heading out. Alex saw him swiftly walking out from a distance, and he ran up to Danny.

"Danny, where are you going?" Alex asked Danny. *Doesn't he usually say 'grandpa?'* Danny thought to himself, but didn't say anything aloud.

"I was given a summons to Washington D.C. the other day. The president wants to speak to me. Something

254

that he doesn't want going over the internet," Danny told Alex.

"Wha—why didn't you say something until now?" Alex questioned.

"I didn't want to alarm anybody, but I gotta go now," Danny told Alex, but Alex grabbed his shoulder.

"At first, I was skeptical. But... I think you know what you're doing. Just don't let anything bad happen to us," Alex told Danny. Danny nodded.

"You don't have to tell me that," Danny commented as he walked outside. But there was another person outside. As Danny looked to the jet waiting for him in the front yard of the Adrenaline Corp. HQ, Amar stood in his way.

"Danny..." Amar started, standing in front of Danny.

"What do you want? Who let him in?" Danny started to question Amar first and then to the guards.

"I just wanted to talk. Especially about why you had that robot out the other day," Amar started. The guards were about to take him away, but Danny put up his hand, motioning that Amar could stay.

"Look, Jareus made that last one. I was studying it so I could make better ones that could actually protect people," Danny started.

"Oh, because that last one turned out so well! First chemical weaponry, and *now* you're trying to make more killer robots. What is *wrong* with you?!" Amar spat.

"Did you just come here to yell at me? I'm just trying to protect people, Amar. You, of all people, should understand the threat of a possible third demon. You should know the amount of casualties that could happen if we're not prepared!" Danny argued back.

"Just because you're in a position of power doesn't mean you get to break laws that have been set. Do you understand that entire *nations* are going to see your private military as a threat?" Amar questioned.

"I don't care, Amar. I'm just being prepared. They wouldn't understand. But you should! You've been through what I've been through and more!" Danny reiterated.

"But wouldn't a war within the world be just as deadly or worse?" Amar still questioned Danny.

"That's why I'm going to meet with world leaders right now, Amar. You wouldn't know, but Regiment Legion only cares about themselves and the people around them. They care about maintaining the status quo. Have you heard any of them talk about the possible threat of a demon? No! They think that's impossible. They think that an apocalypse is impossible. But *you,* Amar, you've seen it with your own eyes! How can you stand such hypocrisy from Cole and the others?" Danny turned the tables on Amar. Amar stood there. He couldn't say anything.

"I... don't know..." Amar stuttered.

"If you came here to convince me to 'cut out the nonsense' and 'return to my old self,' I can't do that. This isn't nonsense, it's adapting to the situation. I know what kind of a world we live in. I shouldn't expect things to just magically go back to normal. Rather, I should adapt to the way things are to maintain our lives. Shouldn't I be doing what I'm doing now?" Danny gave Amar a question to think about.

"I'm... sorry..." Amar whispered.

"What?" Danny leaned in with his hand to his ear, scowling.

"I'M SORRY!" Amar shouted suddenly, "I... I didn't mean to suddenly become your enemy. I got so trapped up at Regiment Legion because... well, you're right. They maintain the status quo. All those smiling faces... It was like I was drawn in by a good sense of nostalgia. But... about this world... you're right." Danny and Amar stood in silence for a second.

"Watch the base for me while I'm gone. Welcome back," Danny smiled, walking past Amar.

"But...! Danny... I don't know if..." Amar was cut off.

"I *do* know. It's okay. Everyone makes mistakes. You're forgiven," Danny shouted back to Amar. He walked forward and got on the plane. Amar watched as the private jet lifted off. Danny was flown from the Adrenaline Corp. HQ in California all the way to Washington DC. The president had summoned him a few days prior. But... he had lied to Amar. He was not going there to have a diplomatic discussion about what he was doing with Adrenaline Corp—he was going to deny any claims they had against him.

"Finally," Danny whispered to himself. He had just landed an hour or so ago, but the president finally had escaped the media to see him. After all, 2016 was an election year. The president had been pretty busy, but he couldn't run for a third term.

"You now may see him," One of the guards by the Oval Office finally let Danny in. The president was currently in the White House.

"Hello, Mr. President," Danny respectfully said as he entered the room. The president wasn't wasting any time.

"Danny Kipper, current CEO of Adrenaline Corporation... the private military company that's threatening this country's security. I've been waiting to meet with you, but I no longer have requests for you. I have issued orders," The president told Danny as he had a seat.

"Orders? Well, let me see them then," Danny didn't deny their existence. The president got papers out from his desk. Danny took them from him and looked at just the first paragraph, but already knew that these orders weren't going to work on him. He stated, "That's odd. Do all of these start with 'in accordance with our partnership?'"

"Yes... why do you ask?" The president wondered.

"Well, you see, I ended Adrenaline Corporation's partnership with the United States Government a few months ago. We no longer needed federal funding. I've convinced not only private investors, but other international security departments to fund the corporation," Danny told the president. He was in shock, nobody had told him this part.

"Continuing plans with the type of weaponry you're making could become an international crime if you're not careful, Mr. Kipper. I'd rather not have that on our hands," The president rebutted.

"I know that. Is that all you had to say? Why invite me all the way here for that?" Danny asked.

"I didn't want this to be publicized. Even if one person had dropped in on this call, it wouldn't have been good. The world knowing that we're at odds wouldn't be good for the already politically-tense atmosphere we're in, with this being an election year," the president explained to Danny.

"You don't want our rivalry being politicized. Got it," Danny acknowledged his concerns.

"But, Mr. Kipper, we still fund Regiment Legion. Regiment Legion is our answer to the demon threat. Don't think that we higher-ups are oblivious of the problem—we just don't think that the precautions you're taking are necessary. To us, it just seems suspicious," the president added.

"So Regiment Legion is still going to be investigating us? That's too bad. They've been up to no good lately," Danny sighed, smiling to himself.

"We have to. If we don't keep you in check, we'll have spies from other countries coming in to do it. They might not know your reasoning behind your actions, but they *will* know the exact moment you decide to use chemical weapons in warfare. Regiment Legion is there to keep an eye on you. It's something I can't avoid," the president told Danny. Danny got up, dismissing himself.

"Well… it's a shame that demons are a real threat as well, Mr. President. I'm just trying to be prepared," Danny smirked. His whole attitude had suddenly changed.

I don't need instructions, Danny thought suddenly as the guards let him through. He headed out to find a place to stay overnight, since it was already dusk there. But right after Danny left, the president made a call to Regiment Legion.

"Hello? Are you there?" The president asked over the phone. It had just been picked up by the other end.

"I didn't expect to be getting a call from the president. What's going on… sir?" Amber Ranatrix asked, suddenly freaked out that she was on the phone with the president.

"Danny is currently in Washington DC. There's not much I can say on call… but the documents just don't apply anymore, apparently," The president told Amber.

"Danny's in DC…? Oh… I get what you mean. Thank you for the information," Amber responded.

"Keep up the good work," He ended the call after saying that. Amber realized the call was over and let out a sigh of relief. She was at the Regiment Legion HQ at the moment, and started to look around for Cole. It turned out that Cole had the day off, so she went to the next person she could think of.

"Bobonson!" Amber got Bobonson's attention while he was speaking to another one of the soldiers, Steven.

"Yeah?" Bobonson turned around to meet her gaze.

"I have a special task for you. You too, Steven," Amber told them.

"What is it?" Bobonson asked.

"I want you two to place a hidden camera inside the Adrenaline Corp. HQ," Amber told them both. At first, they were confused, but Amber told them about the situation. Regiment Legion had been created to be the official response to the demon threat, and to look after Adrenaline Corp. Now that Adrenaline Corp. had left its previous partnership with the United States, things had escalated. Bobonson and Steven were more than willing to accept the mission, and were headed over immediately.

"How are we supposed to get in… Bobonson, sir?" Steven asked as they were off.

"I know of a way," Bobonson told him, and the two of them went through the same tunnel that Regiment

Legion had used in order to sneak into the Adrenaline Corp. building before. The two of them took pistols into the basement just in case, for self defense. Even so, they were in enemy territory. Things would not go well for them if they had to shoot someone.

"Sir... I can hear footsteps!" Steven whispered to Bobonson. The two of them stood back behind a pillar, with Bobonson peering over.

"What the..." Bobonson sweat nervously as he saw a chemical weapon prototype sitting on a desk. Amar was looking at the desk from a distance.

"Oh! Sir, Amar must have beaten us here!" Steven sounded glad to see Amar there.

"Steven...!" Bobonson tried to stop Steven from revealing himself, but it was already too late—Steven dashed out. Amar saw and instantly grabbed the shotgun-looking weapon on the desk.

"No need to worry, sir! Amar! It's just us!" Steven tried to calm Amar down. But Bobonson was already thinking about how Amar hadn't been at their base all day long.

"Us?" Amar asked. Steven had blown Bobonson's cover, so Bobonson came out with the pistol aimed at Amar.

"It hasn't even been that long, Amar," Bobonson scowled.

"Sir! What are you doing?! That's Amar!" Steven shouted at Bobonson, not reading the room. Amar looked pained to see them.

"Look at him. Why would he be here if he hadn't joined Adrenaline Corp? Why would he have run to that gun if he wasn't trying to protect it?" Bobonson was spot on with his guesses.

"You don't know the half of it, Bobonson. I know about Regiment Legion only wanting to protect the reputation of this country. But why does a reputation matter more than human lives, anyways?" Amar gritted his teeth, pointing the gun he held at Bobonson.

"You're really going to just believe that story?! Amar, I trusted you to know better than this! What we're doing has nothing to do with anybody's reputation! It's just that Danny's doing some suspiciously dangerous things…" Bobonson started.

"Suspiciously dangerous?! He's making weapons we can use to defeat any threat that would come our way. We want to adapt to modern threats and keep people's lives safe!" Amar shouted back.

"I've spent six months training to join this regiment, I knew it was right. You're going to tell me you joined Adrenaline Corporation because you think they're protecting people? They've done nothing but shy away from what they once were. After Jareus left, all the soldiers that were usually here dispersed in favor of only a few. Many left because of what's happening, Sir Amar!" Steven pointed his gun up as well.

"Don't you lecture me, you legionary dog," Amar spat at Steven, "To prove it, come have a normal conversation. I'll put down the gun." Amar put down the gun and raised his hands.

"Bobonson, he doesn't seem crazy. Now we're the ones pointing weapons at him. We shouldn't be attacking like this. He's in the right to do that," Steven said, putting down his own weapon. Bobonson, however, didn't.

"Bobonson, you should know that I'm not crazy. Who found you at that bar to bring you here?" Amar questioned.

"Bobonson, he put down the gun. Regardless of what side he's on… he's doing the right thing!" Steven argued.

"He wouldn't let us complete our mission, would he?" Bobonson questioned, still holding up his gun. Amar was getting nervous. He was seriously disarmed.

"Does that matter at this point?!" Steven shouted as Amar got too nervous. Amar broke composure and went to try and grab the gun. Bobonson took no chances, and immediately shot at Amar.

Nothing happened. Amar stood still, his arm now out and his hand in a fist. He opened his hand, and the bullet fell from his palm and onto the ground.

"Wha… what?!" Bobonson shouted, almost angry.

"So it worked," Amar grinned.

"What… did you do…?" Steven was stunned as well.

"I was thinking a lot about how certain powers worked. It seems I've been able to pinpoint an area and focus on it. People with certain abilities can also do stuff like this. I'll call this 'excess energy!'" Amar proclaimed.

"Is he immune to bullets now or something? Maybe we should have been the ones to make more powerful weapons…" Bobonson commented.

"Then don't hold back," Amar played it up as he aimed with the stronger weapon. But he underestimated how quickly they'd continue to shoot. They started to shoot at Amar, but Amar couldn't fire back just yet. Amar also remembered that he wasn't immune to bullets, and implying that he was as a scare tactic was probably a bad idea. He just focused a lot of his power in one area and was able to avoid taking damage. But he needed intense concentration to do so.

"Stop firing or I'll have to fire back!" Amar shouted, not actually planning on firing back. But they did stop firing.

"Just don't interfere anymore, Amar!" Bobonson shouted, but Amar heard footsteps coming up to him. Amar saw a gun, and he shot without even thinking. He watched in shock as Steven crashed to the ground.

"Wha—" Amar couldn't even comprehend what had just happened.

"STEVEN!" Bobonson shouted as Steven started to bleed out.

"JUST GO! JUST TAKE HIM AND LEAVE!" Amar started to scream.

"AMAR... WHAT DID YOU DO?!" Bobonson shouted, pointing his gun at Amar.

"PUT YOUR GUN DOWN NOW!" Amar shouted at Bobonson, pointing his weapon at Bobonson. Bobonson gritted his teeth, doing as Amar said.

"I... just wanted to help..." Steven cried as the air escaped his lungs.

"JUST LEAVE, BOBONSON! Obviously I've gone crazy, right? It's as if I can't feel remorse. I DIDN'T WANT TO KILL ANYBODY! So just take him and LEAVE!" Amar shouted.

"You damn traitor," Bobonson spat, dragging Steven along. Bobonson dropped both of their weapons on the ground as he hoisted Steven's body up. Amar ran back. He didn't even know where they had gone—Amar just wanted to get out of there. But when Bobonson returned to Regiment Legion, Steven was no longer breathing.

Regiment Legion 4: Inability

Steven was given a proper burial the next week. Tensions had been rising between Adrenaline Corp. and Regiment Legion since Danny had visited the president's office, but Steven's death had been attributed to an accident. If they had publicized that Adrenaline Corp. was behind it, the war between the two factions would be cold no longer. Danny scolded Amar for what he did, although realized that it had just been a reaction to having his life threatened. But an old someone they all knew saw the news of Bobonson's involvement in Regiment Legion, since it was reported alongside Steven's death.

"Bobonson… who else would be named Bobonson?" This person smiled. He now knew where to go. He thought that the tensions between Regiment Legion and Adrenaline Corp. were stupid. So he thought that he would fix it himself.

…

"What the heck? Who put this here?" Cole asked as he was opening up the Regiment Legion HQ. Amber was with him and it was in the early morning.

He was talking about a message that simply said "meet me in Jareus's driveway." It was burned into some metal. When Cole and Amber checked the cameras, they saw that a man in a black cloak had broken in and left the message around 3 AM.

"Adrenaline Corp. must be kidding around at this point. First they took one of my soldiers, and now they want me to play along with some stupid game?!" Cole was a little angry, clenching his fist.

"Calm down, Cole. I don't think it was Adrenaline Corp. doing this," Amber tried to mitigate the situation. To find out who exactly had left the message, they decided to just play along with the game. The two of them gave the key to Zach as he came in, and left to go to Jareus's old house. Saskia still lived there occasionally.

"What? What are you two talking about?" Saskia asked when Cole and Amber asked whether she'd seen anyone from Adrenaline Corporation.

"You sure that there's nobody from Adrenaline Corp. here?" Amber asked again.

"Not that I'm aware of..." Saskia told her, yawning. She was still in her pajamas.

"Hey! Why are *you* here?" A voice questioned. Cole and Amber recognized it. They looked to the side and saw Alex, but he wasn't alone.

"Alex?! Amar?! What are *you* two doing here right now?" Cole questioned, reaching for his gun.

"We got a request to come here. It wasn't you in the black cloak, was it?" Alex asked with his hand also on his gun.

"The same thing happened at Regiment Legion HQ. I guess it's a third party's doing," Amber realized. Alex took his hand off of the gun.

"A third party, huh? I wonder why they wanted us all here," Amar pondered.

"Amar... I can't believe you betrayed us the way you did," Cole gritted his teeth.

"He was about to shoot me. What did you expect me to do? He was also on our territory," Amar scoffed.

"HE WAS YOUNGER THAN ALL OF US!" Cole shouted as Amber grabbed his arm to hold him back.

They both stayed silent as Cole calmed himself down. Amar had nothing more to say.

"What... is going on here?" Saskia asked. She had quit Adrenaline Corp. after the fight with Escarere.

"There's... quite a lot going on. It's best not to get involved at this point," Alex said.

"Well, whoever told you to come here clearly isn't here, so you should all go," Saskia slammed the door suddenly. It was a lot for her to take in.

"No, you shouldn't," A voice sounded. Suddenly, the man in the black cloak showed up.

"It's you!" Cole and Alex shouted at the same time. The man jumped off of one of the walls that surrounded the front yard. When he landed, he threw the black cloak off of himself. It was Scar, wearing a red flannel and his iconic hat. This time, he had exoskeleton arms on.

"Scar?!" Amar was surprised.

"I heard you two were fighting—Regiment Legion and Adrenaline Corporation. I need you two to team up again. That way, you can fight me together!" Scar grinned.

"Are you still on about fighting people, Scar?" Alex gritted his teeth.

"Well, honestly... not entirely. I've become more of an assassin in order to live here. I just get an odd sense of nostalgia from you guys, and the two companies' fighting is now interfering with my work. There are people that would pay for me to kill you because they want the fighting to stop. But I'm not going to do that. I just want to stop it as well," Scar explained.

"An assassin, huh?" Amar questioned.

"I don't want to have to beat it into any of you. Especially not you, Amar," Scar looked almost sad.

"So what are you going to do? Just force both of us to stop?" Alex questioned.

"What is at the root of the problem?" Scar suddenly asked.

"They just don't understand! We need to be prepared! Another demon could come any day now. Who cares if we're making more preparations than needed?" Amar shouted immediately.

"They're going as far as to break laws, and they're doing suspicious things to prevent a threat that we already have under control!" Cole argued back.

"Alright! Alright! Stop shouting! It sounds like the root of the problem is what Adrenaline Corp. is doing. Are you sure you need to do... whatever it is you're doing?" Scar tried to sort out the problem as quickly as he could.

"What? Are you kidding? You were able to *see* what Diadem could manipulate. Don't you think we should be extra cautious about anything like that?" Alex argued with Scar.

"We should be. But there are other ways. We don't need to do whatever Adrenaline Corp. is currently doing. I'm sure there are other ways," Scar told Alex. He was acting very out of character.

"WHY ARE YOU DOING THIS, SCAR?!" Amar suddenly shouted. "I don't get it. Why are you coming out of nowhere all of the sudden, wanting us to play nice?"

"It's for completely personal reasons. I used to trust your judgment. But I'm sorry, Amar. Neither you or Regiment Legion are in the right here," Scar said.

"What?! But you just said..." Cole started.

"Cole, you don't need to go as far as constantly investigating and breaking into there. It's just instigating the problem. Did you ever think of formally inviting them out?" Scar asked.

"That would never work!" Amber defended Cole. Scar was getting ticked off, and he suddenly punched both Cole and Amar at the same time.

"OW!" They simultaneously reacted.

"I'm getting so sick of 'yer jabbering! If you wanna do this the old fashioned way, I'll use these exoskeleton arms I stole from Adrenaline Corp. to beat my message into 'ya!" Scar was starting to sound like his old self. They all got into a little skirmish. For a second, Amar, Cole, and Alex went in to try and hit him with a melee attack, while Amber went in to shoot. But they realized they had instinctively started to work together.

"Hey! Back off!" Alex suddenly shouted, shoving Cole.

"Ah ha ha! You guys can't help but want to go back to the way things were! You're just too stubborn! Guess not even I have the ability to break that stubbornness…" Scar laughed, suddenly running off.

"HEY! GET BACK HERE!" Amar shouted as he and Alex ran after Scar. Cole and Amber stayed put.

"Maybe… maybe there's another approach we can try," Cole reflected on what just happened as Alex and Amar lost where Scar went.

"I guess if it's that disruptive, then maybe we'll have to put our pride aside to try and compromise," Amber commented. After that, they all headed back to their bases. Scar wasn't found by either party.

Adrenaline Corporation 5: Northern Rebels

I had to send you guys to Canada. You're my hope to stop the demolition of that base. These are the words Danny had told Jack, Mark, Toshi, Kami, and Devon, along with some other troops. Danny anticipated that they would meet some of their fellow soldiers from training up there, so he needed to motivate them. Of course they would encounter Jill, but also Allison, Odessa, Tanya, and Adam Steel—who were there.

"I don't understand, who exactly are we fighting?" Kami asked as the soldiers from the Sacramento base flew over in a transport helicopter, with others around them. It was four in the morning, and the sun hadn't come up yet.

"We're fighting the northern rebels, Kami. They've tried to burn down the base and actively work with foreign governments against the rest of the corporation," Toshi told her. But Toshi didn't seem happy about it in the slightest—his usual smile was nowhere to be seen. They were all armored in new black and orange bullet-resistant suits, and had newer versions of the exosuit that Jareus made.

"Why are we going to fight our own company, though?! Why are they against us? I just don't know what happened... Where's Harlow when you need him?" Kami questioned.

"Harlow? Harlow Henry? Actually... that's a good question..." Jack muttered more to himself than anybody else.

"I already wasn't a fan of fighting against Regiment Legion. They have a lot of soldiers that used to be on our side. Now our own side is turning against us, and Danny doesn't say much about what's going on. So what *is* the deal?!" Toshi sounded frustrated. They continued to fly near the northern base. As they got close, they started to hear gunfire.

"It seems like they've already started the fight…" Devon remarked, grinning. Mark nodded as he observed the same thing.

"I'll have to get you guys close, but not too close. Otherwise they might shoot us down. Just prepare to jump out," The helicopter pilot told the crew. They all acknowledged him as the helicopter swooped down. It was snowing up at the Canadian base. The sun had still yet to come up, but they were able to see the base from where they were. The Canadian HQ was surrounded by trees to camouflage it—it wasn't around any cities or anything. The base was more of a concrete fortress.

"I wonder why Tanya decided to come here…" Devon remarked to himself, just as they got low enough to land.

"GO, YOU ALL! THIS IS THE FURTHEST I CAN TAKE YOU!" The helicopter pilot suddenly shouted as one of the other helicopters was shot down in front of them.

"What the…" Toshi remarked as the others were jumping out.

"TOSHI!" Kami shouted. He snapped out of it and jumped out as well. They all survived the 40 foot drop with ease—the exo made it seem like nothing. They stood by a forested area, a few hundred feet from the northern base. They saw that soldiers were standing atop the walls on all corners of the base. They were firing EMP bullets first, disabling the other soldiers' exosuits.

"So that's their strategy…" Devon whispered.

"We need to get into that base and retake it. There has to be a side with less coverage," Jack mentioned, getting out his gun. The southern soldiers had all been given an inherent advantage—they had the incendiary rounds that Danny had started to mass produce. More soldiers started to drop from helicopters. Most of them were able to get away safely, but a few helicopters crashed.

"We were supposed to take them by surprise, but it seems they've been too on guard to do that. Apparently, they even took out a round of snipers that were here first. I was listening to our pilot's intercom," Devon explained.

"We should attack the gate going inside then, right?" Mark asked.

"That'd be the plan, but that's the most heavily guarded area. Which makes it hard to pinpoint where to go, since they have this outer wall and an area on the inside before the actual base itself," Jack mentioned.

"The corner..." Kami started.

"What? The corner?" Toshi asked.

"They'd have a harder time aiming at the corners without causing friendly fire..." Kami reluctantly said aloud.

"So we could boost up there, cause chaos at one of the corners, and pierce the initial wall!" Mark exclaimed. Kami nodded, but almost seemed anguished in saying this.

"Yeah... that could work..." Toshi muttered, sharing her pain. Neither of them really wanted to attack other people in Adrenaline Corporation, but that was what they had to do. As more soldiers attacked the outsides and were being shot down, Toshi's squad moved to the forest closest to one of the corners, so they still had cover.

"Alright, so we'll boost up on three?" Devon asked.

"Sounds like a plan to me," Jack grinned. The others nodded, but Toshi and Kami seemed very reluctant to do so.

"Alright… one… two… THREE!" Toshi shouted. They all boosted up onto tree branches and then boosted again, flying up into the air. The people on the corner couldn't react on time, mostly. All of them evaded attack, except for Devon, who was hit by the man on the very corner. But the explosive rounds blew up the area around the corner, creating a weak spot as soldiers wearing dark orange coats flew off of the wall portion that had exploded.

"That worked! Devon… are you alright?!" Jack shouted. Devon's body lay unconscious on the ground. As they all landed, Jack went to feel his pulse, realizing that it was fine, "I'll get you back up!"

"Is he breathing fine? Do we have to get a medic?" Mark asked, half-panicking. But Jack shook his head, taking out a bullet from his wound.

"These… are non-lethal bullets. They just put you under for a while…" Jack shuddered saying those words. They all had a realization that they were using extra-lethal methods of handling the situation while the "rebels" that had "caused the problem" still didn't want to hurt the people that they disagreed with.

"You mean that, besides the helicopter crash, those soldiers on the field were all just unconscious?!" Toshi shouted.

Jack nodded. "I don't even think there were any crash casualties whatsoever. All of us, even the pilot, were able to jump from the helicopter and land just fine. I'm guessing they only shot the helicopters down because they knew the other soldiers would do the same."

"What is Danny making us do?" Kami wondered, staring at her weapon in horror.

"I didn't know we were going to be using explosive rounds either. Why weren't we told beforehand? I thought both sides were just going to be using bullets," Mark explained. Toshi gritted his teeth, looking at the hole in the wall they had just made. Southern Adrenaline Corp. soldiers were pouring into that one weak spot now, and the battle of the outer wall was in the process of being lost by the northern side. The invasion was going as planned.

"Let's take the weapons from these soldiers. I don't want to use incendiary rounds," Toshi declared. Kami, Jack, and Mark agreed with him. But a whole different battle was being fought on the inside now—it was pretty evenly matched.

"ADVANCE!" The four of them heard as they went to the inside of the northern wall. It was Jill. She was wearing a dark blue uniform, standing atop a tank with a whole different kind of exosuit. It was more of a full armor than just a skeletal structure.

"There really are people we know here, huh?" Mark whispered to Jack as a few tanks rolled out.

"So… this is the northern base…" Jack muttered, sweating a little as the real battle started to begin.

…

As this was happening, Danny was busy back at the Sacramento Adrenaline Corp. HQ, but he got a message telling him that the battle was going well.

"The northern wall has been broken into? That's good news, I suppose," Danny said to himself as he was walking down the hallway. He was in one of the upper floors, on his way to meet Alex in one of the rooms.

"Hey Grandpa... why'd you want me to meet you in this room?" Alex asked. They were in a room on one of the top floors that had an MRI scanning machine.

"Alex... your ability. I was thinking of how to reproduce something like that. I don't think anybody's really researched it, so I want to," Danny told him, a blank expression on his face.

"My demon form? Why would you want to do anything with that?" Alex asked.

"Aren't you interested? I want to know what causes it. I wanna know how it works. It may lead to clues as to how my time powers work as well," Danny tried to convince Alex.

"I... I mean, I guess so..." Alex stuttered.

"Good! Good... Alright then. I just need you to get into this chair," Danny ushered Alex into the chair. Alex seemed a little concerned as Danny tightened straps over him, keeping him bound to the chair.

"Okay... so do you want me to transform now?" Alex asked. Danny shook his head.

"No. Not yet. I wanna see if there's a certain something that makes you transform. I want to know how the process works. If we can figure that out first, maybe we can replicate it in other people," Danny explained. Alex was still working up a nervous sweat.

"Oh... okay. Well usually, I just kind of tense up, and my body just sort of does it when I want it to," Alex explained to Danny, but Danny wasn't interested in that.

"Well, Alex. I want to know the science behind it. What's being released as a signal? How does your body form extra parts? That's what I'm interested in. Let's start at where you usually put the most pressure," Danny coerced Alex.

"Oh… okay. Well… I usually start with my wrists, I guess. Those are where I start the transformation," Alex told Danny. Danny came over, hooking up certain wires around his body, in order to monitor his brain waves as well.

"Alright, well, I'm going to use this contraption on your wrists. It's not going to do anything right now, so don't worry about it," Danny told him.

"Oh… okay," Alex gulped as Danny strapped Alex's arms to the back of the chair and locked them in a mechanism behind the chair.

"So… just focus on trying to transform. But don't go all the way," Danny grinned, going over to the computer that was monitoring everything. Alex took a deep breath and focused on his wrists. Danny shouted, "STOP!"

"HUH?!" Alex reacted and he stopped.

"I got it. What is this? It looks like some sort of foreign particle that works its way up to your brain by communicating with many of itself. It activated the sensory cortex of your brain, and the brainstem started to show some activity as well. Could it be that you activate the power, but the rest is taken care of involuntarily?" Danny started to hypothesize to himself.

"Foreign particle? Like a kind of parasite?" Alex asked.

"I mean… I wouldn't personally *say* it's our usual definition of parasite. It's like cells that communicate with each other. But… I have no idea what they are!" Danny proclaimed.

"That's… odd…" Alex pondered what that could mean.

"Okay, Alex! I'm going to try this now! Don't be afraid, there's just a bit of pressure!" Danny cheerfully told Alex.

"A bit of pressure? What do you—" Alex started. He was cut off by the wrist device suddenly clamping down, sending needles into the areas underneath his palms. He felt electric volts coming right into his system and screamed at the top of his lungs as suddenly, he could no longer help it. The demon form started to appear on his body.

"This is perfect! I'm getting all kinds of data now!" Danny said over Alex's tortured screams. He was actively trying to stop his transformation, but he couldn't go back. The machine had him in immense pain as he was forced to exert all his energy.

"WHAT'S GOING ON IN HERE?!" Amar shouted, walking in after hearing all the screaming. Just as he did that, Alex's demon form broke through all the barriers and Alex transformed back to normal, crashing onto the floor.

"Oh, hey Amar. Just running some tests is all," Danny said, perfectly calmly.

"HE… HE…!" Alex started to spit out, while gasping for air on the floor.

"What is all this?" Amar asked, disgusted by what he saw. There were restraints to keep Alex down and what looked like torture devices to him.

"Oh they're just testing equipment. This is only our first test, so don't touch them," Danny warned Amar.

"FIRST?!" Alex sputtered, "HE DID EXPERIMENTS ON ME!" Alex was saying that mainly to Amar.

"Why? Why do you need to do this?!" Amar questioned Danny.

"For my robots. I wanted to see if I could give them the same kind of power that Alex has. There's no way anybody could stop us if that was the case," Danny told Amar nonchalantly.

"Okay… maybe you're going a bit too far with this. Don't you think so?" Amar asked Danny, trying to be nice.

"Amar, you should know. We just need to do what has to be done," Danny responded as Alex got up. Alex looked furious.

"I'm done with this," Alex cried, running out of the room.

"WAIT!" Danny tried to stop him.

"I saw that coming. How could you *not* see that coming? Did you honestly think what you were doing was okay?" Amar asked Danny. Danny stopped for a second.

"Why… Why did I do that?" Danny asked, shaking his head. Danny ran down after him, "ALEX! WAIT! I DIDN'T MEAN TO—" He was cut off.

"I DON'T CARE!" Alex shouted, running out the front door. Danny grabbed his forehead.

"I don't think he's coming back anytime soon," Amar told Danny. Danny started to understand what exactly he had just done. At the same time, Alex bumped into someone as he was running away.

"Alex?" Bobonson asked. He was walking around on the street outside of Adrenaline Corp. HQ at about nine in the morning.

"Bobonson? Why are you here?" Alex asked.

"I needed to take updated photos of the outside of your HQ, to be honest," Bobonson told Alex truthfully.

"Well, screw that place. *My* HQ? I was just tortured there…" Alex told Bobonson.

"Tortured?!" Bobonson exclaimed in shock.

"Yeah. Danny was trying to exploit me for my demon powers somehow. I'm not exactly sure of the full story, but he said it had something to do with robots. So I don't think I can trust him," Alex told Bobonson.

"So… what are you going to do now?" Bobonson asked.

"Well, if you guys don't mind… I'll be your double agent. I don't care if I was on Adrenaline Corp's side. I don't care about agreeing with security measures anymore. I want to expose what happened to me," Alex angrily told Bobonson.

"You sure you're not trying to be the one to spy on us? How do I know that this isn't some ploy?" Bobonson asked. Alex showed him the marks on his wrists. His skin was unmistakably torn up and destroyed.

"Just let me see Cole and Amber. I promise, you guys aren't the ones I'm betraying anymore. I'll go back to Adrenaline Corp. HQ as if nothing happened at the end of the day, and let Danny apologize to me," Alex told Bobonson.

"Oh, alright. I guess I can believe you…" Bobonson agreed, and he took Alex in. Soon, they would go over to Regiment Legion and explain what was going on to Cole. Alex seriously hadn't been lying when he'd said that he was fed up with the way he was being treated at Adrenaline Corporation. Most importantly, however, Alex was going to become Regiment Legion's double agent.

Regiment Legion 5: Double Checkmate

Amber was sitting at a table, eating lunch. It had been an hour or so since Alex came to Regiment Legion. Right after Alex had left, a Regiment Legion spy came in with news regarding a rebellion in the north for Adrenaline Corp.

"Bobonson, sir! I bring news of an internal conflict going on currently in Adrenaline Corp!" The spy rushed into Regiment Legion's cafeteria area.

"An internal conflict? Yeah, I know Alex came in not too long ago…" Bobonson started.

"This has nothing to do with Alex, sir," The spy informed him.

"There's another thing? I want to hear this…" Amber added, going over to where Bobonson was after she'd finished up her lunch. The spy explained to them that they'd gotten information about the rebellion at another Adrenaline Corp. base, which was up in Canada. But "a rebellion" was only how Donny was labeling it—the base simply hadn't been following orders to create weapons. Danny had sent in troops to put someone new in power.

"So now Adrenaline Corp. can't help but fight amongst itself…" Amber commented, after hearing the story.

"It seems more and more people are trying to jump ship. Even Alex can't take it anymore. What does Danny exactly have in mind?" Bobonson questioned aloud.

"I wonder if this has to do with the experimental weaponry that the main base was trying to introduce. We've known for a while that there were new bases and that Danny was expanding… but the thought that one of them might defect hadn't been in our plans," Amber thought aloud.

"I think this'd increase our chance of at least stopping Danny's plans tenfold. One wrong move and we can get the Supreme Court involved," Bobonson grinned.

"That's all the news I have for today," The spy saluted and left the room. Bobonson sighed and thought about what to do next.

"So, what do you think you'll do once this whole mess is over? You were better friends with all those people from Adrenaline Corporation, right?" Amber asked Bobonson.

"Yeah… well… Amar was kinda the one that found me after some years of confusion in my life. It may have been dangerous, but I believe he did show me the right way. I just don't know why he suddenly turned…" Bobonson explained to Amber.

"Well… I'll always be here if you need someone. I know it isn't much, but I can tell you're kind of at a loss when it comes to the people you can trust. You just told me basically that the one person you trusted the most turned out to be untrustworthy, right? I… I can understand that. My sister used to be part of Adrenaline Corporation, but even after quitting, she hasn't given up hope on Danny. She doesn't even want to come see her own sister…" Amber revealed to Bobonson.

"Really, huh? I never had any siblings… but that does sound rough," Bobonson admitted, "I'm glad you came to talk to me, though. In these times, it's hard to just sit back and have a breather every now and then. It's like our world has gone into hyperspeed mode."

"That's definitely true. When all of this is over, maybe we can go get dinner or something," Amber offered, just in time for Cole to come running up the stairs.

"I'M HERE WITH OUR NEXT OBJECTIVE!" Cole shouted as he reached the top of the stairs.

"Oh, really? What is it?" Amber asked, almost disappointed that he had cut Bobonson off.

"We're going to find the footage of when Alex was being tortured! It'll be something we can use against Adrenaline Corporation, and it's footage that Alex personally wants to release!" Cole spoke in a cheery attitude.

"That... well that does make sense," Bobonson added. The three of them discussed it a bit more in detail, and it was decided that Bobonson and Amber would be the ones to infiltrate once more to try to find this footage.

"Alright, let's head out!" Amber proclaimed as she and Bobonson went down the secret tunnel once more. The fact that Adrenaline Corp. hadn't found it was nothing short of a miracle.

"What's the best course of action, do you think?" Bobonson asked as they were just about to go into the basement once more.

"I don't know, honestly. Let's look around when we get inside," Amber told him. They slowly peeled off the fake wall once more and went inside, and were met with nothing but shock as they saw Alex there, waiting for them. Bobonson almost screamed.

"Good thing you came now! Danny isn't up in that room and I can take you there now. However, I'm not the best at figuring out where to get that footage," Alex nervously whispered.

"I can do that. But also, how did you know we'd be here?" Amber asked.

"Well… I actually found out where the secret passage was earlier. I was going to show Danny, honestly. But after what he did to me, I made it a secret he'd never find with me still here," Alex gave the thumbs up. The three of them steadily made their way to the upper floors of the building, being sure to try and stay out of the sights of any security cameras.

"This is the room that has the computer with the footage on it, right?" Bobonson asked as they approached the room.

"That it is. I won't ask how you know that… I'll just go distract Danny while you two get the footage," Alex told Amber and Bobonson. They gave him the thumbs up as they walked in. But as Amber opened the door, she saw the person she least wanted to see: Amar.

"Ehhh, ha ha… hi," Amber nervously grinned.

"You're here for that footage, aren't you?!" Amar gritted his teeth. He closed his eyes and exhaled, "Well… It was pretty messed up for Danny to do that," Amar just walked forward, pretending like he didn't see anything, "But this doesn't mean I'm helping you. I just want Alex to have some sort of justice for what he went through." Bobonson and Amber almost stood in shock as even Amar didn't do anything about them. After that, the rest was history—they got the footage and escaped. Alex covered their tracks, and a day later, Danny was watching the footage on his television, gritting his teeth.

"So they got that footage, huh? I wonder if this is Alex's doing… But it doesn't matter. It isn't enough to be incriminating evidence," Danny commented, watching it on the television. It was from an odd angle, and when

Alex powered up into demon form, it was cut off. Back at Regiment Legion, Cole had called the company lawyer over to see if it was enough evidence.

"Sorry… but this video isn't enough evidence on its own. It isn't exactly the most high-quality recording—it could have been edited. Plus, it just suddenly cuts off without reason. I think you should gather further evidence before we go forward with any legal action," The lawyer explained to Cole.

"Alright. I understand that much. I didn't know the security camera in this room would be so poorly positioned," Cole admitted.

"Also, did you go in with a search warrant?" The lawyer asked.

"We have a contract with the United States Government which was endorsed by the United Nations, allowing us to investigate Adrenaline Corporation," Cole mentioned.

"I see…" The lawyer nervously smiled.

"I'll have more evidence later. Let's just postpone it for now," Cole told the lawyer, and as he left, Amber walked into the room.

"Any luck with the footage?" Amber asked. Cole shook his head.

"It isn't enough. It's a little too sketchy to take everything from that clip at face value, honestly," Cole ended up agreeing with the lawyer.

"So what if I went and stole the mechanism that Alex had to wear in the clip? Couldn't I prove that it was a torture device? We could get Alex to come and say that was what happened to him as well," Amber suggested.

"Actually… that's exactly right!" Cole cheered as he walked down the stairs with Amber.

"I can actually call Alex and go over right now, then. I'm sure he'd be willing to get it to me," Amber agreed.

"That'd be sweet," Cole gave her the signal to go, so she went up the stairs to find cellular reception. But she tried to call Alex where she had service, and he wasn't picking up. So she went back down, only to find that Cole had disappeared.

"Cole? Cole, where'd you go all of the sudden..." Amber looked around the hallway, and trailed off after she found a previously-hidden door that had been left open, "Cole?" She asked as she poked her head in.

"Oh, Amber!" Cole shoved something in a drawer.

"What is this room?" Amber asked in surprise. She noticed it looked like the back room in a pharmacy—there were medicine cabinets all over the place, "Are you hiding something?"

"This is just an experimental room, Amber. I just need a place I can go and take a break," Cole couldn't explain what it was. Amber saw his hand in a fist. She grabbed his hand and forced whatever he was holding out of his hand.

"What is this?" She asked, looking at a small white tablet.

"Hey!" Cole shouted.

"This looks like something you would swallow. Like some sort of pill," Amber said.

"It's not ready! Sure, I was experimenting with what could be done, but that's a prototype. Do not under any circumstances swallow that!" Cole shouted at her.

"I'll figure this out later," Amber scowled at Cole, walking out of the place. She decided not to go to the secret tunnel, but instead, she had a new idea. Amber went to the front of the Adrenaline Corp. HQ with the weird drug that Cole had made.

Danny saw Amber in the security cameras as she just stood waiting for someone. The gates opened as Danny walked out.

"What do you want? Is this some sort of request for Alex? Why are you standing here as if you're waiting?" Danny asked.

"I have something Cole made. I thought maybe you'd want to check it out, since he was keeping it a secret from even me," Amber glared at Danny.

"Hmm... well... I guess you can give it to me," Danny tried to take it from her but she put her hands behind her back.

"I'll come in and bring it to be analyzed. I want to see what it's supposed to do as well," Amber demanded.

"*Tch*, fine. Follow me," Danny rolled his eyes. She followed Danny inside. The two of them went past the room that Alex's torture had taken place inside of. A few rooms down was a room with a machine that'd help them figure out exactly what the drug would do.

"So this is the place?" Amber asked as the two of them walked in. Danny nodded, turning on the computer.

"So what's this with Alex's torture? Why'd you guys interfere and call it something it wasn't? Alex volunteered for that, you know," Danny argued with her.

"I wasn't really involved with that..." Amber fibbed right back as Danny put the drug into the machine and looked at the computer.

"Uh huh. I *see*," Danny rolled his eyes. But just then, something on the computer caught his eye. It was essentially simulating how the drug would affect the human brain and body.

"Uh… what does that mean?" Amber pointed to a lot of red displayed on the computer's graphic of the human body.

"This… well… from what I can tell right now, this is supposed to be a steroid that'll bulk up muscle mass entirely. It'd probably weaken you entirely after the effects are over, but this could make a 'natural' super soldier in a way," Danny explained.

"I… see. I'm going to go speak to Cole about this, if you don't mind," Amber got up, clearly pissed.

"Uh… go ahead," Danny didn't know what else to say to her. Amber ran out, but as she did so, she rushed into the room where Alex had been tortured and grabbed the device that Danny had put on Alex's wrists. She ran out of the headquarters and back to Regiment Legion. Danny, none the wiser, knew he finally had a checkmate for winning over Regiment Legion.

"I guess I'll call him up," Danny grinned as he picked up his phone and gave Cole a call.

"What is it? You haven't called me since before the Escarere incident," Cole spat. He didn't sound happy.

"I know about your drug, Cole. This whole back-and-forth we've been going on, is coming to an end. It's only fair that I get to expose you now," Danny gave his ultimatum.

"That's too bad for you, Danny. You were close to getting me, but I started to realize that maybe that *really* wasn't the best idea. Amber forced me to destroy the rest of the prototypes when she returned to HQ. But she also brought that device you used on Alex. I know you wouldn't want me to reveal this, so I'll make it simple. Neither of us will reveal these things we've found out. There's no time I ever actually used that drug on anyone, either—but as a deal, I won't say anything further," Cole monologues to Danny.

"*Tch*, who would have thought it'd come to this? This isn't over," Danny remarked to Cole as he hung up and threw the phone on the ground. He exhaled, frustrated.

"They won't stop attacking. I have to win overwhelmingly, or leave this country…" Danny said to himself.

Adrenaline Corporation 6: Forcing the Past

"CONTINUE TO ADVANCE! DON'T LET UP!" Jill shouted, still amidst the battle of the Northern Rebellion.

"You got it!" Odessa shouted, boosting straight up. The fight had been going on for a while now. Most of the northern soldiers had been defeated, but a strong few were still standing. Odessa was one of the best soldiers that the north had.

"AH!" Allison yelped as incendiary rounds blew up a wall that she was near. She was in full battle gear, but she couldn't take it anymore. She didn't want to shoot other people, and stood timidly in a hallway inside of the northern base. Allison was sick of it. Danny had drafted her out to the northern base, and when she had asked Danny if she could leave, he'd said that it wouldn't be for the best. She started to question if she had remained loyal to Jareus's dream, and it haunted her on the inside.

"I'm sick of this! I'm getting out of here!" Allison shouted, running down the hall. She jumped onto one of the ATVs in their garage, hotwired it, and flew right out of the garage.

"There one goes!" The southern Adrenaline Corp. soldiers shouted as Allison flew right by them. They shot in her direction, but it wasn't worth it for them to turn around, since the northern soldiers continued to shoot at them. Allison flew out the back gates, and drove off far from the invasion.

"Don't shoot at that one! It isn't worth it! Just let her go!" One of the other southern soldiers yelled at them, but it was too late.

"DON'T UNDERESTIMATE US!" Tanya shouted, already shooting the other few. She was standing back as a sniper.

"Tanya?!" Devon yelled. He was still on the battlefield and had heard her shout. "Tanya… why don't you just come back with us?" Another sniper shot whizzed by him as he managed to just barely duck in time.

"No thank you, horse face," Tanya grinned, "You're the ones attacking us! We've actively tried to not kill your side by using nonlethal ammunition. What does your side do? Use EXTRA lethal ammunition! Do you not see what your actions are screaming?"

"Eh?" Devon started to think about it, but was hit by another one of the non-lethal sniper shots.

"Have a good rest, horse face. Hang in there," Tanya whispered to herself, reloading. She took cover behind a barrier. Just as she hid back, Adam Steel rushed to the battlefield, dodging around bullets.

"Utter foolishness. A company fighting amongst itself?" Adam whispered to himself disapprovingly as he took out a laser rifle. He aimed down sights, hitting a few of the southern soldiers before they found his position. With his exo, he boosted out of the way.

"JUST STOP FIGHTING, NORTHERN REBELS!" Toshi shouted like he was in pain, boosting onto the scene and kicking two soldiers out of the way. As bullets were shot at him, he put up his arms with the exo on to guard his face. Another soldier boosted forward to try and stop Toshi, but Kami suddenly protected him, shooting that soldier down.

"They're not letting up, Toshi," Kami warned.

"STOP RIGHT THERE!" Jill shouted. Her voice came from inside a tank that was moving steadily toward Toshi and Kami, "If you want to resort to true violence and explosive power, we can do that too! I just never really wanted to. But if you move a muscle, you're done for."

"Hey... your name's Jill, right?" Toshi asked, putting his arms up and sounding concerned, "I heard about you from Jareus back in the day! From what he said you certainly sounded nice—"

"I'm not going to suddenly pity you. What are you even trying to convince me of? Jareus is dead. *You guys* are the ones killing my soldiers," Jill shouted to Toshi.

"Fire on the tank!" Other southern soldiers started to yell.

"HOLD YOUR FIRE!" Kami shouted, standing right next to Toshi.

"Oh? This is sure to be interesting..." Jill spoke to herself.

...

"I've just received news that we're almost done with putting down the Northern Rebellion!" Aaron told Danny, back at the Sacramento HQ, bursting into his office.

"Eh? That sounds great… but…" Danny started to tell Aaron. Aaron noticed a glass of rum poured on his desk. It was half-finished.

"But what, sir?" Aaron asked.

"What Northern Rebellion?" Danny asked, entirely serious. Aaron stared at him for a moment.

"Ha-ha. You're funny, sir," Aaron told him, closing the door. But Danny held it open.

"If there's some fighting going on or something, just call it off. I want to see some people," Danny told Aaron. Aaron looked at Danny in shock, as if he didn't know what was happening.

…

"Why do we have to fight like this?" Kami asked, back at the Canadian base.

"I don't know. You were the ones to start it, just leave already," Jill gritted her teeth.

"We were entrusted with putting some new leader in, but I think you could just come back to us, Jill!" Toshi shouted. Jack and Mark even stood up in the distance, revealing themselves. Everything came to a stop.

"Do you even know what Danny is doing? Regiment Legion had to inform me…" Jill told them.

"Oh come on. Those lying spies told you *what* exactly?" One of the southern soldiers from the crowd asked.

"They aren't liars! The fact that you're using the things they spoke of today is undeniable evidence that Adrenaline Corp. is building illegal weaponry. Not only that, but it seems as if Danny's hiding something. Harlow hasn't been back for months now!" Jill shouted. The other soldiers were suddenly stunned, and they looked down at their hands. The very weapons they were holding were proof enough to her claims.

"There's nothing we can do now...!" One of the southern soldiers yelled out, not knowing what to do.

"YES THERE IS! You can all join us! We don't need to listen to anybody in power if they're blatantly wrong," Jill got on top of the tank, staring down at everybody stopped in the middle of the battle, "Are you going to fight for yourself? Or are you going to fight for someone else?" Jill questioned the soldiers, "You all could stand up for yourselves right now if you're against the idea of our leader becoming a tyrant!" Everyone stood as still as the freezing air—until one man moved. One of the southern soldiers threw his gun on the ground.

"I'M THROUGH JUST FOLLOWING ORDERS!" Another southern soldier shouted, throwing her gun on the ground. The northern soldiers started to relax a bit. They continued to stare at the brave soldier, as if expecting a statement of some sort, only to witness an incendiary bullet fly into her chest. Screams of horror erupted from the crowd as she was blown to bits.

"WHAT?!" Odessa, amidst the battlefield, shouted. She turned around to search for where the shot had come from. The perpetrator didn't even try to hide himself. He stood on top of a rock, his rifle still aimed at his victim. He wasn't even a northern soldier—his victim had been the target of friendly fire.

"Traitors are traitors," He projected, reloading. At this point, everyone started to panic, rapidly looking around and wondering who was on what side.

"CALM DOWN! We will prevail—" Jill started to shout as another person in her tank let out a gasp.

"GET OUT OF HERE, JILL!" A soldier inside the tank shouted. She looked down suddenly, just to see another explosion go off. One of the southern soldiers had stuck an explosive to the bottom of the tank, and it hadn't gone off until then. Jill's body was thrown into the sky, for those all around her to see. The exo wouldn't be enough to protect her from this explosion.

What the hell, Jareus? She thought, looking into the sky as her body was launched in what felt like slow motion, *Why did you have to leave so early? If only you were here to stop this...* Tears came to her eyes. She knew what was coming. After that, the pain wouldn't last long. *The rest is up to you, northern soldiers. I'm coming to see you soon... mom... and dad.*

The explosion faded, and the charred body that was thrown into the sky came down with a bang. Everyone stopped and acknowledged what just happened. The one who had stuck the bomb saw everyone staring in shock, and started to sprint away from behind the tank. He was suddenly shot, and he too exploded into bits. Jack took his rifle out of aim and returned it to the sling on his back.

"Our side would do such a thing? What... what scum..." Jack grit his teeth and tensed up his face, walking toward the tank that had burst in flames. "THE FIGHT HERE IS FINISHED! We're going to tell Danny that everything went according to plan, but that we're going to stay here. You all got it?! Those of you still wanting to fight on his side, GET OUT OF HERE!" He shouted in anguish

"Jack..." Odessa wanted to smile at him, but she couldn't bring herself to do so. She was still in shock about Jill's fate.

"I SAID GET *OUT* OF HERE!" Jack screamed. Only a handful of soldiers began to try and boost their way out of there. Jack continued, "Mark, you know what to do."

Mark nodded, jumping on top of the outer wall. Tanya suddenly jumped up there as well. The two nodded to each other, and used tranquilizers to snipe the handful of soldiers.

"We'll have to keep them from spilling the truth for a bit..." Mark commented. As the rest of the base started to organize, Toshi suddenly got a text message that confused him.

"Odessa!" Toshi called out.

"Toshi?! I didn't even know that you were here... I'm glad you're here to join us, though," Odessa greeted Toshi.

"Something weird just happened, Odessa. I sent a message saying that everything was going well at the northern base, and that the soldiers were going to just stay there for the time being. Suddenly, one of Danny's men messaged me back saying to just call off the invasion," Toshi explained to Odessa.

"WHAT?!" Odessa was just as confused, and the two of them pondered the point of all the meaningless bloodshed then. So many of their former teammates were either dead or fatally wounded. The entire base was converted into an emergency hospital, and medics from both sides were now working to revive as many as they could.

"I... I don't know either. We should talk about what to do next with everyone after they recover," Toshi told Odessa. She nodded and the two of them headed into the base.

...

"Who's standing out there?" Amar asked himself, reading a magazine as Danny was working on a robot back at the Sacramento HQ. "Hey, Danny. Someone's outside."

"I can't be bothered right now. This is crucial," Danny told Amar. Amar rolled his eyes and got up. He decided to go outside himself.

"Fine. I'll go look," Amar told Danny, heading out. There was a girl he recognized out front, but he only started to remember who she was when he'd gotten close to her.

"You're Amar... right?" Lexus asked. She had been waiting outside with what looked like a picnic basket.

"Is Danny there? I've been worried about him... I don't know if he's doing well or not. He seems to be so busy all the time, and he never calls or texts me," Lexus admitted to Amar.

"Eh? Danny... well... he's busy, yeah," Amar told her.

"But couldn't he just come out for one moment?" Lexus begged Amar. He remembered what Danny had said about this moment being crucial, so Amar simply chose to do what he thought he'd been told.

"He can't right now," Amar told Lexus.

"But... It's been forever since I've seen him. I brought this basket and everything..." Lexus complained.

"Did you not understand me?" Amar was getting annoyed.

"Just go and ask him..." Lexus started to beg.

"NO MEANS NO! I already did, jeez. Maybe some other time," Amar shouted at her, making her feel horrible. He turned his back on her and went back inside.

"Ah shoot," Danny complained to himself as Amar came back inside, slamming the door behind him.

"What is it?" Amar asked Danny.

"If I could just get this one robot to work perfectly, I could make a ton of them," Danny griped. "There's just one piece that won't work as expected."

"A single piece? What's wrong with it?" Amar asked.

"Oh, there's nothing wrong with it. I just can't remember how to make it work right now. For some reason, my memory on certain things has been in and out," Danny complained to Amar. Amar noticed there was a glass of rum on the table next to Danny.

"Maybe that's why you can't remember," Amar pointed to the glass. Danny looked down at it.

"But I haven't had that much. My motor skills aren't impeded at all. But now that you mention it, whenever I *do* drink, I end up not remembering certain things and wondering why I even *did* some things," Danny mentioned.

"Well, whatever. What is this part anyways?" Amar asked.

"I can't remember the specifics right now, but it's called a cybercore. It's an invention that's essentially the brain of a robot, which functions to help it work independently. It should help power it too, I think. But honestly, I can't figure out how these work—or even how they even keep getting shipped from our base in Norway. I think I'm just going to use a conventional computer, or a dummy cybercore," Danny told Amar. Amar nodded, pretending to know what he meant. Just as Danny turned back to the robot, the two of them heard an explosion coming from the back of the headquarters.

"What was that?!" Amar questioned.

"I don't know either. Let's go investigate. I'll finish this in just a second," Danny told Amar. The two of them geared up.

"This is what wearing an exosuit feels like? This is weird," Amar commented. He wasn't used to the feeling.

"Yeah. It's for safety. I don't care if you've figured out that 'excess energy' or whatever. I'm trying to work on it as well, but the exos are probably still superior," Danny told Amar as they ran to the back door.

"We'll see," Amar grinned as the two of them burst out of the double doors, only to see a delivery truck blown onto its side. There was a gang of four thieves that were trying to load their Jeep with the goods inside.

"Oh shoot! They're here!" One of the thieves yelled. The others prepared to fight.

"Say, let's take these guys out and make it… like old times, why don't we?" Danny asked Amar. He smiled.

"Yeah… like old times," Amar responded. He put his first foot forward and suddenly launched into the air, shouting as he did so.

"You don't know how to use an exo, do you?" Danny asked, shaking his head as one of the thieves laughed and tried to shoot at Amar. Amar was able to grab another bullet.

"I'll figure it out!" Amar shouted. Danny grinned, boosting forward and kicking one of the guys in the face.

"AH! HERE THEY COME!" Another one of the thieves yelled. Amar finally dropped to the ground, and the others continued to shoot at him. He dodged left, right, and ducked as he ran forward. The guy turned his back for just a second, but Amar kicked his back when he did so. The impact was enough to make him pass out.

Meanwhile, Danny boosted straight up, shooting a grapple onto one of the guys. He started to swing his body around like a sort of deranged lasso.

"AHHH!" The guy shouted as the grapple attached to his belt barely held on. Suddenly, he whipped something expected out of his coat. "TAKE THIS!"

"What the...?" Danny hadn't seen it coming, but suddenly he was hit by an electric whip that the guy had taken out, making the exosuit fall off of him and giving Danny a shock. They both fell to the ground as Amar had taken care of the third thief.

"Oh no you don't!" Amar dodged the fourth thief, landing on the ground and trying to whip him. Amar boosted forward, but still didn't have a concept of how to work the exo, so he boosted right past him.

"Heh!" The thief grinned, whipping Amar as he flew by. The whip latched on and electrocuted Amar.

"AHHH!" He shouted as an electric current ran through him. He tore the whip off of him by sending his 'excess energy' to his hands, and tried his best to tough it out and stand up. "Is that all you got?" Amar grinned. Suddenly, Danny came back out of nowhere and took care of the other guy, knocking him out instantly.

"Alright, that's that," Danny patted his hands, getting dust off of them. "Let's escort them to the police. I don't have time for this." Amar noticed Danny's whole attitude had suddenly changed after he'd come out of the shock.

"Yeah... I guess you're right," Amar commented, going back inside. Amar told the story to Martin, and Martin and Aaron called the police. They dropped off the four thieves at the station, and on the way back, Martin started to speak to Aaron.

"It's a little weird how Danny's been acting lately, isn't it?" He asked.

"Hmm… I know what you mean," Aaron agreed.

"Like… it's a little weird how the attack on the Canadian base was suddenly called off in the middle of it, and now we haven't heard anything from them. But Danny just doesn't seem to care anymore," Martin explained.

"Yeah, who would have thought that random kid in Rownert would have a friend that'd suddenly take over entirely. I haven't even seen Harlow this entire time," Aaron added.

"Yeah… I'm concerned about that too…" Martin told Aaron nervously. But they were just about back at the base. The two of them went their separate ways, as Aaron had some errands to run. Martin waved goodbye, but decided he wanted to explore. He was curious about some of the things Danny was doing—especially in one of the other compartments in the basement. So Martin looked around, and initially saw nothing but computers. But as he went into another door, he started to hear noises.

"Huh? What's going on here…" Martin said to himself. There was a portion of the wall that seemed like he could just push through it. Martin pushed through it to a secret room and…

"MMMPH!" Harlow tried to shout through the muffle on his mouth. He was tied to a chair in this secret room.

"Harlow… Henry…?" Martin's eyes widened in shock. Suddenly, a cold arm grabbed Martin's neck.

"You just *had* to go poking your nose where you shouldn't, didn't you?" Danny asked.

Regiment Legion 6: Making a Pact

"So what have you been up to these past months? What is it, like, the end of March already?" Zach asked Saskia as the two of them hung out for the first time in a while. Zach had come to Jareus's old house to talk. They were in the kitchen.

"Well, I was just trying not to get involved. I left right before you started the flood of people that joined Regiment Legion. I just felt it wasn't the same with Harlow being gone all the time, and Jareus wasn't there either," Saskia told Zach, holding a mug full of tea. She took a sip.

"Well, we've essentially been in a cold war, each trying to get enough dirt on the other to shut them down. But some of it we couldn't even use, because both parties had a checkmate against each other. Honestly, at this point, it feels like a war between Danny and Cole," Zach explained to Saskia, having some tea himself.

"What's making it an official thing, though?" Saskia was curious.

"Essentially, Danny wants to be more secure than ever. He's paranoid enough to go above and beyond what's necessary to make sure that everyone's safe from demons, but he doesn't realize the harm he's creating. Admittedly, our argument that "we can be enough without illegal measures," isn't our strongest bet. But now, we need to investigate them because if Adrenaline Corp's actions get out of hand, there will be… an *international* response," Zach continued to explain.

"Got it… so what's so complicated about it? Couldn't you just take down Adrenaline Corporation?" Saskia asked.

"They're on a thin line, but everything we can expose right now—their lawyers would make it seem *technically* legal. They're obviously hiding a lot, and that's our task," Zach finished. She nodded, understanding the situation. Just then, the doorbell rang.

"Who would be here…?" Saskia questioned, but got up to go get it anyway.

"Hey…" It was Allison at the door, still wearing the battle gear from the Northern Rebellion.

"Allison?!" Saskia blurted out, which made Zach come to the door as well.

"It really is Allison!" Zach shouted. But Allison started to slip, and it looked like she was about to collapse. Saskia held out her arms to catch her.

"I think… she just passed out," Saskia told Zach, holding up her unconscious body. After about ten minutes, Allison woke up again on the couch they had put her on.

"Wha…" She started.

"Allison! What the heck is going on?!" Saskia already was in her face. She took a moment to look around.

"I finally got out of there… I'll tell you what's going on in just a second. Let me actually get up," She told the two of them. After sitting upright, she told Zach and Saskia the details of the battle in Canada.

"…I just escaped. I went to the nearest city, got a plane, and then used a rideshare app to get a car to take me here. I couldn't take it anymore. I only joined because of Jareus, and now that it's come to this…" Allison sputtered out, on the verge of tears.

"Things with Danny and Cole have gotten too out of hand…" Saskia commented to herself.

"Especially with Danny! What the heck was he thinking, launching an attack on his own base?! I have to do something about this…" Zach gritted his teeth in anger. He grabbed his stuff, got up, and started to walk away.

"What are you going to do?" Allison asked.

"I started this whole split between Regiment Legion and Adrenaline Corp, and I'll be the one to end it. I have a plan, though, so don't you two worry about it," Zach gave the thumbs up as he left. But much as Zach was nervous about it, he was angry enough to do it now. On the car ride back to Regiment Legion HQ, Zach called Alex.

"Hello? What's going on?" Alex answered, already sounding concerned.

"Alex, I have a plan. I think that if all of us were to make a peace treaty in which we agreed to just work together to defeat any demonic threats, but also disband the illegal weaponry, then maybe Danny would finally crack. But Amar is really the tipping point here. I'll go in the wilderness with Bobonson outside of Adrenaline Corp. HQ, and you take Amar out there. We'll bring him back to Regiment Legion HQ," Zach explained his plan to Alex.

"Zach… do you really just expect this to work all of the sudden?!" Alex questioned Zach.

"Look, I know it's a shot in the dark. But before things escalate and it becomes too late for negotiations, we need to end this. Just believe in it for now, please," Zach begged Alex.

"Alright, fine. I'll see what I can do. What time should I expect you two?" Alex asked over the phone.

"I'm driving to Regiment Legion HQ right now. We'll go as soon as possible. Make it in like an hour. Just sit Amar down at a table and pretend to notice us outside," Zach told Alex.

"Alright… fine. Leave it to me," Alex told Zach.

"Thank you," Zach ended the call. With that, he went back to Regiment Legion and got Bobonson on board with the idea. The two of them were to go outside of Adrenaline Corp. HQ as soon as they could, so Alex just had to get Amar's attention.

"So Amar… what's up?" Alex asked Amar.

"Eh? Not much," Amar was outside, doing pushups.

"You want a snack or something? I was just making some guacamole inside. I also just heard from Danny that all the soldiers from Canada are returning," Alex offered.

"Uh… sure," Amar answered. He wasn't really sure how to react because Alex hadn't really acted this way with him before. The two walked in together, sat down, and Alex got out the bowl of guacamole. They both grabbed a chip each and started eating.

"Amar, why do you keep up the physical training all the time?" Alex asked, trying to sound casual.

"Well… honestly, I just don't feel like I have anything better to do in my downtime," Amar responded.

"WAIT A SECOND! I think I just saw Regiment Legion soldiers!" Alex shot up, looking out the window.

"Are you sure?! Where?!" Amar shot up as well. Alex really did see Bobonson outside, giving him a thumbs up and then hiding behind a bush.

"I think they're behind that bush. I'm pretty sure I at least saw Bobonson, but there was another person there with him," Alex said.

"Well… let's go yell at them to get off the property," Amar muttered, cracking his knuckles. *That was easier than I thought it'd be…* Alex thought. The two of them went outside.

"Right there!" Alex shouted, and Amar ran over.

"Hey! Don't pretend like we can't see you—" Amar was cut off. Alex suddenly went into his demon form and punched Amar so suddenly that he passed out.

"Well… guess I didn't need to be here," Bobonson laughed as Alex carried Amar over his shoulder, turning off his demon form.

"That was a last-minute thing. I didn't know if I'd get the opportunity," Alex added.

"Well, we have Amar. Now all we have to do is take him to Regiment Legion and get him to agree with us," Zach commented. Alex and Bobonson both nodded, and they started to make their way to the Regiment Legion base. When they were finally there, Amar started to wake up.

"What the…?" Amar remarked as he found himself on a bed in the Regiment Legion HQ, next to Zach, Bobonson, Cole, and Alex.

"Sorry, Amar. But this is probably the only way we could get you to reason. You've been a little stubborn in the past," Cole told Amar.

"What do you mean, get me to reason?! You still just want Danny to stop protecting us, don't you?! You want him to cut out his nonsense and just go back to being his old self. What you don't realize is that the world has *changed!*" Amar instantly shouted.

"I *DO* REALIZE!" Zach yelled, stepping into the situation, "What I realized when I left Adrenaline Corp. is that Danny has a way with words—he can make himself *seem* right. But really, we have a bunch of technology here at Regiment Legion at our fingertips that would be enough to defeat Escarere again, if it came down to it. We even have help from the military. Danny has just changed Adrenaline Corp. because of his own paranoia. He even used tested strength on one of his own bases, just to make sure that the weapons were strong enough. After seeing what happened to Jareus, how could he help but become a little crazy about the subject?!" Amar stopped, and gulped for a second. He realized what Danny meant when he said 'like old times.' It was as if Amar was just Jareus again, it was an escape from the reality he was used to. He was allowed to go back to his old self. But that isn't what Amar wanted—he wanted to be the person he'd become, not the person he had once been.

"Oh…" Amar started, "He… he really *has* been different. I just thought that you guys were a bunch of hypocrites when it came to securing safety measures," he admitted.

"Amar… I don't blame you. But please…" Zach started.

"I GET IT ALREADY! But… Zach… what do you even want to do about it? What can we even do now?" Amar defensively asked.

"We're making a peace treaty," Bobonson added.

"A peace treaty…?" Amar questioned.

"It demands the stop of all illegal things on both sides. Regiment Legion swears not to, and requests for the oath of Adrenaline Corporation to do the same. Then there can be peace, and we can work together and toward the future," Bobonson explained.

"Right you are, Bobonson," Amber came in, "And I have it right here."

"Huh. Alex... were you playing on both sides? I was just wondering since you're here now, but you *were* the one to knock me out," Amar asked, as Amber got pens ready.

"Sorry, Amar. I knew Danny would interfere if we didn't do something like what we did. Who knows what would have happened?" Alex apologized.

"Here, Alex," Amber gave him the paper. Everyone in the room signed the paper together. The more signatures they'd collected, the more likely that Danny would sign it.

"However, Amar, don't be prepared to forget about Steven," Bobonson gave Amar a nasty look. Amar couldn't bring himself to say anything, but they all walked together to Adrenaline Corp. HQ.

"It actually feels like maybe we could do this..." Zach commented, seeing the building come into view.

"Let's just hope everything goes as planned," Cole smiled as they walked to the front gates.

"GRANDPA! OPEN UP!" Alex shouted when they all stood outside of the gates. The gates started to open up.

"Here we go..." Amber whispered to herself in excitement. The double doors of Adrenaline Corp. HQ seemed to slide open in slow motion as Danny appeared.

"Alex... what is this?" Danny asked.

"I shouldn't really have to apologize since your apology *to me* was so lackluster, but I've decided it'd be for the best to draw up a peace treaty. The shady activities of Adrenaline Corporation have gone on for long enough.

I even had to be subject to one of your weird experiments. Regiment Legion is more than capable of taking down a demon, especially if it has help from a not-so-shady Adrenaline Corporation!" Alex shouted, holding out the peace treaty. Really, it only needed Amber's and Danny's signatures, since everyone that had gathered had signed it already.

"Let me see this," Danny took the paper and pen. The rest of them looked intently to Danny's eyes as they glossed over the words and conditions of the paper. All of them just wanted him to put his signature on there and finally drop his guard.

"We're so close…" Cole whispered. They all were nervous to be so close to the end of all this corporate nonsense.

"Well…" Danny started. The rest of them looked as his hand raised the pen and started to move toward the paper.

"He's gonna sign it!" Zach whispered in excitement.

"Did you really think I'd give up that easily?" Danny snarled, ripping the paper in two.

"WHAT?! BUT DANNY! EVEN I AGREED TO—" Amar started to shout.

"DO YOU REALLY THINK I CARE, AMAR?! I DON'T CARE ABOUT YOUR FEELINGS! I CARE ABOUT THE SAFETY OF THE WORLD. YOU PREVENTING ME FROM DOING SO MAKES YOU A THREAT. SO—I HEREBY DECLARE WAR ON REGIMENT LEGION!" Danny shouted. The guards outside of Adrenaline Corp. HQ immediately pointed their guns at the group.

"Wha—WHAT?!" Cole shouted.

"Capture Alex and Amar. The rest, I don't care. This'll be over within a few hours anyway," Danny shrugged.

"AH!" Amar and Alex shouted as the guards took them hostage.

"We're booking it!" Amber shouted, running back out the gates with the rest.

"They'll get what they have coming later. Right now, let's get back inside," Danny ordered the guards as Alex and Amar were gagged. "I'll make sure these two don't fall far from me this time."

-4 HOURS UNTIL WAR-

"WHAT THE HELL!" Alex shouted after Danny took off his gag. Danny had brought him and Amar to the planning room.

"Alex, let me explain," Danny told Alex.

"FIRST YOU RIP OUR PEACE TREATY, AND THEN GAG US?! WHAT'S WRONG WITH YOU?!" Alex shouted at Danny.

"LET ME EXPLAIN!" Danny shouted in Alex's face.

"Okay, okay! EXPLAIN then!" Alex dared Danny while Amar was still gagged.

"Okay. What Regiment Legion did to you two was manipulation. They took you in because of your anger, Alex. They kidnapped you, Amar. Their idea of an alternative isn't anywhere near better than ours. Watch," Danny commanded them as he took a copy of the drug Cole made and threw it into a machine. They witnessed as the computer monitor's graphic of a human body turned all red.

"What's this even supposed to mean?" Alex asked.

"This is a drug Cole made. Cole couldn't help but be skeptical in the way I was. While the worst thing that could happen with the weapons is unintended collateral damage or the provocation of other countries, this drug was going to put human lives directly on the line," Danny started.

"I don't get it, what does it do?!" Alex shouted.

"It's a super steroid, essentially. A few hours after taking it, you'd become a muscly superperson. But after its effect fades, your body would be in shambles. I don't even know if you would survive," Danny told the two of them.

"Then why did you gag us and throw the others aside?!" Alex still questioned Danny.

"Would you have truly listened to me otherwise?!" Danny questioned right back. Alex stopped for a moment.

"You have a point," Alex said. Amar started to try and make noises, but the muffle was still around his mouth. Danny took it off.

"I didn't see that one coming. How about you untie us? Don't we have a war to fight?" Amar asked. Danny grinned.

"We have a war to win. The soldiers I sent up to the north should be back soon enough as well," Danny cheered, untying them. Alex slapped Danny.

"That's for earlier," Alex gritted his teeth.

"Yeah, yeah…" Danny held his cheek, "But I have a special task for you, Alex. I want you to control a certain droid." Alex nodded.

"What about me?" Amar asked.

"You'll be part of the war, don't worry. I'll have you in the front lines," Danny told Amar. Amar gritted his teeth but forced a smile.

"Whatever," he responded.

"I've gotta go tend to the arriving soldiers. You two make preparations. If I'm right in my thinking, they'll probably be attacking here to try and get the jump on us. We'll just make this the perfect trap for them," Danny explained, walking away at the same time. He left to go meet the other soldiers.

"This is weird, Alex. I don't like this," Amar commented.

"I know. But I didn't know about Cole's drug. If he was going to repeat what happened to me for his soldiers, then I can't forgive that," Alex responded.

"But who knows if that was just a prototype or something?" Amar asked aloud.

"I'm not taking chances. But I don't exactly want to be loyal to Danny, either," Alex told Amar. Amar shrugged.

"I need a breather before anything happens. You should try to find whatever droid Danny wants you to control," Amar walked out of the room.

"Maybe I should…" Alex commented to himself. Meanwhile, Danny was greeting all the soldiers coming in. A few vans pulled up to the front of the Adrenaline Corp. HQ. Danny stood ready, knowing that this wasn't going to be easy. He had prepared a trump card, though.

"Danny!" Odessa shouted, jumping out of one of the vans. Danny realized that she, a soldier from the north, was with them as expected.

"LOOK OUT!" Danny shouted. Odessa jumped to the side as suddenly, an odd looking robot tried to fly right into her. The soldiers didn't know it, but it was actually a robot that Danny had created to look as if it had come from Regiment Legion.

"What was that?!" Odessa questioned as the other soldiers got back in the vans to take cover.

"It looks like Regiment Legion is already attacking!" Danny shouted, holding his arm out as an exosuit arm suddenly came flying out of Adrenaline Corp. HQ to attach to him.

"WHAT?! Regiment Legion?!" Odessa questioned.

"Yeah… Cole found out that I knew about the dangerous drug he was creating to make super soldiers. He pinched me into a place where I had to declare war on him!" Danny shouted, getting ready for the robot's second impact. It made a loop in the sky and came flying back down. Everyone around Danny observed him using the exosuit arm to smash into the robot at faster-than-visible speeds. The robot, with Regiment Legion written on its torso, had been defeated.

"Thank goodness for your time powers. But seriously? Regiment Legion did that?" Odessa asked as the rest of the soldiers started to come out of the vans.

"Danny! How are we supposed to believe you when you didn't tell us about the weaponry?!" Toshi questioned.

"It was an honest mistake! But we're going to have to fight for our lives now! I need you all!" Danny shouted to them as suddenly a bunch of military vehicles started to pull up all along Adrenaline Corp. HQ.

"What the hell is going on?!" Adam Steel questioned aloud. The United States military formed a circle around Adrenaline Corp. HQ.

"I'm not joking, do you see that?! They're coming now. It's do or die time!" Danny shouted.

"FINE! Whatever! But only because of this situation!" Odessas shouted. The rest of the soldiers just nodded and decided to go with her.

"Danny, is that really what's happening?" Aaron came outside to ask Danny.

"Indeed it is," Danny told Aaron. "EVERYONE! PREPARE FOR INVASION!" He shouted to everyone funneling into the building.

-3 HOURS UNTIL WAR-

"Does it hurt at all, sir?" One of the Regiment Legion soldiers asked Cole as they were tightening his special-grade exosuit.

"Not at all," Cole replied. They were frantically getting ready inside of Regiment Legion as well.

"I just made a call to the military! They've created a barricade outside of Adrenaline Corp. HQ, but that is the furthest that they want to get involved with this," Zach informed Cole as soldiers around Cole were making sure his exo was in the best shape possible. It was matte white with blue markings and bigger shoulder guards than Adrenaline's exosuits had. Amber and Bobonson were arming their soldiers with rifles.

"This is what we have to do, don't we? We haven't really had time to prepare, but I say by default we put more training into our soldiers than Adrenaline Corp. does," Bobonson commented.

"We may have less people, but we have better people, is what you mean to say?" Amber asked.

"I guess so, yeah," Bobonson nervously smiled. Suddenly, his phone rang.

"Bobonson? Is that you?" Jack's voice asked.

312

"Jack?! What's going on?" Bobonson asked.

"Danny has rallied all of the northern troops from the Canadian base as well. They're all getting prepared to go to battle. They were originally against the idea, but Danny fought off a Regiment Legion droid as well as told us of a drug that Cole was making," Jack explained. Amber overheard and took the phone from Bobonson.

"Jack, the drug part isn't a lie. But I forced it to stop before ever being used by anybody. We never sent any robots over there, though," Amber told Jack through the phone.

"I thought so. I'll see what I can do on this side," Jack hung up the phone. Bobonson took the phone back.

"You think he's on our side?" Bobonson asked Amber.

"I think so. He just said he'd do what he could," Amber told Bobonson. Zach overheard them talking.

"Someone's gonna help us out?" Zach asked.

"Jack said he'd do what he could.' Plus, apparently all the northern troops are there, but they are going to work for Danny's side," Bobonson told Zach.

"Interesting. Well, let's get everything ready as fast as we can, then. It won't be easy beating all of them," Cole suddenly interrupted, wearing his exosuit.

"Yeah…" Zach agreed.

-2 HOURS UNTIL WAR-

"Alright Alex, you gotta control this one," Danny told Alex. They were both in the basement control room of a bigger robot.

"What the heck?! When did you make this?" Alex questioned as he stepped in front of a computer. He was able to see through a plethora of cameras on the screens, all attached to the head of the robot. It was a bigger version of a humanoid-type robot, with four legs and wheels on each. It had a dark gray and orange color scheme, and missile launchers and turrets on both arms.

"What do you think I've been doing this whole time? Why do you think that I've been working primarily on the incendiary rounds? Those weapons everybody complained so much about were nothing but a secondary project..." Danny admitted.

"Oh... I didn't know this was your main project," Alex admitted, now thinking that perhaps Danny wasn't *actually* as terrible as people were portraying him to be. Maybe he was just misunderstood.

"This, the Adrenaline Tanker Droid, isn't exactly done yet. But it can be controlled, and it's ready enough. We need it now. I'll show you how to work it. If it stops working, don't sweat it. Put on an exo and go to the battlefield," Danny told Alex.

"Alright," Alex replied, sounding determined. Danny showed him how to work it, but quickly had to move on. Aaron was acting as his general and getting the main troops outfitted for battle. Danny went to check on the other autonomous robots.

"As I thought, I won't have enough time for the Cybercores as of now. We'll have to use the dummy system," Danny thought aloud, activating the Adrenaline Proto-Droids.

"What are you doing?" Jack asked. He had just come to see what Danny was up to, but had never been informed about robots joining their forces.

"Getting these humanoid droids ready for battle. They aren't the best they could be, but they'll do," Danny told Jack. But Jack was angry about being lied to—he even told Mark to leave the battle area.

Meanwhile, Amar was taking a walk. He'd gone outside just to take a breather and just to get away from everything. He looked out to the wilderness behind the Adrenaline Corp. HQ. He remembered the days where he used to go out into the wilderness on his freedom travels. But Amar looked back at the building, and saw Jack shouting at Danny through a window. His eyes widened, his heart raced, and he ran.

"I mean WHY DID YOU LIE TO US?" Jack questioned Danny, getting furious.

"What do you mean?" Danny asked.

"Don't be stupid! You know that I know people from Regiment Legion. All I had to do was ask, and I figured out that your robot stunt was just that, a stunt," Jack shouted back at Danny.

"You know then, huh?" Danny asked Jack. Jack was just about to respond, but it was too late. One of the Proto-Droids grabbed him from the back.

"What the hell?" Jack reacted.

"Then stay here. I don't care. I have a war to win," Danny told Jack.

"WAIT A MINUTE!" Amar suddenly shouted, charging up the stairs. Danny didn't hesitate, sending two of the Proto-Droids forward. Amar leapt over them, jabbing at Danny. Danny blocked with the exosuit arm that he still had on.

"What do you want, Amar?" Danny spat.

"I want to end this war before it even begins. I can't have you ripping apart everyone we know like this. You're forcing our friends to go against each other in combat! For what?! We had a peace treaty," Amar shouted at Danny while dodging the Proto-Droids.

"I have a gut instinct. If I were to give up, there'd be something to kill us. I can just feel it, and I don't know why…" Danny said, suddenly using his time powers to appear right in front of Amar and punch him, "…But if we're not prepared, we'd all die anyway! I just want to overwhelm Regiment Legion into surrendering."

"That won't work, Danny! They're determined!" Amar shouted back at Danny.

"I'll break that. It wasn't like Cole was much better," Danny commented, having a Proto-Droid finally land a blow on Amar. Amar got up slowly, holding his stomach.

"You know what? I QUIT! I don't want to be on either of your sides! I JUST WANT TO LEAVE!" Amar cried, bleeding from his cheek. Before Danny could even respond, Amar sprinted as fast as he could. Amar ran, and ran, and ran. He ran past the military barrier even, yelling to them that he was defecting from Adrenaline Corporation. He ran into the wilderness.

"Danny, if you don't mind, I'm also going to quit," Jack gasped for air, still being held by the Proto-Droid.

"That's unfortunate for you, Jack. You'd tell everyone to go against me, wouldn't you?" Danny grinned. Jack gritted his teeth as Danny continued, "Just stay here for a while. It won't be long." The rest of the Proto-Droids followed Danny to the area with all the other soldiers.

-1 HOUR UNTIL WAR-

"Gather everyone as soon as possible! We're going to invade the rear entrance of Adrenaline Corporation!"

Cole shouted to Zach and the others. The troops were all getting rallied up.

"FOR STEVEN!" Some of Steven's friends shouted. The Regiment Legion's soldiers were outnumbered, but the spirit they carried was mightier.

"ARE YOU READY?!" Zach shouted, loading a gun while putting on an exosuit. The crowd of soldiers shouted back. They started to get in various ATVs and vehicles.

"MEN AND WOMEN OF REGIMENT LEGION…" Amber started. She was in an exosuit of her own, and currently speaking through a microphone. The gates to exit Regiment Legion HQ started to open as she continued, "…TODAY OUR STRENGTH WILL BE TESTED! REMEMBER THAT WAR HAS BEEN DECLARED UPON US, SO SHOW NO MERCY! OUR SMALL BUT SPECIALIZED FORCES WILL GO UP AGAINST THE OUTLAWS OF ADRENALINE CORPORATION!"

"YEAH!" A bunch of soldiers shouted, including Zach and Bobonson. Cole smiled from a distance as the troops started to move out.

"I talked to the president earlier. He isn't happy about this, but he still says we should try and take care of it as fast as we can. Are you sure you can handle the troops?" Cole asked Amber, coming up to her.

"Yeah. You just focus on fighting Danny himself. If he's gone, the line of power should be disrupted for enough time for us to take advantage of the situation. But… are you sure you can fight him? You two were best friends once, right?" Amber fired a question back at Cole.

"I'll be able to. I don't feel like I want to, but I know what must be done," Cole admitted to Amber as their troops exited in floods.

"I see them. It's time," Danny told Aaron, on the phone with him. Danny was in his office, putting on the full U.N.E. exosuit that he upgraded.

"Roger that, FIRE!" Aaron said, first to Danny and then some of the sniping troops. Regiment Legion was just coming over the hill in the wilderness, and they were planning to invade the back entrance. This is just as Danny had seen coming—he knew where they were planning to attack him from because he'd observed the way that the military had set up their barricade.

"Should we still be here?!" The military soldiers shouted to each other, seeing bullets fly over their heads as they stood still.

"Not so fast!" Zach shouted, jumping up in an exo of his own. He used a riot shield to deflect the bullets out of the way.

"ADVANCE!" Amber shouted. All of the vehicles started to go at full speed toward the back entrance of Adrenaline Corp. HQ as the military cleared out of the way. Amber then saw Zach landing, as well as Bobonson beside her and requested, "As much as I want to go with you guys, I have to command the troops from back here. Would you two do your best to infiltrate? Maybe you could get some of the soldiers to defect."

"With pleasure!" Zach grinned.

"You can count on us," Bobonson added. She smiled, and then gave them the hand signal to go forward. Zach and Bobonson, both in exosuits, headed for Adrenaline Corp. HQ. Zach had a long-range pistol and riot shield, while Bobonson had a rifle. There was already gunfire coming from both sides. Zach slid down the hill, with Bobonson close behind.

"Look out!" Zach shouted. Behind a bush, there was an Adrenaline Corp. soldier. Bobonson ducked and shot down at their legs. He hit them and they flew backwards.

"Got it," Bobonson told Zach. Zach jumped up with the riot shield again. He spotted some snipers.

"Spotted. We need to get closer," Zach commented. Bobonson nodded. Zach hit the ground again, and they both ran behind Zach's riot shield until they found cover behind a little bunch of trees.

"Found ya!" An Adrenaline Corp. soldier shouted.

"AH!" Zach shouted, shooting as a reaction. Zach beat him to the kill, and blood splattered on Zach's face.

"Jeez…" Bobonson was a little grossed out. Zach wiped it off.

"This is just what we have to do at this point," Zach told Bobonson. Bobonson nodded as he pointed his gun out from behind the trees. Zach did as well, and they were able to get some good shots in before anybody had noticed their position.

"I just need to reload," Bobonson said, sitting down. But Zach saw something else coming from the direction of Adrenaline Corp. HQ. He gasped.

"Bobonson… there's a problem," Zach sweat nervously. Bobonson reloaded and went to look. They saw a robot the size of a small building, with four legs that all had wheels on them.

"You've gotta be kidding me," Bobonson panted.

"I have a plan. We can shut it down somehow. I have a riot shield to protect you… is there any way you could break it?" Zach asked Bobonson as the giant robot started to take out Regiment Legion soldiers and blow up some of the vehicles with its rocket launchers. Bobonson noticed that every time it launched a rocket, it had to stop after in order to reload for a bit.

"It might not be able to move right after firing rockets. So… I do have an idea," Bobonson told Zach. They also witnessed the Proto-Droids fly into battle.

"We're getting slaughtered right now… we need to do something," Zach thought aloud.

"We will. You just need to protect me with that riot shield," Bobonson confirmed.

"What's this about?" A feminine voice asked. They both freaked out, but she already had a gun pointed toward them.

"Odessa?! Why are you fighting on Danny's side?!" Zach questioned as Odessa stood with her rifle pointed at Zach and Bobonson.

"Cole's droid came in and tried to kill us earlier! It was you guys who trapped us in here!" Odessa shouted.

"What?! We don't have ANY robots on the battlefield right now! We tried to give Danny a peace treaty, but he refused it!" Zach shouted at Odessa.

"What?!" Odessa gritted her teeth, still aiming at the two of them.

"He means it! Adrenaline Corporation declared war on us! We were just trying to find a way to end the feud," Bobonson added. Odessa put down her gun.

"I thought that Danny might be lying. I was ready to punch him in the face the second I got back! Yet… he looked heroic… yelling about how he needed to do what he was doing. I guess I'm a fool for falling for that," Odessa beat herself up over it.

"Hey… don't do that. You'll have your opportunity," Zach grinned. Odessa smiled as well.

"I'll try to get the former northern soldiers to evacuate, rather than be in your way. Better yet, they might even join you," Odessa gave them the thumbs up. Bobonson and Zach jumped out from behind the tree. They moved around, Bobonson following behind wherever Zach went. They were waiting for the robot to fire another missile, but for some reason it wasn't.

"Why's the thing standing still?" Zach muttered. He hadn't accounted for the mental state of Alex, the one controlling it. Alex could barely watch the bloodshed.

"What's wrong Alex? Why have you stopped?" Danny asked, just about ready to go out and see the battle firsthand with his exosuit.

"I can't… I can't keep doing this to people, Grandpa…" Alex cried out, falling to his knees. Danny saw the cameras of the robot as Bobonson and Zach grabbed on to the robot. Bobonson shot near its neck, and Zach used the riot shield to cut all the way through it. The sun was setting as the video display cut to static.

"Grab a gun, Alex. Go to the battlefield," Danny commanded, angry that his creation had been destroyed.

"Grandpa… I really can't…" Alex panted heavily. Danny gritted his teeth and started to walk away.

"I'm going. You should too," Danny spat out, walking down the stairs. Alex looked at the ground behind him. There was already a pistol with incendiary rounds, ready to use.

"I… I can't just run from what I've become," Alex picked up the gun. Danny stopped, listening to Alex run down the stairs from a room on the floor below. He smiled, looking out at the battlefield from behind a glass wall.

"I'll have to update Aaron, things are going better than expected," Danny smirked. He picked up the phone to call Aaron, but as the phone rang, Danny saw something he didn't expect.

"Yo," Cole greeted, crashing through the glass. Cole had on his dark blue shirt with his white exosuit, while Danny wore dark red and bright orange with his gray exo.

Danny grabbed Cole's gun as he aimed it. He was going to try and shoot it at Cole, but Cole ducked and grabbed Danny's legs. Danny dropped the gun on the ground as Cole boosted out of the room, still holding onto Danny.

"Hello? Hello, are you there?" Aaron was still talking through the phone that Danny had dropped on the ground.

"COLE…!" Danny shouted. Cole had flown them off to the right, and they were going to crash into the ground in the wilderness, where there weren't other soldiers. Just as they were about to hit the ground, Danny used his time powers to correct his position and land upright. As Danny let time resume, Cole hit the ground, did a somersault, and got up.

"I'm here to put an end to your tyranny," Cole announced, tightening his fists.

"Tyranny? You call trying to help the world tyranny?" Danny spat, scowling.

"I call your constant lies and cover ups to control the masses tyranny!" Cole shouted, pointing at Danny.

"Very well, then come put an end to this so-called TYRANNY!" Danny shouted back at Cole. Cole gritted his teeth and boosted straight forward. Danny put up his

322

arms to block it. They had all the room they wanted, since they were away from the other fight. Cole flipped backwards, landing on his feet again. Danny slowed down time, boosted forward, and kneed Cole in the gut. As time resumed, Cole flew back. He was barely able to stand.

"What the…?! Oh… right…" Cole remarked to himself, keeping his cool as he went up against Danny.

"Time powers," Danny grinned.

"Does your exo help sustain that?" Cole asked. Danny didn't say anything, staying in his defensive position. *That means he'll get exhausted from it eventually!* Cole thought, boosting forward. Danny went to slow down time again, but Cole caught the moment his muscles tensed up. Cole redirected his boost to straight up as Danny slowed down time.

"What the?!" Danny remarked. He realized that he wouldn't be able to reach Cole, since he couldn't use the exo's boost while time was slowed down. *If he turns this into a midair fight, I'm screwed. Gravity will act against me!* Danny's mind yelled as time returned to normal. Cole flew backwards and onto his feet again.

"You don't look so confident anymore," Cole grinned. Danny's face showed only anger, and he flew forward, slowing time on his way to punch Cole. Cole stuck out his arm before Danny slowed time, and as Danny got close, he launched his own gut into Cole's fist in slowed time.

"GAH!" Danny shouted as the shock of the hit resumed time, sending him flying back. When played back in normal time, Danny essentially threw himself at supersonic speed toward Cole's fist.

"Ahh, that stings!" Cole grinned, pulling his fist back to bring both of them in front of his face.

"But now I know both of your trump cards," Danny told Cole. Cole still didn't stop smiling.

"Do you now?" Cole teased. Danny jumped straight up and boosted toward Cole, who put out his fist again. But this time, Danny anticipated it, and kicked Cole in the face. Cole had started too early, since Danny didn't use his time powers.

"It seems like I do," Danny gloated. But Cole boosted forward through the dust unexpectedly and knocked Danny to the ground. Danny boosted up while lying down and dragged himself on the dirt. Cole ran forward as Danny used a boost to flip himself up. Danny blocked a punch that Cole had thrown and boosted forward into Cole. Danny crashed them both into the ground, but then Cole threw him up into the air. Danny saw the opportunity, used his time powers, and put his foot out. He kicked faster than he ever had before.

"GAH!" Cole cried out, but he grabbed Danny's leg. He threw Danny to the side, breaking a part of the exo on his leg. They both had cuts and scratches all over them at this point.

"Oh? It looks like you've made quite a strong exosuit," Danny commented, looking at Cole's improved Regiment Legion exosuit.

"Yours is too. But didn't Jareus add grapple hooks?" Cole asked Danny.

"I'm the one who made this suit. I might have taken some inspiration from the original, but this is the updated version! It can boost pretty far in midair, so why even have grapple hooks when they add so much weight?" Danny blabbed on.

"I see," Cole wiped blood from his lip, getting back into a battle pose. Danny grinned.

"But I can destroy an exo. Even one like yours," Danny arrogantly taunted Cole. Cole paid him no attention and continued to fight. Danny slowed time as Cole got close and landed a kick with his right leg, as it was only his left leg that had a broken exo part. Danny kicked a specific joint on Cole's exosuit arm. As time resumed and Cole flew back, the arm suddenly became loose.

"Looks like you weren't joking," Cole commented. He was still able to move the arm, but it was closer to breaking now.

"I built these from the ground up. *Of course* I would know how to tear one down," Danny grinned. Danny went in for another punch, but Cole blocked his punch. Cole tried to punch right back, but Danny blocked his punches as well. Danny boosted backwards—he was a little wobbly because of the one leg that was half-working. Cole also noticed that he was getting tired from all of the time power usage.

"Block this," Cole challenged with resolve. He boosted in, uppercutting Danny. Danny took the blow head-on, and flew back a bit. As Danny tried to blindly block his head area again, Cole slid and knocked Danny off of his feet. Cole boosted into the sunlight and prepared to stomp down on Danny, who was finally able to see after unblocking his face.

"NOW!" Danny shouted, pumping himself up. He used his remaining energy to slow down time as much as he could. Cole was practically frozen in the air. Danny, in slowed-down time, broke off the half-working part of his exo and threw it toward Cole's hip joint in his exo. If he could hit it hard enough, it'd split his exo in two. The piece of shrapnel he threw practically stood still in the air until he resumed time.

"What?!" Cole shouted as the exo shrapnel hit Cole's hip joint, and successfully split the exo in two. This made him fly off to the side, rather than flying down onto Danny, but there was one thing Danny hadn't accounted for.

"AGH!" Danny let out as his chest was pierced by another piece of shrapnel. When Cole's suit split in two, the already loose piece of his exo came off. The bottom of it was sharp enough to lodge itself in Danny's chest, but not to go through him.

"Ugh… what the?" Cole questioned. As he got up, the exo fell off of him. But he looked over to Danny. Danny grabbed the shrapnel with both of his hands, "The exo?! It stabbed him?!"

"This is horrible…" Danny's voice trembled as Cole watched. Danny quickly removed the shrapnel, but he was unable to hide his wound.

"What… IS THAT?!" Cole suddenly explained as he looked into Danny's wound. In the wound where Danny had removed the shrapnel, there wasn't just blood—in fact, there was less blood than Cole would have expected. Instead, Cole's eyes widened in horror as he saw the finger that Escarere had fired into Danny's chest. It had lines of demonic flesh connecting to his own flesh, invading him like a parasite.

COLE CAN SEE IT! WE'RE DONE FOR! RUN! Danny's mind shouted at him. Danny suddenly boosted up and grabbed back onto the Adrenaline Corp. building. Cole tried to go after him, but had no exosuit he could use to keep up with him.

"GET BACK HERE!" Cole yelled helplessly.

"Sorry," Danny simply replied, heading right back into the HQ. Cole requested backup and another exo as soon as he could, and while he waited, his mind raced. *What could that mean? Was this all part of some other and bigger plan? This explains Danny's sudden shift in behavior...* Cole thought.

"Cole, we're going to need your help over here. Just get a bit closer and I can give you a new exo, but I can't exactly break off from battle here!" Zach shouted at Cole through the phone.

"Got it," Cole told Zach, but his mind was only thinking of what he had just witnessed. But when Cole went over to where Zach said he was, there was nothing but an extra exo and an ATV waiting for him. Cole wondered where Zach went, but saw the chaos of the battle still raging on. Zach hadn't gone back to battle—he and Bobonson had been captured.

"You said that you wanted these two, right sir?" One of the Adrenaline Corp. soldiers asked Alex.

"Yes, thank you. You can go back to battle now," Alex told the soldier as he looked at Zach and Bobonson tied up to chairs.

"What's the meaning of this?!" Zach shouted out at Alex.

"I'm just conflicted. We had everything ready, didn't we? Then why didn't you tell me about the drugs Cole made, or whatever the thing was with the robot?" Alex asked.

"We don't have any robots at Regiment Legion!" Bobonson shouted at Alex.

"I figured that much, but what about the drug? How come nobody tells me the full truth anymore?" Alex continued to question.

"Look. I don't know. That drug, apparently, was never going to see actual use anyways. Odessa already joined our side, she's evacuating the other northern soldiers. We don't have to keep killing," Zach tried to convince Alex.

"Why would my grandfather do these things? Did I change him too much by coming here?" Alex started to question himself.

"Listen, Alex, we can all find out the truth. All three of us. All we have to do is go out there and end this war. We don't really want to kill Danny, either. We just want to be together rather than separated," Bobonson tried to console Alex.

"Then why didn't you tell me the truth earlier?!" Alex asked.

"We didn't know! We genuinely didn't know!" Zach shouted. Alex sighed. He got up and started to untie the two.

"I guess there's no choice. We'll have to find out the truth for ourselves," Alex sounded determined.

"Guess we will," Zach grinned and shook hands with Alex. The three of them went to the door to find that although the sun had set, the fighting was still going on.

"Where do we even start?" Bobonson asked, looking to the sky. One of the Proto-Droids was suddenly struck down.

"Scar?!" Zach was surprised to see Scar getting involved as well. He stabbed one of the Proto-Droids to the point of it malfunctioning.

"What are you three doing? Aren't you on opposite sides?" Scar questioned them.

"Well... not really anymore. What are you doing?" Alex asked Scar. Scar grinned.

"Well, I'm here helping out Regiment Legion. I hate that the robots are being used for fighting, and I thought they could use some help. See ya!" Scar suddenly ran inside.

"What the…? Well… whatever. The worst he'll do is destroy some other robots," Zach shrugged it off. What they didn't know was that Scar was going in to get valuable information on something he had been researching. Just then, there was a loud explosion. An Adrenaline Corp. missile had just flown toward Cole, but using his exo, he flung it back at the main building. It exploded, blasting a hole in the front of the HQ. The fire started to spread.

"WOAH! WHAT THE HELL?!" Alex questioned. Meanwhile, Cole was frantically trying to get to Amber.

"There you are, Amber! Do you have that microphone from earlier?!" Cole asked her as he boosted right toward one of the vans.

"COLE! You scared the heck out of me. Yeah, I do, what do you need it for?" Amber asked.

"I need to make an announcement," Cole told Amber.

"What kind of announcement?" Amber asked.

"I don't have time for questions!" Cole shouted. She opened the back of the van that had a sound system. Cole grabbed the microphone and put the speakers on maximum volume.

"I hope you know what you're doing…" Amber commented as Cole started to speak.

"ATTENTION, ALL PARTICIPANTS OF THIS BATTLE! DANNY HAS BEEN FOUND TO BE UNDER DEMONIC INFLUENCE. YOU CAN CHOOSE TO BELIEVE ME, OR NOT! I JUST NEED THOSE THAT ARE ON MY SIDE TO CLEAR A

PATH FOR ME!" Cole shouted. His announcement was loud enough to echo over the battlefield. The soldiers shooting at each other even stopped to listen.

"Demonic... influence?" Toshi asked himself as he was leaving the battlefield with Tanya and Kami. They had been contacted by Odessa.

"What the heck is Cole talking about? Is Danny really under some demonic influence?" Bobonson questioned.

"Wouldn't surprise me. In fact, I hope that's the case. He's been acting crazy for months," Zach angrily agreed. But Alex stood in shock. He stood completely still as gunfire and flames illuminated the sky around them. Suddenly, Alex's head began to twitch out of control. His neck moved in an owl-like way it clearly wasn't supposed to.

"ALEX?! What's wrong with you?" Bobonson asked. Alex calmed down, and turned around slowly.

"He's full of crap. It's just another lie. Maybe you two are enemies after all? Were you sent here to blind me?" Alex asked.

"Alex? Why are you acting like this all of the sudden?" Zach asked. Alex shook his head. His eyes suddenly looked lifeless.

"I'm just going to let this pass. Survive if you can," Alex simply told Zach and Bobonson, running off of the battlefield.

"ALEX!" Zach shouted, "What the heck has gotten into him? That was... a weird sight. But do you think Cole's lying to us?"

"Lying or not about demons, all he asked was for us to clear a way for him to get in the HQ again... After it started to burn, right? Then let's do so," Bobonson answered.

"Right. But why does he need the front way?" Zach questioned.

"It might have to do with Danny's position and the amount of soldiers that could interfere here," Bobonson added. Zach nodded, and the two of them went to work on making as much of a way as they could—naturally, with as few casualties as possible as well.

"Danny, don't you worry. I'm going to rescue you," Cole told himself, dashing down the hill and through the battlefield. Explosions were going off left and right, lighting up the way as Cole dodged bullets and had people covering for him. Cole didn't want to kill Danny, but to extract that flesh from him.

"GO SIR! GO!" Regiment Legion soldiers cheered Cole on as they fought their own battles and as Cole flew down the hill, running at speeds only an exo could carry him at. This second exo wasn't as good as the first, but it would do. Cole boosted forward and crashed through the door of the headquarters. He looked around quickly as the place began to catch fire. Cole rushed down to the basement to make sure that Danny wasn't there when he saw two people tied up, trying to inch their way across the floor.

"Harlow...?!" Cole reacted, a nervous sweat forming across his forehead. Cole boosted down to where Harlow and Martin were.

"Thank goodness… someone finally came…" Harlow gasped as Cole took off a gag that had been on his face.

"Harlow, is this where you've been?!" Cole asked.

"The day before Danny was going to meet with you all, I saw him physically collapse for a second. He didn't seem to remember it right after, but I could tell that it just didn't seem like he was alright anymore. Later, he suddenly tied me up without explanation and threw me down here. Every now and then, a robot came down here, ungagged me, and gave me food for a bit," Harlow explained, gathering his thoughts.

"I found him, but Danny didn't seem to be happy with that. He threw me in there with him," Martin explained as Cole also took his gag off.

"Remember when Escarere shot her own flesh into Danny? It's still there…" Cole told the two of them. Harlow's eyes widened.

"So that's what it was…" Harlow grabbed his face, "I was wondering what had happened. All I knew is that whatever put me in here *wasn't* Danny."

"You guys get out of here. I'll call Bobonson to come get you guys through the battlefield outside," Cole told the two of them.

"What *IS* happening outside?" Martin asked.

"Danny declared war on Regiment Legion. This is the result of that. Luckily, most people have just been leaving the battle after feeling endangered, or if their exosuits have stopped working. I think our side is winning now, but Adrenaline Corp. certainly started off stronger," Cole told the two.

"I thought that this might happen…" Martin responded.

"I'm going to find Danny now. Trust me, I'm going to try my best to just make him pass out so we can remove whatever's in him," Cole continued, running back up the stairs with the two of them.

"Do whatever you can, Cole," Harlow reassured him as he split off from the two of them. Harlow and Martin went to the back door to meet Bobonson while Cole charged up the stairs. The place was now essentially engulfed in flames, and Cole was starting to sweat, charging up to the next floor. Cole looked around as part of the roof collapsed near him, and he barely dodged it.

Half of the lights weren't functioning, but the flames lit up most of the way. Cole ran up another flight of stairs, and that's when he found what he'd been looking for—most of the walls had collapsed on the top floor, and in the wreckage, there Danny stood. He was using an emergency kit he'd made to tend to his injury. There was now a metal plate over the wound in his chest.

"DANNY!" Cole shouted as Danny stood, looking down. Flames behind Danny illuminated his figure as Cole flew up the stairs, running straight to Danny. Danny gritted his teeth and braced for impact. The two crashed right into each other, each standing their ground as they reeled back.

"COLE...! WHY DID YOU COME HERE?!" Danny shouted back at Cole.

"I KNOW WHAT'S GOING ON! YOUR FACADE IS OVER WITH!" Cole shouted back at Danny as the two boosted off of each other, landing face-to-face again.

"Do you now? How unfortunate for me. But can you really stop what's going to happen? I had a plan to take care of the rest of your army," Danny spat.

"What?!" Cole reacted as suddenly two spears flew to Danny's sides. They each had two prongs at the ends of them. The two floated to his sides as if controlled by telekinesis, however, they were powered by small jets to create that illusion.

It looks like those two connect to his exosuit, Cole thought as he saw them float in coordination with Danny's arms.

"I'll make your suffering short-lived," Danny scowled at Cole, sending one of the spears flying at him. Cole boosted up, dodging out of the way as he noticed the other one closing in on him. He raised up part of his arm with the exo on it to stop the oncoming spear. It blocked the spear successfully, but Cole was sent flying back by the pressure. He almost flew right into the fire, but he used the exo's boost at the last second to save himself. The fire gave the spears an almost red glow as Cole hit the ground, balancing himself again.

"It's going to take more than that to get rid of me..." Cole wiped the sweat off of his cheek. Danny still hadn't moved from where he was. Cole grabbed a gun from his belt. He hadn't come ill equipped this time, and dodged out of the way of the next spear attack. Cole shot at the spear, but it was so thin that he couldn't land a bullet on it.

He decided to boost toward the spear, but it evaded his attack as Danny moved his arms to control the spears. However, Danny didn't notice that Cole had aimed for him. Cole fired a bullet at the top of Danny's right exosuit arm, which broke it and skinned the top of Danny's arm as well.

"GAH!" Danny shouted out. One of the spears fell to the floor, and Cole picked it up. Cole wielded the spear in his left hand and the gun in his right. Suddenly, Danny's spear smashed right into Cole's gun, breaking it in two with the high velocity of the weapon.

"You seem angry," Cole commented, blood seeping out of his cuts. Danny's eyes widened, and his face of fury was shown.

"It's always been you. This whole time, you've been the one to interfere with all my plans, Cole. You've now even seen right through me. If I don't end this now, it won't end," Danny pointed at Cole, sending his spear to attack again.

"BUT I'LL BE THE ONE TO END IT!" Cole shouted, blocking the flying spear with his own. The spear's jet system pushed Cole backwards, but Cole ran forward at full force, shoving both toward Danny. Danny finally decided to jump into action, grabbing the spear that had flown and using it to vault himself over Cole. Danny kicked Cole in the back, sending him flying forward. Cole almost crashed face-first onto the ground, but held on to his spear to save him. Cole boosted straight up and spun to meet his line of sight with Danny's as he boosted once more down right onto Danny. Danny blocked his attack with his spear, and shoved Cole backwards. They stood, facing each other on both sides of the room. Suddenly, a large portion of the floor between the two of them fell, leaving a giant hole between them.

"We don't have much time. If neither of us end this, it'll be the end for both of us," Danny shouted out to Cole.

"That's fine by me! I just need to bring the real you back," Cole responded. Danny gritted his teeth, but a smile crept onto his face. Danny stood still as he sent his spear forward. The spear kept trying to hit Cole as Danny began to look for a way out. Cole was getting barraged by the spear, but kept hitting it back with his own spear.

Danny saw that he could potentially get out if he just crashed through the glass of one of the windows, but there was fire in his way. Cole saw Danny looking to escape and realized that he needed to act fast. Cole boosted straight up and stabbed the other spear to the ground with the two prongs of his own spear. Danny didn't see it coming, but Cole sprinted toward the gap in the floor and boosted across it as fast as he could. Cole smacked right into Danny.

"GET OFF OF ME!" Danny screamed in anger, shoving Cole to the ground. But Cole boosted forward, crashing right into Danny again and causing him to trip. Cole kicked straight up and Danny flew into the air. Danny flipped and boosted straight back down onto Cole, but Cole barely dodged. As Cole went in for an uppercut, Danny slowed down time and slammed his body right into Cole. As Cole flew back, Danny didn't realize that Cole had grabbed onto his arm.

"TO HELL WITH IT!" Cole shouted, bringing Danny with him as he boosted through the fire. The two crashed into the ledge of where the floor had fallen through.

"ARE YOU INSANE?!" Danny questioned, infuriated as the floor beneath them started to crumble as well.

"MIGHT AS WELL BE!" Cole shouted as the two started to fall. Danny boosted right into Cole, but Cole grabbed on to Danny. The two of them tried to keep themselves up with as much boost as they had, all the while shoving each other around. Danny decided he'd had enough and grabbed onto Cole's exo. He tried to fling himself to safety as Cole started to fall again. Just then, Cole hurled a piece of his exosuit arm into the fragile flooring above Danny. They both watched as another piece of the floor came crashing down.

"NO!" Danny shrieked as a large floorboard crashed into him. Cole saw this opportunity and hit the falling floorboard to fling himself to temporary safety. Cole's arm nearly split open because of the unfortunate position he was in, but he knocked himself onto one of the remaining floor pieces.

"DANNY!" Cole shouted as he saw Danny fall under the floor piece, all the way through all the holes to the basement floor. The flames were getting out of control, and Cole's arm was bleeding. Cole could have left then, but he wasn't satisfied with that. Danny couldn't just be left to die. Cole ripped off a part of his shirt and tied it around the injured part of his arm. He jumped off the ledge deliberately.

I said that I'd save you, not kill you for good! Cole thought as he fell through all the floors of the building. He tried to boost up at the last second near the ground, but it didn't negate all of his damage.

"OW!" Cole shouted as his bleeding arm hit the ground, but he didn't have time to worry about himself. He looked up and saw where Danny had fallen. He was in a large pile of debris from the floors collapsing, and there was fire surrounding him on all sides. But Cole didn't care. He marched forward, boosting right through the fire. Cole used all of his remaining strength to lift the debris off of Danny. He checked Danny's heart rate, relieved to find that he was still alive.

"Let's go, then," Cole muttered to himself, throwing Danny over his shoulder and carrying his body out of the flames. Cole boosted up to the first floor and crashed onto the ground. He picked Danny up again and continued to push through, kicking open the front doors as the firefighters arrived and saw the two of them.

"HELP!" Cole shouted as the battle finally started to die down. All of the soldiers looked their way, shocked at what they saw. Firefighters ran over to begin putting out the fires, and medics came to help the two stand upright while they got stretchers for the two of them.

"GET THEM TO A HOSPITAL, QUICKLY!" One medic shouted to another, and the two of them were put into the back of an ambulance, both on stretchers.

"You better live..." Cole muttered, passing out as well.

...

"Looks like he's waking up," Danny heard a voice as he slowly regained consciousness. His eyes felt heavy as he looked around the barren hospital room.

"What... happened?" Danny asked. The voice from earlier had been Harlow's, and Danny now saw him sitting at his bedside. "Harlow! There you are. How come you've been gone for so long?"

"You really don't remember it, do you?" Harlow asked as Cole walked into the room. Danny was on guard again.

"What do you want, Cole?!" Danny was already defensive.

"Enough, that stuff is over for now. I'm just glad you're okay. Thank goodness they were able to remove that flesh from you," Cole told Danny.

"Flesh? What do you mean? How did I get like this anyways?" Danny asked, looking down at his still battle-bruised body.

"You don't even remember locking me up?" Harlow asked. Danny looked at him in confusion.

"Locking you up? Why would…" Danny's memories returned to him as he spoke. He remembered everything as if it was a movie playing back to him, and he was forced to watch.

"Hm? Are you remembering now?" Harlow asked as Danny silently looked into open space.

"A little too well…" Danny stated grimly. Harlow and Cole went over everything with Danny as he regained his memories, figuring out when he was and wasn't conscious of what was going on.

"For almost half of the time you couldn't remember things?!" Cole questioned after making a quick comparison in his head.

"Well… every time someone would bring up a detail of what I had ordered to do, it would kick back in. For some reason, it never felt wrong, so I didn't question it. The only time I could ever really question things was if I was a little intoxicated. It seems like alcohol could block the effects of Escarere's demon flesh. But what was the plan there? She was obviously using me for something, but the only thing that happened was war. Maybe that's what she wanted?" Danny stated, still confused about the whole thing.

"Well, now that we've got that down, let's talk about the future," Harlow said. Danny nodded and Harlow continued, "Originally, Amber and I had agreed to just do away with Regiment Legion and Adrenaline Corporation. But, it'd put a lot of people out of a job, and the government still wanted to fund a version of Regiment Legion, knowing the possibility of a supernatural threat. So, we had the two merge. We simply call it, Adrenaline Legion."

"Yup! And since we're all sorta over the whole corporate battle for now, Bobonson was the one who really stepped up and decided he wanted to be the head of Adrenaline Legion," Cole commented.

"Wait a second... How long have I been out?" Danny asked.

"It's April 7th now, so about a week," Harlow finally told Danny. This shocked Danny, knowing he had been asleep for a full week. He even touched the place on his chest, where he now had a scar and stitches. *It really put me out for that long?* Danny thought.

"So... now what?" Danny asked.

"Well, Zach and I moved back into Jareus's old place for the time being. Saskia and Allison were there. Alex arrived there too the other day, and he's staying there. Do you wanna join us?" Cole asked. Danny thought about it for a minute.

"Yes, but I have something to do first," Danny told Cole. Cole was a little confused, but went along with it. He and Harlow accompanied Danny to Adrenaline Legion, where he explained what had been happening to everyone over the loudspeaker. At first, people immediately had a hostile reaction to his voice, but as he continued to explain... people began to understand more.

"That's really what happened to you, Danny?" Odessa asked, coming to see him. Most of the soldiers that Danny had met personally had transferred over to Adrenaline Legion.

"Yeah, unfortunately. I can't help but feel horrible for it. I just... feel like there was something I could have done to stop it. But you guys in the north seemed to have the right idea. I put Jill in charge up there. I gotta give her a call sometime..." Danny smiled, knowing that the north

340

soldiers remembered what he really would have done. But Odessa suddenly stood still, not saying anything.

"You really don't remember…" She mentioned, coldly. Danny was only confused by this statement.

"What…?" Danny asked. Odessa looked him in the eyes.

"Jill died in the battle of the Canadian base. You suddenly just called it off without reason," Odessa's voice trembled.

"She… what…?" Danny's eyes widened in horror. They stood there in silence until Danny spoke up again. "I had regained my own thoughts for a bit. I didn't even know that there was a battle in the north. I called it off because it just didn't seem like a good idea."

"Well it wasn't," Odessa icily told him. "Now I've got work to keep up with, especially because of the mess that just happened a week or so ago. So I'll have to see you later," she finished, walking out of the room.

Later, Danny found Jill's grave. He stared at it for hours, just thinking. But when the sun started to set, he finally drove back to the house he and Jareus had become owners of so long ago.

"There you are!" Lexus shouted to him, stopping him before he went to the door and hugging him suddenly.

"Wha—Lexus?! What are you doing?" Danny asked.

"I knew it wasn't you! It couldn't have been!" Lexus cried, still grabbing him. Danny was embarrassed. Cole and Zach headed outside as well when they heard the news.

"Yo," Zach smiled as Danny and Lexus walked inside.

"YOU!" Allison shouted. Danny braced for impact, "You MADE me stay inside of that DUMB company!" Allison karate-chopped Danny's head.

"I'm sorry..." Danny moped.

"But I guess it isn't your fault... but you had that coming!" Allison shouted, turning around and going to eat.

"Jeez... well. I guess you deserved that one," Saskia laughed as she saw the situation. They all got reacquainted, and made dinner together. Danny questioned if he deserved such happiness and hospitality after all of what happened, but it wasn't as if it were entirely his fault, either.

"It's been weird, honestly. Being against each other has made me tired. Amber made sure I was working day and night," Cole yawned.

"Amber? Like, as in Amber Ranatrix?" Lexus asked.

"Actually, yes," Cole blinked in surprise. "How did you know that?"

"She's my sister," Lexus said simply. Everyone's eyes widened.

"SISTER?!" Danny and Cole jinxed.

"Yeah. I'm Lexus Ranatrix," Lexus told the two. Zach laughed at them.

"Who would've thought..." Saskia commented. Alex came by and quietly ate his food as well. The rest of them started to get tired, and all eventually went to bed. Danny, through all of his guilt, still wondered where Amar was. He thought that Amar had gone through something similar, so he knew that it wasn't impossible to have a true change of heart. Knowing that gave him the peace to sleep.

342

But Alex stayed up later, choosing to step outside to watch the stars above. He sat, watching, as he knew the planet was moving on its axis and the stars appeared to move across the sky.

"Well. I guess the plan is still in motion," Alex said to himself, going back inside. —*END OF CONFLICTING DIVIDE*

Fun Fact: Escarere was originally going to come back in her entirety, and Danny and Cole were going to team up against her. But it felt unnatural to suddenly make them friends again immediately after that big of a conflict, So I scrapped the idea.

COMING IN VOLUME 3—

Part 8: Vengeful Memories
Part 9: Eternal Solstice

Look forward to the continuation!

ACKNOWLEDGEMENTS

My friends, family, and all those who helped me get through life as I worked on this text, I thank you first and foremost.

My editor, Alexandra Tack, made sure I knew my "then"s from my "than"s. Thank you for controlling the mess of my early writing. As well as the cover artist, Ellie Reis!

And of course, the biggest thanks to those childhood friends who helped me make the original version of this story on a camcorder in the early 2000s. Including but not limited to:
Donathan Luck
Kenneth Riles
Alex Salcedo
Zach Leith
& many more.

ABOUT THE AUTHOR

Justin Ferrante, also known by many nicknames (including the one on the cover), is someone who loves stories. Seeing so many good stories in the world inspired him to try and make stories of his own.

He hopes to give readers a good story to enjoy, and also wishes to produce a good story for himself. Most importantly, he aims to give readers an emotional enriching experience through the eyes of the characters.

One story read is another lifetime lived.

FROM PART 8: VENGEFUL MEMORIES—

"You *built* his current form?! Does that mean... you know how to take him apart?!" Alex shouted.

"I wish..." Danny whispered, clearing his throat. "The thing is, I don't know the full story. I only know about this through these visions. Escarere was sent with the intention of building that *robot body*, obviously. I can't remember how to make him because it wasn't me."

"You got my hopes up there, Danny," Alex said, laughing. "But it's alright. The past is the past, we need to fight given our current situation," He tried to motivate him.

"Thanks," Danny laughed as well, "But didn't you usually call me grandpa? You think you're all buddy-buddy with me now?" he joked, chuckling.

"Right, my bad," Alex said, quickly turning the other way.

That... was a little odd, Danny thought. *I hope he knows I was just joking around. He hasn't been acting like himself lately...*

COMING IN—

VOLUME 3